ALIVE

COURTNEY KONSTANTIN

Dedication

To the readers who have connected with the Duncans.

Your belief has brought them to life.

CHAPTER ONE

One Week Before the Outbreak -

The end of winter still held tight to the Montana skyline. Large puffs of snow floated to the ground, collecting and turning the landscape white. Though spring had arrived, Mother Nature had failed to inform the Montana weather. The forest was quiet, the animals still hid away. They waited for warmer weather to wake them from their slumbers.

Rafe Duncan stood in front of his wall of windows, as he drank his morning coffee. He was accustomed to the randomness of the snow in the Montana mountains. His view was the back-side of the small slope that his home was built on. He could picture the gravel drive below, that led to a large metal gate. The gate was the entrance to the large rock wall that surrounded his property. He ran his hand over his closely cropped black hair. He focused on his reflection in the glass, his blue eyes looking back at him.

My property, Rafe thought to himself. He couldn't seem to get used to calling the compound his. He had lived in town while his father was still alive. When a heart attack took Mitch Duncan's life three years before, Rafe was the one to find him. Rafe didn't think of that moment often, he didn't see a reason to agonize over something that was just life. Death was the end and it came to everyone.

When his father hadn't shown up for one of his jobs, Rafe was listed as a contact. Mitch had been scheduled to set up a security system for a wealthy rancher, who was having issues with his animals going missing. He wouldn't have worked, except he needed the income to continue to build the compound he had spent his life on creating. The place that he was sure would save his family someday. In the end, he should have been more concerned with regular physicals.

Rafe turned away from the windows. He would need to leave a little earlier for work himself. The snow would cause traffic. No matter how often it snowed, drivers didn't understand how to handle the icy conditions. Unlike his father, Rafe maintained the property, keeping it in working order. However, he wasn't obsessed with survival like his father. A lot of what he did was out of habit and not fear of the apocalypse to come.

He ducked his chin as he emerged into the snow and ran to his pickup truck parked between the house and the root cellar. Though it was early and he was headed to his day job, he had been awake for hours. His morning chores had to be done, snow or sun. As he circled back to the driveway, he could hear the cows mooing their goodbyes as they did every morning. This morning he had packed them back into their stalls in the barn, to protect them from the snow. As long as they were fed and milked they were happy animals.

His father wouldn't have approved of the relationship Rafe had created with the animals on the compound. In the mornings when he trudged out to the barn to milk the ladies, he talked to them and he found them to be great listeners. Mitch believed animals were for nothing but food. Rafe didn't see a reason to butcher the ladies while he was getting milk from them, so they were still functional. The rooster, on the other hand, Rafe had plans for that bird. He swore to himself that if that mean animal attacked him one more time when he was collecting eggs, he was having him for dinner.

With a push of a button, the large gate rolled open and Rafe pulled into the forest beyond. As was his habit, he waited just outside the gate for it to close completely. He kept his eyes moving, to ensure nothing got into the compound while the opening slowly closed. He may not have had the same paranoia his father lived with, but the compound was still his home.

The drive through the trees would be considered magical if Rafe wasn't used to seeing it. The puffs of snow caught on the trees, creating a white canopy over the dirt road that led him to the main asphalt highway that passed his home. He stopped at the entrance and looked both ways, noticing how the snow was starting to stick to the ground, creating a white wonderland. He could see tire tracks from other drivers passing through and he easily maneuvered his truck to the tracks already cut through the snow.

The drive to his work was uneventful most days. He arrived in good time to the facility he worked at as a security associate and showed his badge to the man in the box next to the entrance gate. The man waved him through with not even a crack of a smile, even though Rafe had been working with the man for over a year. He wound behind the complex to where the security vehicles were parked and left his own truck outside a door.

Rafe had called this job his main income for just over a year. His actual employer was an outside security company, who was often contracted for government work. The medical facility he worked at now was typically a quiet place to be. Many days Rafe wondered why they needed security at all. But it was a paycheck and it helped keep his home in working order.

Inside the building, Rafe followed a hallway to the security center that was a hub in the middle of the building. All of the doors were only accessed with keycards. Throughout the hive of pathways, additional locked doors sat allowing only certain employees through different doors. As security Rafe could access any door as needed. As a standard, all of the locked doors stayed closed at all times. According to the man he reported to, a government suit that knew nothing about security, many of the rooms were on a need to know basis.

He arrived at the fishbowl security room and relieved the guard from the night shift. Rafe always found it odd that there was 24-hour security in a medical facility. However, from the logs he had reviewed, there were many people coming and going throughout the evening. There were so many different titles and people, Rafe was never able to determine what exactly people did in the middle of the night. Whatever it was, it was important to them.

The security room was referred to as a fishbowl because it was a room made of glass. It had taken Rafe some time to get used to being on display as people bustled from place to place around him. Once he realized no one cared about him, he no longer cared about who was there. One wall was partially covered with monitors, views from every angle, showing hallways, labs, and offices. Two desks also sat in the room, though there were never two officers in the room at any given time.

Rafe sat in front of the monitors to start. He reviewed all of the footage coming in and found his partner officer making rounds like she was scheduled. Liza was a husky woman, that most likely could kick the crap out of Rafe if he stepped out of line. But her temperament was sweet and friendly, clear on her face as she smiled at the group of lab coats she passed in the hallway. Liza looked at her watch then. Next was the customary wave to Rafe in security as she knew he would have taken his post.

"Hi, Liza," Rafe said into the mic attached to his shirt. He watched as she saluted him and continued on her rounds. With their normal hello out of the way, Rafe began to cycle the views. There were way more cameras in the building than video monitors. Security associates were expected to cycle through all cameras three times a shift.

It was breakfast time, so people were milling around the cafeteria. Rafe cycled again and found a lab with four coats working inside. They had a wall full of mice in individual cages and what had to be hundreds of beakers and glass containers stored in every extra space of the room. The group of doctors seemed to work in silence, each a spoke on the government wheel. Rafe often watched the labs, curious about what was being tested, created, or observed. It was moments during these observations where Rafe really questioned the high-security facility and what was happening in it.

Mitch Duncan had been full of paranoid theories about the government. Rafe figured he had rolled over in his grave when his only son worked contract work for the same entity he didn't trust. However, Rafe had inherited his father's understanding of security and systems, so the work came naturally to him. Rafe's previous assignment was at a bank that had been robbed and was revamping their security. That type of job made sense to Rafe. There were materials to protect that were valuable to people.

Now, Rafe felt like he was protecting secrets. For a year Rafe had warred with his inner demons, feeling he was betraying his own belief of right and wrong by working at the facility. The people he met throughout the lab were kind and friendly, none setting off any warning bells in his head. He assumed that meant one of two things. One, they were very good actors and didn't feel their work was wrong. Or two, they had no idea what they were really working on either and they were all in the dark together.

He sighed and pulled his gaze away from the doctors. Leaning back in his seat, Rafe set the monitor to auto-rotate. Images of hallways, offices, storage rooms, and labs passed in front of his ice blue eyes. Eyes that had been commented on to look cold and unfeeling, more than once. He relied on his eyes, the sharpness of them and his mind as he watched the images of the building. People moved as they were meant to, going from place to place.

An alarm suddenly began to beep in the security station and Rafe sat forward quickly. He scanned the monitor attached to the alarm and pulled up the camera it indicated. It was the same lab he had been watching before. In the lab, the doctors scurried frantically. Blood was dripping from one woman's hand as she tried to cradle it against her chest.

Rafe realized the emergency was medical, so he started the proper procedures. He called to Liza over their radio and let her know he was leaving the fishbowl to attend to a medical emergency. He gave her the location and she agreed to meet him to assist. As protocol, Rafe also notified the guard at the entrance that there was a medical emergency and Rafe would advise if emergency services were needed. Rafe made these calls as he grabbed his security medical bag and headed out of the door.

When he arrived at the lab, the doctors inside seemed to have calmed down a bit. The sight of Rafe at their glass doorway prompted one to motion for him to wait before they opened the door. One by one each doctor exited the lab through the air shower entrance. The first was the woman with the bleeding hand, which was wrapped in a towel now.

"Hi, I'm Rafe with security," he said, as he set down the medical bag and motioned for her to sit on the bench outside the air shower door.

"I'm Tammy," the hurt doctor replied, a little shaky.

"What happened?"

"One of the mice, it attacked me."

"Attacked you?" Rafe asked. He raised an eyebrow, not understanding how a mouse could have injured the woman badly enough to produce the amount of blood he saw on the towel.

"He bit into my hand, wouldn't let go."

When Rafe took the woman's hand in his gloved ones, he

found a large chunk of flesh to be missing from the web space between her thumb and forefinger. Gingerly he turned her hand to see how bad it was, and he found additional bite marks with less severe wounds on her palm below her thumb. He pressed gauze to the deepest wound and began to bandage it up with a little pressure to help stop the bleeding.

"That was one pissed off mouse," Rafe muttered.

"I don't know why. They are usually such docile animals," Tammy replied.

As Rafe worked the other doctors from the room stood around watching. Liza arrived and once she realized Rafe had everything handled, she radioed for a decontamination team to come to the lab to handle the biohazard situation. The alarm had alerted the lab executives on site and it didn't take long for a suit to arrive on the scene to supervise and handle the situation. If Rafe didn't know any better, this situation was much worse than the chance this woman had rabies.

The other doctors were each taken aside by 'The Suit' individually and Rafe watched from the corner of his eye. He couldn't hear anything, but he could see the doctors' faces as they were being questioned. One woman, who Rafe knew to be named Charlotte, stared up at 'The Suit' with defiant eyes. It made Rafe pause and turn full on to see what was happening. As 'The Suit' asked her a question, Charlotte's hands started flying around in gestures of accusation and anger. Her eyes, which were a noticeable green, were stormy and vivid. *Something is definitely going on here*, Rafe thought to himself.

"Do I need stitches?" Tammy asked, breaking Rafe's concentration on the argument raging nearby.

"Probably. I can't do those here, they don't give us those types of supplies. I don't think you need an ambulance, but I would go to the hospital directly. Also, to make sure you don't contract rabies."

"Oh, the mice don't have rabies. We make sure of that."

"Well erratic behavior like what happened today could indicate someone made a mistake," Rafe said.

"We don't make mistakes."

Rafe just shrugged his shoulders as he cleaned up the area, shoving all of the bloodied items into a red biohazard bag. Everyone made mistakes, he knew, these doctors were no different. Being smart didn't mean something couldn't happen that wasn't in your control. He knew better than to ask or insinuate that whatever tests they were doing to the mice could have caused this. When he started his contract, he was expressly forbidden from speaking to anyone about their work in the facility. So, he left it up to Doctor Tammy to figure out why the mouse had attacked her so viciously.

Raised voices caught Rafe's attention and he was pulled back to 'The Suit' and Charlotte's conversation. He was suddenly reminded of his sisters, Alex and Max. Alex, the oldest of the siblings, had a calming manner; motherly and patient. Max, on the other hand, was the youngest and full of fire if you got her going on something that she believed in. He tried to picture Max now and had to smother a grin at how the small spitfire of Charlotte would do even Max proud with her current tirade.

Finally, Charlotte stormed away, and 'The Suit' put a phone to his ear. With the lab shut down for decontamination, the doctors were sent home. Rafe gave Tammy one more suggestion of going directly to the hospital because she probably needed stitches. She agreed and was gone a moment later. The alarm and injury was the second incident in two years Rafe had handled. Ultimately, he knew that was a very low rate of issues and his job was quite easy.

Later that evening Rafe walked into snow flurries coming down again. He climbed into his truck and set the heater on to keep himself relatively warm on the drive home. The temperature would drop as soon as the sun disappeared behind the mountains. He pulled out, waving at the night security associate, now at the gate.

Traffic was easy, with no accidents clogging up the roads Rafe needed to get home. Once away from town he could feel the release of tension he held when being in close contact with so many people at once. He wasn't antisocial, he liked people well enough. But in small doses. He preferred seclusion and quiet. It was one of the things that set him apart from his sisters. Though Max didn't really care for emotional connections outside of the family, she knew how to manage around people. Alex was a people person and they tended to gravitate toward her heart.

Lost in thought, he almost missed the lights flashing from the trees. Rafe let his foot off of the gas pedal slowly as hazard lights caught his attention about ten feet off the road, into the trees on the right-hand side. He pulled his pickup over to the side and jumped out to check on the driver of the car. When he approached the door swung open and a very angry Charlotte jumped out. She swung a crowbar in his direction.

"Stop right there!" She yelled. Rafe noticed her green eyes again. They seemed to be even more green when she was angry.

"Whoa! Calm down. I just saw your hazards and was coming to see if you were ok," Rafe said, his hands up so as not to frighten her.

"Easy explanation. You could have been the one that just ran me off the road!"

"Ran you off the road? Someone did this to you?" Rafe scanned the road as far as his eyes could see. Nothing moved. No lights except his headlights and Charlotte's hazards showed in the area.

"Yes! I don't just drive into the forest for fun." She seemed to lose some of her momentum of attack and the crowbar started to lower a bit.

"Who would run you off the road? The snow does create some careless drivers. Maybe it was an accident?" Rafe asked the question, but something in his gut had him believing it was as Charlotte said.

"Can you help me get my car back on the road?" Charlotte ignored his question and seemed on edge. Rafe walked to the car to see what type of situation they were dealing with. He didn't have his equipment for towing on the truck currently. The car was pretty stuck into an embankment, it's front tires dug in from where Charlotte had tried to reverse on her own.

"I can't do it right now. I don't have the supplies. I can take you where you need to go," Rafe offered.

"I don't even know you."

"I'm Rafe Duncan," he said pointing to his chest, then he pointed to her, "You're Charlotte Brewer." That caused her to squint at him as if she couldn't place his face.

"Oh, you work in security at the lab," she said suddenly. Rafe just nodded his head. He motioned toward his truck and Charlotte thought for a moment. Decision made in her mind, she turned back to her car and fished out a duffel and her purse. She trudged up the small hill and climbed through the door Rafe held open for her.

Inside the truck, Rafe found Charlotte shivering and leaning toward the vents. He cranked up the heat and she sighed. He pulled back onto the main road and headed toward the small cottage he knew she was renting. Word got around out in his area of the happenings of residents. When the old couple that owned the cottage decided to move into the city and rent out their little home, everyone heard about the young doctor that moved in.

"I saw you today, helping Tammy. You saw me arguing with the facility head," Charlotte said.

"Yup."

"I shouldn't have argued with him."

"Why not?"

"I just shouldn't have. He didn't like it," Charlotte said softly.

"From the argument I saw, you didn't seem to care what he liked."

Charlotte didn't answer. Rafe glanced over at her quickly and he could swear she was blushing. He swung his gaze back to the road quickly, not quite sure what else to say.

"Thanks for stopping," Charlotte said finally, filling the void of sound in the truck cab.

"Why do you think someone ran you off the road on purpose?" Rafe asked, remembering she had avoided his question earlier.

"I think I was being followed," she said, her voice uncertain.

"You think? Or you know?"

"I saw the same black SUV a number of times behind me in town. I ran errands and it was always behind me. I went to yoga and I swear it was parked down the street. When I got out here, there's usually not a lot of traffic in the evenings. The same SUV was behind me."

"There are a lot of SUVs in town. Many of them are black."

"You don't have to believe me," Charlotte shot back, her chin lifted defiantly. Rafe was again struck by how she reminded him of his sister Max. The thought almost made him grin, but he knew it was the wrong time for that.

"I'm not saying I don't believe you. I'm just trying to talk the situation out with you."

"It was the same SUV. Same tint on the windows. I'm pretty sure it was the same license plate, but to be fair I wasn't paying close attention at first."

"How did it run you off the road?" Rafe asked.

"I was driving carefully like I always do when there's snow on the ground. The SUV came up kind of quickly and I was a little nervous about it already. It accelerated like it was going to pass, but just as the back bumper was at my front wheel it started to come into my lane. I had no choice but to move over and it just kept coming. I slammed on my brakes, but it was too late, I was already in the trees."

Rafe sat in silence for a moment. He imagined Charlotte trying to slow down, honking her horn probably, to alert the other driver she was there. Her car was small, but not so small the driver wouldn't have noticed her panicking as they almost hit her. The addition of not stopping once they caused her to drive into the trees, Rafe came to the conclusion that Charlotte was right. She was ran off the road on purpose.

Not long after, Rafe pulled into the driveway of her little cottage. Charlotte sat in her seat for a moment, staring through the windshield. She seemed lost in thought, so Rafe sat quietly waiting for her to let him in on what was happening in her head.

"How did you know where I live?" She asked without looking at him.

"People talk. A doctor moving into the neighborhood was big news when you came."

She still sat staring, as she nodded in understanding of his explanation. Rafe wasn't entirely sure what she was waiting for. For a moment he wondered if she wanted him to open her door. Though his father never taught him the intricacies of being a gentleman, Rafe knew well enough that if they were on a date it would be appropriate for him to open her door. However, that was not what this was, and he didn't want to do something strange.

"Would you mind waiting until I get inside?" Charlotte asked him finally.

"Sure. Do you want me to walk you to the door?"

"Would you mind? I know it's cold out."

"I think I can handle a little snow."

Rafe jumped out of the truck just as Charlotte climbed down and put her purse over her shoulder. She had her keys in her hand as she approached the door. But when they got to the door, she stepped back with a gasp. Rafe moved around her to find the door open, the jam broken where someone had kicked it in. He instantly went on alert, turning and looking around the woods that surrounded the little house. It was too dark to make out anyone that might be an intruder. Rafe wasn't armed and didn't feel confident enough that the intruders were gone.

"Come on," he said. He took Charlotte's arm and led her back to his truck. Her shock kept her from fighting him as he opened the passenger side door and lifted her in.

"Stay here. I'm going to look around the back."

Reaching into the bed of the truck, Rafe grabbed the crowbar he had taken from Charlotte when he picked her up. Normally Rafe had a gun in his truck, but he had to admit to himself he had become lax with the items he knew he should always have. He hefted the crowbar for a moment, deciding that against a would-be attacker it would work in a hand to hand situation. However, against a gun, he would be at a severe disadvantage.

He crept up to the cottage and went to the first window in the front of the house. Charlotte seemed to keep all of her drapes pulled, leaving a clear view into her home. Rafe slid to the side of the window and slowly peered around the edge. He watched the shadows in the house created by his headlights that shined across the front windows. Nothing moved as he stood stock still watching.

Deciding that the front room was clear, Rafe moved to the side of the house. The first window he came to was higher, and he guessed it was a bathroom. He doubted someone was hiding in her bathroom at that moment, so he moved on without trying to find a way to see in the room. The next window was a large double window. He peeked in to find a nicely made bed, dresser with tv, and armchair with a robe draped over it.

As he noted all of the items in the room, he realized the room had been ransacked. The dresser drawers were out of the dresser and clothing was thrown on the floor. The small drawer from her nightstand was open and hanging at an odd angle, items on the floor below. Someone broke in and they were looking for some-thing specific. Her TV was left, so if the break-in was all about theft, the wannabe thief missed a large item.

After Rafe finished a circle around the house, he was fairly certain the intruder or intruders were gone. Other areas in the house seemed to have been searched and items possibly taken. Though without actually seeing the house intact, Rafe couldn't be positive anything was actually missing. When he came around to the front of the house again, Charlotte jumped out of the truck and came running to him.

"Is there someone inside?" She asked.

"I don't believe so. Did you call the cops?"

"Yes. They said to not go inside until they get here. But I need to go in!"

"Charlotte, wait outside. Let the authorities do what they do. They might be able to figure out who did this."

"Charlie," she said suddenly.

"What?"

"Stop calling me Charlotte. No one calls me that. Call me Charlie."

Rafe looked at her, stunned. A few times during the day she had made him think of his sisters. Now to find out she went by a nickname, a typically male name, it was all too much for him. His parents couldn't decide on a name for his older sister. Mitch Duncan didn't know what to do with a girl. The story he told to his children later was, after much debate they had agreed on names for the girls that could be shortened to boy names. Alex's name was Alexandria and Max, Maxine.

Ten minutes later a cop car came screaming down the road, lights flashing through the darkness that had fallen. Rafe explained in detail what he had seen, touched, and done. The cop seemed fairly impressed with his assessment. Weapon raised, the officer entered the house. Moments later he was flipping on lights and talking into the radio on his shoulder. Additional cars pulled up and a crime scene team started their investigation.

"Ma'am, I'm Officer Brown. Do you think you could come inside with me and indicate if anything is missing?" The initial officer that had arrived on scene spoke softly to Charlie, treating her like a fragile creature.

"I've been wanting to do that, Officer, but I was told to stay outside," Charlie answered, her chin hitched up.

With a slightly disbelieving look and Rafe following in bewilderment, they entered the house. Charlie went directly to a desk she had set up in her kitchen area. From the doorway, Rafe could see cords that were leading to where a computer may have sat. A large monitor set up was left, with one monitor knocked over on the desk.

"Well the bastards took my computer," she said, confirming Rafe's suspicions. She began patting under the desk and a creak could be heard before she pulled a piece of wood out. She then palmed a small thumb drive and an envelope. The officer made a move to take the items from her to log into evidence, but Charlie refused adamantly, stating they were her personal documents and she would need them for an insurance claim. Rafe knew without asking that they weren't just personal documents.

"Ma'am, do you have somewhere to stay until you are able to get the locks replaced?" Officer Brown asked.

Charlie looked at him, her face similar to a deer in headlights. It hadn't occurred to her that she would need somewhere to go for the evening. Something about the lost look in her eyes pulled at Rafe. He was speaking before he had thought it through.

"She'll stay with me."

CHAPTER TWO

Sitting in his truck, waiting for the metal gate to roll back at his property, he glanced over at Charlie in his passenger seat. What had gotten into him? This woman's life had nothing to do with him. He hadn't meant to offer his home to her. However, he was even more surprised when she agreed. *No sense to not stay with a stranger*, Rafe thought to himself.

"You live here?" Charlie broke into his thoughts.

"Yeah."

"Alone?"

"Yeah. Why?"

"It's so big," she said, trailing off as they pulled up next to the house.

Rafe parked his truck in its normal spot at the top of the driveway, next to the house and facing the three large shipping containers not far in the distance. In the dark, she wouldn't be able to see the root cellar entrance that was on the other side of the driveway. She got out of the truck tentatively, as Rafe grabbed the small duffel she had packed for herself. He waited silently as she turned and took in the land that surrounded the house. In the moonlight, he knew she couldn't see the large rock wall that surrounded everything.

"Come on in, make yourself at home," Rafe said as he finally walked up to the door.

He flipped on the kitchen light, illuminating the mudroom as he removed his shoes. Charlie followed his lead, leaving her sneakers next to his on the ground under a bench. Rafe walked into the house, turning on lights as he went so Charlie would see where she was going. He could navigate the area in the dark most of the time, but he didn't want her to trip or run into a wall.

In the hallway, Rafe paused, suddenly not sure where to have her sleep. The Duncan house didn't have a guest room, Mitch never planned to allow people to come to visit. He felt wrong putting anyone in his sisters' rooms. Not that his sisters were coming to visit anytime soon, it was still their space. Decision made, Rafe turned into his own room.

"You can sleep here," he said, leading the way into the room. He set her duffel on the bed, which he was thankful he had made that morning. He glanced around for a moment and didn't see anything embarrassingly out of place. Luckily, he was similar to his father when it came to things, Rafe was more of a minimalist.

"This is your room?" Charlie asked.

"Yeah. I'll sleep in my dad's room."

"Oh, where will he sleep?" Charlie looked back out to the hall as if she expected someone to be standing there.

"He won't be. He passed away."

"Oh, I'm sorry," Charlie said, her cheeks flushing slightly.

"It's ok. It's been a few years. It's hard to not think of the room as his still."

"Rafe, thank you for this. I'm not sure why you offered, or really why I accepted."

"You needed a bed. I have beds to offer," Rafe said, shrugging.

"It's more than that. You don't even know me. I don't know you."

"And yet, you're here in my house," Rafe said, laughing a little to lighten her mood. It didn't work. She suddenly sat on the bed and he realized she was clutching something to her chest. He started to walk back to the door and leave her to sleep or do whatever it was she wanted to do.

"I think I know who broke into my house."

Her words stopped Rafe in his tracks. Her voice was laced with fear and she spoke so quietly he wasn't sure he had heard her accurately. At the doorway he turned back and leaned against the doorframe, looking back at her. Her little frame was curled in on itself, while she softly rocked back and forth. He felt cold, thinking about how small and broken she seemed at the moment.

"Why didn't you tell the cops?"

"Because I can't."

"You can't, or you won't?"

Her eyes blazed then, as she looked up at him in anger.

"You think I wouldn't say something if I could, if something could change?"

"I'm not saying you wouldn't. I'm just trying to understand why you didn't tell the cops if you knew who trashed your place."

"It wasn't about trashing it. They were looking for this," she said, holding out her hand, the flash drive in her palm.

"Why would someone be looking for that? What's on it?"

"I...I can't tell you," she said quietly.

"Really?" Rafe raised one eyebrow at her in disbelief.

"It's dangerous. Obviously. Look at my day! I was ran off the road. My house was ransacked!"

Her anger gave her fuel and she stood up again. She began to pace around the room. Her blonde hair had been falling from the knot she had it tied in. Now she pulled it all down and Rafe was shocked to realize it was well beyond the middle of her back. Absently he noted he had never seen her with her hair down at work. She now twirled a long strand around her fingers as she moved.

"I'm thinking I can take care of myself, Charlie. If you know something, you should tell the authorities. They could try and protect you from whatever is happening," Rafe said. She was making him dizzy with her movements. He wanted to grab her and make her still.

"Do you ever wonder what goes on at our facility?" Charlie caught him off guard with her question. He had always wondered but had never asked so he didn't risk his job or the company he contracted with.

"Sure. But there's all sorts of confidentiality clauses I had to sign when I started working there. So, I just don't ask."

"You should. You should ask lots of questions."

"What questions would I ask? I'm not a doctor. I don't understand what it is you lab coats do in your decontaminated rooms," Rafe said. He smiled at her slightly, again hoping to lighten the stress of the situation. She looked at him and just huffed out a sigh.

"I'm tired. This has been such a long day. I just want to go to bed. Is that alright?" Charlie asked.

"Of course. But if you change your mind, you can find me just upstairs."

Rafe showed Charlie the downstairs bathroom, provided her with towels and let her know she was welcome to anything in the kitchen. She declined dinner, claiming she was just too tired to do anything but take a shower and sleep. So Rafe ate a quiet dinner of leftover chili he had made the day before. He stood eating at the kitchen bar, letting the warmth of the chili slide through his stomach and warm his chilled body.

His mind couldn't seem to wrap around everything that had happened that day. Whatever information Charlie she had, she was scared about. Her being ran off the road and her house being broken into on the same day were too wild to be a coincidence. She led him down the path to believing that whatever the problem was, it all tied back to the facility. He started to wonder what he had gotten himself into with helping Charlie and with working at the facility.

Sleep was difficult, causing Rafe to toss and turn in what was his father's bed. He hadn't spent much time in the room since Mitch died. Laying on his back and staring at the ceiling, Rafe reflected back on his father's beliefs. Working for a government facility would have horrified Mitch. He didn't trust anything the government did. Rafe's own feelings were indifferent. He understood much of his father's thoughts were eccentric and not normal.

Now he found himself thinking about the work that was happening in the lab. Charlie said he should ask lots of questions. However, he wouldn't know what to ask. The facility was cloaked in secrecy and urgency at all times. Even when he had worked night shifts, there was never a slow in the number of people working and rushing from one point to another. Employees were two distinctive groups, separate from security. There were the doctors, or the coats, as Rafe called them. And then there were the suits, the business people that would randomly show up in the facility.

Access to the facility was on a need to know basis, and Rafe in his security position didn't know anything about who came and went. Faces changed often. Charlie was one of the coats he recognized because she had been around a little longer than others. The high turnover didn't really raise questions with Rafe before. Previously he had thought projects changed so the scientists needed changing. Now his mind went to a very dark place and he wondered what happened to those that disappeared from the facility.

Morning came before Rafe was prepared, but he drug himself out of bed to start his daily chores. Toweling off his hair, Rafe walked out of the bathroom shirtless, just as Charlie came out of his room looking rumpled and sleepy. His chest was broad, and his body toned from the constant physical work he did on the compound. The skin showing was still glossy from the water of the shower. She stopped suddenly and Rafe was aware he should have put a shirt on with a literal stranger staying in his house.

"Uh, Morning," Charlie said.

"Morning. Coffee is made. What time do you need to be at work?"

"Nine. If that works for you."

"Sure. I just need to feed the animals and handle a few chores. Your car will be towed to the office this morning as well," Rafe said. He had taken the time after she went to bed and called his friend at the local auto body shop. He knew he had his own tow truck and would give Charlie a discount on a tow.

"Thanks for doing that. Uh, are you done in there?" Charlie was outwardly calm, but her voice revealed she was uncomfortable trying to get around a shirtless Rafe. It made him want to laugh, but he kept his face void of any emotions. He nodded and stepped away from the bathroom, so she could scurry in and shut the door quickly.

Outside the sun was coming over the trees and the sky was clear. Rafe was glad they wouldn't have more snow that day. The slush that was left would melt within the day, as spring tried to push its way into Montana. He slipped on his muddy work boots and trudged to the barn. Stepping in, he started with his list of daily chores. He was greeted by the songs of the cows that were waiting for their milking.

He propped a stool next to the first cow and sat down as he ran his hands down her flank. She looked back at him for a moment with big dark eyes but then went back to eating the hay he had popped in front of her.

"Disinterest, huh? Well, that's alright. I'm still here for you," Rafe said as his hands methodically completed the milking. He didn't have to think much about what he was doing, as he had been milking cows since he was six. He hummed while he worked, feeling calm with the repetition of processes he knew.

After milking the four cows he had, he filled five glass jars in preparation for freezing. He rotated frozen milk so there was always a supply. He also always had a glass jar in the fridge for his use. Whatever was left went to mix with the scraps for the pigs. Since he lived alone, there weren't always a ton of scraps for them, so they often got feed, mixed with any food that was starting to go bad and the extra milk. They fattened up nicely every year and he always had a freezer full of pork.

After throwing open the barn doors, allowing the cows to roam free in the pasture for the day, Rafe headed to the chicken pen. He waited outside for a moment, watching the rooster. When he was furthest from the coop, Rafe took the chance and headed inside. As he was pulling the eggs from the nests he felt the familiar sharp pain on his leg and he looked down to see the pissed off rooster. Rafe made one kick at him and the rooster dodged as if he could foresee Rafe's movements.

"Damn you bird. I'm going to kill you, tear out all your feathers, and eat you! You are not the boss around here!"

Laughter from the side of the pasture caused Rafe to look up. In his distraction the rooster took the chance to attack again. He launched off the ground trying to attack Rafe with his claws. One poked through his jeans and made contact with skin. Rafe yelped in surprise and pushed the rooster away from him before fleeing the pen. Charlie's laughter continued from her place by the fence.

After storing the eggs in the outdoor storage area in the barn, Rafe met Charlie.

"You have some interesting friends," she said, a grin on her face.

"He's gonna to be dinner, not a friend," Rafe said. That only caused Charlie to laugh again and clutch her stomach. Her laughter was infectious and Rafe even had to smile along with her.

"You do have quite the set up here," Charlie said, once her giggles had subsided. They were walking together back toward the house, but Rafe led her to the greenhouse first.

"I do."

"All just for you?"

"It's my home, but also my family's place. It belongs to my sisters too."

"But they don't live here?"

"You sure ask a lot of questions," Rafe said. He opened the greenhouse door and motioned her to step inside before him. The room was warm, the glass ceiling doing its duty of letting in the sun and warming the air.

"I can't help it. You're a stranger. But a nice one that rescued me not once, but twice yesterday. I'm naturally curious."

"No, my sisters do not live here. But they could if they wanted to, at any time."

"You're close? I always wondered how having family would be. I don't have siblings. And my parents died when I was young," Charlie said. She walked the rows of plants that Rafe had started earlier in the month. It was early to plant. But in the greenhouse, he was able to get his seedlings started. The stronger plants would be moved to the garden bed once spring took full hold.

"We're close. Not in the, we talk every day all the time way. We grew up...interestingly. That bonds people I think."

"Interestingly?"

Rafe looked at her, his eyebrow raised at the additional questions. She blushed a bit and looked away.

"You're a doctor?" Rafe asked, his attempt to change the subject.

"Yes. I do more studying now then handling patients. But at one time I just wanted to have a private practice."

"How is that possible? You're so young?" Rafe asked, noting that it seemed Charlie was too young to have gone through medical school and all of the official training after the fact. She didn't answer, only shrugged her shoulders and continued to look at his plants.

Sensing she didn't want to talk about it, Rafe let the subject drop and turned on the water. The small irrigation system he created turned on and water began to flow into the seedling containers. He moved around, putting down fertilizer where needed and mixed plant food in the dirt for some of the bigger plants. After he was done, he circled back to the water valve and shut the system off. Charlie was staring out of a window, lost in thought.

"Ready to get to work?" Rafe asked.

"Not really."

"Maybe you could call in. You had a rough day yesterday."

"I can't do that. Then they will know they are getting to me," Charlie replied.

"Who?"

Charlie turned to look at him. She seemed to contemplate what to tell him. In the end her gaze seemed to shutter, the decision made to continue to keep him in the dark.

"Are you done here? Is it time to go?"

"Yes. We can go," Rafe replied.

The drive to the facility was quiet. Charlie fidgeted in her seat as they got into town and closer to the place she seemed to be afraid of. At the security gate, for the first time ever the guard took notice of Rafe. If it wasn't such a serious situation, Rafe would have laughed. But instead he explained that Charlie's car had broken down, so he offered her a ride. He showed both of their ID's and they were let into the gate with no question.

Rafe pulled his truck back to the normal spot he parked. He popped open his door, but realized Charlie wasn't moving. She sat still in her seat looking at the door in front of them.

"Charlie?"

"I just don't want to go back in there," she said quietly.

"You've said as much. I can take you home if you want?"

Charlie shook her head, her hair back to the pile on the top, with little strands escaping around her face and neck. Her decision made, she got out of the truck and marched up to the door without a look backward. The two split to go their separate ways, after Rafe promised to wait for her so he could give her a ride in case her car hadn't made it to the facility in time.

In the security fishbowl, Rafe went through his normal morning routine of talking to Liza and checking monitors. He found himself watching Charlie in her lab. She was changing into her lab coat and about to step into the air shower before entering the sterile room. Rafe had noticed all signs of the previous day's issue completely wiped away from the white room. Some of the cages were now empty and he assumed the attack mouse had been taken care of. However, he wondered why there seemed to be more than ten cages empty instead of just the one.

Watching Charlie and the other coats in the room, Rafe realized the injured woman from the day before wasn't present in the lab. He thought back to her wound, thinking it would have been easily handled at the ER if she had gone like he instructed. A few stitches would have closed it up. But as the wound was on her hand, she may have felt it was too painful to work the day after and had called in sick. Rafe made a note to ask Charlie about that.

The day seemed to pass slowly, but without incident. Rafe liked quiet. He shifted through the labs, watching the movements as he always did. Nothing seemed out of the ordinary to him for most of the morning. It was after lunch that he found the same suit Charlie had yelled at walking through the corridors. He wore wire-rim glasses and the security cameras couldn't quite see his eyes as he moved. Rafe knew 'The Suit' wouldn't know he was being watched, so he switched through cameras to follow his path straight to Charlie's lab.

Suit man tapped on the glass wall of the lab, pointing directly at Charlie and motioning for her to come out. Her face went pale from what Rafe could see, her mouth slightly open in shock. Was this man the one she was afraid of? Was he the one she thought had sent someone to follow her, run her off the road, ransack her house? Rafe didn't think twice about his actions as he grabbed his portable radio and left the fishbowl. He radioed Liza to let her know he was stir crazy and was going to walk. When really, he was walking straight to Charlie to find out what was going on.

Rafe arrived at the lab, just as Charlie was exiting the air shower. Rafe hid around the corner, waiting to see if he could hear any of their conversation. Different than yesterday, Charlie spoke quietly, professionally. She didn't raise her voice or yell at the man. Rafe could hear 'The Suit' ask about Tammy and where she was. Charlie replied that she didn't know, but that she hadn't come to work today. There were more whispered words that Rafe couldn't make out and he had to take a chance to glance around the corner to even make sure the two were still standing there. He could see the side of Charlie's face and her eyes were round with fear.

Again, Rafe acted without much thought. He walked calmly around the corner, as if he had just arrived. Charlie caught sight of him first. 'The Suit' had his back to Rafe, but Charlie's eyes shifting caused him to turn and focus on what had caught her attention. Rafe smiled professionally at them both as he stopped near them.

"Hello, Doctor. I was just coming to check on my patient from yesterday. Tammy, I believe?" Rafe said, smiling at the word patient to show he was being jovial.

"Um, well, she's not here," Charlie stammered, clearly not sure where Rafe was going with the conversation.

"You are?" 'The Suit' spoke. This close, Rafe could now see the man's eyes. They were hazel and cold. Fixed on Rafe, the look was menacing without saying a word.

"Security. I treated Tammy's hand yesterday. Had suggested she go to the ER. Wanted to check on the progress," Rafe said. He kept his stance and voice nonchalant, not phased by 'The Suit's malicious attitude toward him.

"Right. Well security doesn't have patients. You can move on," 'The Suit' said.

"Doctor? Is there anything I can help you with?" Rafe said,

ignoring 'The Suit' and focusing on Charlie. His gaze willed her to say something, to give him a sign she needed his help. Her eyes met his for a moment before she shook her head no without saying anything.

Not being able to stand in the middle of their conversation any longer, Rafe moved past the pair and turned the corner down the hall. He waited a moment, to make sure the conversation didn't escalate. The sound of clipped heels started his way and he knew 'The Suit' was about to discover him hiding around the corner. Light on his feet, Rafe ran to the next turn in the hall and headed back toward the security office.

He arrived back at the fishbowl just as the phone was ringing. Rushing, he grabbed the phone out of the cradle and answered with his normal brisk security greeting.

"What do you think you're doing?" Charlie's irritation flowed across the line. Realizing who it was, Rafe turned to the monitors and pulled up the cameras in her lab. Her face was turned up at the camera, a silent accusation of his spying.

"I saw 'The Suit' come back. I was making my rounds. What's the problem?"

"You don't make rounds. The woman guard does. I've never seen you do that before."

"Been watching me?" Rafe joked.

"I'm observant. I notice what's happening around me. And you have never walked near our lab during the day. You can't get involved in this, Rafe," Charlie said. Her voice was in a harsh whisper, but she didn't take her eyes off of the camera, making sure he saw the exact emotion she was trying to convey.

"You seemed uncomfortable, so I tried to help," he said.

"I'm not uncomfortable."

"No, you're right. Not uncomfortable. You were scared. Is 'The Suit' who you're afraid of? Is he the one that you think sent the people after your car and house?"

"Rafe. I'm only saying this one more time. Stay out of it.

Look, thank you. Thank you for all you've done for me. But this is something you need to stay away from. It's for your own safety."

With that, Charlie hung up the phone. She glanced at the camera one last time and turned back to the counter that held her work. Rafe watched her for a few minutes more, before continuing to scan the cameras through their rotation. He watched the other images, but his mind was still with Charlie. He could take care of himself. Eventually, even Charlie would realize Rafe wasn't someone to be challenged.

CHAPTER THREE

The morning sun streamed into Tammy's bedroom. The room was simply decorated, with her bed, dresser, and armchair taking up most of the space. Her general idea was to just have items that were functional. She didn't worry about colors or matching. She just knew in general what she liked and clean colors were what she chose. Her light blue bedspread that was typically pristine, was stained with blood now. Her work clothes from the day before hadn't made it to the laundry basket. Instead, they were left in a bloody, crumpled pile at the foot of her bed.

As she tried to peel her eyes open, her body began to tremble, making it impossible for her to turn off her alarm. Her hand hurt, burned almost, where the mouse had bitten her. *Damn mouse*, she thought to herself. She hadn't listened to the security guard who told her to go to the emergency room. It was just a mouse bite. However now, she was thinking she should have listened. Her foggy brain still couldn't comprehend why the mouse had attacked her. The small thing had done quite a bit of damage to her hand before she had flung it across the lab. She knew that mouse, along with the others of the testing group, would have been disposed of as soon as the attack had happened.

It took all of her strength, but Tammy finally was able to fling back the comforter. It was then she realized that the bandage on her hand was soaked through and there was blood all over her bed. She groaned. She was never going to get the stains out of her light-colored sheets. She tried to hold up her hand, so she could examine the bandage. But she couldn't keep her eyes open long enough to really focus. She was sure that some places were so thick with blood, they were black. The bandage had been tight enough, putting pressure on her wound. Tammy felt more confusion as she tried to work out why she hadn't started to clot yet.

Tammy rolled to the side of the bed, attempting to put her feet down on her hardwood floor. The moment she put weight on her legs, she collapsed weakly. *How sick am I?* She thought to herself. The floor felt cool against her cheek, giving her an additional sign of some sort of illness. She tried to breathe deeply but her chest rattled, and she started to cough. It felt like her entire body was convulsing. To distract herself from how bad she was feeling, she began to categorize her symptoms. Her doctor brain tried to reason that she had some sort of flu that had come on fast and hard.

She was so late for work. Even though she felt like death, she realized that not calling in would reflect negatively on her. Tammy had not missed a day of work since she began her time at the facility. When she was hired and moved from her position with the CDC, Tammy had been excited about the change. Once she started working in the lab, her mind focused on the work at hand. She rarely thought about the reason they were working on the projects that were given to them. With the CDC she was always investigating pathogens and the effect they had on the human body. Her work in the facility was quite similar, except the pathogens she worked with had no names. Just numbers to identify the batch being tested.

The sun shifted, and the shadows changed in her bedroom.

Tammy wasn't sure how long she had laid on the ground. But she worked her way slowly to her bathroom, where she hoped to reach her thermometer and medications. Her body didn't want to respond the way it should. Using her uninjured hand, she tried to pull herself. It was a long painful process, with many moments when she would begin coughing again. When she reached her bathroom floor, she was exhausted beyond belief. She fell into a deep sleep, her injured hand seeping across the white immaculate tiles.

Darkness seeped into Tammy's bedroom, finding her still sleeping on her bathroom floor. She hadn't been able to reach her medications. In the short moments she was awake, she would think she had the energy to get to the pills she knew she had. Coughing woke her again and she was disoriented. At first, she was shocked, believing she had gone completely blind. After blinking her heavy eyelids a number of times, she was able to make out the clock by her bed, though it was a blur of color instead of clear numbers.

Tammy was in trouble, she knew it. What she thought she could handle on her own had quickly spiraled out of control. She had only recently moved to Montana, relocated from her home in Georgia. The only people she had locally were her co-workers. Her mind tried to sift through who she could call. Any of them would be a good option, as they were all doctors in their own ways.

Decision made, Tammy turned her body to angle back toward her bed. Her cell phone was plugged in on the bedside table. She needed to call a co-worker. Or even 911. Her injured hand no longer hurt, which was a blessing Tammy thought. For a moment she thought she couldn't actually feel the fingers on that hand, but she told herself it was her exhaustion and flu causing her to feel numb. The darkness hid the blood she had trailed to the bathroom and the additional she trailed heading back to her bed.

Just feet away from her bed Tammy's body no longer responded to her mental commands. The woman lay sprawled across her floor, one hand looking to pull her further, her legs spread in useless angles. Blood matted her hair, her nightgown, and the floor. It was in this horror that Tammy's body shut down and her breathing stuttered to a stop.

CHAPTER FOUR

Rafe finished his evening chores just as darkness settled across his compound. He stood outside for a moment and looked up at the stars. The evening was crisp and clear. He loved nights like this and often opted to sleep in a hammock within the trees that lined the property. He could name the majority of the constellations across the sky. According to Mitch Duncan, Rafe's obsession with the stars was a foolish way to spend his time. But as a child whenever there were no chores to do, Rafe would lay on his back outside and just study what he saw.

He was just turning to head into the kitchen from the mudroom when the alarm from his gate went off. A few long strides took him to the monitor in his room that projected the camera angles and let him speak with people at the gate. He was astonished to see Charlie's face looking directly into the camera that was positioned to look into the driver's side window. She waited, patiently but with nerves. He saw her eyes darting around the dark forest that sat outside his stone walls. He pressed the button on his intercom.

"Charlie?"

"Rafe. Can I come in?"

"I guess. Did you forget something here?" Rafe said, as he turned to look around his room, the room she had slept in the night before.

"No. Can I come in and then we can talk. It's....well....it's creepy out here."

Rafe didn't blame her for that. The woods, when you weren't familiar with them, could hide all sorts of nightmares. Though they weren't real, and all imagined, it didn't stop your brain from conjuring beasts. He reached to the opener he kept in his room for this exact reason and buzzed her in. He watched the monitors until her car had passed through the gate and then pressed the button again to close the entrance. He didn't stop watching the monitors until he knew for sure she was the only thing to enter the compound.

He was waiting for her when she pulled her car up next to his truck in the gravel driveway. She seemed to prepare herself for his questions before getting out of her vehicle. When he approached, he noticed bags in her backseat, more than the single duffel she had brought for her previous stay. He just waited for her silently. He was learning he couldn't push Charlie into giving him any information she didn't want to give up. Their last conversation over the phone at the facility had a finality to it, making Rafe believe she wouldn't be turning to him for help again.

She finally opened the door and got out. At first, she looked around the compound again as if she were waiting for a monster to jump out of the shadows.

"Did you want to come inside?" Rafe said. He thought maybe the lights inside could help her feel more at ease.

"Yes. Can I....can I stay?" Charlie asked timidly.

"Stay? What's wrong?"

"I just don't feel safe. I had my locks changed. The doors fixed. But, they know where I live."

"They?" Rafe asked though he was pretty sure she wouldn't tell him who "they" were.

"I can't tell you. I won't put you at risk."

"It's not a risk for you to be staying in my home?"

"This place?" Charlie laughed as she gestured around. "This place is a fortress. But also, we have no connection. No one even realizes we have met. They wouldn't send people here looking for me."

"So, you didn't come here to see me, just to use my fortress?"

"Correct," Charlie answered with no hint of a smile. Rafe couldn't judge her motives by her expression.

"Come in. You can stay."

Bags in hand, Charlie followed Rafe into the house. Once inside she waited for his cue and he motioned for her to take his room again. He followed to grab his essentials. While he sorted through his dresser, Charlie sat silently on the edge of the bed, waiting for him to be done. His arms were full of clothing when he turned toward the doorway. He stopped and looked over his shoulder, finding her staring at the wall across from him. He decided silence was his best option at the moment and left her to her thoughts.

In his father's room, now his room he supposed, he put away the things he had brought. The dresser had long been emptied of his father's clothing. Rafe was wider than his father, so his clothes were useless to him. As he sorted and organized he could hear Charlie moving around the house and soon walking up the stairs. He waited for her to speak, trying to not pressure her into talking before she was ready. She stood at the door of the room watching him before clearing her throat.

"Thank you," she said.

"You're welcome," Rafe replied. He continued his task of getting the room sorted for his use.

"I know this is asking a lot. I'm sorry to put you out of your own room."

"Charlie, it's alright," Rafe said as he turned to finally face her.

"It's really not. I've never been this scared before," she said, her voice getting very quiet at the end.

"Then why don't you hand whatever is on that flash drive over to the proper people?"

"Because I can't."

"You can't? Why can't you just do whatever you want?"

"It's not safe. I told you that."

"Yes, you keep talking about safety. But you never give any details and it's getting old. Look, I have no issues helping you out here. Frankly I feel some sort of strange obligation to protect someone that's in need like you are. But if I'm to help you, I need to know what's happening."

Charlie seemed to mull that over for a moment. She looked around the room while he waited for her response. His father's extensive collection of knives were in a glass case against one wall. She stopped in front of the case, staring at the blades, their intricate handles and sizes. Her eyes looked back at Rafe, a question on her face.

"My father liked knives. And being prepared."

"Clearly," she said as she looked back at the case.

Rafe was about to give up on any additional information from her when she spoke again.

"My job is not what I thought I signed up for. And if I didn't have a contract I would leave immediately. But I don't know what they would do to me now if I tried to walk away."

"Isn't it like any other job? You quit and maybe don't get paid. But they don't chop off your hand," Rafe replied.

"No. It's definitely not like any other job."

"What about it isn't what you signed up for?"

"You realize it's against both of our non-disclosure agreements to talk about this, right? If I tell you what's happening, we are breaking all the rules," Charlie said, her voice holding a warning tone.

"Ok. Thinking we are beyond that now."

"The experiments that happen in that lab. They aren't normal. I worked for the CDC before, did you know that?"

"No. But I figured you had to be someone that knew labs and the work that needed to be done. So many seem to come and go," Rafe said.

"I know. That's what scares me. I was friends with one of the last doctors. We had drinks a few times. When all of a sudden it seemed like she just disappeared. It was around that time she was talking about the strange things we seemed to be testing and how she wasn't sure she could keep doing the job. Then one day, she didn't show up to work. And she never answered her phone. I had just assumed, ya know, she moved away and was distancing herself from the facility."

"You never heard from her again? Ever?"

"I received an email," Charlie answered, her voice quiet, almost sheepish. Rafe guessed she knew what he was thinking. But that didn't stop him from voicing what was on his mind.

"You didn't think to notify anyone that your friend was missing?"

"I got an email. Said she was done with the facility and had moved on. Basically, it explained exactly what I had guessed, so I didn't try to contact her again."

"Remind me to not go missing and hope you'd come looking," Rafe commented sarcastically.

"Really? That's what you're going to needle me about?"

"I'll let it go for now. Talk more about the experiments."

"Well, with the CDC I was always working on cures. Ways to solve health epidemics before they happened. If some small outbreak did somehow start, I would be sent to see if the cures we had manufactured would work for the strain that was infecting people. It felt like good work, helping people kind of work," Charlie said. She was wringing her hands again and twirling a piece of her long hair. Rafe noted it as her obvious tell that she was nervous or scared.

"Sounds like it would have been fulfilling. Why did you accept the job at the facility?" Rafe asked.

"I was approached by one of my supervisors. He told me about the opportunity at the facility. I was pulled into a joint meeting with my supervisor, the director of the CDC, and some government executives. It was explained to me as a chance of a lifetime to really make a difference. Looking back now, my supervisor seemed uncomfortable. But I had assumed she just didn't want me to leave," Charlie explained. She turned to face Rafe then, waiting for his reaction. He just motioned for her to continue.

"This isn't the chance of the lifetime. I no longer create cures. I create toxins and viruses first. Then if they are what the executives are looking for, we figure out if we can cure it," Charlie finished.

"Wait. You're making illnesses? Why?" Rafe asked. He had a sneaking suspicion he already knew the answer to that. But he wanted to see what Charlie thought the purpose was.

"They don't tell us what it's for. At first, I thought it was the idea of us creating things before anyone else. If we created it in our lab safely and then we could create the cure, if someone else did the same thing in their lab it wouldn't work well against us. We'd be ready for it."

"Ok, that's what you thought at first. And that does make some sense. But you're saying you don't believe that now?"

"No," Charlie said.

"Why?" Rafe asked, sounding a bit repetitive.

"The last few experiments, the executive has been angry with the failures. I thought the last one was going to be what they were looking for, but then the mouse attacked Tammy. The guy you saw me talking to..."

"The one you were yelling at you mean?" Rafe interjected.

"Yes, that one. I was yelling that day because he didn't care that Tammy had been injured. He wanted to know which experiment the mouse had been injected with and if there were any clear signs of infection. When I told him, I didn't know for sure because it hadn't been long since the experiment was started, he was very angry," Charlie said.

Rafe leaned against the wall, looking over at Charlie who was now sitting on the bed, her hands gripped in her lap.

"He was angry that you didn't succeed with that round of experiments? What happened to the mice after? I noticed a bunch were missing."

"Protocol for an incident like this is the animals with that specific control group to be disposed of immediately. Then the room had to be decontaminated. We had to wait a day to go back to the lab to ensure its process was done."

"You didn't see the mice taken away, right?" Rafe asked.

"No. I just assumed it happened because they were gone when we got there."

"What were you trying to create?"

"A biological substance that could create large mood shifts in the subject, mainly focusing on anger. We utilized large doses of antidepressant chemicals and noradrenaline to cause a large shift in the serotonin in a subject's brain. This dip can create the chance of violent behavior with the right instigation."

"And it didn't work? That mouse was angry enough to bite Tammy," Rafe commented.

"There's no way that mouse was affected that quickly by what had been injected. It had only been a few minutes before Tammy was bitten."

"Is there any way to know that? Were there any tests done?"

"Before the mice were disposed of? I wouldn't think so. It was a standard accident with one animal acting out," Charlie said absently. She seemed to weigh what Rafe was suggesting, staring into space. She shook her head as if to wake herself up before looking at him.

"No. There's no test. But I just can't imagine that the test injection had affected the mouse that quickly."

"And your tests with that chemical? Are they done? Or will you have to run another round through mice? What does 'The Suit' want you to do?"

"'The Suit'? That's a good name for him. Well he wants us to test it again. It was possibly the most promising version of the current assignment. I'm going to put it off as long as I can. But that's why I came here. If I don't comply, I'm not sure what they will do."

"Probably get someone else for the job," Rafe said.

"Maybe. But I'm the lead in the lab right now. It would take time to hire someone else and bring them up to speed. I just need to stall, until I can gather more information. And I have to gather that without getting caught."

"Ok. Well, while you're doing all this, you can stay here. My gates and walls are all alarmed. Someone tries to come in here that's not welcome, we'll know with plenty of warning."

"And you know how to use those?" Charlies asked, as she pointed at the knives on the wall.

"That and more."

The next few days were not without issue. Rafe had a hard time acclimating to living with someone in his house, let alone a woman. He had to remember to not walk out of the bathroom after a shower with only a towel. He had walked in on Charlie showering on the first day. He almost ran into the doorjamb in his rush to get out of the bathroom with his eyes squeezed shut. Her dainty laugh followed him, which only needled him.

They were careful to not lead anyone back to Charlie's hiding place at the compound. They still drove separately to work. They didn't speak personally at the facility, following their individual routines. Charlie almost slipped on the third day when she passed him in the hallway and she asked if he had remembered the lunch she had packed him. He quickly looked around and felt fairly certain they were alone before answering. The domestic feeling of the situation bothered him. But Charlie insisted on helping around the house while she stayed.

"I'm not a freeloader," she had said.

Rafe went about his normal chores morning and evening. Charlie would follow, watching everything he did and then the third day she offered to help milk the cows. After much laughter and a spilled bucket of milk, she got the hang of it and they were able to feed the pigs and create a meal for the chickens. After seeing the rooster with Rafe the first day she was at the compound, she absolutely refused to enter the chicken coop. She did enjoy standing by the fence laughing in her loudest laugh as the rooster insisted on attacking Rafe. The obscenities Rafe yelled at the rooster were partially directed at her as well.

The weekend arrived and with nothing else to do besides chores, Rafe walked Charlie around the rest of the compound. He showed her the root cellar, bunkhouse, and storage containers. She marveled at how Rafe was knowledgeable in storing vegetables in a root cellar. When he began to talk about canning fruit, she stared at him as if his head had rolled off his shoulders. He looked back at her, amused by her reaction.

"Well it's not nuclear science. But I make sure I always eat well," he finally said. He pulled an apple from a nearby crate and rubbed it against his pants before handing it to her. She took a bite and smiled at him. Looking around they talked for an hour longer about how he stored carrots, garlic, onions, and sweet potatoes. They looked at the different jars of pears, peaches, pickles, and beans. As he told her the process he went through once a month or so to rotate jars and pack up fresh foods, Charlie was enthralled.

"I don't understand. How did this all end up here? How did you learn all of this? Your mother?" Charlie asked.

"No. My mother died when I was two. My father built all this. Mostly on his own, but when I was old enough I helped with a lot of it. Then he passed away and I've just continued things as he did."

"So, your father was afraid of the world ending?"

"Oh, he was afraid of a lot of things. But the world ending in one way or another was his top concern. He wanted this place to be safe and successful for my sisters and me."

"You have a lot of land around here. Is it all walled in?"

"Yeah. My father insisted on the rock walls. He used a tractor to build the majority of it himself. After he passed, I set up a security system with a closed-circuit system with video and alarm. It all runs off of the solar power batteries in the back."

At the mention of the solar-powered batteries, Charlie insisted on a more detailed tour. They left the root cellar and walked to the back of the bunkhouse to show her the solar power panel bank he had created for his father. They then went to the wall and walked the perimeter of the property. Rafe showed Charlie where the fruit trees were, where they picked from a tree of winter pears, filling a basket to take back to the house.

Evening was dropping across the house as they arrived back from their long walk. With the fresh pears, Rafe began the task of washing and drying the fruit. Charlie sat down heavily at the kitchen table and watching him.

"Too much for you today?" Rafe joked.

"No. It was fun. Thanks for showing me around. I haven't been sleeping well."

"Do you need something else in your room?"

"Your room you mean?" Charlie said with a small smile.

"Well it's yours right now. If you need something to be comfortable, just let me know."

"It's been four days. It's not your job to cater to me, Rafe," Charlie said.

"I know. But it's my house and I feel like it's my responsibility."

"It's nothing to do with the house. Or the room. Or you.

Tammy still hasn't come back to work. I'm concerned. No one has heard from her. It almost feels like the first friend I had at the facility. She's just disappeared. I want to go to her house and check on her."

"Where does she live?"

"In town at a small townhouse that was rented for her I believe."

"When do you want to go check on her?"

"Today?"

"Slow down, speed racer. We need a plan. Her house could be under surveillance since she hasn't returned. But I don't want you going there without me, in case it's something worse," Rafe said.

Charlie absently nodded, as if she were thinking of something else. Rafe was surprised that she agreed to wait. The woman was always ready to run head first into any dangerous situation. The smartest thing she had done in Rafe's opinion, was come to his compound. They talked the plan out over the weekend. It was decided Rafe would follow Charlie in his own truck. She would lead the way to the townhouse but wouldn't stop directly near it. Rafe would check Tammy's house before letting Charlie know it was safe for her to enter.

Monday came, bringing all of their plans to a halt. Arriving to work as they had done the week prior, Rafe entered the security gate first, with Charlie's little car following behind. Rafe didn't watch the security guard as he drove away. He didn't see the man watching their two cars and picking up the phone to dial the number he had on speed dial.

CHAPTER FIVE

The facility loomed in front of her car and Charlie just sat looking at the door she needed to walk through. She knew Rafe had driven to the back of the building, parking in his normal spot. He would be on his way to the security office now. But Charlie continued to sit in her car, just staring. She thought about just driving away. When that thought entered her mind, it immediately left, chased out by the fear she felt. 'The Suit', as Rafe liked to call him, was a formidable enemy. Though she didn't have the proof on him she wished she did, deep down she believed he was responsible for so much more than just management of projects.

Charlie was in her own mind as she entered the building and headed for the locker room set up for the employees working in the labs. Changes of clothes were provided to keep the environments sterile. She changed into her scrubs and white lab coat before heading to her assigned lab. The halls were lined with white rooms, doctors just like her flitting from one place to another. It had always bothered Charlie they weren't allowed to know what projects were being worked on in labs they didn't belong to. The secrecy seemed odd when they all had signed the same non-disclosure agreement.

The air shower blew her loose hairs into her face. She closed her eyes and waited for the process to be completed. Once the beep sounded she opened her eyes to find the green light for her at the door. Stepping into her lab, she realized she was the first to arrive that morning. She checked the clock and found herself to only be about five minutes early. She began her preparations for the next solution she was creating. While the one they previously tested on the mice hadn't been completed, they had a timetable to continue. They would circle back to the previously unfinished tests when they had open time scheduled.

From behind her, the air shower turned on again. Charlie was used to the noise and didn't turn to see who was entering the lab. When the door opened though, Charlie looked up when she heard coughing. A lab technician, named Aiko entered the room. Charlie noted immediately how pale she looked.

"Aiko? Are you ill?"

"Charlie, oh my god. I'm not feeling so well," Aiko started. She stumbled to a chair near the desk inside the lab and sat down. Charlie followed and when she stood next to Aiko's seat, she noticed her arm was bandaged.

"What happened? Did you just come down with something today?"

"Yeah. But, I only came to work so I could talk to you. I don't have a phone number—"Aiko's sentence was cut off by coughing that shook her body.

"You needed to talk to me? Why?"

"Tammy. I went to see Tammy last night. It was late. I was driving by her townhouse and saw a light on and what I thought was someone moving around," Aiko said. Her breathing was labored, and she gripped her chest as she tried to continue.

"Aiko, I think we should call someone to help you."

"Tammy bit me," Aiko blurted out finally.

"Bit you?"

"Yes. It was dark. But I know it was her. She didn't answer

when I knocked, so I tried the door. I was concerned, ya know?" Aiko's words came out as a mumble, as she laid her head on the desk.

"Yes, we were all concerned. What happened next Aiko?" Charlie asked. She shook Aiko slightly, waking her from whatever daze she was in.

"When I opened the door, I heard a growl, so I stepped back out on the dark porch. Tammy doesn't have a dog, right?"

"I don't think so," Charlie said.

"Well, it was dark on the porch. And suddenly she was on me. Tammy. She grabbed my arm as I was stepping back. And before I knew it, she bit into it! I was able to yank away and run," Aiko finished.

Charlie took Aiko's arm in her hands, inspecting the gauze that covered the wound. Looking closer, she saw what looked like very dark blood. If she wasn't mistaken it was black, not dried blood, but black blood trying to ooze through the gauze. Her mind raced. She was qualified to be a primary care doctor when the need arose, but she wasn't sure she knew how to handle whatever was wrong with Aiko at the moment. The woman laid very still, her breathing very shallow. However, there was one more question burning in Charlie's mind.

"Aiko, did you call the police? Go to the hospital or anything?"

"Hmmm? No. I called here. Talked to the director. Told him I was hurt. He said they would send authorities to deal with Tammy. Isn't that what we have to do? Call here? Not the police?"

The agreement all of the employees signed at the facility did specify, should there be an emergency, injury, or questions, they were to never call the local authorities. Always call the facility first. If you needed emergency medical attention, the staff at the facility would be sent to you by way of a private ambulance. All of this seemed like overkill to Charlie before, but now as her mind worked through these details, she realized how foolish she had been. All of their considerations. All of their rules. They were all ways to keep the lid on whatever happened inside or outside of the facility.

Charlie turned to the phone, knowing she needed help for Aiko. She first called the local emergency staff. Told them she had an injured and sick employee. Explained it wasn't a workplace injury but she was extremely ill and needed help. Once off the phone with them, Charlie risked the call to Rafe she needed to make.

"What's wrong with her?" Rafe asked immediately, no hello, just right to business. *Always the gruff one*, Charlie thought. Charlie looked up to the nearby dome that held the camera she knew he was using to look at her.

"She's really sick. She is saying Tammy bit her last night! I don't know why Tammy would do that," Charlie said in a rush.

"Charlie, are you sure the virus you guys created didn't get passed to Tammy?"

"No. It couldn't have. All of the viruses we create and test, have specific mutations to not allow crossover. It's a safety protocol. And I told you, it was too fast. There's no way Tammy got this from that mouse," Charlie said. Her voice went into a hushed whisper when the air shower came on but was bypassed by the emergency team.

"Hang up so they don't ask who you're talking to. I'm watching for any signs of trouble," Rafe said and then the phone clicked.

She did as he instructed and turned to watch the emergency team working on Aiko. Questions were shot at her in rapid-fire succession. Where was she when she first got sick? Was she infected in the lab? How long had she been ill? Her symptoms when she arrived? Charlie answered to the best of her ability, only having the limited information Aiko had relayed to her before passing out.

One EMT laid Aiko flat on the floor to start checking vitals. It was then they realized she had no pulse and wasn't breathing.

Charlie cried out and covered her mouth with her hand. She stepped back, in shock and dismay. This young girl had always been bubbly and sweet. And now she lay lifeless on the floor of her lab. The EMT ripped open her shirt, to place the pads of the defibrillator in place, while the other worked an oxygen bag at her mouth. As they waited for the charge on the machine, the EMT started manual compressions, counting out loud.

Charlie's mind was a jumbled mess. She stepped to her work console and pulled out the thumb drive she had in her pocket. She was no longer afraid of anyone seeing what she was doing. *What if Rafe is right?* She thought. *What if the virus jumped species? What if Tammy has it?* Those questions pushed her to begin the download of all information about virus 302RD onto her drive. She thought about the name of the virus. The 302 was put into place before she had come to the lab. She never figured it was for 302 tries, but now she guessed it was. The RD stood for "Rage Disorder" describing the desired effect of the virus.

"Clear!" One of the EMTs yelled from Aiko's side. Charlie tried to not cringe as she heard the sound of the defibrillator doing its job.

"Nothing," the other EMT responded.

"Wait...she's moving...." EMT number one said, his voice incredulous.

"She doesn't have a heartbeat. You're seeing things. Resume compressions," EMT number two said.

The EMT fisted his hands together and laid them back on her chest. Suddenly Aiko's hand snaked out and she grabbed the EMT doing compressions and pulled him down. Charlie at first thought in her foggy mind, Aiko was playing around and was going to try and kiss the EMT. The scream that tore through the lab next, cleared Charlie's mind of that thought immediately.

"Oh my god, what the hell!" Screamed the other EMT as he pushed away from Aiko on all fours. Blood poured from the EMT in Aiko's grasp, pooling around her face and onto the white tile.

"Aiko! What are you doing?" Charlie screamed. The words were out of her mouth before she thought and almost immediately she knew it was a mistake. The EMT with the face half gone was pushed to the side. Aiko's dead body moved to sit up and then climb to her feet. Charlie felt rooted to one spot, not able to comprehend what was happening. It was Aiko's eyes that finally shook her from her stupor. The black orbs, which used to be Aiko's brown eyes, stared at Charlie where she stood. Charlie stared into the darkness, her mind trying to determine where the whites had gone.

Aiko's body stepped toward Charlie, completely ignoring the man moaning on the ground with a large hole in his face. The growl that split the air, made Charlie think of what Aiko had said about Tammy's house. *No, she didn't have a dog*, Charlie thought. Convinced then that Aiko was no longer alive, Charlie grabbed her thumb drive and bolted for the door to the air shower. She reached the door two steps before Aiko, whose hands were now up in claws, attempting to swipe at her.

The gauze that had covered Aiko's wound had been removed by the EMT as they inspected her body. Charlie gasped when she saw the round black mark with flesh missing from her arm, that looked like a human bite. Tammy had bitten her and now she was dead, but not? Charlie didn't want to wait around to find out. She tried to slam the door between her and Aiko just as the infected woman was reaching through to grab her. The door tried to close with a crunch and Aiko's fingers stopped moving as her arm fell at an awkward angle. There was no response from the infected woman and Charlie stared at her face in horror through the glass.

The black depths of her eyes were dead but focused clearly on Charlie. Her mouth chomped before a deep hissing growl seemed to come from her throat, though Charlie was sure she had never heard that noise from a human before. Aiko continued to throw her dead body against the door, trying to get into the air shower. Charlie held onto the doorknob with all her strength. Making a decision, she opened the door wide enough to push Aiko's now broken arm back into the lab. Once clear the door slammed shut and locked for the decontamination sequence.

Charlie stood in the middle of the air shower, shaking as she watched Aiko through the glass window. Charlie knew as soon as the shower stopped the doors on both ends would disengage, allowing the person to leave decontaminated. She wasn't sure if Aiko could open the door once it was unlocked and that had her pushing herself against the exit, so she could escape. As she did this Aiko's face suddenly moved away from the window. Charlie waited but she didn't come back, so she crept back to peek into the lab.

Horror gripped Charlie like a vice. Aiko was on her knees, leaning over the EMT she had bitten earlier. The man tried to weakly fight, but it seemed he couldn't get the small woman off of him. Blood spilled from where Aiko was biting into his exposed middle. Charlie began to gag when she realized that Aiko was eating the man, eating his skin. Just as the air shower stopped, Aiko dug her fingers into the hole she had made, ripping at the EMT's insides. The man stopped struggling, lying dead on the lab floor.

She was so focused on the nightmare happening, that she was caught off guard as someone threw themselves into the door, throwing her to the ground. The other EMT, who had somehow hidden from Aiko's attention escaped through the open exit door. Moments later Rafe appeared in the doorway. With no hesitation, he reached into the air shower, grabbed Charlie off the ground, and drug her out the exit door. The EMT was nowhere to be found.

"What the hell is happening, Charlie?" Rafe yelled.

"I....I.....she....." Charlie stuttered.

"Charlie!" Rafe yelled as he began to pull her down the hall.

Charlie looked back in bewilderment, allowing herself to be led away. Behind her, she could see Aiko making her way slowly from the air shower room. She focused on them trying to flee and began to amble their way. Charlie found herself categorizing symptoms in her mind. Her body didn't move fluidly like a living being. Each joint seemed to move and pop on its own, not moving with the entire body. And yet she was still moving forward at a speed that could catch someone walking along unknowing.

The tug on her hand had Charlie moving faster to keep up with Rafe's long strides. He led them straight to the security fishbowl and locked them inside. He then began to flip through the cameras, until he found his counterpart walking the halls. From what Charlie could tell she wasn't far from her own lab, not far from Aiko and the murderous scene that happened there.

"Liza! We have a situation. There is a woman who has murdered an EMT in the halls. There's...well there's something wrong with her. Approach with caution," Rafe said into the radio. They watched as Liza listened to his message and then began walking as Rafe gave her instructions to Aiko's location. Aiko, now that she didn't have sight of Charlie and Rafe, was wandering aimlessly around the halls near the lab.

The pair watched Liza approach the lab. She looked into the glass windows and her hand flew up to cover her mouth. She reached for her radio and began yelling into it, the sound echoing in the security room.

"Jesus, Rafe, call the police!" Liza called.

"Liza, we need to follow protocol," Rafe said, his voice calm and soothing.

Liza didn't answer again, her radio dropped from her hand and just hung. She turned in the direction that Rafe had instructed. They didn't carry weapons in the facility, leaving Charlie to wonder what Liza was going to do when she got to Aiko in the first place. As Liza turned the corner, Charlie saw something that turned her blood to ice. She grabbed Rafe's arm and pointed at the monitor that was showing the camera directly outside her lab.

"How is that possible?" Charlie whispered.

They watched as the dead EMT, with his stomach contents dripping down his legs, stumble out of the air shower. With the doors both open there was nothing to stop him from exiting and getting into the building. Charlie had a grip on Rafe's arm as they watched and Rafe let loose a string of expletives under his breath. He grabbed for the radio and tried to raise Liza. The dead EMT was following the same path as Liza and Charlie realized the panic from Rafe was because Liza would be caught between the two with no weapon.

"I have to go help her," Rafe said, not taking his eyes off the monitors.

"You won't make it there in time," Charlie replied.

Not listening to her, he grabbed a baton that sat in the corner of the security center. Giving her swift instructions to lock the door behind him, he was gone. Charlie looked at the buttons in front of her and the screens Rafe had left up. She couldn't see Aiko anymore; the infected body had wandered away from the cameras that were pulled up. Charlie didn't know how to change anything, so she watched in fear as events unfolded where she could see.

Liza must have heard the EMT coming because Charlie saw her spin when the infected man came around a corner behind her. There was no sound from the cameras, but Charlie knew that with her mouth being wide open Liza was screaming at the horrific sight of the EMT in front of her. She began to back away, panicked at what she was seeing. Charlie still didn't believe her eyes. She knew the man was dead. She knew Aiko was dead. Yet, both were on their feet and moving around the building.

Rafe's running form flashed on one screen, pulling Charlie's attention. When she turned back to look at Liza, she cried out seeing that the EMT had collapsed onto the woman. He was tearing at her neck with his teeth, his head making a back and forth motion that seemed to shake Liza's whole body. Charlie felt detached from everything. She could see the pool of red spread and grow from under Liza. The woman fought, but eventually, her arms fell awkwardly at her sides as the EMT continued his meal.

Suddenly Rafe came around the corner, his face distorted in pain and rage. He wielded the baton and swung at the head of the EMT, knocking him from Liza. Unfazed by the injury, the infected tried to get back to his meal. Charlie could imagine the smell, copper from the blood filling the floor. She could still hear the growling noise coming from Aiko and she assumed that was what Rafe was hearing now. Rafe swung again, this time the head of the EMT slammed into the wall and the body stopped moving completely.

Charlie felt sad watching Rafe. His face was full of anger and grief. He leaned over Liza, but without touching her he knew she was dead. Suddenly an alarm began to sound in the facility, loud and piercing, causing Charlie to jump back as if she had touched something she shouldn't have. Rafe looked up at the red flashing lights and seemed to make a decision. He dropped the baton and ran. Charlie sunk to the floor, sliding back against the wall in the office. *What is happening?*

It seemed like an eternity before Rafe was banging on the door for Charlie to unlock the manual deadbolt that only the security office had. She crawled to the door and opened it. Rafe entered without looking down at her. He locked the door again and went straight to the monitor. He began pushing buttons and the views on the screens rotated.

"Where did she go?" Rafe asked, more to himself than to Charlie, who was still sitting on the ground just watching everything happen around her.

"Who?" Charlie finally asked.

"The lab tech. The first one. Where did she go?"

"I didn't see. I wasn't sure how to follow her with the cameras," Charlie replied.

"Look. There, blood on that door frame. That door leads

outside. Someone must have been walking in when she was nearby," Rafe said, as he pointed at the red smears down a white door.

"What do we do?" Charlie asked.

"Well the alarm is going, someone knows what's happening. I think we need to go. Do you have everything you need?"

"My purse and clothes are in my locker," Charlie said.

"We can come back for them. For now, this happened in your lab. I think it's best we get out of here."

Charlie couldn't help but agree. Rafe helped her off the ground and she took a moment to hide the thumb drive in her bra. He looked at her strangely but didn't make a comment. They split up in the halls to get to their cars which were parked on separate sides of the building. Charlie could tell Rafe wasn't crazy about the idea of splitting up, but she had wanted to drive her own car in case someone was watching them.

The screaming reached her when she was just about to open the door to go outside. She turned to see a woman running in her direction, clutching a bleeding arm to her chest. As she pushed Charlie into the door in her rush to get out, the woman screamed about being attacked. Charlie jumped to the side when they were outside to avoid being trampled by the injured woman and others that started to stream out. Everyone was panicking and running. The scene gave Charlie a sick feeling in her stomach. If Aiko was outside somewhere, who was attacking people inside?

The dead stare of Liza, looking at the ceiling entered Charlie's mind. She looked back into the facility and realized that it was Liza attacking people. Everyone attacked, starting with Aiko, was dead. However, they were walking, functioning, biting, and eating live people. She thought back to Aiko's eyes, black but focused on Charlie. The animalistic noises the dead woman made were not human. Her body was no longer being driven by brain power, but some other instinct that reanimated her dead body. And that dead body wanted Charlie's live one.

The sounds of panic and fear echoed out of the open doorway.

Charlie stepped back slowly before turning and sprinting to her car. As she rounded the building to the entrance of the lot, she found Rafe sitting in his truck waiting for her. When she finally came into his view she could see him throw up his hands in exasperation as if to ask where in the hell she had been. As they approached the security gate, they didn't even slow. The gate was already open, possibly ran down by the number of cars fleeing the lot. Charlie noted that the security officer that was typically at the entrance was missing.

Once they were in town, Charlie slowed to the speed limit. She checked the rearview and confirmed that Rafe was still cruising behind her. The town seemed to be moving at a normal pace. Unlike Charlie's heart, which wanted to rip free from her chest in fear. She carefully drove the route to the compound. When she turned down the dirt road and approached the gate, she had to thank her lucky stars that she had met Rafe on the side of the road.

The metal gate began to slide open as soon as Rafe's truck was within distance to use the opener. Charlie parked her car in her normal spot, next to Rafe's spot on the gravel drive. She laid her head on the steering wheel for a moment, listening to the crunch of gravel under Rafe's large truck tires. The tears that came then were hot and fierce. Her mind couldn't make sense of the carnage she had just seen. The carnage that only took a total of twenty minutes to happen before they escaped.

The car door was pulled open and Rafe stood, waiting for Charlie to get out. She went to reach for her purse but realized she didn't have it. Slowly she climbed from the car and faced Rafe. Her face was a tear streaked mess, but she couldn't bring herself to care. Rafe watched her warily for a moment before finally speaking.

"Ready to tell me what in the hell just happened?"

CHAPTER SIX

Tammy's last thought before dying on her townhouse floor was that she should have gone to the ER like the security officer had told her. She laid against the floor as her body cooled after her heart stopped beating the blood through her veins. Her open eyes started to cloud until they were black and shiny like a hematite crystal. Her body began to twitch.

Infected and walking dead, Tammy wandered the townhouse. Her mind was no longer human, no longer thinking rationally about movements, no longer in control. The only driving thing now was a hunger that couldn't be quenched while locked in her townhouse. She bounced off of walls, wandering aimlessly. With no meal present, the infected didn't have anywhere to go.

During the day she could hear the children behind the house. They played loudly in their backyard, swinging and climbing a jungle gym. The infected was drawn by the noise, stumbling to the back of the house. Without the human thinking or the control to do small things, she couldn't move the drapes to see the children over the fence. She couldn't open a door to try and attack the meal she knew was just outside. Her unresponsive body continued to bang against the window until a noise from the front of the house pulled her that way.

This went on for days. Tammy's infected body never rested, never stopped moving. Her hunger and desire to spread the infection were the driving needs of her body now. Nothing could stop that need. If her uncoordinated movements caused her to fall to the ground, she would pull herself to the nearest noise she heard. Eventually, her body figured out how to get back on its feet. Then the stumbling back and forth started again.

The ringing of the phone would cause Tammy to growl and hiss as she looked for a living body to claw and sink her teeth into. The ringing would stop as the call would go to voicemail and Tammy would be aimless again. Missed calls from co-workers and family continued to come in as Tammy's body tried to figure out how to get out of the confines of the townhouse.

Soon the smell of rotten flesh wafted throughout the house. Though the smell didn't bother Tammy in the slightest, her nose no longer communicating with her brain, it would be putrid to a living nose. With no windows or doors open, the smell continued to grow but didn't reach the outside. Until Aiko came calling.

Tammy's dead ears understood that something living was at the door. The knocking called to her and her infected body stumbled toward the noise. Before dying, Tammy had been so distracted she had forgotten to lock her door when she arrived home. It was a mistake that meticulous Tammy would normally never have made. But the infection was already roaring through her body, causing her to lose focus and forget things. The doorknob turned reluctantly, as Aiko tried it. When the door clicked open, Tammy, infected and driven, was waiting for her.

"Tammy?" Aiko called.

She then gagged as the smell of dead flesh began to come out of the door. The hesitation of her prey was all Tammy needed to put her clawed fingers on the door and pull toward Aiko. Aiko's small body stumbled forward, not expecting the door to move and she was face to face with dead Tammy. Growling while black ooze came from her hand where the mouse had bitten her, Tammy stepped forward toward Aiko. The living woman was confused by the sight of her co-worker and she stood still for a moment.

As Tammy tried to attack, Aiko lifted her arm to fend her off. Tammy's teeth sank into Aiko's soft flesh immediately. The bite didn't change Tammy's drive, her need to feed, to spread and rip apart the living. Aiko screamed and panicked, pulling her arm away and running down the stairs of the porch. She clutched her bleeding arm to her chest before getting back into her car and speeding away.

The door was left open in Aiko's haste. Of course, she didn't know what was wrong with Tammy. She had no idea that Tammy was dead, but walking, infected with an illness that they had all worked together to create. Aiko couldn't have known, as the infection raced from her arm to the rest of her body, that she was already dead. She didn't know that the infected Tammy, clumsy and on the hunt, fell down her porch stairs toward the sounds of other people.

Aiko had no idea, she had just released patient zero.

CHAPTER SEVEN

"Ready to tell me what just happened?" Rafe asked. He looked at Charlie, her face still wet with her tears. He tried to not feel bad for her. In his mind, he knew that whatever craziness they worked on in that lab caused this. Liza was dead, because of the experiments Charlie and her co-workers had done.

"I...I don't know what you mean?" Charlie said.

"Really? You don't know why seemingly dead people are coming back to life?"

"I don't think they are coming back to life," Charlie said.

Rafe's mind flashed back to the EMT with his body cavity ripped open and his organs and blood flowing on the floor. There was no way that man was alive. But he was walking and attacking.

"Is that your professional opinion?" Rafe asked, his voice laced with sarcasm. He was trying to not be too tough on Charlie, but he was angry. Even when part of him realized he was being irrational.

"I'm not sure what you're trying to get at here, Rafe," Charlie's defenses rising to the fight. "I had nothing to do with this. Yes, my professional medical opinion is that the wounds those people had, well minus Aiko, were deadly. There's no way they were still living. I watched the EMT shock Aiko numerous times and she didn't have a heartbeat when she started to move again."

"Had nothing to do with this? How do you know what you did in that lab didn't somehow cause this? Tammy was bitten by the mouse, Tammy then attacked the other woman. She died shortly after and attacked the EMT," Rafe said, spelling it all out. Charlie stood staring at him in horror.

"You're suggesting whatever this is, passed from the mouse to Tammy in that bite? And then Tammy's bite passed it to Aiko?"

Rafe could see the wheels turning in Charlie's mind. She seemed to finally join the page he was on.

"I don't see how it's possible. We didn't have the virus set to pass between species."

"Isn't it possible someone made a mistake? Is it possible something mutated?"

"Anything's possible, I've learned that. But it seems improbable," Charlie said.

"Improbable as dead people walking and attacking other people?"

"Not only attacking....eating," Charlie whispered.

"Eating?!" Rafe exclaimed.

"Yes. Before I got out of the air shower, you must have been on your way to the lab, Aiko started to....eat....the EMT." Charlie's voice broke on the word 'eat'. Tears began to well in her eyes again, and Rafe felt the need to act quickly to avoid a meltdown.

"Ok, let's just get inside. We'll switch on the news. See if anything comes out about this. We are safe here."

For the rest of the morning, the two stayed glued to the local tv channels. Game shows, soap operas and many commercials for medications passed along. But there was no breaking news. No news came on at all. When the afternoon came, Rafe made them sandwiches and insisted Charlie eat something. She claimed to feel queasy. Rafe couldn't really blame her, his stomach wasn't feeling food either. However, he believed in keeping their energy up.

By the evening Charlie had only moved from the couch to use the restroom. Rafe started to become concerned with her mental stability as her hair started to fall from its bun in a disarray from her messing with it so often and he had to convince her to remove her lab coat after she sat in it for five hours. He could imagine someone not able to handle these circumstances, breaking down and falling into fear. Most of the day she barely spoke, so when she did after the evening news, Rafe physically jumped.

"How is there nothing about this on the news?" She demanded.

"Maybe it looked worse than it actually was," Rafe said. Charlie had shot him a look that clearly said she thought he was stupid.

"We saw people, dead people, walking around. This was very bad. Someone had to have reported it to the news by now."

Rafe had to agree with her. In his mind, there was no way that none of the employees would break their NDAs and call the authorities. Or call the news to report what had happened. An attack like this should be headline news across the country. Especially if it was a virus that could be spread. A warning for others had to come out. To avoid anyone that was injured, had black eyes, or was trying to eat them. These are things the public needed to know.

By midnight they were both exhausted. Charlie had fallen asleep on the couch, while Rafe continued to surf the local stations. To his surprise, nothing was ever mentioned about the facility or the attacks. His own eyelids began to grow heavy and he figured they would need to turn in for the night. Looking over at Charlie, she seemed comfortable enough. He pulled a throw blanket over her and headed up to his room. He didn't think he would sleep. It was surprising that once the adrenaline crash came, he felt like he had run a triathlon, twice. His body was running on empty and needed to recharge.

Morning came faster than he had expected. Charlie bursting into his room woke him from a nightmare where he was trying to bite one of his cows. His confusion was apparent as he sat up in bed looking at Charlie as if he had no idea who she was. He rubbed his eyes for a moment and looked at her. He saw panic on her face.

"What?" He asked.

"It's on the news. You've got to see this."

Rafe jumped out of bed to run after Charlie down the stairs to where she had the morning news on. A pretty woman was looking into the camera with a smile. The small picture near her head showed a building, but it wasn't their facility. The headline said, "Local Attack." Rafe watched as the woman reported about an attack that happened downtown. There were no witnesses to be interviewed. The victim had died. But it was when the woman talked about the description of the attacker, Rafe sat heavily on the couch.

"The attacker is described as female, 5'3" with short black hair, of Asian descent. She was last seen wandering the area in a lab coat. After the attack her whereabouts are unknown, and her trail has not been picked up. Authorities are warning anyone that spots her to not approach and to call the number at the bottom of the screen immediately," the news anchor said.

"Why would they call a number? Why not 911?" Charlie asked.

"They don't want the local authorities involved would be my first guess. That sounded like the woman from your lab, right?"

"Aiko, yes. Sounds exactly like her. But why aren't they giving additional details? How do they have a description if there were no witnesses?" Charlie shot off her questions at a rapid pace.

Turning the TV up louder, Rafe walked into the kitchen to make coffee. He was surprised that Charlie, who typically couldn't handle life without coffee in the morning, was so wired without a pot of coffee on. Once he had his mug he wandered back in to finish watching the morning news. He was surprised there wasn't more about what was happening. His mind rolled over the events and facts. The only conclusion he could really come to was the facility was owned by a branch of the government. Being that, the experiments and activities in the facility were considered secret, possibly from other branches of the government. They wouldn't want the information of yesterday's attacks to go public.

He left Charlie where she sat in front of the TV. As the situation grew in his mind, something dark formed. He felt that something more was happening in town, but because they were on the compound they weren't seeing it. He milked the cows in silence today, without the normal banter he had with his ladies. He stored more milk in the freezer this morning, telling himself it was just in case. The paranoia of his father seemed to seep into his pores and he felt himself mentally trying to push it back into a box. Somewhere it couldn't affect his way of thinking and behaving.

Noon rolled around and Rafe decided they needed to go into town. Charlie was reluctant to leave the news watch, but Rafe explained to her they would see more in town than sitting in his living room. She left to get dressed out of her previous day's clothes and Rafe decided to get ready for town. He went to the gun safe that was located in his sister Alex's room. It was biometric for his hand as well as his sisters'. Once open he grabbed his 9mm. He slid in a full clip and slid it into a belt holster he had that could be hidden under his shirt. He then pulled out his 12 gauge tactical shotgun and loaded it as well, ensuring the sleeve was also loaded with extra ammo.

Rafe went to his truck and mounted the shotgun in his rack on his back window, just as Charlie came out of the house. She saw the gun and had no reaction. They had decided driving together was no longer a problem. Rafe also didn't want to be responsible for her if she was in a different vehicle, so Charlie joined him in the truck, wringing her hands as they drove. Rafe saw her watching the side mirror as the metal gate closed behind them, clearly concerned for the stability of the compound she had come to rely on for safety.

As they drove toward town, cars seemed to pass them leaving town at an incredible rate. Charlie watched each of them as they went by.

"They are packed to leave. Something is wrong," she said.

"Well let's go find out what it is."

At the edge of town, Rafe noted that beyond the cars everything was seemingly quiet. He pulled the truck into a small supermarket parking lot when he noticed what looked like looting of the store. Getting out of the car, he grabbed his shotgun before closing his door. Something wasn't right here. Charlie jumped from the truck and followed him as they slowly entered the store. The doors had been broken off their hinges, pulled outward by a vehicle possibly.

Inside the store, lights were on, but everything seemed silent. A smell wafted through the store, Rafe guessed it was food. However, he noted that the power was still on, so he couldn't imagine why something was spoiling already. He walked slowly, shotgun at his shoulder as he swung from side to side checking all possible hiding places. Now that he had a good view inside, it confirmed his suspicions that the store had been looted.

"Why are people breaking into the store?" Charlie asked. Rafe shushed her quickly, still not convinced they were alone. She shot him a dirty look at being admonished, but she didn't speak further.

The sound of crinkling plastic reached their ears, spurring Rafe into action. He swung the shotgun toward the sound, pushing Charlie behind him with one hand. She complied without question, feeling the safest place was behind the shotgun. Rafe slowly walked down the aisle next to where he thought the noise came from. No additional noises could be heard, but he was sure it wasn't a natural noise. When they reached the end of the aisle,

Rafe did another full circle, checking the direction they had come and found nothing different. He pointed toward the half-looted shelf and pushed Charlie gently toward it. She understood and pushed herself against the shelving.

Shotgun leading, Rafe moved around the end of the aisle. As he stepped into the next aisle, he was immediately faced with what had caused the noises they had heard. The ground was splattered with blood, a shelf pulled down with products strewn across the walkway. In the middle was a body, the source of the blood, Rafe assumed. He watched in shock as the body, which had to be missing quite a good deal of blood, climbed to its feet.

It was a woman, who at over six feet tall was almost as tall as Rafe himself. Her black eyes didn't distract from what was a beautiful face. She was blonde, lean, and almost looked living. He found himself at odds with what he knew to be happening and what he was seeing. She faced Rafe and immediately a growling noise began to come from her mouth. He couldn't see the bite on her and assumed it was somewhere on the back of her body. Rafe found himself strangely questioning the volleyball uniform she was wearing, including spandex shorts and kneepads. She was someone that was just going about her business, maybe on the way to a volleyball game. But her life was cut short by whatever infected caught her in the supermarket.

"Rafe," Charlie whispered from behind him. The growling had pulled her from her hiding place and she stood to watch in shocked fear as the volleyball player slowly made her way toward where she wanted to spread her illness. Rafe swallowed hard. He knew what he had seen in the facility. Now faced directly with one of the dead, he wasn't sure about pulling the trigger. He stepped back until he was touching Charlie.

"Is there a cure?" He hissed back to Charlie.

"I...to cure this? No. I don't think it can be cured," she answered.

"Are you sure?"

"I can't be completely positive. I need to review my notes."

"If I end this, for this woman, how do I know it's not murder?" Rafe said, mostly to himself. He pushed Charlie back further as the volleyball player got closer.

"It's defending our safety, isn't it?"

Rafe nodded, knowing that was true. But somewhere in his mind, he couldn't accept just killing the woman. Decided, he used the shotgun and aimed at one of her long legs. The shot caused the knee to buckle and the volleyball player collapsed to one side. No normal reaction came, no hand out to break her fall, no pained noise. The infected just fell into the shelf and tried to crawl forward. She was now a single-minded killing zombie. Rafe had seen enough.

"She's slowed down. Let's grab some groceries and get out of here."

"You're going to leave her like that? What if she tries to get someone else?"

"I'll deal with it before we leave. Now grab what you can and let's get the truck loaded."

The pair went out to the truck first, backing it as close to the broken windows as possible. Rafe checked the area again, finding everything still. The quiet was eerie. He was waiting for someone to jump out in front of him. Rationally he realized they hadn't made it very far into town before stopping at the market. People were fleeing and stopping on the outskirts of town wasn't the plan. Despite that, he knew the area couldn't possibly stay quiet for long.

Charlie argued about stealing at first. Rafe moved around the market, bagging perishable groceries that they could eat for the next few days. He ignored Charlie's arguments at first, but he grew annoyed with her constant barrage of questions and reasons for why they shouldn't steal. He loaded his third bag into the truck before she had started packing anything. Finally, over her not understanding the situation he whirled on her.

"Charlie, rules do not apply anymore. Have you noticed the people walking that should be dead? Natural law doesn't apply. Things are happening here that are not going to fit into the world you seem to want to live in. So, either catch up so we can survive together or figure things out on your own. Either way, stop arguing with me and get out of my way."

He left Charlie with her mouth hanging open as he headed back into the supermarket. He felt bad at first for being harsh to her and then leaving her out in the open on her own. Nonetheless, he felt she needed to understand their situation and work with him. When he turned back to look for her again he saw she was moving toward the bakery. *Better than nothing*, he thought to himself. He decided he would later find the time for why he suddenly needed to make sure Charlie survived.

He found himself back in the aisle where the volleyball player tried to crawl. When Rafe entered her line of sight her noises intensified as her fingers tried to claw and get purchase on the slippery tile floor. It was her face that made Rafe stop to watch. If it wasn't for the black orbs where her eyes were and the gray pallor of her skin, he wouldn't believe anything was wrong with her. She probably stopped traffic on a normal day when she was warm and healthy. He had to shake himself from his thoughts as the dead volleyball player continued to find a way to get closer to where he stood.

Moving down the aisle, Rafe stepped far to the side to avoid the claws of the infected and started grabbing canned foods as he passed. Once his hands were completely full again, he went back to the truck. He arrived just as Charlie did. Her hands were full of bags of bread, sliced, French, bagels and more. He looked over at her and nodded as she loaded the softer items on top of his canned goods. She then produced two containers of soft cookies, with an inch of frosting on top of each. Her smile was sheepish, but she handed the containers to him in a sign of apology he assumed.

"They're my favorite," Charlie said, looking up at him.

"Well then grab them all. I'm sure we could find time to eat them," Rafe replied. He was rewarded with a wide smile from Charlie as she went back into the market for the rest of the cookies.

Standing outside, Rafe stood to survey the parking lot. There was no nearby movement, though he could hear vehicles moving in the distance. He could hear sirens at times and far off gunshots. In his gut, he knew the city was falling into chaos. It was what his father always preached. Faced with a real society ending event, services would break down, people would panic and life as they knew it would be over. Normal people wouldn't be prepared to handle themselves in a situation like this. Mitch Duncan was more convinced it would be some sort of electromagnetic pulse attack, believing the United States would be the victim of an attack by one of its many enemies. If he ever imagined the dead would walk and be attacking people, he never told his children.

Once Rafe thought they had stayed long enough at the market, the volleyball player had drug herself almost to the front check stands. He glanced at her for a moment, wondering if Charlie was right and he should end her. However, for some reason, he couldn't bring himself to do it. They climbed back in the truck and Rafe left the shotgun between them for easier access. Charlie looked at him for a long moment, before turning to look out her window.

"What?" Rafe asked.

"You're all heart," Charlie said.

"Yeah, that's not exactly the case," he replied.

"Keep telling yourself that," she said with a small laugh.

After some discussion, Rafe convinced Charlie they should drive further into town. They needed to see what was really happening, as the news wasn't discussing the truth. Charlie was worried about their safety, but she conceded after Rafe pointed out his truck was tough, and they wouldn't get out of the car unless completely necessary. He understood her fear. Rafe didn't doubt that she was a tough woman, after seeing her stand up to 'The Suit' at the facility. She had a fire in her. But this was different than words. This was a fight for survival.

Kalispell was a fairly small sized city. Rafe had lived there the majority of his life until his father passed away. He then moved to the compound closer to Flathead Lake. The small town life was what Rafe had always wanted and Kalispell had been his place. Seeing it now, he felt shocked deep in his core. People ran from all directions, from their homes to their cars. There were numerous accidents that he had to maneuver his truck around. They passed a gas station that was overrun with people trying to get gas. When Rafe glanced over he watched as two men came to blows over the pump that they both had tried to pull up to. A gunshot rang out and Rafe stepped on the gas to get away from the station. The last thing they needed was to be next to a station when someone was using a firearm around gasoline.

A loud noise caused Rafe to pull into a restaurant parking lot and slam on his brakes. He risked putting down his window, so he could look up at the sky, just as a plane took off from Kalispell City Airport. His jaw dropped open as the implications raced through him. Initially, he had thought this could be just be stopped in Kalispell, maybe only reach a few nearby towns. People died so fast from blood loss and the illness, spreading further would be impossible. But somehow, he hadn't thought about planes. If planes had been taking off all day like they tended to do, sick people could be everywhere.

He rolled his window up and looked at Charlie. Without saying a word, he could tell her mind was in the same place. Her skin had taken on a pale look, her eyes red with unshed tears.

"Why are they letting people fly? Don't they know what's happening here?" Charlie asked.

"Maybe people are trying to escape? Or maybe because the news has been limited, not everyone knows what's happening."

As he spoke gunshots sounded again and he watched as a family fought off three infected that tried to attack them. The parents with two children were in a state of panic, searching cars they came to, apparently looking for a ride. Rafe took a moment to evaluate, realizing the father didn't know how to use the gun he was pointing. Grabbing his shotgun, he told Charlie to stay put and he jumped out of the truck. He racked the slide on the shotgun and stalked toward the infected. He felt his remorse for the beautiful volleyball player disappear as he looked at the blood-stained men that rambled toward children they wanted to feast on.

His first blast was enough to take the head off of the nearest infected. The body fell into the next infected causing the pair to fall. The noise of his shotgun pulled the attention of the third infected, exactly as Rafe had planned. He racked the slide on his shotgun, as another wild shot went between him and the infected. He looked over at the father that was still holding his pistol toward the infected. The man was terrified, so Rafe swallowed the amount of yelling he wanted to do at the man.

"I have this handled. Please don't shoot me," Rafe called to him. The man focused on him for a moment, before his arm fell and he hugged his children to him.

Rafe turned back to the infected that was advancing toward him. Without realizing it, he had decided the brain was the only way to stop the dead beings. Without a head, there was no way they could continue to hunt for the living. He switched the safety on the shotgun and slung it on his back before he pulled the six-inch hunting knife that was on his hip. The infected was within attack distance now and the mother that he had just come to the rescue of cried out in warning. That noise was all it took to pull the attention off of Rafe, causing him to pursue the infected instead of waiting for the attack. He sighed before he took three long steps forward, slamming the hunting knife into the skull of the infected. One quarter turn and he yanked it back out.

As guessed, the infected fell to the ground, now truly lifeless. Rafe found that he felt more powerful having a solution at least to the immediate threat. With that knowledge, he went to the infected that was just fighting back to its feet from under the dead body of his teammate. One swift downward strike and there was one less infected wandering his small town. He leaned down and cleaned the blade on the infected's clothing, not wanting to carry the disease in his sheath.

"Thank you," the father said, as the family approached.

Rafe just nodded and shrugged. He may not have been a people person, but he would never be the person that stood by while a family was slaughtered.

"Do you have a vehicle?" Rafe asked the man.

"We did. But we were in an accident. We were trying to find something else..." the man looked around at the carnage and nearby wrecks as his voice trailed off. Rafe joined him and looked around.

Rafe immediately located a vehicle that had been abandoned near his truck. He walked toward it with purpose, calling for the family to follow him. He continued to keep his head on a swivel, looking for any additional nearby threats. He could hear the adults murmuring behind him and was pretty sure he heard the wife worry that he was crazy. Rafe almost laughed out loud. For years people thought his father was crazy. But his talents were useful. Thinking he was crazy didn't stop people from taking advantage of those things.

At the car, Rafe pulled out his multitool and kneeled so he could reach under the steering wheel and steering column. The older model was a perfect candidate for hot-wiring the car. As he ripped out wires to find the ones he needed the man behind him cleared his throat.

"We aren't going to steal someone's vehicle," he said.

"What were you going to do if you found one with keys? Leave a note?" Rafe shot back.

"Well, no."

"I don't think the person that left this vehicle, if even still alive, had plans to come back," Rafe explained.

"So, you're saying it's not stealing," the man said.

"Right. It's called salvaging."

"Ok. I guess I can live with that."

"Well that's good if you want your family to live you will need this," Rafe said as he touched wires together and the car turned over and caught.

The children were loaded into the back of the car. Rafe explained to the father which wires to touch together to start the car and which to not touch together to save himself a nasty shock. Before they drove away, Rafe put together a supply of food from what they had taken from the supermarket. He leaned into the back of the car and handed a container of overly sugared cookies to the kids with a smile. As they drove away, Rafe wasn't completely confident that they would survive. The smiles on the children's faces as they looked at the cookies would stay with him for a long time.

CHAPTER EIGHT

Rafe sat in the driver's seat of his truck, looking at his phone as it restarted. As soon as he realized planes were taking off from the local airport, he knew he needed to call his sisters. They needed to be warned. They needed to come to the compound. He needed to start Sundown. The faces of his nieces and nephew went through his mind. Billie, Henry, and Jack were the next generation in their family. Since their births, his sisters would bring their families to Montana to visit. He loved the children as if they were his own. He couldn't think of a world without them safe.

"Why would cell service not be working?" Charlie asked. In the seat next to him, she was fiddling with her phone. She had resorted to taking out the battery and SIM card, hoping that would get a signal. But there were no bars.

"Why would there be no news about this? Why would there be so little presence of emergency services? Where are the evacuations? Where is the government?" Rafe shot questions out in rapid fire. Then he cursed and slammed his phone into the dashboard when it still came up with no service.

"Your sisters, they don't live nearby right?"

"Nevada and South Carolina."

"They'll be fine then. That's far enough away."

"There are planes leaving, Charlie. We both are aware that distance doesn't matter right now," Rafe said. He beat his hand into the steering wheel a few times before starting the truck back up.

"Maybe landlines are working?"

"Maybe. Let's stop at another store on our way back to the compound. I want to make sure we salvage while we can. And we should probably get you some additional clothes. I don't have many female items at home."

They drove in silence through town, winding through side streets when there were accidents blocking the road. The neighborhoods were silent as graveyards, doors left open, possessions were strewn across driveways. The fear was palpable by the way people chose to run immediately. Rafe slowed the truck at one garage that was in complete disarray, blood splattered the outside walls of the house and the concrete driveway. He waited, to see if anything moved. The sound of his running engine brought an infected out of the shadows. An elderly woman, her pink robe now smeared with red and black. Her gray hair was still perfectly in rollers on the top of her head. Her skin was now a mottled gray.

Rafe felt sorrow at the sight of the woman. Sadness for what the woman's life should have been, though coming to an end in age, she should have been able to enjoy her last years in peace. He found himself wondering if she had a family nearby. Did she have a husband in the home? Was he dead now too? So much went through Rafe's mind as he sat and watched the woman try to amble her way to the truck.

"Rafe?" Charlie roused him from his thoughts.

"I can't leave her like that," Rafe said.

"You left the woman in the market," Charlie pointed out.

"I know. I was wrong. These people, their lives have ended. And it's wrong that their bodies are left to wander like this. Also, you were right. If I don't end them now, they could hurt someone else in the future."

"You can't fix this, Rafe."

"I can do something to help."

Rafe pulled out his 9mm and opened his truck door. Stepping onto the quiet street, he could clearly hear the noises coming from the woman. She didn't sound like a grandmother now, more like a wild starving dog. Rafe took aim carefully and took his shot. The bullet entered the woman's face just below her right eye. With the brain gone, the body crumpled to the ground in a heap. Rafe turned and motioned for Charlie to come with him, which she did warily.

"I want to check the house. Make sure she didn't have a husband or someone else that is now turned too. Didn't think you'd want to stay outside alone," Rafe said.

Charlie agreed with a nod of her head and followed Rafe toward the house. At the old woman's body, she stopped and crouched down. Rafe stopped and watched her. She seemed to move clinically, looking at the woman's wounds and eyes. The infected had a large piece of her neck and chest missing where something had bitten and ripped at her. The wound was blackened, oozing still with no clotting starting. Her eyes were the same black coal of all other infected. Charlie checked her legs and hands quickly and then stood up.

"Nothing different. I wanted to check to confirm what I've seen firsthand, with Aiko," Charlie said.

"You have research about this illness, will what you find help with possibly curing it?"

"I honestly don't know. When a pathogen is created, we don't test cures until we know the pathogen does what it's intended to do. This one was destroyed with the mice. We never got to the curing step."

"So, you were working on unknown pathogens for the govern-

ment, with no cures, and you never thought you should quit?"
Rafe asked.

"I thought I was doing good work for my government. I
thought they wanted to be prepared for the worst," Charlie said,
her voice angry and loud.

"You were creating biological weapons! Isn't that clear to you
now?" Rafe demanded.

"Now? Well, my view has changed just slightly now, Rafe! And
I told you I had started questioning things. That's why I have that
thumb drive. I took information whenever I could!"

Their argument continued to rise in decibel, yelling at each
other in frustration and anger. Rafe couldn't understand how
Charlie had been so foolish to believe she was doing good. Here
they stood in the middle of a society ending plague. A plague that
the government had contracted Charlie and her team to create.
Without question, he knew she was a brilliant doctor. Internally
he did admit that one of the first things she told him was she
didn't like what they were doing at the facility and that she had
taken information. However, she never gave him enough information to understand what was actually happening.

The sounds of their voices carried through the previously
quiet neighborhood. Movement caught Rafe's attention behind
Charlie down the street. He cursed, wanting to kick himself for
letting them dawdle in the open and fight loud enough to literally
wake the dead. Charlie. believing he was cursing at her, got more
angry and started to get louder. Without explaining, Rafe covered
her mouth this his hand and turned her around to see what he
saw. She fought his grip at first, but she froze in fear when she saw
what he was bringing to her attention.

Between houses, from open garages and the shadows of
hedges and trees, the infected were flowing out. The sounds of
the argument between Rafe and Charlie had been like ringing a
dinner bell. Rafe was in shock at the number of people that were
now infected. Anger burned hot in his gut as he realized there was

every shape, age, and gender in the crowd. *How did this happen so fast?* Rafe thought to himself. He finally loosened his grip on Charlie's mouth, but she continued to lean against his chest and he allowed her to stay there. They were going to have to stick together, like it or not.

"How...I don't understand..." she whispered, echoing Rafe's exact thoughts.

"I don't know. But we need to get back to the truck and go. We're going straight for the driver's side door and you will climb across. Got it?"

He waited for her nodded agreement before pulling his 9mm again. He didn't have anywhere near enough ammo with him to fight off a horde like this. But he could clear the way to the truck. A few of the closer infected had stepped into their path, blocking their way. Rafe easily took out the nearest ones as he pulled Charlie behind him with his free hand. When they reached the truck, Charlie opened the door and started to climb in immediately. Rafe spun to face the infected that continued to follow. Before he had the chance to raise his 9mm, the door was pushed shut on him and he was smashed against the truck.

"Rafe!" Charlie cried out.

Rafe had more to worry about than Charlie's concern. The infected that was against the door was a large man, ripped with muscle and such large shoulders that he had no neck. Those shoulders seemed to have been his downfall, as one was ripped to tatters by bites and chunks missing. His teeth snapped furiously at the glass that was between him and his meal. Rafe couldn't climb up and he couldn't shoot the infected. He decided his only option was to push and move.

With all his strength he planted his feet and shoved the door away from his chest. The infected stumbled back a few steps, not capable of keeping his balance when someone pushed back. Rafe moved away from the door and allowed it to slam shut as he pulled his hunting knife for the closer attack. The burly muscleman of an infected gained his traction again and came at Rafe with a renewed vengeance. Considering the uncoordinated nature of the infected, when the clawed fingers reached for him, Rafe stepped to the side and shoved the arm away, practically spinning the infected. With the knife, he quickly used all of his strength to slam it home and bring down the large man.

His breathing came in hard pants as he spun and found two more infected close to him. His instincts, though buried for some time, raised to the surface. The first infected reached for him and he front kicked the small man off his feet. The second arrived just in time for Rafe to sidestep, sliding the knife blade into its skull. As that body dropped the first infected was fighting to its feet and Rafe quickly handled it without issue. He took a moment to clean his knife and look at the infected he had dropped. They were typical people. People that had probably been trying to run from whatever this was. But they were caught in it anyway.

The area finally partially clear enough for him to get into the truck, Rafe took a few running steps and the door swung open as he reached it. Charlie had watched the entire encounter and was waiting for him. He jumped into the truck and slid the key home quickly.

"Next time, give me the keys," Charlie said.

"Why?"

"Because if you die, I need to be able to drive," she replied sarcastically.

The Wal-Mart parking lot was worse than Rafe had imagined. Crashed cars littered the area around the entrance to the store. He pulled in and tried to get as close as he could. Eventually, he stopped the truck next to a car that had been turned on its side. Infected wandered through the wreckage, attention caught by the moving vehicle. Others seemed to still be feasting on their last meals and Rafe knew those would rise soon and also be looking for food.

"This doesn't seem safe," Charlie said.

"It's not. But once we get on the compound, I'd like to stay there until some of this clears itself out," he replied as he motioned to the infected that were bumping into cars trying to get to the truck.

"I have a few changes of clothes, I should be fine."

"We have plenty of a lot of things there. But right now, power is still on. Meaning meat, eggs, fish are all still good. If we get as much of that as we can, we can stock the fridges that are in the barn and the house."

"What happens when the power goes out there too?" Charlie asked.

"We switch to solar. I have full batteries charged already that we run off of some of the time. I also have a gas generator just in case."

"Prepared," Charlie commented.

"For anything," Rafe replied.

Making the decision to salvage whatever they could as they were in town, Rafe took down his shotgun and made sure it was loaded. He then handed Charlie a crowbar he always had under his seat. She looked at it and then at him strangely.

"In case we get separated, hit them in the head and run."

"We should probably just not get separated," Charlie replied.

"Best plans can go wrong. It's a just in case."

It was easy to avoid the infected in the lot. They were spread out across the spaces, many having difficulty getting around things to get to them quickly. They entered the store cautiously. Rafe waved Charlie toward the carts, thinking they would load it full of everything they wanted and just go straight to the truck. The squeaky wheels made him wince, but his guess was if they moved fast they would be ok.

First stop was the women's clothing area. Surprising to Rafe, not much of the looting had happened in clothes. He could see the jewelry area down the aisle and broken glass glittered on the tile. People really didn't understand what was most important. He

surveyed the store with his shotgun at his shoulder. Running footsteps pulled his attention to their right and he turned in time to
see a man trying to run out with a TV. He looked right at Rafe
and his shotgun. Rafe signaled for him to stop, thinking the man
was about to run into a situation he couldn't handle on his own.
However, the man was too intent on his TV and continued to run
out the doors.

Can't save everyone, Rafe thought to himself. He turned back
around and found Charlie piling jeans into the front area of the
cart. She then turned and grabbed a handful of shirts without
looking at designs, only glancing at the sizes to ensure they would
fit. Rafe then led her to the back of the store. They passed electronics to find more people breaking into cases and taking things
they wanted to loot. Rafe left them to do as they pleased, and
they continued to the camping section.

Rafe was in his element here. He found a sturdy hiking backpack and handed it to Charlie to start putting clothes in. He
wanted her to have a bug out bag. The bag needed to be filled
with all the essentials she would require should they need to evac-
uate or be away from the compound. He always had his own
packed and ready. But his sisters took theirs and he had disman-
tled his father's. He started tossing things into the basket for her
to add. First aid kit, flashlight, batteries, flint, waterproof matches
and more. Charlie didn't question, just unzipped all the pouches
and started shoving things in.

As Rafe tied a sleeping bag to the bottom of the pack, a
scream ripped through the store. He froze, trying to judge where
the scream came from. Another cry followed, seeming further
away. Rafe grabbed two handfuls of freeze-dried meals. They
wouldn't be as hearty as the MREs he had at home, but it was
something for now. Meals Ready to Eat weren't the most delicious items out there, but they were fast and convenient for
travel. In addition to the most important thing for survival, fuel
for the body. He quickly added two tarps and was turning away

from the camping section when the sounds of fighting reached them.

"Time to go," he whispered to Charlie.

They crept through the back of the store, heading for the food section. The electronics section was now empty. Rafe assumed the fighting and screaming came from those people as they were confronted with the dead. As they passed one large aisle, Rafe could see blood pooling near the entrance of the store. The infected had entered. He quietly got Charlie's attention and pointed toward the mess. She nodded nervously but continued to push the cart forward. Rafe readied himself with his hunting knife in one hand. A fight in the store was going to be close, too close for his shotgun.

At the refrigerated section that held the meat, Charlie started grabbing everything in her reach. Rafe continued to keep an eye out, with his back to Charlie and the meat. As he waited, his mind wandered to his sisters again. He found himself hoping that news outside of Montana was informing people of what was happening. All three of the siblings had been raised with the same ideals, the same plan and the same need to be prepared. If his sisters saw the news and realized how bad this could get, they would start their evacuation plan. The plan they were raised studying always. Sundown.

Mitch Duncan had believed the world could never stay stable. After the death of his wife, he raised his children in his ideals. One of his most important lessons was Sundown. Mitch knew someday his children wouldn't all live on his compound, despite his desire to keep them under his thumb. However, his goal was to always have the compound as a functional survival location. He built it to be self-sustaining in almost all ways. After he died, Rafe continued his work to ensure the safety of his family. Now they all needed to be together and he couldn't reach his sisters.

"Rafe?" Charlie's voice came from behind him.

"Hmm?"

"I've got almost a half cart full of meat. I think we should move on to the next item."

Rafe had been so lost in his thoughts he hadn't been paying attention to Charlie's progress. He nodded and led the way to the aisle he knew held the long sustaining meals. He started pulling large cans of stews, egg powder, honey powder, pancake mix and rolled oats. The cans were all meant to be emergency food, so they didn't expire for years. With these items, he knew it would be possible to create decent meals if they were to run out of produce, fresh milk or eggs. By the time he was finished, the cart was overflowing, and Charlie could barely see over to push it. But he felt good about having the extra provisions. *If—no, WHEN— Alex and Max get here, I'll have it ready for them,* he thought to himself.

He unslung his shotgun, swinging it back to the front so he could face any threat as they were leaving. Now that they were headed back to the entrance, Rafe knew they would face infected somewhere. Closer to the door, they approached the blood splashed across the tiles. In the produce section, apples had rolled across the floor where a body had fallen into it. For now, it seemed the body was still just dead, not rising yet. However, ten yards away three infected shuffled from dead bodies they had taken down there. The corpses were mutilated and the infected were painted red.

"Keep going," Rafe instructed as the infected noticed them and started toward fresh meat.

Rafe stayed at Charlie's back, walking backward to keep an eye on the infected coming their way. He didn't want to use his shotgun until they were closer to the truck. The noise would draw more unwanted attention. The three infected shuffled closer, arms raised clawing at the air in front of them. The slow progress of the heavy cart was making them an easier target than Rafe wanted. He turned and took the cart from Charlie, pushing with all his strength to get them outside.

Once outside, the situation was more complicated than before. The cart was caught on a box and Rafe pushed harder to move beyond it. Finally breaking free, he realized it was a TV box he was caught on. The TV could be seen smashed a few feet away where it must have fallen from the box after being dropped. The TV was covered in spray, almost impossible to see on the black surface. TV thief must have fought back after dropping his haul. Rafe looked around the parking lot finding more infected near the truck than before, attracted by the noise and movement of the living.

They stopped at the back of the truck and Rafe grabbed his shotgun again. He took aim at the first two infected that followed out of the store. His buckshot tore through the head of the first and into the shoulder of the second. The first body collapsed at the entrance of the store, while the second was spun away slightly. The blow of the buckshot didn't stop the infected from trying to follow Rafe and Charlie. It tried to step forward and found itself caught on the body at its feet. Rafe took the reprieve to check the surrounding areas and realized he was gonna have to fight their way out.

"Keep loading. I'll watch your back," Rafe said to Charlie, as he stepped away from the truck and into the fight.

At first count, he saw eleven infected heads in the parking lot. His goal was to end them before they could reach Charlie and before they could kill anyone else. He racked the slide on his shotgun and aimed at the nearest infected head. The sight of black gore spilling across the concrete was one that made Rafe's stomach turn. He didn't hesitate to continue his assault. His shotgun clicked empty and he slung it over his back quickly before pulling his hunting knife.

Rafe's mind went blank and his body fell into a necessary survival mode. As required in his family, he had learned hand to hand combat early in his life. He had continued his training throughout his adult years, honing his body. Little did he realize, that all of that training would come in handy when he needed to kill the dead. These were the thoughts that came to Rafe's mind as he ducked and pivoted away from the jagged fingers of an infected. Rising behind the attacking woman, Rafe used his knife and ended her dead life. He pulled his blade back and wiped it quickly on the infected's clothing.

He turned to check on Charlie, who was still loading groceries into the back seat of the truck. He was startled to see an infected moving closer to her. Flipping his knife in his hand, he called Charlie's name and told her to duck. She complied quickly, and he let the blade fly. Throwing knives was one of his favorite pastimes with his father. His sister Alex rebelled against Mitch's lessons and Max soaked up every word to become a prepping machine. Rafe was more in the middle. He didn't revel in fighting like Max did, though he honed his skills to ensure he wasn't useless in a fight. The one thing he could always do with his father was knife throwing.

The blade had struck home, embedded through its left eye. Charlie stood on shaky legs and looked down at the infected that had fallen five feet from her. Rafe jogged over and yanked the blade free, causing the eyeball to pop out of the socket. He was shocked at the result, holding the knife slightly away from him, looking around to figure out how to fix it. Behind him, he could hear Charlie retching and he felt guilty for what she must be feeling. Finally figuring no other way, he used the shirt from the infected and carefully slid the eye off of his blade. It dropped to the ground with a quiet plop that Rafe only barely heard over Charlie's throwing up.

Checking on Charlie was his first thought, but he realized that there were more infected streaming into the parking lot. He didn't count the number he had taken down, but it was everything close to them for the moment. After being sure they had a few minutes before anything else threatened them, he turned back to Charlie and the cart. She immediately stepped back from him and

Rafe assumed it was fear on her face. He just looked at her uncertainly.

"You are covered in...." She said, trailing off.

Rafe looked down and confirmed what Charlie was trying to say. His close combat with the infected had left gore on his clothing and boots. At first, his stomach wanted to follow Charlie's example and let loose. Rafe swallowed down the sickness and helped throw the last items into the truck. He put an old towel on the driver's seat, to try and keep the nasty substance out of his truck. As he started up the engine the infected were getting within the reach of the vehicle. A tall man smeared himself across the driver's side window and Rafe just looked at him. A part of him was still waiting for this all to be a joke, a large flash mob. Suddenly everyone would be healthy, and the sickness would fade away. But as the infected chomped at his window, he knew this was just getting started.

CHAPTER NINE

Rafe's sigh of relief was audible when they pulled through the compound gate and it shut solidly behind them. He pulled the truck up the driveway and parked. Neither of them got out immediately. Charlie laid her head back on the headrest, her eyes closed. Rafe just sat staring out of the windshield. He was having a hard time putting his thoughts into working order. His mind was at least understanding that what he had done wasn't murder, but protection. Putting the infected down ended their mindless attacking and he saw that as a gesture of humanity.

"It was so stupid of me to go with you into town," Charlie finally said.

"Why?"

"The thumbdrive. I have too much information. I don't want to lead 'The Suit' or his men to the thumbdrive."

"I think they probably have more pressing matters to deal with right now," Rafe said.

"I hope you're right," Charlie said.

Getting out of the truck, they both acted as if they had run a marathon. Though tired, Rafe needed to handle the evening chores, especially with the animals. He trudged to the barn. Once there he stripped out of his shirt and left it in a burn barrel. For a moment he thought it was wasteful, but his tired mind answered he had plenty of shirts and he would wash the next one. There was a landline phone in the barn and he immediately picked it up, thinking of his sisters and starting Sundown. He didn't feel surprised when he found the line to be completely dead. Somehow, he had expected the general utilities to keep running. But nothing was going as expected now.

He hurried through the milking, much to the annoyance of the ladies. But he allowed them to roam free in their pasture for the evening, something he rarely did. It was a pleasure for the cows and at that moment he didn't have the energy to fight with them and keep them in the barn. He fed the pigs their mixture of milk, grain, and slop. They seemed to snort in pleasure as they dropped their faces into their dinner.

When he got to the chicken coop, he waited until the rooster was on the far side before dashing in. He dropped the feed for them quickly, attracting most of the chickens. With haste, he grabbed the eggs that had been laid throughout the day and ran for the gate. Escaping the chicken coop without an attack by the rooster was always a good day. Rafe had a hard time feeling good about it. Instead, he partially wished the rooster had gotten him good, to remind him he bled red. He stood watching the animals for so long, darkness fell, and he felt a chill.

"Rafe? Are you alright?" Charlie called from the barn. Her arms were full of packages of bacon they had taken from the store.

"Yes, I'm ok. Just thinking. What's up?" Rafe replied.

"We ran out of fridge and freezer space inside. I guessed you wanted the rest out here?"

We, Rafe thought. They were a we now he supposed. He hadn't meant to take on anyone at the compound. His sisters would arrive, sure. However, he hadn't planned on taking responsibility for anyone else's safety. It would seem he couldn't turn Charlie away. It felt like so long ago that he had found her ran off the road and then her home broken into. The fear she was feeling at the time was nothing compared to what they faced now. Rafe couldn't leave her to fend for herself, no matter how tough she seemed to act.

Together they stored the rest of the supplies in the large freezer and refrigerator he had in the barn. The dried goods they took to the root cellar to stay relatively cool and it was just good storage. While there, Rafe retrieved a jar of apple butter, deciding they needed a sweet treat after a day like today. They walked together back to the house. Rafe noticed the small looks Charlie threw in his direction and he finally had to ask her what the problem was.

"Do I have more black crap on me?" He said, turning to try and look at his back.

"Ah, no. Not at all. Well, your pants and boots are still filthy," Charlie pointed out.

They were. In the mudroom, Rafe kicked off his boots and thought about spraying them down. He just couldn't muster the energy and decided to handle it the next morning. He went straight to the bathroom where he took the hottest shower he could manage without blistering his skin. When he came out, he felt relatively normal and clean. He still stood in front of the mirror and turned around to make sure there was nothing on him.

After dressing in his room, he came to find Charlie sitting back on the couch with the news on. This time she was scouring national news. Rafe watched as she flipped and when she finally stopped he felt horrified to see that there were attacks happening in other cities.

"So finally, someone is reporting the truth," Charlie said.

"It would seem so. Where are they saying the attacks are?"

"This story is Florida. I've heard a number of different states though."

"My sisters will see this. And then they will come," Rafe said, his voice matter of fact.

"How will they get here from across the country?" Charlie asked, baffled.

"You don't know my sisters," Rafe said. And he genuinely laughed thinking about it. "If you think I'm extreme, living out here, the guns, the knives. You haven't seen anything until you get the three of us together. Mitch Duncan's finest recruits."

"Your dad was serious."

"Very. When it came to survival and the end of the world, it was no joking matter to him. My childhood was interesting, to say the least," Rafe said. He lost himself in thoughts of Mitch and the lessons he taught.

Living a normal life wasn't a possibility with Mitch Duncan. He remembered the time he was sure his father had completely lost himself. Rafe was a typical ten-year-old boy. He was interested in sports, playing with his friends, and the introduction of video games. None of those things were an option in his life because his dad didn't see their benefit for their prepping lifestyle. Mitch had a one-track mind, only concerned with preparing his children for the worst. Rafe went along easily, but at times he just yearned for something normal. He started sneaking things into the house that he enjoyed, baseball cards, a football and comics. They were all items he could trade for at school with items he found at home. That was until Mitch found out.

At ten-years-old Rafe wasn't naturally sneaky. When Mitch found the items hidden under his bed, Rafe wasn't even sure how to lie about them. Instead, he told the truth. Mitch didn't get angry like other fathers. He got quiet and contemplative. When he didn't say anything, Rafe knew he was in for some sort of punishment. Mitch had left his room telling him to be prepared for a campout the next day.

"What about school?" Rafe had called after him as Mitch left the room. It had been a Tuesday.

"There's nothing that school can teach you that I don't teach here," Mitch had said, stalking away.

That was just like Mitch. He didn't believe in traditional school. If the truancy officer hadn't shown up when he took them out of school too much, he would have pulled them completely. Rafe knew that Alex was especially thankful for being able to leave and go to school during the day. She had bright dreams of going to college. Where Max would have been happy to never step foot in another classroom if she could have prevented it. Rafe was right in the middle. He loved his home, the wildness of it. But he also wanted things that normal life had to offer.

Wednesday morning, Mitch woke Rafe an hour before his alarm was set to go off. He gave his son no time to get up and grab his bug out bag and follow outside. Rafe hastily pulled on the clothing he had set out the night before, a sturdy pair of hiking pants, thermal shirt with vest, and boots. He ran out the door to catch his father climbing into his truck. Rafe noted that there was no other equipment in the back of the truck. The missing things like a tent or food gave Rafe a nervous tremble in his stomach. His father rarely wasn't prepared for whatever was to come. He clearly wasn't concerned about shelter for his son.

An hour later, Mitch pulled off of the asphalt side road onto a dirt trail. When the trail came to a dead end, Mitch exited the vehicle without a word. Rafe knew that he was meant to follow. With his bug out bag, Rafe followed Mitch. While they walked, Rafe remembered a few years before when Mitch had left Alex out in the wilderness alone. She had come back injured and while it seemed like Mitch cared his daughter was hurt, he also believed he had taught her some important lessons. Alex still refused to drive alone with him anywhere, afraid he would just leave her again. Rafe was prepared if his father was going to repeat his form of punishment.

Instead, they came to a large pine tree. Mitch looked up at its branches for a few minutes before motioning to Rafe.

"Climb it. There's a good v section up there that you can set up camp. You will stay there for two nights. You will not come down. I will know if you do. Do you understand me?"

Rafe had looked at him dumbfounded but had nodded anyway. His father was going to leave him, but unlike Alex, he told Rafe what he was doing. Also different, Rafe had to stay in a tree for two days before Mitch would retrieve him. Rafe had accepted his punishment and with his bug out gear on his back, he started to climb. He had always enjoyed climbing trees and being out in nature. Since they were little, he and Max used to camp away from home on their own. But they always had tents and were well prepared. Sleeping in a tree wasn't his idea of safe.

Once Rafe had settled on the branch Mitch had instructed, his father disappeared back down the path. From his perch, he could hear the truck start and see the brake lights as he drove away. The world closed in around him, quiet and calm. Thinking, Rafe had known he would be in trouble if his father found his prized items. He took a few deep breaths and decided how he was going to handle the days. His father had no idea that he had hidden comics in his bug out bag, just in case. As well as a Hardy Boy's book he was reading. He would keep himself occupied as necessary and stay in the tree as instructed.

"So, he just left you? In a tree?" Charlie asked, pulling Rafe back to the present.

"Yup. That was what he would do as punishment. Something to prove that the skills he was teaching us were more important than the things we wanted."

"What did you do?" Charlie asked, her attention rapt on Rafe and his story.

"Well, I tied myself to the tree. I used a length of paracord that was made into a survival bracelet. My dad used to make those before they got big and commercialized. Anyhow, we all had something like that in our packs. So, I tied myself to the tree to sleep. My biggest fear was falling out and breaking my neck. At night I wrapped myself up in a sleeping bag and slept sitting up. It was uncomfortable, but I was fairly warm."

"Of course. You were only ten-years-old. How did your father never have the police called on him?"

"Out here? No one knew what was really happening to us. I don't know about my sisters, but I never talked about my crazy father to my friends. They never came over, because we lived so far from town. It was easy for no one to find out. And in my father's mind, this wasn't abuse. It was teaching." Rafe said.

"Did you eat in the tree?"

"Yeah. I had MRE's stored in my pack. So, I ate them cold, using the water I had also hauled up. I did start a small fire in a can after I ate the fruit from it, to warm my hands a bit. But I was really careful because a forest fire wouldn't have helped me at that time," Rafe explained.

"This all seems so crazy to me, but you talk about it like it was so normal. My family, well we were lucky if we took vacations together. And those were never camping. The closest we ever got was a hotel room that wasn't a suite," Charlie said.

"It wasn't a vacation for us. It was just our lives. I didn't know anything different. And though I saw my friends with normal parents, I did enjoy living out in all the open like we did. Like I do now."

"So, you stayed in the tree for two days, two nights. What happened on the third day?"

"My dad showed up like promised. He always meant what he said and did what he promised. I had succeeded in living through the days and nights. I climbed down when allowed. He never praised us. But when I came down, he patted me on the shoulder in a way he rarely did. We got in the truck and came home. Life was back to normal after that, minus my hidden contraband." Rafe said.

"Wow. I really have no other words. I guess you're right. If your sisters are like you, they will have no trouble making it here. But then what?" Charlie asked.

"Then we survive. I'm not sure what's going to happen to society. What the government is going to do. We are meant to be self-sustained here. That is what we always prepared for."

"When your sisters come, I mean the house will be pretty full I assume? I can move back to the cottage. It's away from town, so I should be fairly safe from the sick," Charlie said. When she spoke, she looked down at her hands, the subject making her uncomfortable.

"You trying to get away from me already," Rafe said, a smirk on his face. The tone made Charlie look up with a retort, but she bit it back when she saw his smile.

"I don't want to be an inconvenience."

"You aren't. You'll pull your weight. You aren't going back to that cottage. It's completely unsecured. You're safer here," Rafe said. His tone left no room for arguments.

"What will your sisters think of some random woman living with you?"

"They will probably be more interested in the work you were doing that could have caused all of this. Maybe we should work on that after dinner?" Rafe suggested.

Charlie agreed, and the pair went into the kitchen to work on dinner. Rafe found it amusing that at every turn he was a surprise to her. When he put out the apple butter he had brought from the root cellar, she didn't believe he had made it himself. He laughed harder when she tried it, claimed it was heaven and then called him a liar. They put together a dinner of cheeseburgers with all the fixings, canned pears, and Charlie's favorite cookies. They ate mostly in silence. Rafe figured Charlie was horrified by the story he told her and wasn't sure what to say to him now. He didn't really blame her. In the regular world, leaving a child in a tree for two nights was considered child abuse. For him, it was a lesson in survival.

The dishes cleaned and put away, Charlie brought out her thumb drive. Rafe brought his laptop to the dining room table. Side by side they waited as the laptop recognized the new thumb drive. Charlie worked the computer, finding the specific files on the pathogen that was in the mouse that bit Tammy. The information that came up could have been in a different language to Rafe. However, Charlie read along, murmuring to herself, touching the screen at points to follow something specific. She then got very silent, her body going stiff.

"What does it say?" Rafe finally asked.

"It's a lot of data. I didn't work on this stage as much. My part was to find the cures to these pathogens. But I understand enough to know something is missing here. There is a protein that is supposed to be in every test pathogen. That protein ensures the inability for the pathogen to transfer to humans, no matter the vector. Looking at this, I don't see that protein was added," Charlie explained.

"Ok. That I can understand. Maybe that step hadn't been done before the mouse attacked Tammy?"

"No. The protein should have been in the pathogen before the idea of tests even started. Someone messed up, or...." Charlie said.

"Or, someone did it on purpose?" Rafe finished for her.

"Why would someone do that?" Charlie asked. She sat back, letting her long hair down so it flowed around her shoulders. She began to twist a piece around her fingers in a nervous habit.

"I said it before. Biological weapon." Rafe said. Charlie cursed and pushed away from the table. She paced from the kitchen to the far wall and back again.

"How did I not see this? Were they having us create illnesses they could use against enemies? Maybe I just wasn't the one getting the orders. I usually only worked on the cures for the pathogens. There wasn't many I couldn't cure. Those that I couldn't, none were deadly, so it was never brought up again. I feel so stupid," Charlie said.

"You aren't stupid. They probably only gave everyone a small piece of the puzzle. If you had all talked about the work, the pieces would have fit. But it didn't occur to you."

"There were four of us on these projects, so each of us got different instructions. We all put our details into a specific file and that is where 'The Suit' could pull the information he wanted," Charlie said, as she worked things out in her own mind.

"That's how I would do it. For something you want to keep a secret."

Charlie stopped pacing and faced him, her face set hard in determination. Her eyes that so easily gave away her moods, were dark and clouded. She was worried and scared.

"I need more information, Rafe. The pieces I pulled, they are mostly just mine. I never got enough time to grab any other information from the folder we worked in."

"How do we get that?"

"Only one way. Without the internet working, we can't hack into the system from here, even if I could have figured it out."

"Ok. So, what's the way?"

"We have to go to the facility."

The next morning, Rafe rose with the sun after a sleepless night. He tossed and turned thinking about having to go back into town. The facility was a windowless box, which could easily be a coffin if they weren't careful. Rafe argued with Charlie for hours the night before, trying to find any other way to handle the situation. Charlie insisted if she didn't have the other information, she couldn't attempt the curing process. Looking at the documents she did already have, she didn't feel there was a positive chance of her fixing whatever had been unleashed on the world. Rafe didn't understand the depth of what the infection was so he couldn't feel comfortable with the risk. However, he did know it was important to attempt to fix what had happened.

He wandered out to the barn and noted that all of the snowfall from the previous days had melted away. The day promised to be clear. He hoped that was a good omen. As he robotically went through his morning chores, Rafe thought about the news they had watched flowing in. The TV reception finally stopped near midnight, going to a static. Rafe and Charlie had sat on the couch staring at the black and gray for a long moment before Rafe switched the TV off. The stories from around the country were the same. Violent attacks, deaths, the word zombie was used often. International news was only talking about the states. Some countries had turned away any planes coming from the United States. Rafe couldn't blame them. If there was a way to stop the spread, he would do the same thing.

His mind wandered to his sisters again. Alex and Max were the smartest women he knew. *Might have to add Charlie to that now*, Rafe thought. Charlie was clearly brilliant when it came to the medical field. Even if this plague was created in her lab, it wasn't her fault that it was released out to roll through the human population. Part of Rafe wanted to scold her for not asking questions sooner. But that was the part of Rafe that was like his father, who questioned anything the government did. Rafe knew working at the facility that he was involved in government secrets. He had no idea it was biological weapons being created in those labs he watched on the security cameras.

Back inside the house, Rafe took his coffee back to his father's room. Charlie hadn't come out of her room yet and Rafe hoped she had gotten some sleep though he doubted it. Knowing that walking dead people were wandering miles away, made sleep pretty uncomfortable. He set down his coffee and went to his father's closet. A footlocker was on the floor of the closet. After pulling out drawers and sorting through things, Rafe had five of the knives that Mitch had used to teach him to throw. Rafe didn't know what they would be facing at the facility. His hope was whatever died inside found its way out, looking for a new meal.

But in the chance that he had to go in fighting, he wanted to be prepared.

He was shrugging into the shoulder sheath he had for the throwing knives when Charlie knocked on his door. He turned to see her studying his knives. He tightened straps that had loosened over years of non-use. Once comfortable he picked up his coffee and motioned to Charlie for them to go down and have more. Once she had a cup in her hand, she breathed in the smell deeply before taking a breath and sighing.

"Didn't sleep much?" Rafe asked.

"No, you?" Charlie answered with a shake of her head. This morning her long hair was secured in a braid down her back.

"No. Coffee is the fuel for today. I'm not sure what we will be facing at the facility. Or driving around town."

"That's what I'm worried about. But like I said last night if I have a chance at this, I need more data. Nice knives by the way," Charlie said, changing the subject of the arguments they had the night before.

"Thanks. It's been a while, but it feels like riding a bike. Muscle memory and all that," Rafe said. He pulled a knife and flipped it a few times in his hand to make the point.

The shotgun was loaded, and the extra rounds were added to the shell holder. Rafe reloaded his 9mm and added two extra magazines to his cargo pants pockets. He was sure he would never feel prepared enough to handle what they were going to face at the facility. Charlie loaded the truck with their bug out bags, just in case, and a cooler of food she put together. Rafe commented on how being prepared was coming naturally to her, to which she just snorted in response.

The drive to the facility was quiet. Along the roads, there were cars abandoned, crashed and smoldering. No explanation was needed for some, where the scene was clearly marked with blood and gore. The infected bodies found their meals wherever they could. Rafe drove slowly through a congested section close to town. The road was blocked by green military grade hummers, both with large caliber weapons on the top. Charlie gasped and pointed to one, where a hand was holding onto the gun still, but no other body was visible. Rafe looked away, finding no need to stare at the horror story unfolding in front of them.

"They didn't know what they were dealing with," Rafe said quietly.

"They should have. They wanted it created," Charlie said defiantly.

"Maybe. But these soldiers, they are just following orders. They don't know what happens up the chain."

As they slid through the tightly packed vehicles, Rafe started noting a trend of bullet holes that ripped through many of the cars. Holes that size could only have been made by the weapons on top of the hummers. Either the soldiers didn't care about killing civilians or there weren't healthy people there when the fighting started. The situation haunted Rafe, a sick feeling gnawed at his mind. Something didn't feel right about the scene. He tried to shake off the distraction as they pulled up to the entrance of the facility.

The security gate had been obliterated by people escaping from the outbreak. The security guard station at the gate was, of course, empty but marked by bloody handprints on the outside and inside. Though the man was never kind to Rafe, he hoped he didn't meet a painful fate. Rafe tried to judge the closest door to the lab Charlie needed. She realized what he was doing, and she pointed out where she always parked because it was the easiest access for her. He parked the truck and left it running for a moment, waiting. Nothing stirred around the parking lot. The door they needed to enter was closed in front of them, but blood marked the outside.

"When we get inside, you need to stay with me. And do exactly what I say. You see something don't scream unless that's the only way I'll hear you. Try to stay calm," Rafe said. He looked over at Charlie, who already had the crowbar in her hand.

"Got it," was all she said in answer.

The pair approached the door carefully. Rafe continued to scan the parking lot for any threats that may be nearby. He guessed any infected would have been drawn by the noise and movement of the truck. But nothing was popping out from dark corners yet. At the door, Charlie swiped her badge. The power was still on to the building and security of the doors was still intact. Rafe wasn't sure that was good or bad. He didn't want to get caught against a locked door when an infected was attacking him.

The door swung out toward them. Rafe had his 9mm in his hand as he rounded the door to confront anything that was waiting directly inside. His heart was slamming against his chest, waiting for the first nightmare to jump out at him. The entrance hall was empty. But the pristine white was no longer. Blood washed the walls and windows of the labs. Handprints showed where people may have tried to pick themselves up or possibly the infected bouncing from wall to wall. Drag marks were on the ground, bodies dragged by the infected was Rafe's guess. Slowly he stepped into the building, his eyes easily adjusting from the sunlight to the florescent lights still on inside.

The quiet was eerie to his ears. Though the facility was never loud, it was always full of people. Doctors, security, custodians, and suits wandered the halls day and night. Now it was silent. In the distance, deeper into the facility movement could be heard. It was loud enough to reach them at the entrance. Rafe knew it was infected bodies, with no direction, slamming into walls and doors. He carefully picked his steps around the blood splatters, pointing for Charlie to do the same. They made no sounds as they made their way to Charlie's lab. It wasn't before long that they reached one of the middle security doors. Charlie handed her badge to

Rafe, who swiped it, cursing silently at the loud beep the reader made.

They stepped through and after two more turns, they arrived at Charlie's lab. Rafe looked at the air shower, realizing that it would make quite a bit of noise when they stepped in. But once in, as long as no infected found out a way in, they would be safe for Charlie to gather her data. He looked back as Charlie grabbed his arm. He wasn't sure where it came from, but an infected who was once a custodian was trudging toward them. Rafe didn't want to shoot anything until it was totally necessary, knowing the noise would echo throughout the entire building.

He walked away from Charlie, pulling his hunting knife as he approached the infected man. Rafe tried to look at him without really seeing him. The man was a worker that was in the building during the day, like Rafe, and they had crossed paths a number of times. Seeing him now, flesh hanging from his teeth, blood caking his face and clothes, made Rafe want to vomit. He hung on to the idea that ending the man's dead walking, was releasing him from the horrible existence he was trapped in. As Rafe reached the man, the infected had his hands out immediately trying to claw at Rafe's skin. Rafe blocked his advance, sending the infected into the wall with a hard redirect. Before he could turn back to attack Rafe again, Rafe had sunk his hunting knife into the man's skull.

Sadness washed over him as he leaned down to clean his knife on the man's uniform. Rafe didn't even know his first name but saw him almost every day as he decontaminated labs and took out the trash. Walking back to Charlie, he pushed her into the air shower and followed. The shower came on with a loud hiss and the doors locked while the decontamination happened. Rafe didn't speak, though he could feel Charlie's eyes on him. He knew she wanted to ask him questions, ask him if he was ok. He didn't have the words for how he felt, so he avoided her gaze and avoided the subject.

Once inside the lab, Charlie went directly to the computer

station that all of the doctors loaded their files on at the end of the day. Each small station in the lab had only a tablet for working throughout the day. At the end of the day they were required to take all of that work and put it on the network files. Rafe searched the room to ensure they were alone. The blood for Aiko's kills a few days before was still dark on the stark white tile. He stepped around the murder scene and checked all corners just for good measure. They were alone in the lab.

A bang on the window from the hallway informed Rafe that it wasn't the same case outside. The sounds of the keypads and the air shower had attracted two infected so far. They could see their desired meal and were working themselves up into a frenzy to get to them. Rafe watched them, studying their movements, their facial expressions. Teeth gnashed and snapped at the glass, with clearly no understanding of the barrier between them. Every few moments they were back up and slam back into the window. Rafe knew if the glass was anything less than what it was now, they would find a way to break through. He didn't believe that showed specific intelligence, just luck that they would throw themselves against whatever was between them and food.

"How much longer?" Rafe asked.

"I'm trying to access the files now. Once I find what I'm looking for, it's just a few moments to get the data to the external drive," Charlie answered from the computer.

"We have a few guests. I'm not sure if the attendees will grow, so move as fast as you can," Rafe said.

"Doing the best I can under the pressure of imminent death," Charlie shot back.

"Oh, is that what it takes to get you moving? I could let one of these lovely guys in to visit?" Rafe said, gesturing toward the infected at the window. Charlie just looked at him with a perfect eyebrow raised in challenge.

Rafe turned away from the infected, doing the best he could to ignore the noises coming from them. He wandered the lab looking through things. A first aid kit caught his attention and he pulled it out to inspect it. Inside were all of the normal items you would find in a basic kit. He set it aside, deciding on a way to take it with them. It made him think of the large med bag that was in security. Looking back at the window to see now a third infected there, Rafe started to plan in his mind. He wanted to get to security, get the med bag. There he could grab a security badge and enter other labs. They would also have useful items. He didn't doubt that he could handle the infected at the door to get them moving toward security.

Ten minutes later, Charlie felt she had moved all of the files onto the external drive she had brought. She tucked it safely in an inside pocket of her denim jacket. The same three infected were still at the window, their threat rising as they saw their prey moving around inside. Standing at the door of the air shower, Rafe told Charlie to wait until he was out and had ended the infected. She protested at first, but he asked her to just listen. With a stubborn huff, she crossed her arms, crowbar in her hand.

Rafe entered the air shower. The noise of the alarm and the machine whirling pulled the infected over to the door to watch for him to exit. He came out prepared, 9mm at the ready. He shot the first infected at almost point-blank range in the forehead. The body was blown back off its feet, knocking into another infected. Rafe pulled his knife and shoved it into the head of the infected on the ground. He left it before standing and heading toward the third who was just moving away from the window. He palmed a throwing knife and with quick precision the blade embedded deep into the infected's face. The body crumpled to the ground unceremoniously and stopped its movements.

Behind him, the air shower turned off and Charlie stepped out with crowbar raised. She brought the metal whistling down on an infected that was coming up behind Rafe. The blow was enough to crack the skull and impact the brain, throwing the infected to the ground truly dead. Charlie stood there looking at Rafe as he put two and two together. He hadn't heard the infected coming, as he was concentrating on the three in front of him. He realized Charlie had been watching his back from the lab and saw the threat before he could be bitten. He pulled his knives from the skulls of the infected and cleaned the blades, before sliding them back into their sheaths.

"Thanks," Rafe said.

"Next time don't leave me behind," Charlie replied.

CHAPTER TEN

From a bunker miles away, 'The Suit' watched as the intruders entered the facility. As soon as the outside door was opened, an alarm had sounded on his system. Immediately the cameras were activated for him to watch the pair walking through the halls. When they entered the lab, he immediately recognized Charlotte Brewer, the nosey doctor that had been hired for the Mars Project. Of course, those hired didn't know the project they were associated with. 'The Suit' found the doctors worked better not knowing the whole picture.

He sat forward in his plush office chair, watching as Charlotte went to the main terminal in her lab. She had a small black drive and 'The Suit' knew immediately what that meant. The separate parts they worked so hard to keep secret, Charlotte would pull them all together. It would be like a puzzle for her, but all of the pieces fit into a large picture that she would understand. The Mars Project.

Charlotte had become a thorn in his side a few weeks prior when it was discovered by IT that someone was taking information out on a portable memory drive. After scouring through camera footage, it was finally discovered that Charlotte was taking home her information. His men broke into her house but weren't able to find the drive she was using. A search of her private computer didn't show that she had been storing the information there. Now she was clearly adding pieces to her information.

'The Suit' tapped his chin as he watched the infected humans wander down the halls and part of him wished he had the ability to open doors with a button. If Charlotte and the security guard were killed, 'The Suit's worries would die with them.

The Mars Project, playing off of the name of the Roman God of War, was the secret project of a faction of the US Government. 'The Suit' was part of that faction and ran the biological division of their efforts. Those efforts were to create new and deadlier ways to handle their enemies. Enemies that this faction believed needed to be handled swiftly and immediately. They didn't believe in talks and summits. Instead, they felt the ultimate goal was to eradicate everyone that opposed the United States. Not even the President knew what happened in the black sites that the faction owned and ran.

'The Suit's eyes were glued to the screen, watching the security guard wandering the lab. He picked things up and looked at them. 'The Suit' knew the man didn't have a clue of what he was looking at. For a moment, 'The Suit' turned away from the video screen and pulled up the file on the outside contracting company he had hired for security at the facility. He scrolled through the photos of the guards hired and finally found the one that matched the man with Charlotte. Rafe Duncan. He read his file quickly, not finding any red flags he felt he had to worry about. He did, however, find his address and that would be useful information. 'The Suit' had already been informed by his inside man that Charlotte seemed to be staying with the Duncan man, arriving to work together and leaving together.

Movement on the video screen pulled 'The Suit' back to the happenings in the lab. It was clear that Duncan and Charlotte were arguing about going out into the hall. Duncan clearly winning his argument entered the air shower alone, leaving Charlotte to watch. 'The Suit' had to admit he was impressed with the movements of the man. He easily dispatched three infected, one with a throwing knife, which made 'The Suit' wonder more about the background of the man. As he watched Duncan finish the last infected, 'The Suit' caught sight of the fourth infected wandering toward Duncan. He held his breath, hoping the infected would get Duncan before he could get away. 'The Suit' cursed when Charlotte appeared from the air shower and killed the infected herself.

"Damn it," 'The Suit' breathed as he drummed his fingers on his desk.

The Duncan man seemed to be a more formidable opponent than 'The Suit' had originally assumed. He followed the pair through the halls of the facility. Instead of leaving directly, Duncan led the way to the security vestibule. He retrieved the medical bag and a badge, which 'The Suit' was sure would be a problem. But as he watched, it seemed Duncan was scavenging supplies that could come in handy in the future. They stopped in the locker room where no official camera was positioned due to questions of privacy. However, after a few clicks, 'The Suit' had the hidden camera pulled up. It wasn't that 'The Suit' was a voyeur. The camera was placed for the safety of The Mars Project.

Duncan and Charlotte seemed to find nothing of importance in the locker room, except Charlotte's personal items that were left behind in her locker. The pair exited quickly, only to be faced by another infected. This one was a woman, a security officer, 'The Suit' guessed from her uniform. The hesitation in Duncan only confirmed his suspicions. It was someone he knew and had trouble killing. Charlotte was saying something, and 'The Suit' wished he had audio on the cameras. She seemed to step forward toward the woman before Duncan did, but the man grabbed her arm and pulled her back. Hesitation over, Duncan pulled one of his knives from his shoulder harness and let it fly. As before 'The Suit' found himself grudgingly impressed by his skill and accuracy. The infected woman hit the wall and slid down into a heap.

'The Suit' watched as Duncan pulled the knife from the face of the woman. He carefully wiped it on her shirt before putting it back in its place on his belt. He stood looking down at the woman for a long moment. 'The Suit' sat forward watching. Duncan had deadly accuracy, but his weakness had to be the people around him. 'The Suit' wondered, who was Charlotte to this man. Before the recent issue in her lab, 'The Suit' had never had an indication that she was involved with anyone at the facility. And 'The Suit' was very good at keeping tabs on his people.

He turned then and began to flip through the file he had on Charlotte Brewer. She was alone in the world, one of the reasons she was chosen for this project. No husband, no children, her parents both died in a car crash when she was twenty-one. She was an only child and didn't spend time with any extended family. She moved to Montana without much, just a small trailer hooked to her car. This indicated to 'The Suit' she didn't have much sentiment. As far as they knew, she hadn't dated or done anything outside of drinks with her co-workers since she came to work at the facility. 'The Suit' looked back at the screen just in time to see Charlotte put her hand on Duncan's shoulder, the two sharing a small intimate glance as she was clearly consoling him. *When had this happened,* 'The Suit' thought to himself.

Duncan led the way back through the halls for them to exit where they had started. Pulling up an exterior camera 'The Suit' confirmed they were driving together. They sat in the truck and seemed to be discussing something before they eventually pulled away. 'The Suit' watched the truck until it disappeared from his visual on the last camera on the property. He spun away in his chair, checking the footage he had on a different system. These views were pulled from all of the cameras around Kalispell. Deep in his bunker, 'The Suit' watched as people attacked others, blood was spilled, and the plague raged. It took a moment, but he finally picked up the truck Duncan drove pulling into a camping store. He picked up his phone.

"Yes," a voice came across to answer 'The Suit's call.

"We have a complication," 'The Suit' said.

"Something different than what is already happening?" The voice was thick with accusation and annoyance.

"Listen here, Callahan, you answer to me in this hierarchy. You will handle the things I tell you to handle, without complaint," 'The Suit' shot back. The line quieted for a moment.

"Yes, sir," Callahan answered.

Major Callahan was the military muscle of the government faction 'The Suit' was a part of. He was their inside man in the military, making decisions that were for the good of the faction and not the general government. When processes in war zones needed to be fulfilled, Callahan was the one to be called. He could infiltrate the troops on the ground and arrange for them to complete the missions the faction needed for their goals. Callahan liked being known as the faction's fixer and that wasn't far from the truth.

"Good. The Mars Project. There's evidence that has been taken from the facility. I need your men to get it back."

"Yes, sir. Where is it?" Callahan asked.

'The Suit' switched back to the folder with the hiring details for Duncan.

"I have an address. Callahan, this man Duncan, tell your men to watch for him. He's a fair adversary."

CHAPTER ELEVEN

The truck came to an easy stop at the camping supply store. Charlie didn't really want to stay in town. Her fear had ratcheted up while they were at the lab. The enclosed space with the infected wandering the area made her feel uncomfortable. Being back in the place where she had assisted in creating the virus that now was killing everyone, made her feel sick to her core. She was sure they were being watched and she mentioned it to Rafe a few times. His attention was so divided that he didn't really acknowledge her feeling.

She looked over at his silent form now. He had barely spoken since he had to kill Liza. Charlie felt sadness for him. She wasn't sure what Liza was to him, but his emotions were clearly intense after seeing her as an infected and having to end her. Charlie wanted to console him somehow, but she didn't know him well enough to reach out in that way. Instead, she just waited for him to make a move and tell her why he insisted on coming to the camping supply store.

Charlie surveyed the area, mimicking the way Rafe looked all around them before making a move, In the distance, movement could be seen everywhere. But unlike before, no infected came out of hiding at the sound of Rafe's truck. The glass in the store was broken in. From where they sat she couldn't tell if it was vandals or looting. She suspected a little of both. The sound of Rafe readying his weapons made her turn toward him and watch.

"Do you want to talk about it?" Charlie asked suddenly. She hadn't meant to ask, but she couldn't stop herself from caring. Rafe had taken care of her, been there for her and given her a safe haven.

"About what?" Rafe asked. His voice was quieter than usual.

"Your friend. You had to kill your friend. We should talk about it," Charlie said bluntly.

"Liza. Her name was Liza. We weren't really friends. Just co-workers."

"Someone you saw every day at the facility. I know it bothers you that you had to do that. I would have done it for you."

"It's only right that I took care of her," Rafe said. His eyes still scanning the surroundings, without landing on her.

"Maybe. And I understand that. But if you want to talk, well I'm here. I'm kinda the only one here," Charlie replied.

"I think we're in the clear. You ready to go in?" Rafe asked, avoiding the subject for now.

Charlie held up the crowbar that she wielded and just nodded her head. She knew that Rafe wanted to get whatever they could while they were in town, so they didn't have to leave the compound often. She agreed with that and wanted to follow his lead. It was clear to her that Rafe had skills and knowledge she had no idea of. She trusted him. That was a big thing for her after discovering what she did at the facility. She had trusted the job, the government, the people around her. She shouldn't have. It was a mistake to believe in any of that. Now she was with a man she only truly met less than a week before and she trusted him with her life. It was baffling to her but felt natural and she didn't question it.

She followed Rafe out of the truck. Once outside sounds

reached their ears. Sounds of fighting, groaning infected, screaming, and crying. Rafe hesitated next to Charlie, looking toward
the noise. She watched his face, waiting for a decision. Without
asking, she knew he was warring with the need to help those that
might be trapped and under attack.

"If I asked you to wait in the truck, would you?' Rafe asked.

"Probably not," Charlie answered honestly. That got a grunt of
laughter out of Rafe.

"At least I know what to expect with you. I want to check out
what's happening. Maybe we can help," Rafe said.

"I'm with you. If you think it's the right move, I'll follow."

That caused Rafe to look at her strangely for a moment as if
he didn't believe her words. The look quickly changed to determination and he turned toward the turmoil. Charlie stayed close on
his heels, not wanting to be separated from the man with the gun
and knives. When he started throwing knives she had been in
absolute shock. His accuracy had been perfect. She wondered if
there would be a day when something Rafe did, wouldn't surprise
her. She looked at his knife sheath now, the metal of the knives
glinting in the sun as he moved. They looked small, but they were
deadly in his hands.

They rounded the end of the strip of stores, coming to a small
alley between buildings. Charlie gasped in shock, her mind trying
to comprehend what they were seeing. The first thing she knew
was, they were too late. It was a group of survivors that somehow
ended up in a dead-end alley. They weren't able to defend themselves because they all fell to the infected. Now over a dozen
infected were bent over bodies of their victims, gorging themselves on fresh flesh. Rafe groaned a pained noise before he used
his 9mm on the nearest infected. The loud echo of the shot
brought attention to the living pair in the alley.

Groans, hissing, and growling began from the infected as they
dropped their fresh kills, to follow the newest additions. Charlie
began to back up, but Rafe stood his ground. In her fear, she

missed the noise of an actual animal nearby. As she watched Rafe prepare to engage the infected coming at him, a white streak of fur flew past Charlie. The fur was snarling and attacking the infected, the noises it made so similar to those of the zombies. Black gore flew and Rafe called out to the animal trying to protect it from the infected. Rafe's calls went unheeded as the animal continued its unrelenting attack.

Charlie finally focused and realized it was a dog. A large dog, attacking the infected with no concern for its own safety. In her mind she found herself thinking odd thoughts, wondering if the dog even knew it was in danger. And how hard would it be to clean its fur once it was soaked in the gore from the infected. Rafe was fighting his way to the dog, clearly wanting to save someone or something from the infected that had come into the alley.

Rafe reached the dog, only to have to jump back because the dog was so absorbed in the fight he didn't recognize friend from foe. Charlie spurred into action, as she watched infected trying to circle back behind Rafe. She cried his name as she ran in to smash the crowbar across the skull of a nearby infected. Her voice brought Rafe around to see how the infected were circling him. He cursed aloud and grabbed for his throwing knives. A few moments later two knives were embedded in two skulls and the infected nearest to Charlie fell. Even in the midst of survival, Rafe was defending her. She was both parts pleased and aggravated. She was trying to take care of herself too, but Rafe wouldn't allow it.

Resorting to gunfire, Rafe finished the situation, leaving two alive humans and one dog gasping for breath in the alleyway. Rafe regarded the dog warily and the dog watched him for any sudden movements. Charlie, on the other hand, was attracted to the beauty of the dog immediately. She dropped the crowbar and knelt down cooing to the dog and calling it to her.

"Come here, pup. You did such a good job. Who do you

belong to?" Charlie said softly. The dog cocked an ear her way and he seemed to relax when she spoke. It occurred to her that he probably knew she wasn't an infected because she spoke to him. He slowly came to her, head down in submission. When he got close to Charlie he stopped and looked at her again.

"It's ok, baby. You are such a good pup. Come here," she continued to coax, keeping her body relaxed and easy to not scare the dog.

"Charlie, you don't know this dog. Didn't anyone tell you not to pet other people's animals?" Rafe asked. He inched their way as well, gun still at his side. Charlie guessed he thought he would need to protect her from the dog.

"Rafe, stay back. He's scared. But he's not dangerous," Charlie said softly, keeping her voice low and calm. She could see Rafe go stiff trying to fight his basic instincts.

The dog was gorgeous, a husky, with white and gray fur. His eyes were deep and full of emotion, as he looked into Charlie's face, one blue and one brown. His coat was splashed with blood and gore from his vicious attack. But now that he didn't find an obvious threat, he whined softly at Charlie and came to sniff her outstretched fingers. He licked her once before putting his head under her hand. Charlie took that as an approval for a pet, and she sunk her fingers deep into his fur. She ran her hand to his neck and encountered a collar. She turned it and read the tags.

"Storm. Your name is Storm." At the sound of his name Storm let out a little yip, as if agreeing. It made Charlie smile. Then Storm did what she didn't want him to do, he turned and leaned his filthy body against her. Charlie let out her own yip and Rafe stifled a laugh.

"Ok, Storm, you are clearly in a need of a bath. Maybe we could help you with that," Charlie said to the dog as she stood up and looked at Rafe. Her face held the question and she waited for his decision.

"If he wants to come with us, we can bring him home and

clean him up. He'll have to behave around the other animals," Rafe said.

"Yay!" Charlie cheered, and Storm did a little prance around her feet as if he knew exactly why she was happy. Rafe just shook his head and retrieved the knives he had used during the fight.

As Charlie and Rafe walked away from the alley, Storm followed close to Charlie's heel. She could tell he was a well taken care of dog, his coat—without the gore—was shiny and well brushed. As he followed without instruction, he was clearly trained and loyal. Charlie wondered where his family was. She was saddened thinking they must have been dead, or he would have been with them, protecting them from the infected.

Suddenly, Storm stopped, his hackles rising as a low growl left his lips. Charlie and Rafe froze and looked at him. For a moment Charlie wondered if she was wrong and Storm was going to turn on them. But the thought disappeared as soon as the hissing and growling came from the camping gear shop they were approaching. Storm stalked ahead of Charlie, ignoring her whispered calls to come back. Rafe followed closely with Storm, his hunting knife pulled. They entered the shop as a team, Charlie following up behind them with her crowbar. Storm shot off to the left and his growling became louder than the infected that he jumped and took down. Rafe quickly ran after the dog and used his hunting knife to stop the infected from attacking.

Charlie came around the corner to find Rafe pulling his knife clear and patting Storm on the head.

"He's a good watchdog," Charlie said. Storm trotted to her, tongue lolling out of his mouth. She smiled down at him and gave him a quick rub for the job well done.

Now that the camping store was cleared of the infected, Rafe got to work collecting the items he thought were useful. Charlie picked up a new, larger bag for her bug out bag. When she came across a section of food, she ripped open a beef jerky and threw a piece to Storm. The beautiful dog jumped and snapped it out of the air. He seemed pleased with the taste, so she filled her bag with all of the jerkies from the rack. Dehydrated foods, a mess kit, a thermal blanket, and a dog bowl for water followed. Rafe called her over to add a few knives, a multitool, and ammo to her pack.

Thinking of the story of ten-year-old Rafe in a tree, Charlie grabbed multiple rolls of paracord to add to her pack. Rafe saw her and smiled, realizing why she was grabbing it. She was trying to learn from what she saw Rafe do and the stories he told her. Charlie knew that Rafe was determined to protect her. However, she wasn't the type of girl to sit around and hope a man did what is needed. Strong and smart, those were words Charlie thought described her. Determination sat in her heart to prove to Rafe that she could be a partner to him, not a responsibility.

They loaded the truck with their additional supplies. Rafe filled the bed of the truck with boxes of MREs he had found in the storage room of the camping supply store. Charlie laid down a tarp in the back seat and showed Storm where to lay down. The dog jumped up with no assistance and laid down exactly on the tarp. She looked at him for a moment, trying to think about what they would do with him when they got back to the compound. First, she dug into the cooler of food and gave him one of the turkey sandwiches she had made. He swallowed it before Rafe and Charlie were in the car.

"Poor pup, he's probably not seen a normal meal in a few days," Charlie said, looking over the seat to where Storm laid.

"He has you wrapped around his paw already," Rafe mentioned.

"He's been quite helpful, don't you think?"

"As long as he doesn't bring fleas to the compound, he's ok," Rafe said.

"This pretty boy doesn't have fleas. I know it."

Without a word, Rafe pulled into a small parking lot with a

few shops. One read "Pretty Paws," a high-end pet store. He looked at Charlie with a smirk and pointed.

"We're gonna need some supplies for a dog. I've never had a dog at the compound."

Charlie was excited to shop for their new addition. Storm jumped from the truck to join them. And Charlie already found herself looking to him as an early warning alarm. The dog walked to the building as Rafe went to the front windows. The business had not been ransacked yet, so everything seemed intact. But Charlie knew that wouldn't stop Rafe from being very sure that everything was clear. She stood back as Rafe crouched with a small pouch in his hands. After a few moments at the lock, he had the door open and Storm walked in sniffing along the way. When he didn't bark and just came back to the doors, Charlie and Rafe entered with him.

Walking the aisles Charlie filled the cart she had. Rafe began to transfer bags of what seemed to be the best dog food out to the truck. Storm was well behaved, staying right with Charlie and never trying to wander off or pull things off of shelves. If something caught his attention he would stand near it and whine to get Charlie's attention. She added whatever he wanted to her cart. Storm soon had a large collection of squeaky toys, bully sticks, pig's ears, and bones. Charlie also added every bottle of shampoo for long hair dogs to the cart. Looking down at the dog covered in infected blood, she knew the process of bathing him would be a long one.

They loaded back into the truck after they scavenged what they believed the essentials were. To ensure the business would stay intact a bit longer, Rafe locked the door behind them. Charlie didn't suspect that any business would be reopening anytime soon, but if the doors stayed locked maybe they could come back and get more items if they needed them for Storm. The dog in question put his muzzle next to Charlie's shoulder and she stroked him softly, watching Rafe.

"He's got skills," Charlie said to Storm. The dog just nosed her cheek and Charlie laughed.

"So do you. Don't be jealous," she laughed.

Rafe climbed into the truck just as her laughter echoed in the cab. He looked at her strangely and Charlie felt blood rise in her cheeks.

"What?" He asked.

"Storm is jealous of you," Charlie said.

"A dog? That we just met?"

"He needed people. Clearly, he's made us his," Charlie said, and Storm nosed her cheek again.

"Well, I don't know that we needed a dog. But whatever you want to do," Rafe said.

"He'll warn if there are infected around like before. Maybe we didn't know we needed that. But I think we know that now."

"Ok," Rafe answered because he clearly didn't want to argue with Charlie about the dog she was making hers.

Rafe pulled the truck away from the pet store and headed away from town. Charlie stared out of the windows at the effective destruction of their city. She couldn't believe that this one pathogen, started by one sick person, had grown the way it had. She thought about Aiko getting out of the facility. She remembered that all it took was for Aiko to have one bite and she died of the illness a day later. Death was what started the change and she came back moments after that. Charlie assumed people that died completely changed even faster, not going through the illness phase. That made the destruction faster because the infected feasted on whatever living person they could find.

"Where did you go?" Rafe asked.

"Hmmm? Just thinking. It happened so fast. I wouldn't have thought it could spread like this."

"No, me either. But no one would have known how to fend off the sick in the beginning. That only multiplies the amount of infected on the hunt."

Charlie agreed and went silent again. Internally she was beating herself up over her part in this. As soon as she felt things were off, she started taking pieces of information away from the facility. But it was never enough to clearly explain anything. Her plan had always been to get more information off of the main terminal. There were always other doctors around. Thinking back, she realized she wasn't ever sure who to trust in her lab. She knew how she had been hired and sometimes they talked about their lives and pasts. In the end, though, Charlie couldn't be sure that none of them were reporting directly to 'The Suit' and his people.

They arrived at the compound with no additional run-ins with the infected. During their drive, Charlie could hear the sounds of gunshots and even explosions in the distance. Rafe didn't intend on being a one man hero and continued to home. She had a feeling that not saving the people in the alley bothered Rafe, but he would never admit it to her. One thing that was clear about him was he didn't wear his emotions easily. She knew to see his co-worker as an undead infected had bothered him greatly. But he refused to speak about it. At least with her. Inside she accepted that they didn't even know each other.

Storm bounded out of the truck when Charlie opened the door. He ran to the nearest grass spot and relieved himself. Then he stood and sniffed. The cows mooed from their pasture and Storm's head looked that way. Charlie wondered if he had ever seen larger animals or if he was a home animal only. She walked with him to the barn area, letting him sniff around the cow pasture, pig enclosure, and chicken coop. He barked once at the rooster who tried to attack the fence as Storm stood there and Charlie laughed. The rooster clearly liked no one.

"It's alright, boy, that rooster is a mean thing. You just stay away from there, you hear me?" Charlie said.

Storm's ears twitched in Charlie's direction as he looked at her with his head cocked to the side. It was almost unnerving how it seemed he understood every word she was saying. She reached down and scratched behind his ears and his tongue lolled from his mouth. Rafe met them there with his hands full of shampoo bottles and the brushing implements Charlie had brought.

"Maybe we should give him a bath. I'm assuming you're going to bring this beast into the house," Rafe said jokingly.

"Of course. Where else would he sleep?" Charlie asked, her voice innocent, though she knew she was needling Rafe.

"My father never allowed animals in the house. Animals weren't for pets," Rafe said.

His admission made Charlie sad for a moment. Clearly, his childhood wasn't a normal bright one that most children had. However, he didn't seem upset over that. When he spoke of his father and his childhood it was very matter of fact.

"Well, dogs are pets. But they can also be protection. So, having him in the house is just another level of defense. Think of it that way," Charlie said.

Rafe shrugged and made his way to where the hose was. Charlie insisted on towels so Storm wouldn't be too cold after the shower. After much scoffing, Rafe went into the house to retrieve old towels for the dog. They sprayed the dog down and used an entire bottle of soap on his coat. Storm didn't help them much in the process by shaking every time they put water on him or when he was covered in soap suds. Rafe had many curse words to use as they were soaked by the dog's antics. Charlie just laughed, not only at the dog but at Rafe's face and the soap that stuck to his short hair.

Once clean, Storm's coat turned out to be more white and silver than Charlie had guessed. He was mostly bright white with some silver around his face and down his back.

"He's such a beautiful dog," Charlie said, and Storm promptly rolled around in the grass

"When he's clean," Rafe answered, making Charlie laugh

again. Rafe smiled at her and it caught her off guard. It was a genuine smile, instead of the smirks he gave normally.

"Why do you think the infection doesn't spread to him?" Rafe asked suddenly.

The image of Storm's teeth embedded in an infected crossed Charlie's mind and she understood why Rafe asked. She looked at the dog for a long moment as her thoughts processed, trying to understand a pathogen she couldn't even study. She put together what she knew from the infected mouse, to Tammy becoming infected. All it took was a bite from the mouse. For Tammy to infect Aiko, she had to bite her. But both she and Rafe had been in contact with blood from the infected. Neither of them showed any signs of the pathogen. Then there was Storm, who clearly had ingested blood and who knew what else during his fights with the dead.

"Without studying anything, I can only create a general hypothesis," Charlie started. She looked up to see that Rafe's smirk had returned.

"Well, Doctor, enlighten me."

"Something mutated at the time of transfer from the infected mouse to Tammy. I guess we'll never know what, since the mice were destroyed right after the incident. This pathogen must only pass to humans now. The mutation doesn't go the other way. And it's possible the blood isn't a vector for infection. Only the bite of the infected is. Something in their saliva meeting the blood of an uninfected, creating the chance for the infection to spread," Charlie explained.

"That's a general hypothesis? You must be dangerous when you have real data to work with," Rafe joked.

"I'd like to think I was good at what I did," Charlie replied.

"I need to handle the evening chores. Why don't you take the beast inside and let him see where he'll be sleeping," Rafe said.

Storm ran in front of Charlie up the steps to the house. In the mudroom, he waited patiently as she took off her boots and set her purse down. She wasn't sure why she wanted it from her locker. Maybe someday they would need their government-issued ID's again. For now, most of everything inside was useless. It just felt personal to her. She also found where Rafe had put a bag of dog food in the mudroom. The bags of items she had taken were all lined up along the wall. She sorted through and found the food dishes she got. Thinking, she decided Storm could eat inside the house too, so she found a place for his food mat and bowls. The dog sniffed around her and what she put down. He seemed to perk up when he realized there was going to be food involved.

Water was first, and Storm immediately began to lap at the bowl Charlie set down. She watched him for a moment, feeling satisfaction in taking care of the animal. She wondered if that was how Rafe felt about his cows. Next, Charlie filled the bowl with a few cups of food. Unsure of what Storm needed, she looked at the bag for directions. He sniffed at the food for only a second before digging in. It made her smile, feeling like she was completing such normal daily chores. Instead of feeding the dog that had helped them kill the infected just a few hours before.

Rafe had grabbed a dog bed and Charlie thought that was a sign that he liked the dog more than he admitted. She placed the big pillow in the corner of her bedroom. Being honest with herself, she felt better having him nearby. Rafe had tight security, but could anything really be better than the instincts of a dog? Storm, finished with his dinner, padded into the room. He constantly sniffed around, everything being new to him.

"Hey, Storm, this is your bed. See here?" Charlie said as she patted the cushion.

Storm came to her, pushing his head into her, looking for affection. She willingly gave it to him, then showed him the bed again. The dog got on and circled a few times before laying down. He put his muzzle on his paws and looked at her as if to say "I did as I was told. Am I a good boy?" Charlie gave in and ran her fingers through his clean, soft fur.

That night, Rafe whipped up a surprisingly delicious meal of tomato basil soup, with produce he had grown. He accompanied it with chicken thighs, green beans, fresh salad, and canned apples. Charlie moaned as the food hit the spot of her hunger. Storm was laying at her feet as they ate. He never begged and Rafe tried to argue the table was no place for a dog.

"We aren't exactly living a typical society setting right now," Charlie pointed out.

"True."

"We barely know each other and we're living together," Charlie said with a laugh, causing Rafe to join with his own deep laugh.

"You aren't wrong. Ok. I'll let you do whatever you want with the dog."

It was only a few minutes later that Charlie caught him passing Storm pieces of chicken.

In the kitchen, as they put away leftovers and cleaned, Rafe started the conversation about them needing to know each other better. He asked Charlie to tell him about her family since he had spilled so much about himself already.

"Well, I'm pretty much alone when it comes to family. My parents died a few years ago, a car crash. I found it sad of course, I was heartbroken. But then it was very motivating. I always wanted them to be proud of me. We were close. I don't have siblings. That's why I find it interesting when you talk about your sisters."

Rafe's eyes went distant and he looked away. Charlie caught the change in his attitude and put down the towel she was using and turned to him.

"What is it?" She asked.

"Nothing," Rafe answered his standard response often enough.

"Rafe, I feel like at this point we have to consider ourselves friends. We have no one else right now. Tell me what's bothering you," Charlie said softly.

"My sisters. It's been a few days. Alex could have been here by now if she saw the reports when we did. I don't know, I just have a bad feeling."

"I'm sure they are fine. Getting out of town and on the road will probably be hard. Look how bad the roads are around Kalispell. Even for a smaller place, some roads were completely blocked by cars."

"That's probably it. I know they should be fine."

Charlie was about to say something consoling but Storm let out a low growl by the door to the mudroom. It stopped Charlie and Rafe in their tracks. Rafe looked at Charlie before looking at Storm. They waited to see what else he was going to do, already learning to listen to his reactions. His hackles rose, he crouched as if ready to attack, but didn't bark.

"Infected?" Charlie asked.

Rafe turned off the light in the kitchen, allowing them to see into the darkness outside. Charlie's eyes quickly adjusted, though she couldn't see anything moving in the yard. Rafe walked from window to window, finding nothing. He then went to his room to check his monitors. He came back a few minutes later, joining Charlie back at the door with Storm. The dog was still growling low in his throat.

"None of the alarms have tripped, there's nothing on camera."

"Are you sure the alarms are set?"

"Uh, yes. I set up the system personally. Everything is set accurately. Nothing can come through the gate or over the walls without setting off an alarm," Rafe said.

"Not trying to insult you. But we've seen Storm in action. Something is bothering him."

"Could be an animal on the other side of the wall," Rafe suggested.

Charlie had to admit that was possible. She stood, her hand on Storm's head, waiting to see if anything came out of the shadows. Nothing appeared, and Charlie had to coax Storm from the door.

Rafe and Charlie agreed it was probably something on the other side of the wall causing him to be protective. His senses were heightened and would probably smell the rotting odor of the infected if they wandered into the trees around the compound. Charlie brought Storm to his bed and pet him for a few minutes before crawling into her own bed. She fell asleep as Storm paced her room.

CHAPTER TWELVE

Patient Zero continued her hunt through the residential area she had stumbled into. Her bite was infectious, and she had feasted on numerous bodies since she was released from her prison. The body that used to be a healthy and vibrant Tammy, was now covered in a ripped and bloodied nightgown. Her skin had grayed, and scratches were ripped through her arms where her prey had tried to fight back. She felt no pain as she walked, looking for the next attack.

Her foot was turned unnaturally inward, causing her step to falter and sway. In her dead mind, nothing told her that there was something broken. Instead, it only sent signals of feeding to the body. The woman had been clipped by a car when she tried to attack a family inside. The injury didn't stop the need for prey. She drug the broken foot along as necessary.

Each of her limbs moved as if controlled separately, yet somehow the infected was able to stay on her feet and move forward. The noise of crying made her change her direction quickly and she almost stumbled. But the body caught itself and headed directly for where the crying sounded. She found herself with other infected attacking people that were trying to fight out of a business building. Patient Zero had no need for the infected around her. They were just in her way. She pushed her body through the throng, fighting to the front to sink her teeth and nails into warm flesh.

The sound of screeching tires and brakes sounded behind the horrific scene. The noise attracted some of the infected near the back of the mob, but the others pushed forward as healthy people fell beneath the attack of too many infected to fight off. Patient Zero was just about to dig into a leg that was near her when a mesh hood fell over her head. With no desire to comprehend she continued to try to fall onto the meal at her feet. Instead, she was lifted off the ground.

Patient Zero fought and tried to claw into the hands holding her. A collar was fit around her neck, controlling her head easily. She had no desire to save herself, only thought of eating. The men were so close. The sounds of the attack happening nearby made her go into a frenzied state, growling, and hissing coming from her mouth. Her teeth were bared but when she tried to attack the hood prevented her teeth from reaching anything. And she was yanked by the collar, attached to a thick chain.

At the end of the chain was a man in all black, his face covered in a hood and night vision goggles. Around Patient Zero a group of heavily armed men fought off the infected that were coming toward them. They cut down every dead thing that was within reach. But Patient Zero was controlled and led to the black armored vehicle that was parked in the street. The back door was open, and she was lifted and drug into the interior of the truck. Metal shackles were attached to the ankles and wrists. One of the men gagged at the feel of her broken ankle as he secured the shackle.

"Straighten up, Bradley," another figure said, talking to the man that almost threw up his stomach contents.

"Its ankle is completely snapped, it feels like jello in there," Bradley answered.

"That's no concern of ours. Callahan wanted Patient Zero and we found her. Let's get her transported."

The black truck disappeared into the night, no headlights giving away it's position. They headed East, to deliver the goods as requested.

CHAPTER THIRTEEN

An alarm tore through the house. Rafe was on his feet before
thinking and was shoving socks and shoes on. Pulling a shirt over
his head he ran down the stairs, almost tumbling from the lack of
being awake. Charlie, with Storm on her heels, was just coming
out of her room when he was about to throw open the door. Rafe
ran past her and went to the monitors he had on one wall. The
alarm that was showing was from the top of an outside wall.
Something or someone had tried to come over the rock barrier.

Rafe scanned the cameras, all equipped with night vision. It
took a moment, but he finally found them. Five men, in black,
wearing night vision stalking toward the house. They all had what
looked like government-issued weapons. Rafe opened the gun safe
immediately to get out the shotgun and his rifle. He threw the
rifle over his back and loaded the shotgun while watching the
men. They were trying to surround the house. He knew it was
impossible for them to know exactly where everything was, they
never filed any sort of plans for this property with the county.
This was exactly what his father assumed would happen if anyone
knew about them.

"Who are they?" Charlie breathed.

"My guess? Whoever was after you. They found you and now want what you have," Rafe said.

That sent Charlie running from the room. Rafe took one more long look at the camera feeds to figure out their best options and he followed. Charlie was shoving the external drive she had into her bug out bag that was left in the kitchen. She then turned and started grabbing Storm's canned foods and throwing them in another pack they had scavenged. Without Rafe saying a word, Charlie already knew there was imminent danger. Rafe had to approve of how she was catching on.

Rafe strapped on his throwing knives and grabbed a flashlight. The first man to breach the house was getting a face full of light and a shot to the head. He wasn't playing around. These men came on his property to do him harm. He wasn't waiting to ask for any explanations. Rafe brought Charlie to the front door he rarely used and had her crouch down behind him. As long as he kept her behind him, he could protect her. Storm was next to him, growling. The noise was making it hard for Rafe to concentrate and he told Charlie as much.

"Storm, you're a good boy. But shhhh," Charlie said to the dog.

He didn't look back at the woman, but his ear twitched and he silenced the growling. As a team, Rafe and Storm waited. Rafe knew the house better than anyone. He knew every creak, every door hinge that squeaked and every entrance point. He waited to hear where they were going to attempt to enter first. The creak of a step outside of the mudroom had him moving slightly so he would have a clear view of that entrance. They wouldn't have known that Rafe never used the front door. They would assume the back door was the easiest entry point.

The door slowly opened and Rafe waited until he could see the man in the dim moonlight. As soon as his face was visible, Rafe hit him with the flashlight, causing the man to yell and step back. Rafe then sighted his 9mm and shot the man in the neck and shoulder. If he was wearing something bulletproof, which was likely, Rafe hoped his shots landed on flesh. The intruder went down hard into the mudroom. Rafe stepped slightly to the side to see around the kitchen counter that blocked his vision of the floor. All he saw were boots. And they were moving.

"Time to go," Rafe said to Charlie.

He stood and spun to grab the bags he had brought next to them. One was his bug out bag. The other was the med bag they had brought from the facility. He opened the front door carefully and looked around. Seeing no one, he stepped out with Storm and Charlie following him. He knew the shot at the back of the house would attract the team to their fallen member. Rafe turned the opposite corner of the house, hoping to put enough distance between the attackers and them before they realized they had fled the house. Storm launched himself forward just as a quiet shot rang out.

The burning pain that lanced through Rafe's side was immediate. It wasn't nearly as bad as he would have expected, being that he had never been shot before. He folded to one side for a moment, as Storm jumped landing his front paws on the chest of the shooter. The shot had been close to silent. *Silencers*, Rafe thought to himself. They would have wanted to attack quietly. Maybe they thought they could take Charlie without Rafe even knowing. They were clearly not prepared for the security system Rafe had set up.

Storm was tossed to the side, his teeth never making a purchase into flesh. Charlie cried out as the dog skidded. Rafe had to grab her from running after him and leaving the safety he provided.

"Stay back," he quietly growled at her.

Rafe sprung forward, catching the man in the chest with a front kick, sending him sprawling back. The recovery was quick, and he was back on his feet moving toward Rafe to strike out. The man's first blow went wide and Rafe crouched to strike out with two sharp punches to the man's abdomen. The second punch from the attacker connected with Rafe's shoulder as he tried to pivot away. The man then tried to throw a knee at Rafe's face, that barely missed, as Rafe moved back to allow himself more room. This created an opening for the man to raise an additional weapon Rafe didn't know he had.

Noises from inside the house caught Rafe attention. The men had come to find out about the shots inside. Quickly and not wanting to draw additional attention, Rafe pulled a throwing knife and hurled it at the shooter. It impaled the man in the neck and he immediately dropped his weapon to reach up and grab at it. With the blood flowing, the handle was slick, and the man couldn't pull it out on his own. Rafe moved forward to grab the dropped gun. He checked the magazine finding it full. He then patted down the attacker to pull any additional magazines. He loaded them into his cargo pants pockets.

The dog was back, and he was pissed. Rafe thought he almost lost a finger as Storm locked down his jaws on the man's arm and began to shake. Charlie whispered to the dog to stop him, but he was full on in attack mode and he wasn't hearing the woman. Rafe pulled the knife from the man's throat finally. He was too far gone and wasn't feeling anything the dog was doing at the moment. The pain in Rafe's side flared and he put his hand to the wound area. It came back covered in blood.

"Oh my god, Rafe! You were shot," Charlie exclaimed, trying to yank his shirt up.

"Charlie, quit. We don't have time for this. There are still at least three more. Probably in the house looking for us. We need to move and fast," Rafe said.

She didn't immediately remove her hands from his shirt. He could barely see her face in the light of the moon, but she was pale and beautiful. He had no idea where the word beautiful had come from as it crossed his mind. He gently pushed her hands away and handed her the shotgun.

"Do not use this unless I expressly tell you to. I haven't taught you to use it and I don't need you killing me or the dog," Rafe said. Charlie didn't answer, just nodded.

The attacker at their feet was clearly dead. Storm, realizing this and knowing his job was done for the moment, finally let go. He stepped away from the body and panted harshly. Rafe let out a low whistle to get his attention and Storm immediately was at Charlie's side again.

"I always wanted a dog," Rafe said as he began to walk away.

"I knew you liked him," Charlie whispered.

Rafe would have laughed if they weren't in such a precarious position. With the M16 pushed against his shoulder, Rafe led them away from the house. He was aware of Storm in a constant state of unease as the dog would let out low growls every few moments. Once they reached the greenhouse, Rafe stopped so he could look back around the corner toward the house. He could now see flashlights in the house. Still only counted three, but that didn't mean someone wasn't out hiding waiting for them to run for it. Their next target was the barn. Rafe instructed Charlie to stay low and run straight to the far side of the building.

A shout sounded from the house just as they reached the barn and moved behind it. Rafe realized there were a number of reasons for this but didn't feel the need to stick around and find out. They moved along the barn wall, when another shout sounded, closer this time. Rafe assumed they found the dead man next to the house. They didn't have much longer before their route was easily discovered.

"Charlie, listen to me. There is a door, hidden, at the back of the compound. My father installed it for this exact reason. We will go straight to that and into the woods. They will have a hard time tracking us from there," Rafe said.

"The woods? Can't we just kill them and go back in?" Charlie asked. Rafe was slightly surprised by her cutthroat attitude.

"If these guys don't report back, more will come. We need more help."

"Your sisters?"

"Hopefully," Rafe said quietly.

He pointed her in the right direction of the door and she and Storm ran for the wall. Rafe waited a moment longer and followed. As he ran he heard a bullet whiz by his head. Pivoting quickly, he knelt and turned with the gun. He had only shot an automatic rifle a few times. Finding two of the three men running toward them from the barn, Rafe opened fire. One dropped almost immediately, from a shot or to get cover, Rafe didn't know. The second began to stagger his running pattern realizing he was taking fire. But he wasn't shooting back while out in the open.

Rafe realized he had to slow these guys down, or they would be on them too quickly to get away. The grounds beyond the barn and pasture were mostly long grass and weeds. Until Rafe decided to put something in, he let nature do its thing. Rafe decided to use this to his advantage and found a patch of fairly long grass. He crouched near it, hoping he could hide long enough to ambush the next mercenary that ran their way. His breathing was ragged and harsh. The pain in his side radiated throughout his chest and abdomen. He had no idea how much blood he was losing, but his side was hot and wet with the blood that was seeping from the wound.

He didn't have to wait long for the mercenaries to follow. They didn't come as a group, making Rafe believe he had hit at least one with the M16 fire. The two left alive came and Rafe was sure they were trying to flank them at the door. Knowing it was unlikely they were aware of the door, the men probably believed they were going to catch them at the far wall with no issues. Rafe waited until they had passed his position. He pulled two knives from his sheath and threw one deadly blade at the nearest man. He fell heavily, pulling the attention of his partner, who swung his view toward Rafe.

Rafe dove back into the grass before popping up slightly to the left of the aim of the M16. He threw the second knife at the man's thigh, wanting to maim and not kill. The injury had the desired effect as the men started to fall to one side, trying to hold his gun up but having a hard time keeping his body straight. Rafe stalked to the man who was trying in vain to pull the knife from his leg. With a foot on the mercenary's injured leg, Rafe reached down to grab the handle of the knife. He turned it harshly a quarter turn, causing the mercenary to cry out, before yanking the blade free. Taking the M16 from his hands, Rafe threw it into the grass.

Staring into the man's face, Rafe wiped the blood on the man's pants before replacing the knife. He pulled his 9mm in a smooth motion and pointed it at the mercenary's face. Rafe leaned down and yanked the night vision goggles and mask off the man's face. He was surprised to find a man that couldn't have been older than himself. Not a seasoned killer like Rafe was assuming. Despite the pain in his own side, Rafe stepped down on the wounded leg harder and the man's face screwed up in pain.

"Who are you?" Rafe demanded. When the man didn't answer, Rafe clicked off the safety on his 9mm. That little movement was clearly a warning and the man knew it.

"Just kill me. I can't tell you anything," the mercenary gasped.

"I didn't say I wouldn't kill you. I asked who you are. Who sent you and from where?"

"You can't fight them forever. More will come," the man said.

"I figured that already, genius. I don't think your boss knew much about me when he sent you here to die. What was the plan?"

"We weren't supposed to come near you. Just take the woman and leave," the man admitted.

"So, it's about Charlie. You're from the government. How can our own government send mercenaries in to kill its own citizens?" Rafe demanded. His anger caused him to push down harder on the leg.

"We aren't mercenaries," the man said, reaching up to his

shoulder to pull on a piece of his black shirt. A patch came down and the US flag showed.

"You're a soldier?" Rafe asked, incredulous.

"Yes."

"When did the military start conducting black-op operations on their own land?"

"When the dead stopped being dead," the man replied, his voice sarcastic as if to say Rafe should have known this already.

Rafe thought for a moment. He knew he couldn't bring himself to pulling the trigger and killing the soldier, defenseless on the ground. He also figured that if he left him living, he would follow them as far as he could and report back to whoever was commanding him.

"When you come around, you let your boss know Charlie is off limits," Rafe said.

"Come around?" The man asked just as Rafe brought the butt of his gun down on the side of the man's head, knocking him out.

Charlie was at the door, but she didn't have the code, so she had crouched to one side waiting for Rafe. Storm stood in front of her, defending against any unknown threats. When Rafe arrived, she stood up quickly, relief on her face.

"What took you so long?" She demanded.

"Didn't want to be followed," Rafe said.

"You scared me. I thought they had gotten you."

"Well you have the dog now, you don't really need me," Rafe said sarcastically. Charlie shoved his shoulder a little in frustration and Rafe hissed in pain.

"Crap, I forgot. Are you ok?" Charlie asked, again trying to reach for his shirt. Rafe pushed her away.

"Yes. Let's get out of the compound before anyone comes looking for these guys."

Rafe entered the code quickly and the door swung out. As soon as they were through, Rafe slammed it shut and put the M16 to his shoulder again. He surveyed the area and found nothing moving. The attackers had probably parked near the entrance road and just entered from that side together. There were no roads behind the compound, nothing but trees and nature.

The forest was dark and ominous at night. The moonlight only made it through in patches through the towering trees. Rafe picked his steps carefully to not jostle his wound. Now that he wasn't running and being immediately chased, the pain was getting deeper and more vivid. Charlie followed him silently, lost in her own mind. He wanted to tell her something to reassure her. But there was nothing to make the situation less dangerous.

"Where are we going?" Charlie asked some time later.

"I know these woods like my home. There are a few places we could hide," Rafe said.

"Ok. Hide in the woods. I like it," Charlie commented wryly.

"It'll be roughing it, princess, but I'll make sure you're fed and have some sort of roof over your head."

"I'm not a princess," she said stubbornly.

"Well, you better not be. We might be out here for a while," Rafe said. He stopped and checked his direction by the moon and stars that he could see through the opening of trees. He adjusted course and Charlie followed.

"Why awhile?"

"I talked to one of the mercenaries. Well, they weren't mercenaries actually. Soldiers."

"Soldiers? Attacked your house?" Charlie asked, surprise lacing her tone.

"Well, I don't think they knew what they were getting into. I wasn't the target," Rafe said, as he stopped and turned to look at Charlie. He wasn't sure how she was going to take the news that she was in someone's crosshairs.

"I don't understand," Charlie looked at him, neither of them completely illuminated.

"They were after you. They were supposed to break in quietly, take you, and leave."

"US Government soldiers are after me? That's how important this is to them?" Charlie began to do what she always did when upset, she paced.

"I guess. I don't think these men knew why they were getting you. Just that they were ordered to do so," Rafe replied.

"They want to cover up what they've done. They want to hide that this plague, was caused by research and work they had us doing in their hidden facility. And I have all the info needed to prove it," Charlie said, reaching behind her to touch her bug out bag.

"Right. And my guess is someone, probably 'The Suit', knows you have that information. It's why you were ran off the road, it's why your house was ransacked. And somehow, they put two and two together and realized you were with me out here. So, they thought it would be an easy strike."

"They clearly didn't know who you were," Charlie replied.

"Not many do. Part of my father's teachings was always to keep a low profile and keep our home with its security a secret."

Rafe turned back in the direction he was wanting to go. His mind was going a little fuzzy and he could feel the adrenaline leaving his bloodstream, causing him to crash. His steps began to slow, feeling like he was trudging through quicksand. He shook his head violently trying to bring everything back into focus as he sat on a large fallen log to go over it. Charlie easily followed, and he could see her watching him from the corner of his eye.

On the other side of the tree, he stopped for a moment to put the packs down he was carrying. Charlie had carried the heavy med back to the wall, while Rafe was fighting. Now he was struggling on the weight of so much packed into the bag. His bug out bag was feeling like it weighed as much as he did. He dropped it to the ground and he fished out a bottle of water he had inside. He took a few drinks, testing the sensation in his stomach. It was cool and welcomed so he drank more.

"Rafe?" Charlie finally asked, standing next to him. He just looked at her as his vision began to feel unfocused again.

"Are you alright?" Charlie said.

"I think....we....should bind my wound," Rafe said weakly before he collapsed at Charlie's feet.

CHAPTER FOURTEEN

Watching Rafe fall was the scariest thing for Charlie that night. It didn't matter they were running from soldiers determined to kidnap her. It didn't matter that she had seen Rafe kill more than one man. Even when Rafe hadn't arrived at the door in the wall right behind her, part of her knew he was on his way. None of that caused the panic-stricken feeling she could feel welling up as she looked at Rafe on the floor of the forest.

"Rafe, Rafe," Charlie said, as loudly as she dared. She crouched next to him, patting his face lightly trying to bring him around.

Charlie immediately went into doctor mode. Though the last few years she had been working in labs, she had done the rotations necessary in the emergency rooms and private practices that were required for her Ph.D. Crouching next to Rafe, she first checked his pulse and found it weak. She finally was able to pull up his shirt and look at the wound he continually pushed her away from. She hissed as she looked at the perfect black hole that was in his side. She reached behind and found the exit wound and that was a welcome relief. She was pretty sure the bullet hadn't hit any major arteries or organs.

Turning to the medical bag from the facility, Charlie had to shush Storm who was whining at Rafe's feet. He was clearly concerned for one of his new friends, but Charlie couldn't concentrate while worrying about the dog as well. Storm set his face on his paws and just watched Charlie as she moved. She unzipped the medical bag, throwing the entire thing open. She was grateful to see the overabundance of items that were kept in the bag.

Looking around, Charlie felt nervous using any sort of light in the woods. What if the men followed them? What if there were infected in the trees? She knew she couldn't stitch up Rafe's wounds without adequate light and it definitely needed stitches. Her mind moved through the options she had. Rafe needed fluids first, his pressure needed to be handled. She pulled out a bag of saline solution and hung it from a small branch above their heads. She put a flashlight in her mouth and carefully stuck Rafe in the arm to run the line. With the fluid going full open, she started to decide what to do with their shelter situation.

Rafe had collapsed next to a large fallen log. They were in the v of that log and a large tree. Charlie started to sort through what was in their bug out bags and pulled out the green tarp Rafe had decided to shove in her bag. It was large enough to cover Rafe and leave room for her to lay if she were to sleep. She attached one side of the tarp to the standing tree, wrapping a piece of paracord through the hole of the tarp, and around the tree. Tying it off, she then grabbed the farthest side and stretched it down and taunt. She then tied that end off on the fallen log near Rafe's feet.

She stood back and looked at her handiwork. She liked that the green was mostly matching their surroundings. But if someone came close it would be obvious. Charlie looked around and decided to lay fallen branches across the tarp. At least those would be slightly more camouflage for them. *Rafe would know a better way to do this*, Charlie thought to herself. But right now, Rafe needed her to figure things out. He could tell her later what she did wrong.

Charlie had to stoop and crawl to get back under the tarp. She reached behind her and pulled some of the branches to hide the light she was going to turn on to see Rafe's wound. Storm didn't like the close quarters, Charlie could tell as he adjusted his position a few times. She scratched him behind the ears and settled him before turning back to Rafe. She pulled out the lantern that had been packed in her bug out bag. The light was stark against the darkness, but she could see Rafe clearly now.

"You should probably stay out for this. That way I don't have to worry about any pain you might feel," Charlie said to Rafe's sleeping form.

She ran her hands under alcohol before getting out the tools she needed. There was a package of sterilized medical tools and Charlie wondered what a security medical bag was doing with them. Ripping open the bag that held the surgical suture kit, Charlie carefully placed it on the sleeping bag she had laid out. Using the scissors, she cut open the front of Rafe's shirt, leaving the exit wound resting on the backside of the shirt instead of the forest floor.

Charlie cursed quietly seeing the wound again. She hadn't known Rafe long but seeing him incapacitated didn't seem possible. He was a force to be reckoned with. A storm that took out anything that tried to get in his path. He was strong and capable. However, Charlie knew from her time in the ER, blood loss would take down the biggest man the same as the smallest frail person. She sat and studied his body a little longer than necessary. The only other time she had seen him without a shirt was a surprise and burned into her brain. He was a handsome man, she could admit to herself.

With gloved hands, Charlie cleansed his wound with the sterile liquids in the suture kit. Squeezing the hole together she used the pre-threaded needle to make small stitches. She leaned close, moving the lantern to be right by his side. She wanted to make the stitches as close as possible, though she doubted Rafe was concerned by scars. She noticed a number of other small scars on his chest and arms, from accidents during his training and chores she assumed. Once the stitches were completed, she easily tied it off with the ease of a practiced physician. She slathered it in antibiotic cream and taped a piece of gauze over the cleaned and prepped wound.

Sitting back on her heels, Charlie was feeling accomplished having the one wound stitched. Now she needed to turn him to his stomach, so she could get to the other. The space being what it was, she was going to have a chore of moving him. She slid the sleeping bag closer to him and carefully rolled him onto it. She had to turn his head, to ensure he could still breathe while lying on his front. She adjusted his IV line to make sure it wasn't hung up on anything and was still flowing. Before starting the second set of stitches she checked his pulse again. It was feeling stronger and she was so thankful.

Repeating the steps she'd done with the front wound, she stitched his back carefully. Rafe twitched once, causing Charlie to hold her breath thinking he might wake. But he didn't move again, and she continued the delicate sutures. Once she had the back covered in ointment and gauze, she carefully removed the rest of the tattered shirt. She knew he had something else in his bag. She removed his boots, leaving the rest of his clothing to deal with later. Carefully she then maneuvered him into the opening of the sleeping bag, bending his legs to get him completely in. She left the arm out with the IV and covered his chest.

She guessed it was almost dawn. Her strength was waning, she couldn't keep her eyes open any longer. She positioned her bag next to his. Charlie prided herself on making sure the shotgun was near her and his weapons were within reach. Everything else she left at the foot of their shelter. Storm nosed his way up to lay between them and Charlie fell asleep with her hand on his head.

Sunlight streamed across Charlie's face, waking her from a dark dream. She couldn't find Rafe. Somehow, she was lost in the forest and the trees were hiding the horrors of the infected. Each turn she made she came in contact with a corpse trying to grab her and make her their meal. She screamed for Rafe, but he never came. In her dream, she was sure something had happened to him and she ran blindly trying to pinpoint where he had gone.

She shook herself, wiping away the darkness of the memory. Leaning over, she reassured herself that Rafe was still breathing and alive. She checked his eyes, finding them to be the normal blue and pupils to be reactionary. But he wasn't waking up. And that worried Charlie. She checked his head again, making sure there wasn't a wound she missed. Not finding anything, she sat up awkwardly in the little shelter. She looked around, a little proud of how she had protected them throughout the night.

Storm whined, and Charlie moved the branches blocking their entrance for him. He darted out sniffing. Charlie was thankful to have him. Without the security of the compound surrounding them, Storm was her early warning sign for any approaching danger. He was a good animal, clearly trained by someone that had time and knowledge. Charlie wondered what happened to the family that had him before. Storm came back into the shelter carefully, like he didn't trust Charlie's construction.

"Hey, I kept us safe last night, right?" Charlie said to him sarcastically. He licked her face and she laughed.

Charlie's stomach growled, and she was surprised she could be hungry. The night had been so panicked and hectic, something she had never dealt with or had been prepared for. Her body clearly didn't care about the events of the night before. It only knew when it needed fuel. Storm looked at her expectantly and she knew the dog was hungry too. Digging into the bag of dog food she had thrown together, she opened a can and set it in front of him. He dug in immediately with vigor. She touched his ear, reveling in the softness of his fur. Without breaking his onslaught of his food, Storm pushed his body toward Charlie, insisting she pet him.

"You are quite the attention hog, aren't you?" Charlie asked. But she still abided by petting him for a few moments before her stomach reminded her that she needed to eat.

Her bladder also calling attention to itself, Charlie decided relieving herself was the first need. She poked her head out of the shelter and looked around. She trusted Storm's instincts and knew he would have let her know if something was in the woods. However, her own brain was still on the verge of fear and imagined every bad thing that could happen. Eventually, she crawled from the shelter and stretched her arms above her head. Looking back at the little shelter she built she was pleased to see that it was well hidden between the trees and branches that she used.

With her business done she pulled out her bag to find something to eat. A can of fruit cocktail seemed like a good choice and she sat against the fallen log. Storm came out of the shelter again and wandered around the area. Charlie shoveled fruit into her mouth while watching the dog for any sign of danger. He happily played, running around trees and coming back to Charlie dropping sticks at her feet. She would throw them, but he would bring more than one back and she wondered if he was playing or doing something else. By the time Charlie finished her can of fruit, there was a pile of wood by the shelter. Storm stood watching her, waiting for praise.

"Are you collecting wood on purpose?" Charlie asked him.

The dog yipped at her and laid on his back next to her leg. She rubbed his stomach realizing someone had trained him in survival tactics. It was as if this dog was meant to be with Rafe because training him in survival seemed like something right up his alley.

Whoever the family was to the beautiful husky, they'd clearly loved him very much. And sadly, Charlie knew they had perished, because Storm would never have been on his own if they were still alive.

"Maybe I should work on this shelter?" Charlie said.

She stood looking at what she had concocted in the dark and she was proud of it. But if Rafe slept much longer, they would need something a little better for another night. She checked his vitals first, happy to see his pressure regulating and his color returning to normal. She checked both of his wound sites, noting no signs of infection or seepage. Nodding to herself, she felt like her stitch work was adequate and she replaced medications and bandages for the time being. She removed the IV line and just knew it was a waiting game for his body to allow him to wake up. Beyond the wounds, Rafe was probably exhausted from blood loss and a crash after his adrenaline left his body.

Collecting additional large branches wasn't hard. She found a folding ax in Rafe's bug out bag. Using that, she chopped some smaller branches from fallen trees. Propping these up against the fallen tree they laid near, she was able to lift the height of the tarp above their heads. The night had been chilly, but in her exhaustion, Charlie hadn't felt extremely cold. She slept solidly. Thinking of another night in the freezing cold made her shiver in the sunshine she stood in. She took the wood that Storm had collected and made a pile near the entrance of the tent. At the fall of darkness, she would light it if Rafe wasn't awake to do it himself.

By mid-afternoon, Charlie sat next to Rafe's head. Minutes passed, and she found herself more and more concerned that he wasn't waking on his own. She checked his pupils again and found normal reactions to light. She felt mostly positive that he didn't have a head injury, but she didn't know about the fight he had with the mercenaries before he reached her at the door.

Thinking back to their escape, she ran her hand over his closely cropped dark hair. He had risked so much to protect her, to save her from a group of men that would have taken her. They would have taken her to 'The Suit' and whoever else wanted to hide this plague. They wanted to silence her and the fact they created the plague that was wiping out the country.

CHAPTER FIFTEEN

Rafe woke, to Charlie calling his name and smacking his face lightly. He looked up at her and realized it was bright and light out. Panic welled in his chest. *We aren't far enough away from the house*, he thought to himself. He tried to sit up, but Charlie pushed his shoulder. He was feeling so weak, it was easy for her to do. He laid back and looked up again, realizing it wasn't the trees he was looking at. It was a green tarp and he was lying next to a log.

"What happened?" Rafe asked.

"You passed out," Charlie replied simply.

"I got that much. Where are we?"

"Still around the area you fell. I couldn't move you far. You're heavy," Charlie said.

"You hid us?"

"Yes. I used a tarp to protect us, but also covered it with fallen branches. We're between a couple of logs, so unless someone is right on top of us we wouldn't be spotted. Storm will tell me if someone comes," she said, gesturing to the dog that was laying at Rafe's feet. He barked once when Rafe lifted his head looking at him.

"You built a shelter?"

"You don't have to sound so surprised," she shot back.

"How long have I been out?" He asked, safely changing the subject.

"About twelve hours I think. I didn't look at the clock last night. A lot was happening."

Rafe tested his body while lying there inside the sleeping bag. He wondered how she was able to get him into the bag, moving his body around on her own. Running an inventory, Rafe found everything to be in working order, except a tight painful sensation in his side. He ran his hand down his body, finding no shirt and a bandage on the front of his abdomen. Reaching behind, he found a matching one on his back.

"I stitched you up. It was a clean through shot, so it wasn't too hard. No major organs or arteries hit," Charlie said, noticing his evaluation and answered the questions in his head.

"You stitched me up?"

"I'm a doctor, you know. I had to do real doctor stuff before working at the CDC. And you had some great supplies. You carry sterilized suture kits. Get shot often?" She joked.

"No. But you obviously never know when you'll need stitches," Rafe said.

"Clearly. How do you feel otherwise?"

"A little weak, but only slight pain in the injured areas."

"You lost quite a bit of blood by the time you passed out. I tried to get some fluids back in you by a bag of saline. Once your pressure came up, I figured you wouldn't want me to waste the second bag if not needed," Charlie explained.

"Good call. I'm starving. Can I eat?" Rafe asked.

"Yeah of course. Want an MRE?"

"Have you eaten?" Rafe asked.

"Sure. I had a can of fruit earlier," Charlie said.

"That's it?"

"I was busy doing things. Oh, and the strangest thing. Storm collected wood for a fire," Charlie said, gesturing again to the dog, who was slowly inching his way closer to them.

"On purpose?" Rafe asked.

"It seemed so. He kept bringing it to me but didn't want me to throw it for him or anything. It was strange. But we now have wood for a fire if we want."

"It will have to be small and only during the day. The light at night could give away our position."

"I hadn't thought of that," Charlie said quietly.

Rafe felt bad, he didn't mean to make her feel as if she wasn't doing a good job. The last few days had been a lot for any person to handle. Rafe admitted to himself he was unnaturally prepared to handle what had been thrown at them.

"It's ok. You're doing a great job. This shelter is quite good," Rafe said motioning with his hand to the ceiling over his head.

Charlie blushed slightly. She busied herself with the MRE she had pulled from his pack. She read the instructions and Rafe just let her figure it out on her own. Her need to be useful and knowledgeable prevented Rafe from instructing or doing it himself. He wanted her to learn. *What if something happens to me?* Rafe thought. He needed to know Charlie could somehow fend for herself if he was gone. He thought about the mercenaries and how Charlie would have survived that attack without him. The concept made him feel cold to his bones and he didn't want to contemplate not being around to protect her.

The MRE was settled, laying to the side to allow the heating element to do its job. Rafe was impressed how easily Charlie just handled the things she was learning. She helped him sit up. Though his head swam, he was determined to get back on his feet. They were still too close to the compound. If the mercenaries were to return, with reinforcements, it would be too easy to find them.

His mind ran through the possible locations they could head toward. Heading back to town was not an option. If the mercenaries were looking at his home for them, they probably went through town as well. That wasn't even considering the previous population of people living in town. He had to assume the majority of those people were turned or fighting their way from the infected. He didn't want to drag Charlie into a war between the living and the dead. It would be a fight he felt the need to participate in.

No, town wasn't an option. Going back to the compound immediately, wasn't an option. He needed to think outside of the normal. And that put him back to his childhood and the lessons from his father. Wandering into the woods, camping, and not coming home at dark were all normal occurrences for Rafe and his sisters. Mitch never thought anything of them not being home for dinner. Their father just assumed they would survive on their own and heed his teachings. The children got hurt and lost, but somehow, they always found their way home. Mitch was never impressed and never surprised.

Thinking about the times they had camped in the woods, Rafe ran through options. Charlie handed him his MRE and he started to shovel food into his mouth like he was going to waste away. They had food for a few days at least. Rafe carried five MRE's in his pack. He had added five to Charlie's pack. They also had canned goods that they had thrown in. He thought about the food stores at the compound and he found himself angry that he couldn't take Charlie back there and be safe.

Staying in the woods was going to be their only option for now. They would forge and Rafe would hunt as needed for additional food until he could sneak back and get more of what they needed. Now that he had that set in his mind, Rafe thought about locations. By the time he finished his MRE, he had decided on the furthest location he knew of. It would be close to a two-day hike. He wouldn't push Charlie through the night, as Mitch would have done to him. She wasn't used to this type of environment.

"So, we're going to go deeper into the forest. Into the mountains. It's a hard hike. But it will be safest for you," Rafe said.

"What about you?" Charlie asked.

"Well, me as well. But it's you the government is after. Not me. So right now, keeping you and your information hidden is our number one priority."

"Ok. But what if we need to get back to town?" Charlie asked, her mind working through the situation.

"It will be about two days to hike in or out of where we're going. Maybe a little less if you make a straight beeline for town instead of the compound. If we really run out of supplies, I'll go to town to get things," Rafe explained.

"You'll go? Without me?"

"You really ask a lot of questions," Rafe said.

"I'm just trying to understand. Why is my life priority here?" Charlie asked.

"Because you're the one with the information. You're the one with the brain that might be able to fix this plague. And if the government wants you, especially enough to send mercenaries, well I'm against anything like that," Rafe said.

"I'm not sure I can fix it..." Charlie trailed off, her voice unsure.

"Well, that's not a solid no. So, there's always the chance. And even if you can't cure it, maybe you can understand it. If you understand it, we could possibly better beat it."

"I guess. But I still don't like the idea of your life being put in danger," Charlie said, lifting her chin in defiance.

"Listen, we can argue about this all day. But the fact is, I'm more equipped to handle what we're in the middle of right now. I will take the additional risks that need to be taken. At this point, living is a risk. So, we're all taking that same risk together," Rafe said. He laid back down, hoping she would take that as a sign he was done talking.

The sun had started to move lower in the sky, night coming.

Rafe marked the movement by the shadows he could see through the opening of the shelter Charlie had built. She had crawled out with Storm on her heels. Rafe was thankful that she was quiet, though he could assume she was playing with the dog. Every few moments he would see Storm race by the shelter and then race back. The dog was clearly in a good mood and wasn't sensing any danger. That gave Rafe peace of mind, something he never thought he'd have without the walls of his compound.

Night fell, the air was chilly in the darkness. But Rafe stood by his decision to not build a fire. They didn't need any additional reasons for outside parties to be attracted to their location. He had pulled a long sleeve shirt on before huddling back into his sleeping bag. Storm had wiggled his way between Rafe and Charlie's legs, finding him a nice place to sleep. Rafe looked at the dog, knowing he definitely wasn't feeling the cold through his thick fur. The white and silver were bright in the limited moonlight.

It was early to sleep and Rafe knew it. But he laid quietly while Charlie adjusted next to him. Being between the fallen logs, the two of them could barely lay on their backs at the same time. Rafe wasn't able to lay on his side yet, afraid to rip out the stitches Charlie had expertly sewn into him. Before he laid down, Charlie insisted on checking the wounds and putting on additional ointment. Rafe had commented on the small precise work and then had laughed when Charlie made a snide remark about not wanting to add scars to his poor body.

Rafe laid and stared at the green tarp, making plans in his mind for the next day. He was hopeful that after an additional night's sleep he would be ready to start their hike into the woods. He thought about the cave that was their destination. When he and Max were children, Mitch had sent them on a summer hike. He was busy building the wall around the compound and small children were nothing but a distraction as he worked the machinery he needed to move the large stones he had purchased.

Rafe and Max loved the woods and they hiked for days,

coming upon a small cave against the base of a small mountain. Above the cave was nothing but a sheer wall. They found the cave to be empty of any wildlife and they set up camp inside for a few nights. It was a fun trip with the two of them competing over who could form better snares and who caught dinner. Whoever didn't catch dinner was responsible for cleaning the animal and cooking. Rafe beat Max two out of three nights. And he remembered how angry her little face was when she had to clean the rabbits he had caught in his snares.

Beside him, Charlie sighed and Rafe assumed she had fallen into slumber. She was busy while he was sleeping, causing exhaustion. On the other hand, Rafe had been sleeping for a while, his body recovering from his blood loss. He was tired but found it hard to fall into sleep with the cramped confines of the shelter. He looked over at Charlie and saw that she had turned to face him. Her lips were slightly parted, her hair spilling around like a halo in the darkness. The word beautiful crossed his mind again and he shook it away.

His sisters had bothered him about women since he became an adult. Alex had found her Blake early on, getting married and having kids in quick succession. Rafe wasn't like Alex. He had never wanted or imagined a normal family life. Max, on the other hand, she never did anything the normal way. She was pregnant out of high school, something that Rafe couldn't believe. But Max's daughter Jack was the most beautiful thing he had ever seen. He had been grateful to be close by when Jack came into the world. And for the time he got to spend with the infant before Max moved to the East Coast.

No, neither of his sisters' experiences made him want something different than what he had lived all his life. The years since Mitch had died had been easy for Rafe. He lived solitary, with his specific responsibilities to only himself and his animals. He never had any desire to add complications to that mix. He saw meeting women as a ritual that just sucked his time from other things he could be doing. Often, he was sought out by friends trying to hook him up. He had earned the title of Mr. Mysterious and Handsome throughout the single women in Kalispell.

Now, Rafe felt an unfamiliar feeling in his stomach. Having Charlie so close, her sweet natural scent filled his senses. He didn't like it. He liked his status quo. Laying there, Rafe made a firm resolution to himself. He was going to protect Charlie because it was the right thing to do, but he would stay far away from her otherwise. He didn't need complicated feelings during a time that was completely too dangerous. He needed his concentration to be prepared for the infected and now the government.

Rafe finally fell asleep with his goals in his mind. Number one, get them to the cave. Number two, build a survivable shelter. And number three, stay away from Charlie.

Morning woke a cranky Rafe. He hadn't slept well, despite being warm and comfortable inside his sleeping bag. Carefully he crawled out of the shelter. He walked a few yards away to relieve himself, happy to do it without Charlie helping him. He stretched, careful of the side that was healing. The ache was still there, but it was manageable. Storm came to his feet and Rafe turned to find Charlie out of the shelter and breaking things down. He went to her to help, feeling awkward having someone else around.

"Morning," he said.

"Good Morning. How are you feeling?"

"As good as expected I would think. Little pain in the side, but other than that, I'm good to go," Rafe replied.

"I figured you'd want to get an early start."

"I think that's best. We'll camp again tonight and hopefully we make it to the cave by evening tomorrow," he said.

"Cave?" Charlie asked.

"Yeah. Our destination is a cave I once camped at with my sister. It'll keep us dry and hidden. And with the cave at our backs, we don't have to worry about someone sneaking up behind us."

"I trust you," she said softly.

"Umm, thanks?" Rafe said, not really sure how to respond.

"I'm just saying, I realize and accept you know better than I do right now. I'm trying to learn and not slow you down," she said.

"You aren't slowing us down. I got shot, remember? And you fixed me up. I'm thankful you were around, or who knows what would have happened," he replied.

Charlie just nodded and continued to pull the branches off of the tarp. The two of them folded the tarp tightly together. Once they were mostly packed, Rafe insisted they eat something before heading off. They shared a can of fruit and beef jerky. Not as hearty as Rafe would have liked, but he decided they would have MREs for dinner. Once at the cave he would set snares and see what he could catch for them to keep their protein intake up. They were going to need food if they were going to live in the wilderness.

Rafe hid the pain from Charlie, as he hoisted his bug out bag onto his back. The med bag was in his hand. Weapons were slung over his shoulders and back. He realized now how pack mules felt. Charlie tried to take things from him, but he had her only carry her bug out bag and the shotgun. Rafe was used to hard hikes, he did them for fun at least once a month. Charlie seemed fit, but he didn't know what type of regiment she kept to make her prepared for their day.

They walked in silence mostly. Storm often ran off ahead, coming back panting. Sometimes Rafe wondered if the dog was smiling at him. As if to say, "You're taking so long, human, and it's comical." Then he would lean against Rafe's legs waiting for confirmation that he was a good dog. Then he was off, a streaking white blur between trees, jumping fallen logs and dashing through bushes. Rafe appreciated the dog's fun attitude, knowing that if there was danger nearby he would alert them immediately. Storm's running gave him the chance to smell everything nearby and Rafe knew that was their early warning system.

Stopping near lunch, they dropped all of their gear near a large pine tree. Charlie sat down, pulling a bottle of water from her pack and drank deeply. She then pulled an empty can out for Storm to drink from. The dog lapped up the water hungrily, before laying down at Charlie's feet, breathing heavy. Rafe didn't want to admit it, but the walk was hard for him. Something he had done a hundred times in his lifetime and he was having a hard time keeping pace. His side screamed at him any time he shifted and pulled at the stitches. He got light headed a few times and slowed, without telling Charlie why.

Rafe sat against a tree and leaned his head back, closing his eyes. The world was spinning, he needed it to stop so they could keep moving. Hands pulling on his shirt caused Rafe to sit up painfully. Charlie just gave him a wry look and gently pushed him back. His bandages in view, Rafe could see blood had seeped into the front one. Charlie glared at him and cursed softly.

"What?" Rafe asked.

"I think you pulled a stitch. Do you have pain?"

Rafe looked away, pretending to check their surroundings. Charlie just waited, knowing his game and a willing participant to challenge him.

"A little, maybe," he said.

"Why didn't you stop sooner?" Charlie was clearly exasperated with him. However, Rafe didn't play invalid. He didn't know how to slow down and not get where they needed to be.

"We need to get to our main camp. I want to set up. And then after a day or so head into town for supplies," Rafe said. He had made plans in his head as they walked, knowing they would need more to survive for a long period of time in the woods. The problem he had was making the decision of going back to the compound to look for his sisters.

"I will need to fix this stitch, so you don't keep bleeding. I might be able to just butterfly it, which would be easier. But I think we should stop for the day."

"Stop? Already? We've only been walking maybe six hours. We have at least another five before we need to make camp," Rafe argued.

Charlie looked at him, her face blank, but her eyes were the fierce green he'd seen on occasion. Rafe waited for some sort of storm to hit, sure that she was angry at him for insisting they keep moving.

"Ok. Well, I'm tired," she finally said. With finality, she turned and pulled the medical bag closer.

Rafe realized she was playing him. She knew if it was just his hurt, he would push through until they made it to their destination. But, if it was Charlie struggling, he would look at it differently. He watched her work for a moment. Her hair was in disarray. Her hands and face were smudged with dirt in places. She had dark circles around her eyes. If he didn't know better, he would admit that she could be looking tired. Yet, he did know better. He was sure she was lying but couldn't bring himself to push her if she was claiming to be too tired to continue.

Storm's low bark broke into Rafe's musings. Charlie froze in place as Rafe got to his feet slowly, grabbing for the shotgun that was propped next to him. The dog was up, feet planted and head down and he stared off into the trees. Rafe waited, trying to see what the dog was clearly sensing. The first indication Rafe got was the sound of breaking branches off in the near distance. He moved to stand next to Storm. The pair stared into the trees, waiting for the attack.

Suddenly, Storm broke away barking through the trees. Rafe waited a moment before following him, realizing he didn't want the dog to get hurt. He was getting used to having the mutt around. As he ran the way he believed Storm had gone, a woman screamed. Rafe slowed for a moment before he realized the scream wasn't from behind him, but from the direction Storm had gone. Rafe slid into a small clearing to find Storm bearing down on two people standing outside of a tent.

"Storm! Down!" Rafe yelled. He held the shotgun at the ready, watching the woman and man carefully. Storm was spooked by the people and Rafe had to admit there was probably a reason.

Storm, hearing Rafe's voice, stopped barking. Rafe glanced down at the dog and saw his hackles still raised and his teeth still showing. He turned back to the campers and studied them for a minute. They both seemed bedraggled. The woman was on the short side, wearing a dress and jacket. The man wasn't much taller, and he looked to be wearing pieces of a business suit with his jacket. Rafe found the scene strange and scenarios in his head failed to explain the two so far out in the woods without proper gear.

"Is that dog yours?" The man asked roughly.

"Yes. How did you come to be out here?"

"Why did your dog almost attack us?" The man shot back, avoiding Rafe's question.

"He didn't. If he was going to attack you, you'd be bleeding," Rafe said. He had little patience for the run around the man was starting.

"Well, he sure scared us. You should keep him leashed."

The irony was not lost on Rafe that he was being lectured about a leash in the woods, while dead people walked the streets. He cocked his head at the man, waiting for him to answer his first question. When it seemed like the man was planning on staying silent, Rafe decided to continue.

"You don't look like you were prepared for the woods. What are you doing out here?"

"Hiding. What else would we be doing?"

"Hiding, dressed like that? That doesn't seem smart. You ran quickly I'm guessing. You don't camp much either or you would have the equipment to bring instead of what you probably grabbed at Walmart," Rafe explained.

"Well, it was all we could think to do, with those things wandering the streets. After we ran into the first ones, we knew the town wasn't safe," the woman said, her voice low and wheezing.

The sound of the woman caused Rafe to take another closer look at her. At first glance, he hadn't noticed the pallor of her skin, pale and gray. She seemed to hug herself in the large jacket she wore. When she spoke, the man shot her a glance as if to tell her to shut up. He didn't want Rafe hearing her speak.

"Are you sick?" Rafe asked, not one to leave the situation unaddressed.

"That's none of your business," the man said without hesitation.

"If she was bitten, which I am about ninety percent sure she was, she will die soon."

"You son of a bitch! How are you going to come here, into our camp, and tell us who's going to die," the man yelled, as his hand reached behind him.

Rafe didn't hesitate, he took the safety off of the shotgun and leveled it at the man. Storm started a low growl, easily realizing his new master was going on the defense.

"See, my dog here," Rafe said, nodding his head toward Storm, "doesn't like the infected. He reacts the way he did because she's infected and he knows it. I'm sorry for that. I really am. But unfortunately, a bite is all it takes. You need to be prepared."

The man's hand came back to his side, a small revolver held there now. He made no move to point it at Rafe, just let it hang as if to show strength. Rafe knew he would let off a shot before the man could raise the revolver. He didn't want it to come to that. Killing living people, scared people, wasn't something Rafe could stomach. He wanted all living people to survive. But hiding away wasn't going to help the woman not turn. She was the same as

Aiko, Charlie's friend. One bite was all it took before she died, turned and attacked.

"I don't want to hurt you. We will head back the way we came. Just be careful," Rafe said.

The couple didn't speak as Rafe slowly backed away. He didn't believe the man could aim his small gun, but he wasn't turning his back on the chance he was wrong. Twenty feet away, Rafe whistled for Storm. The dog also backed away without turning, keeping his eyes trained on the infected woman. She was crying openly now. Rafe felt guilt for blurting out what he did. The attitude wasn't something Rafe handled well. The short man pressed the buttons that turned off Rafe's filter.

Once they were out of direct eyeshot of the pair, Rafe finally turned and ran back the way they had come. He didn't need to worry about knowing the way, Storm led them right back to Charlie. She sprang up from where she sat.

"What happened? What was out there?"

"We need to go, now," Rafe said as soon as he had his breath back.

He started pulling on his bag and guns. Charlie watched for a moment, before following his lead and getting her gear back into place. She closed up the medical bag, realizing there was no time for a fix on Rafe's wounds.

"Rafe, what happened? What spooked Storm?"

"The woods won't be safe, the infected will be here soon."

CHAPTER SIXTEEN

"Home sweet home."

Rafe's flashlight beam crossed walls of stone and floor that was covered with dirt and debris. The shallow cave didn't leave room for animals to hide, but he kicked around some of the sticks and leaves just to make sure. Small animals may have used the space for hiding at one point, but now it would become a refuge for Rafe and Charlie. He turned to her now and watched the determination on her face as she looked at the cave in the waning sunlight.

The hike took them the full two days, longer than Rafe had anticipated. He knew it was mostly because of his injury. After they hiked away from where Rafe found the sick woman and her male friend, they had gone well into darkness. Rafe had wanted to put as much distance between them and the soon to be infected. Once they stopped for camp, Rafe had collapsed from exhaustion. Charlie fussed over him, butterflying his injury closed where he had pulled stitches. She would have spoon fed him the soup they warmed over a small fire if he had let her.

The second day was a little easier on Rafe, the pain in his side diminishing daily. He still wasn't moving as fast as he wanted.

When the sun started to set, he was determined to make it to the campsite before the light was completely gone. He almost cheered when the cave came into sight. It was a sweet thing to see after all those years. Though he hiked in the woods often, he never found a reason to come back to the spot where he and Max had camped for so long. It was like visiting a family member's home, a place you only wanted to swing by for a little stay, not permanently live.

"Well, it's manageable," Charlie finally said, setting her bug out bag near the back wall.

"I think so. We will hang the tarp and a camo net I have in front of the entrance. That will give us protection from the elements. We should also be safe to use some light and fire if we keep the tarp down well."

"Very homey. Where do we start?" She said, rolling up her sleeves.

Together they pulled the tarp tight across the entrance of the cave, using paracord tied to trees on either side. The tarp was cut to hang like curtains. Then Rafe used rocks at the bottom to anchor it, testing it for when they wanted it closed. Next, the net was hung as well, woven with the paracord to hang with the tarp. It didn't slide easily but all they needed to do was be able to duck under when they wanted in or out.

It will have to do, Rafe thought to himself. He pictured getting back into town and bringing a tent back out. If he could pitch that in the cave, Charlie could have privacy whenever she wanted. Rafe was sure this was well below any standards she had, but Charlie never complained as she used a branch as a makeshift broom. After a few minutes, the inside was fairly clear of any debris and Charlie was proud of herself. Rafe smiled, thinking of the next task he could give her.

Storm wandered in and out, pushing the tarp out of the way with his nose. Rafe knew the dog was just insulting his makeshift door. They didn't worry about Storm running off. The dog hadn't been put on a leash yet and he had always chosen to stay close to them. It was both comforting and frightening. Rafe worried they would wake up one morning and he would be gone. The worry was odd to Rafe, he didn't even realize he liked the dog. He also knew that Charlie was quite attached, and he didn't want her upset by the dog disappearing.

Rafe decided to put their beds at the far end of the cave. That way if there was a storm, rain and wind wouldn't bother them greatly. He explained to Charlie that they needed branches, that had just recently fallen, to make beds.

"Trust me. It will be better than a sleeping bag on the rock."

"Makes sense. What about cooking? Are we going to do that in here?"

"Mostly. If it's safe we might be able to have a bigger fire outside sometimes. But mostly everything needs to be small inside. When I go into town, I'm going to see about getting a small camping stove or barbecue," Rafe said.

He ducked under the tarp and swung his light around. He didn't see anything while Storm stood calm next to him, tongue lolling out and relaxed. Charlie quickly followed behind him and she grabbed his arm before he could walk away.

"Go to town? Why are you going into town?"

"We're going to need supplies if we are staying out here for a while. I can hunt and fish. There is moving water not far from here that can be sanitized. But we need more than that, in case there are problems," Rafe explained.

"Why do you make it sound like you're going alone to town."

Rafe knew he was in for an argument by the way Charlie's fists went to her hips. He couldn't clearly see her eyes, but he knew from experience they were looking greener than before.

"I am."

"Rafe Duncan, you must be the most stubborn man on this planet. Hell, you would rival the most stubborn animals," Charlie said, exasperated.

Rafe looked at her as if she had lost her mind. He had no idea what stubbornness had to do with keeping her safe. As he thought about it, he decided leaving Storm with her was also a good idea. But Charlie wasn't done with her argument.

"You just got shot, I had to stitch you up. Remember that? You are still recovering. And yet, your macho attitude isn't diminished at all is it?"

"Whoa. Ok. So, enlighten me here, since you clearly know me so well, what is it I'm doing that is so macho?" Rafe said, his sarcasm apparent.

"Leaving me behind. Always trying to protect me. Thinking I can't do anything." Charlie used her fingers to punctuate and count each of her issues.

"Who showed up on who's doorstep wanting help?" Rafe knew it was a low blow, but he had enough of the argument.

"I....well ok. Sure. I needed some help. It's ok to ask for help. Did you know that, Rafe? You can ask for help. People can help you. I can help you. Watch your back. Like I did back in that alley. Remember me braining an infected as it tried to come up behind you?"

Rafe did remember and he held back the wince realizing she had a decent point. His instinct was to protect her. To do that he believed he needed to leave her behind, keep her away from the infected. And away from any mercenaries that may come calling. However, he now had a different idea.

"What if I teach you?" Rafe suddenly said.

"Teach me what?"

"How to fight? How to shoot? How to survive?"

"So, you will show me how to handle myself on my own?" Charlie asked.

"Well, I hope you won't be on your own. We are a team right now, so I need you to have the skills to watch my back," Rafe said.

Charlie seemed to mull that over. She bent to pick up a branch that was at her feet. As she turned it around, Rafe couldn't see her face in the darkness. He was about to shine his flashlight on her to get an answer when she finally spoke up.

"Deal. You teach me. We watch each other's backs."

"Deal. Now can we make our beds? I'm exhausted," Rafe said.

Rafe carried a small ax as they looked for green branches nearby. When they didn't find as many as he wanted, he started to chop younger branches. Storm picked up sticks around their feet and ran them back to the cave, working his wood collection trick again. After a few trips to the makeshift homestead, Rafe had enough branches to build two small cushions. He showed Charlie to interweave them some, so they didn't just spread out after you laid down. Then he used a little paracord to tie it into a bed at the foot and head. Charlie laid down to test hers and sighed quietly as she found it to be comfortable enough.

They ate by lantern light that night. MREs were eaten quickly in exhaustion. With the light turned out, Rafe worked on getting comfortable in his sleeping bag. He felt around remembering where everything was. His knives were nearby, his 9mm at his head, his hunting knife on the other side with his flashlight. He wanted to move quickly if anything came near their them. Storm was curled up by Charlie, his normal chosen sleeping place. Rafe was confident if anyone was to come within his senses, Storm would be up and waking them immediately.

With these thoughts, Rafe fell into a deep sleep. The fresh air, the quiet sounds of the woods, and Charlie's deep breathing, seemed to lull Rafe. His body was still fighting to mend itself and gain back the blood loss from the days before. He wasn't allowing it the time it needed and part of him knew that. But the rest of his mind knew that they had to get to safety. His body won out now, dragging him deep away from consciousness, allowing the black of dreamlessness to keep him.

Rafe wasn't woken by the morning sun, but instead by the lick of a dog to the face. He sat up faster than he intended and hissed as his side woke up in pain as well. Storm sat next to him, head cocked to the side, waiting. Rafe glared at him and then at the woman that was sitting against the wall trying to not laugh. She had a book in her lap and was watching Rafe with a smile on her face. He gave in and leaned over to pet the dog. This was all the invitation Storm needed. He practically climbed into Rafe's lap to get his love. Charlie's laugh was now audible, echoing lightly in the cave.

"Afternoon, sleepy head," Charlie finally said, once Rafe fought his way out from under the fur ball.

"Afternoon? Are you kidding me?" Rafe said. He looked out the small opening in the tarp that Charlie must have left. The lack of shadows nearby told him she wasn't kidding, it had to be around noon.

"Yup. We've been awake for a few hours. I think your body finally decided to have its own way and make you rest."

"Guess so. What have you been doing?"

"Reading. Storm has collected some more firewood. I figured wandering far wouldn't be a great idea, since I'm not sure I would find my way back yet," Charlie explained, putting the book on her bed and standing up.

"Smart. How about we head to the stream and clean up a bit?" Rafe asked.

"Oh, I would love that, even though I'm sure it's freezing."

"Snowmelt tends to be cold," Rafe said ruefully.

They walked slowly today, with no emergency on their heels. Rafe was still armed with his knives and gun. He didn't want to become too comfortable. It was unlikely the government mercenaries could follow the path they took. Rafe had covered spots where their footprints may have showed too deeply. The rest of the forest floor was hard and covered in natural debris from the surrounding trees. As unlikely as the event may be, or for the infected to find their way there, Rafe still need to be prepared.

Charlie chatted about the forest and how they never camped when she was a child. Rafe listened but didn't need to say much.

Charlie liked to talk, and he didn't mind letting her do it. It was interesting to hear about how a person grew up that wasn't raised by someone like Mitch Duncan. The trees were a second home to Rafe, had been since he was young. Yet, seeing it through Charlie's eyes he realized some of the beauty he had forgotten about. His view was always looking for things that were useful. She saw an adventure and pretty things, as she pulled a flower from the ground and smelled it before putting it behind her ear with a small laugh.

Getting to the stream was easy. It was swollen this time of year with the snow melt flowing down, creating more of a small river. Charlie scooped water and splashed her face, sighing as the cool water cleared away some of the grime that had collected during the last few days. She then dropped the pack she was carrying and pulled out a piece of cloth she had found. She soaked it and turned to Rafe with it in her hand.

"Let's see your stomach and back. This is cold enough that if there's any swelling, it could help a little," she instructed.

Rafe took his shirt off and let her remove the bandages. She inspected her work, muttering under her breath about sutures and lack of infection. The cold compress caused Rafe to jump and goosebumps to break out across his skin. Charlie laughed, a little too happy to torture him with the cold. He sat and held the compress as she instructed. The cold seemed to help with some of the pain as well at the stitch site and Rafe enjoyed the reprieve.

Charlie kicked off her boots after approval from Rafe. Setting them and her socks aside, she pulled her pants up to wade a little into the water. The weather was bright and clear, but in the mountains where they were, a chill still hung in the air. Charlie proceeded to give herself a small sponge bath without removing any of her clothes. Rafe pulled out a large empty water bottle he had in the pack they carried down. He filled it with the cold water. He was sure the water was clean but decided to boil it for safety when they got back to the cave.

He found himself thinking about the animals back on the compound. He knew the cows would be miserable without someone there to do the milking. On any normal day, Rafe could never sleep beyond his normal dawn wake up. Chores had to get done, animals relied on him, the compound was his to maintain. But out in the wilderness with an injury, his body just wanted to rest. He leaned against a tree, letting his eyes droop closed again.

This time, he didn't find darkness behind his eyelids. He was back in the grocery store, with the volleyball player that he hadn't ended. The pretty woman was now starting to decompose, no longer holding the youthful look of life as she did before. When Rafe came up behind her, he found that she wasn't alone. No, the infected woman had found a meal and she was relishing in the fresh meat. When she sat up from her kill, Rafe was able to see the face of the now dead person. Charlie's green eyes stared dead at the ceiling. Rafe found himself screaming no over the sound of cackling. In his dream, he couldn't understand where the laughing was coming from. But when he looked at the infected volleyball player, he realized she watched him and laughed. Laughed at him making the mistake of leaving her to live her dead life.

A cold feeling on his face brought Rafe abruptly out of his dream. He sat forward too fast, hurting his side and smacking his head into Storm's nose. The cold sensation on his face was Storm nosing at him, trying to wake him from the nightmare. Rafe's heart continued to pound as his eyes searched for Charlie. She was still in the water, looking at her feet as she walked to the far side. Only Storm seemed to be wise to Rafe's troubled mind and the dog pressed against Rafe's side in a moment of comfort. Rafe hung his arm over the dog, hugging his warm body as he willed the nightmare to drift away.

Later that afternoon, the trio sat inside around a fire. Rafe had used the wood that Storm seemed to collect and created a small enough fire to boil the water he had collected. He watched it, waiting for the roiling boil to start so he would know how long he had before pulling it off. They had six small water bottles between the two of them, plus two hydro flask bottles that could hold hot or cold beverages. During their hike from the compound, they had used most of their water for cooking and drinking. Rafe wanted to make sure they had some stocked up in case they couldn't get back to the stream for a day or so.

"I think we should go to town tomorrow. We've been away from the compound three days now. We should get lucky and miss anyone looking for us," Rafe said.

"We're betting on luck?" Charlie replied.

"I'm betting they will come back. They will assume we will return to the compound once we think it's safe. I don't think we can go back there until my sisters are there. We need more people to defend the place."

"What happens if they get there when the military is there?"

"They didn't want me. Only you. I don't think they will go after civilians on the random chance of finding you," Rafe said.

When he said it, he realized he was really hoping that was the case. He was torn between going back to the compound to wait for his sisters, so they could deal with the government head-on, or just waiting for them at the cave. He thought about leaving Charlie behind, so he could check the compound. However, he knew she would never go for a plan that left her behind, even to protect her and the information she carried. The town was the only other place they could venture for supplies, so they would have to take that risk.

"I hope you're right. I didn't mean to bring the entire weight of the US Government down on you and your family," Charlie said quietly.

"I know you didn't. And it's as much my responsibility as yours. I took you in, knowing you had something serious from the facility."

"I was studying it a bit while you slept this morning. I didn't want to use too much of the laptop battery, but I couldn't just leave it. I'm not sure I understand this illness at all. It shouldn't have presented this way. It shouldn't have killed people from a bite from someone infected. According to the notes, it was meant to be airborne. But clearly, we have seen that's not the case," she said.

"Glad we didn't find out it was airborne the hard way."

"Me too. The only thing I can think of is, the mice that were infected for testing, it changed there. When that mouse bit Tammy, something was different about the pathogen coming from the mouse. It somehow mutated inside the animal. I'm just not sure how that happened or how to solve it."

"If you were to figure it out, how would you need to do it?"

"I couldn't do it out here," she said, motioning around their cave. "I would need lab equipment. I would need samples from the infected, more than one and at different stages of turning. If I could get a sample from a recently bitten person, before they died, that would be extremely helpful as well. But these are all tests I can't just run without contact with the infected in some way. And with a lab."

Charlie seemed defeated and Rafe felt guilty about that. Solving this world plague couldn't be all on Charlie's shoulders. The facility had a lot of people in the dark about the true intentions of the work done inside its walls. The secrets were tightly kept. Rafe couldn't help wondering if Charlie would have made a difference if she had started gathering information sooner. He didn't voice this to her though, not wanting to weigh her down even more.

"Well, that's a lot of needs. We'll have to work toward it. You may be the only person left that understands how this happened," he said.

"I'm not the only one. 'The Suit' knows. He may not be anything more than an executive. But he knows the projects and the purpose of what we were working on. The orders came down from people like him. He knows. He just wants to silence me, because he knows I know the truth too."

"Guess we just need to not give him the satisfaction."

They ate quietly that night, sipping water and eating beef jerky with their MREs. Storm napped in the corner, full from his own canned meal that he wolfed down. Rafe watched the dog while he ate. They had left the fire going into the night to keep the cave warm until they went to bed. The tarp had to be slightly open for the smoke to find its way out. Rafe was slightly concerned with the light drawing attention. Yet, he knew if anything was within earshot, Storm would alarm them.

That night Rafe laid in bed, staring into the darkness. He thought about the dream he had earlier and the guilt he felt for not killing the infected volleyball player. It made him wonder if she had found any living. Or did someone else handle ending her? He knew the dream he had by the stream was the mixture of the pressure of protecting Charlie, her knowledge, and the idea that someone could have lost their life due to his inaction in the grocery store. He made the promise to himself that when they hiked into town, he would go back to that store and fix his mistake.

Morning brought gloom and rain with it. Rafe stood inside looking out around the tarp. The rain pelted the trees, a steady white noise flowing across the forest. It was less than optimal travel conditions, but they were running low on food and while Rafe could hunt and fish, nothing would be caught in this weather. Hiking into town was their best choice for the time being. It would also give them a sense of how things had been going the last few days.

"Do you want to wait?" Charlie asked from behind him. She was strapping on the rain jacket that had been carefully stuffed into her new bug out bag.

"No. I think we just have to go. We can't base our choices

around the weather. If we do that, we could be stuck here for good."

Storm didn't seem to agree with them. He stood by Rafe's feet, looking out at the rain and back to his new masters. His look was clearly one of disgust. But when Rafe and Charlie headed out, Storm was close on their heels. Rafe made sure the tarp and net were secured down against the rain. They took a lot of their gear with them, in case someone found their camp. He hoped that their set up was hidden enough that they would have somewhere to come back to.

Hiking to town was faster than the compound. It was a middle distance between the two places. Rafe was feeling better after all of the rest he had gotten the last two days. Now that he was feeling closer to normal he was able to hike at faster speeds and further distances without breaks. Charlie kept up with him and she barely seemed to break a sweat. Rafe had to admit he was surprised. She admitted herself that she wasn't an outside kinda girl. Hiking seemed to come quite naturally to her and she enjoyed it even in the pouring rain.

Midday approached quickly. Rafe knew the area they were coming into and slowed a bit for Storm to check things out. They were coming up to the first of the houses they would need to pass. Storm seemed to sense that something was different, and he went off toward the direction of the buildings. Rafe followed carefully, shotgun at his shoulder. A house came into view and Rafe motioned for Charlie to crouch with him behind some trees. Their vantage point of the house was clear, giving them the chance to know who was around before they accidentally stumbled upon them.

Storm slowly crept toward the house, his nose to the ground. He would stop and look around before continuing his sniffing. When he disappeared around the side of the house, Rafe felt himself hold his breath. He waited, listening for a bark. When nothing came, Rafe decided it was relatively safe. He slowly came out from behind the trees, Charlie following carefully behind them. Storm appeared again then, whining at them softly.

"What is it, boy?" Rafe whispered.

Though the dog and man weren't trained together, their communication was clear. Rafe knew the sound Storm made was distress, not fear or trouble. Storm knew what Rafe was asking and he turned to lead him to the back door of the house. Here the door and screen sat open. Rafe could see the kitchen behind the door. The room looked trashed, food littered every surface, mud had been tracked across the tile, cabinet doors sat ajar. Rafe looked down at Storm, who just whined again and looked inside.

"What do you think happened?" Charlie said from behind them.

"I'm not sure. But something upset Storm. I don't think it's dangerous or he would be ready to attack. I'm going to check it out," Rafe replied.

"I'm coming with you."

"Even if I asked you to stay out here, you wouldn't, would you?" He asked.

Charlie just gave him a look that said all he needed to know. He shrugged his shoulders in defeat and reminded her to stay close behind him.

Together they stepped into the ransacked kitchen, Storm leading the way through the house. Rafe noted the farmhouse was homey with pretty yellow curtains on every window. A floral tablecloth was across the kitchen table, with a metal flower pot in the center. The flowers were long since wilted, the gesture losing importance with a plague raging outside. Storm led them down a hallway where the walls were lined with photographs of smiling family members. As they passed open doorways, they could see a child lived here. Rafe started to get a sick feeling in the pit of his stomach.

"Charlie, I think you should go back outside," he started to

say, but they were already at the destination Storm wanted them
to be.

Storm stopped outside a closed door and looked at Rafe again.
He whined quietly and pawed at the bottom of the door. A quiet
noise from the other side caught Rafe's attention. He leaned in,
pressing his ear to the wood. Whimpering could be heard, almost
too quiet for Rafe to pick up on. He was sure it was human.
Leaning back, he looked down at Storm. Thoughts whirled in his
head. The dog wasn't signaling trouble for them, but something
behind the door had him upset. It wasn't infected, the noise was
clearly that of someone healthy. But that left the question of why
Storm was concerned and brought them to that door.

"What is it?" Charlie finally asked quietly, breaking the silence
in the hallway.

Without answering, Rafe put his hand on the doorknob. He
turned it slowly, finding it to be unlocked. Swinging the door
wide, they were looking into a small bathroom. Food wrappers,
bags, water bottles and other trash filled the floor. Except for a
path through the middle that led to the bathtub. There were toys,
stuffed animals, and books on the counter, neatly set in rows. Rafe
started to wonder what had made the sound he heard when a
little blond head appeared in the tub.

"Where's my Mommy?"

CHAPTER SEVENTEEN

"You're not my mommy and daddy," the little blond haired boy said.

Rafe was frozen in place, staring at the boy. He couldn't be more than five years old, his size reminding him of the last time he had seen his nephew Henry who was turning six soon. The little face was dirty with what looked like chocolate and other sticky substances. The blond hair was in complete disarray, dirty and unkept. His blue eyes were wide with fear as he stared at the strangers that had just opened his bathroom door.

"You have a dog," the boy spoke again.

"Yes, we do. His name is Storm. What's yours?" Charlie said as she nudged Rafe out of the way.

Children were something Rafe only had limited experience with. He had spent a great deal of time with his niece Jack when she was an infant. But after that first year, it was just short visits from either of his sisters with their kids. His mind was racing, trying to figure out if parents would be showing up and shooting them on sight for being in their house. Rafe looked up and down the hall again, not seeing any sign of additional movement.

"I'm Aiden," the boy said softly.

"Hello, Aiden. I'm Charlie. This is my friend Rafe," Charlie said, as she stepped into the bathroom toward the boy. Aidan shrunk back against his bedding, causing Charlie to stop and stand still.

"Are you waiting for your mommy and daddy here?"

Aiden nodded.

"When are they coming back?"

"Don't know," Aiden said.

"Do you know where they went?"

"They left," the little boy said, as his lip began to tremble.

"Did they leave you here? Tell you to wait?" Charlie asked softly. As she spoke, she took another small step toward the tub. Aiden didn't seem to notice, his attention on their conversation.

"Yes. My daddy said he was going to see the people that were at the door. But Mommy said she would help him. Mommy went out the back door and the weird people went after her."

"The weird people?" Rafe asked, finally speaking up from his spot in the hallway.

Aiden's little blue eyes swung back to the man. He seemed to study him for a moment and Rafe could see how he looked at his knives and guns.

"They walked funny. And Mommy and Daddy were scared of them."

Charlie and Rafe shared a look, knowing the people were infected that had been drawn to the house somehow. Aiden's parents probably knew they needed to draw them away.

"How long ago was that, buddy?" Rafe asked in a kind tone.

"I think four bedtimes? I've been sleeping in the tub cause Daddy said the bathroom was safest with the small window," Aiden answered as he pulled his blanket up his legs a little.

"You've been taking care of yourself?" Charlie asked, her voice sad.

Aiden nodded his head quickly.

"How old are you?" Rafe asked.

"Four. You're strangers. Mommy said I couldn't talk to strangers." With that statement, his little lip trembled and Rafe started to panic thinking the boy was going to cry.

"Well, you know our names now, remember? Your Mommy was right, you shouldn't talk to strangers. But now we are friends," Charlie said, talking fast to head off any tears.

The boy thought on that for a moment. He seemed to debate Charlie's logic. When he looked back at the new adults, he seemed to understand what Charlie was saying and agreed with her.

"Ok. Where are my mommy and daddy? I want them to come back."

"We haven't seen them, sweetie. We were headed into town. Maybe we could look for them together?" Charlie replied.

After some coaxing, Charlie was able to convince Aiden to leave the bathroom. While he showed Charlie his room and she tried to get him into clean clothes, Rafe walked around the house to close and lock doors. The rain was still pelting down outside, but he could see some blue sky in the distance. What he didn't see were Aiden's parents or anyone else wandering the area. Without saying it, Rafe knew he and Charlie were on the same page about the parents. They were gone. Aiden had been left alone in the world, with no one to care for him. *Now what,* Rafe thought to himself.

A much cleaner Aiden and Charlie joined Rafe in the kitchen. Rafe was sorting through what was left in the cabinets and fridge that was no longer on. Power seemed to be off in the house, making Rafe wonder if power was out all over town. He had found a jar of pickles and olives left in the fridge that were safe. He was crunching on the pickles when Charlie walked in with the little boy.

"I don't like pickles," Aiden said, seeing what Rafe was eating.

"No? Well then, is it ok I eat them?" Rafe replied.

Aiden nodded his head. He went to a cabinet and pulled out a box of fruit snacks. With no assistance from the adults, he opened a packet and ate the snacks from the bag. Rafe watched him, realizing this was how the little boy survived four days without adults. He just ate the foods he liked and could reach around the kitchen. It explained some of the mess, but not all of it. Rafe wondered if someone else wandered into the house but left when they realized there was a little boy inside.

"Aiden, has anyone else been inside the house before we showed up?" Rafe asked.

"Just the men with the guns and masks," Aiden said, as he shoveled fruit snacks into his already full mouth.

"They didn't try and take you with them?" Charlie asked. Her eyes were wide when she looked at Rafe. Again, Rafe knew they were on the same page. The mercenaries were still nearby.

"No. They were looking for someone they said. Then they told me that they would come back for me. But I told them Mommy and Daddy would come to get me, so I wouldn't need them."

His young logic was so simple, Rafe almost snorted. If they wanted to help the little boy, they would have done it immediately. They left a small boy alone, knowing his chance of survival was slim without adult help. The thought banged around Rafe's mind. They left a child to die. He felt that rage in his blood again. The same that pumped through his veins as he fought the mercenaries on his own property. What type of government didn't help little children?

"Rafe, can I speak with you?" Charlie said, signaling for them to speak in the dining room away from Aiden's ears.

They walked away, the little boy only interested in his snack at the kitchen counter. Rafe looked back at him and he could feel the blood pounding in his ears. If Storm hadn't alerted them to his presence in the house, they probably would have moved on to town, thinking nothing of the empty house.

"They are searching for me," Charlie whispered.

"And nothing else apparently. They aren't even helping people along the way. Only looking for you," Rafe replied.

"Leaving Aiden like that, they had to know..."

"That he wouldn't survive alone," Rafe said, finishing her sentence.

"What do we do?"

"We can't leave him here. But we can't wait here either. I don't think his parents are coming back. Nothing would have kept them away four days," Rafe said.

"Except dying."

"Right. I think we have to take him with us. And I can't believe I'm even saying that. I have no idea what to do with a four-year-old."

"I don't really either. But we'll just have to manage. I'm going to find a bag and pack some of his clothes and toys," Charlie said.

Back in the kitchen, Rafe pulled a stool next to Aiden. He watched the boy spread out the fruit snacks and eat the colors he clearly liked the best, first. Then he ate the others. But all one at a time. Rafe found it fascinating. Cleaned up, the boy's age showed more, making him look even younger and more vulnerable.

"Aiden, do you have a rain jacket?" Rafe asked.

"Uh huh," the little boy said.

"Where is it?"

"Am I going somewhere?" Aiden asked.

"We are going to town, buddy. Maybe we can find your parents. But if not, we'll leave them a note and let them know you're with us. It's not safe for you to stay alone. Do you understand?"

Aiden's eyes were round when he turned them toward Rafe to listen. He nodded when the question was asked, but Rafe was sure he didn't really comprehend what danger there was out there. The little boy helped Rafe find paper and a pen to write a note. Though he knew Aiden couldn't read quite yet, he really did leave a note with their information on it. Just in case the crazy happened, and Aiden's parents were alright and came back looking for their child. Rafe didn't put specifics on the paper but told them Aiden was safe and they were looking for them.

With Aiden's bag packed, Rafe went through the kitchen once more. He packed all of the kid snacks he could find, thinking if he couldn't figure out what Aiden ate, at least he had granola bars and fruit snacks. Charlie buttoned up Aiden's bright yellow rain-coat. Rafe thought if the infected didn't see their movement, the bright yellow would bring them like someone clanging a bell. However, at least the kid would be dry. They tied on his toughest hiking shoes and made sure there was another pair of slip-on shoes in his bag, so his hiking shoes could dry out once they stopped for the night.

As they walked away from the house, Aiden stopped at looked back for a moment. It was as if the little boy knew he wouldn't be back. Storm stood at his side and pushed him softly with his head, causing Aiden to giggle for a moment before catching up with Charlie again. He immediately grabbed her hand and Charlie looked down in surprise. Rafe was glad the boy seemed to like Charlie. He wasn't sure how to provide the right emotional support for the child. She seemed much better equipped for the situation.

Rafe decided with the boy they would make the walk into town easier by staying near the paved roads. With their hoods on, a little boy and dog with them, they weren't recognizable as the two people running from government thugs. That wasn't a sure way of hiding, but Rafe hoped they had luck on their side. If the mercenaries had checked the area within the last four days, Rafe hoped they had a few days before they came through again to check for them.

They walked mostly in silence, Aiden chattering once in a

while about the trees or how Storm looked funny soaked. He seemed to carry on a conversation by himself, with little addition from the adults. As they approached cars that seemed to have crashed into each other off the road, Storm was suddenly at Rafe's side. His growl was deep and menacing and Rafe immediately pulled his shotgun to his shoulder. They got closer to the cars and suddenly a head lifted from the far side of the crash. Rafe knew it was an infected man. The thought struck him that the man looked familiar. It took a moment to realize it was the man in the suit that he had seen in the woods days prior. He told Charlie as much as they slowly approached.

Storm didn't wait for any sort signal as he launched himself at the hissing infected. Rafe slung his shotgun back over his shoulder, preferring his hunting knife when the dog was involved in the fray. He carefully circled the cars. The scene on the other side of the wreck made Rafe backstep for a moment, his brain not wanting to take in the graphic event. The infected man had pulled someone from the wreck, the body hung halfway out. Blood painted the side of the car where the infected was left to feast with no interruptions. Flesh, blood, and entrails pooled below the body.

Without thinking, Rafe shoved his blade into the head of the dead body. He knew the dead wouldn't stay dead. Turning, he found Storm tearing at the throat of the infected. Black gore and red blood colored his light fur. Rafe whistled loudly to get the dog's attention. He didn't want to reach in while Storm was in the thrall of attack. He may not know the difference between friend and foe at that point. On the second whistle, Storm finally looked up to see Rafe waiting. Knowing the process well, Storm stepped back and let Rafe shove his blade into the still moving infected. The damage Storm did, not changing the need to feed in the infected.

Turning, Rafe found Charlie holding Aiden in her arms, hiding the boy's face against her shoulder. Her face was pale, but she looked determined to protect the boy. Aiden was gripping her neck strongly, legs trying to wrap around her waist. Rafe motioned to Charlie to go the long way around the cars, on the road, not wanting either of them to see the gruesome scene Rafe had to see.

While they walked around, Rafe looked into the cars, finding other signs of life, but no other blood. He hoped the other occupants were able to get away. Rafe knew there was one other infected with the man in the forest. The woman that must have bitten him. If the man didn't kill her before turning himself, that meant she was wandering somewhere nearby. Rafe found a few bottles of waters in one car and he packed those into his bag. The lack of other items told him these people were either not prepared to leave town, or they took what they had with them. Rafe hoped for the latter.

It didn't take much longer for them to reach the edge of town. Aiden had no limit to his energy and he kept up with the adults easily. Once in a while he would ask for a drink and Rafe would help him with a water bottle, reminding him to take sips so they had enough for the whole trip. The boy followed directions well, giving Rafe flashbacks to his own childhood. At the first group of buildings they came to, Rafe gathered them near a wall and told everyone to stay silent. Aiden made the symbol of zipping his lips and throwing away the key. The gesture made Rafe smile.

The rain had stopped for a moment, giving the sun a chance to shine through. The asphalt was shiny with water across the parking lot Rafe watched. Few living people were around. In the distance Rafe could see cars moving at times, people fleeing or coming for supplies like they were. Once he felt it was safe, he motioned for Charlie and Aiden to follow him around the buildings. They were behind a strip mall and Rafe knew of a small bar that was in the area. He wasn't really a drinker, but he knew the place served food.

When they got the bar, Rafe wasn't surprised to see the

windows and glass door shattered. Looting an alcohol establish-
ment seemed right up the alley of some people that needed to
drink themselves into oblivion to handle life. Walking dead would
be a reason to lose yourself in a bottle. From outside, Rafe could
tell no one was in the front of the bar, but the back was a dark
shadow. Stooping, he grabbed a piece of glass that was on the
sidewalk. He threw it into the pile of glass, making a clinking
sound. They waited, listening, but no sound came.

Looking at Storm, Rafe told him to stay outside. He wasn't
sure how to protect the dog's paws from the glass. Storm seemed
to have an attitude for a moment, but he circled a spot and sat,
watching outside. Rafe knew he would come barking if anything
threatened them while they scavenged.

"A bar? Really?" Charlie said.

"They served food. Sandwiches, fruit, things like that. I was
hoping the food stores would still be intact. I think people were
more concerned about the booze."

Charlie lifted Aiden into her arms again, as she walked over
the glass. Rafe moved ahead of them, in the direction of where he
believed the kitchen was. Entering darkness, Rafe clicked on a
flashlight immediately, illuminating a small silver room. He went
to a cabinet and opened it carefully. He grabbed the loaves of
bread that were there, putting them into a backpack carefully. He
moved to the fridge and found more pickles, making him wonder
if they would end up living on pickles. He found chips which
Aiden asked for immediately. He opened a bag and the boy was
happily munching while Rafe did his searching.

Rafe cheered quietly when he held up unopened packages of
dried salami and pepperoni. He slid these into the bag with the
bread. Charlie looked at him strangely when he cheered while
muttering to himself about not having to live on pickles. The
bar didn't have as much as Rafe had hoped, but he thought it
was worth checking all places that weren't typically thought of
as food sources. Coming back to the front of the bar, they

found Storm in the same spot he had been, watching ever vigilant.

The group carefully moved away from the strip mall. When they rounded the next corner, Rafe stopped solidly, causing Charlie to bump into him. He backed them up slowly, away from the next parking lot that housed a gas station and strip of small stores. The parking lot that was now overflowing with infected people, wandering aimlessly looking for their next meal.

"What?" Charlie asked.

"We can't go that way," Rafe said.

Neither of the adults saw Aiden peer around the corner into the parking lot. Storm's barking set off a flurry of events that Rafe knew he would have nightmares about.

"Mommy!!!"

The scream tore from Aiden as if he were holding a megaphone. Rafe wheeled around just as Aiden disappeared around the corner, running for the woman he believed was his mother.

"Aiden, no!" Rafe bellowed.

The boy didn't hear Rafe, too focused on his mother's form. Rafe immediately bolted for the corner and skidded around it pulling his knife as he saw Aiden running into the arms of a waiting infected woman. The woman may have been his mother before, but now she was hoping to dine on his living flesh. Storm was running with the boy, trying to stop him, but the boy kept pushing the dog away, believing him to be playing. As he got closer to the infected, Aiden's steps began to falter and Rafe could see why. Aiden's mother was missing part of her neck, muscle and skin flopped down where it had been torn from her body.

"Aiden!" Charlie screamed from behind Rafe. She was also sprinting to reach the boy.

In Rafe's mind, the run he made to grab Aiden was endless. His legs felt like they were running through quicksand, he was too slow. Just as he was sure the infected woman was going to grab Aiden, Storm grabbed the little boy's jacket and tugged him back a few steps. The clawed fingers swiped and missed the boy's face. At the same moment, Rafe reached the boy. He hauled him off his feet immediately before running back a few steps to give him to Charlie.

"No! That's my Mommy! Put me down!" Aiden's screams were knives piercing Rafe's ears.

"Aiden, honey, I'm sorry. That's not your Mommy. You can see," Charlie was trying to reason with the hysterical little boy.

As they tried to back away from the horde without having to fight, Rafe turned and found they were slowly being circled.

"Oh shit," Rafe muttered under his breath.

He pulled his shotgun again, knowing he would need to shoot if they were going to get out of this without someone dying. He whistled for Storm, who was growling and barking, not being able to decide who his target should be. Rafe's whistle brought the dog back to them and he looked up at the human trying to decide what to do. Rafe told him to stay with Charlie and Aiden, but he couldn't be sure Storm understood the order.

"Stay behind me, Charlie, no matter what. I'm going to be shooting. I do not want to accidentally shoot you," Rafe said loudly.

He had to raise his voice, to be heard over the cacophony of inhuman noises coming from the infected horde. Seeing Rafe and his gun, Aiden started to realize something was really wrong. He cried into Charlie's shoulder and Rafe hoped the boy didn't have to see his mother put down. Rafe stepped forward toward the edge of the circle with the fewest infected. He aimed his buckshot rounds toward the heads of the nearby dead. He was happy when two went down in heaps, causing others to trip over them. He pumped and let off rounds until the shotgun went empty. He had effectively created the start of a hole for them to escape through.

Behind them, the infected were closing in. Charlie cried out and Storm's barking began more urgently as he pounced on an infected that reached out for Charlie. Rafe pulled his knife out and started striking out at the infected in front of them. They had to get out of the horde if they were going to survive. He had to get Charlie out of there. She was the only one that knew what had happened, how this had all started. And Aiden. Little Aiden who had to see his mother as an infected. Rafe had to save him.

His mind was in turmoil as he danced the grotesque dance with the infected. He counted their uncoordinated movements to his benefit as they had a hard time following him as he moved. Two infected came at him and Rafe turned to back kick one to the throat, sending the small infected man off of his feet. Rafe smoothly stepped away from the other and stabbed it in the temple, before ending the one that was struggling to its feet.

Wheeling around, Rafe found Storm pouncing on infected as they tried to get closer. Once the dog had them on the ground, he would back away, realizing it was a fight he couldn't win. Strangely Rafe found himself admiring the dog at that moment. Shaking himself from the thought, Rafe called Charlie to him and she came rushing with Aiden wrapped in her arms.

"Are you alright?" He asked quickly, Charlie just nodded.

Turning back to the thinned herd, Rafe wondered if they could make it out now. But the infected seemed to keep coming. As he stood, the head in front of him exploded and Rafe jumped back. A moment later the crack of the report from the gun sounded and Rafe was searching for the source. Again, an infected's head jerked to one side and the body fell to the ground. Not sure where the help was coming from Rafe decided to take it anyway and with Charlie's arm in his hand, he slowly led them toward safety.

As they moved, Rafe continued to fight off the infected that were within arm's reach. He fought, blood and black ooze coating his jacket and his knife. The sound of the gun continued as they moved. As soon as an opening was there, Rafe pushed Charlie and told her to run. He didn't have to encourage her further, she took off like a shot, with Storm hot on her heels. Rafe followed, keeping an eye out for whoever had assisted them. No one showed and Rafe didn't want to stop and find them with so many infected nearby.

They ran straight for a shopping center that was down the street. Grocery store, laundromat and nail salon were housed in the center. The front of the store was broken out, unsurprisingly. Rafe ran directly for the broken door. When they got to the opening they crunched over broken glass. Without thinking, Rafe bent and grabbed Storm to get him over the shards. The dog didn't fight and Rafe was thankful because he wasn't a light animal. All that was on Rafe's mind was getting into the shadows of the store before the horde came around the corner where they could see them.

Charlie had run with Aiden in her arms, keeping the boy protected from the infected as well as seeing his mother again. Inside the store the group ran for the back, Rafe searching every corner for anything living or dead. They hid in the back behind a low shelf, their breaths coming in heavy gasps. Charlie gathered Aiden into her lap as the boy's cries continued. She looked helplessly over his blond head at Rafe, but he had no answers for her.

"Where did the shots come from?" Charlie whispered.

"I don't know. It was a rifle. I'm wondering friend or enemy," Rafe replied.

"They saved us."

"The mercenaries probably would too. They want you alive."

Moaning from outside pulled Rafe's attention back toward the door. He carefully crept to the edge of the shelf, peering around. The horde had wandered into the road, but without a clear direction, they seemed to meander down the street. He leaned back and took a deep breath, calming his pounding heart. The image of Aiden running straight for his infected mother was burned into his mind. The little boy had just come into their care and they had almost lost him to an infected horde. Rafe started to question whether he was equipped to care for a small child.

The sounds from the infected seemed to quiet after a few minutes and Rafe leaned back around to check. He could only see a few stragglers that were wandering the area, the bulk of the horde had wandered off in another direction. He finally took a sigh of relief when he turned back to Charlie and Aiden. The little boy's face was streaked where tears had fallen, but he had calmed down a bit. His arms were around Charlie, hugging her to him. Charlie looked exhausted and terrified, much how Rafe felt. He wanted to say something to comfort her, but nothing seemed adequate in the situation they were in.

"Let's see if we can scavenge anything from inside here. We might need to camp in town tonight," Rafe said.

Charlie didn't answer, just nodded and tried to stand with the boy. Rafe motioned her to stay where she was, deciding that someone watching the little one was the best bet. He also didn't believe Aiden was going to let go of Charlie anytime soon. Rafe stood carefully, to not draw attention and moved away from Charlie. Storm followed him, the dog walking in a crouch as if he knew he didn't want to be seen.

Not far from where they had hidden, Rafe found a section of canned goods that had been ransacked. There were still cans left and many on the floor. Opening his backpack, he started adding cans until he was sure he could barely lift the bag. He took the full bag back to Charlie, leaving it on the floor next to her. Taking her bag, he moved to the section that held the rice. On his way, he passed a section of portable mac and cheese containers. He picked one up and read that all you needed was to add hot water. He thought of Aiden and guessed a small child would eat mac and cheese for every meal if possible. All of the containers went into the bag.

A low growl sounded from Rafe's feet and he crouched to hide just as Storm started growling louder toward the door of the store. Rafe put a hand on the dog's head, whispering for him to stay. He wasn't looking to get into a loud fight with any infected, knowing they could draw the horde back. Storm pulled at Rafe's arm, wanting to attack the invader, but he obeyed and didn't take off. Rafe was just about to pull his 9mm and confront what was coming when a voice whispered through the store.

"What in the world are you doing hiding in a grocery store?"

CHAPTER EIGHTEEN

Rafe immediately decided that the voice didn't belong to a mercenary. If it was the government coming for Charlie, they wouldn't have said anything coming into the store. They would have attacked. The voice didn't mean that it was a friend and Rafe wasn't sure who could be trusted anywhere. Rafe waited where he was, trying to send a telepathic signal to Charlie to just stay quiet.

"I saw you run in here. I don't know why you didn't keep running. You can come out."

Weighing his options, Rafe pulled the 9mm from the holster on his hip. He released his hold on Storm but hissed a stay command to keep the dog from attacking. Carefully Rafe stood and leveled his gun at the shadow standing in the front of the store. He immediately saw the rifle the man was holding, putting Rafe on edge even more. He moved to put himself between the man and the spot where Charlie hid with Aiden.

"Why were you watching us?" Rafe hissed back, lifting his voice only high enough to be heard within the store walls.

"I wasn't. I tried to help. I'm the one that was killing those things," the man said, lifting the rifle a little higher. The movement only caused Rafe to raise his gun as well.

"Calm down, man, I'm not gonna hurt you or your family," the man said, immediately lowering the rifle and then slinging it over his back with the strap.

Rafe stood solidly for a moment, Storm at his feet baring his teeth silently. The man was still completely in the shadows, the light from outside making it difficult to see his features in the dark store. From his voice, Rafe was guessing he was middle-aged, maybe a little older. He was a fantastic shot, someone that probably hunted or had been in the military at some point. That thought struck Rafe with a cold icy shiver down his back. He wondered if the mercenaries would send in a spy to grab Charlie. Paranoia ran through Rafe's mind, but he lowered the gun, not seeing a weapon the man could use on him now.

"Why did you help us?" Rafe asked.

"Why wouldn't I? The little boy was running toward them, you were surrounded. I couldn't just leave you to die, could I?"

"You could have. You are a good shot," Rafe said, hedging to get information.

"I've hunted this area all my life. I should know how to shoot at this point."

"Well, we thank you then. We aren't staying. We will move on as soon as the infected get further away," Rafe said. He signaled to Storm to go back to Charlie and the dog did so begrudgingly.

"Do you have somewhere safe to go?" The man started to walk into the store and Rafe stood his ground between the stranger and Charlie.

"Yes," was all Rafe was going to give up.

"Good. You should go there. That horde just grows by the day. You were lucky I was on my roof. I have a business just over that way, and I've been going to the roof to watch what's happening. That horde has been by a few times and it's almost doubled in size the last few days. I'm Issac, by the way."

The man was now close enough that he was in the darkness with Rafe. His features became clearer and Rafe realized he was off on the man's age. The man was completely gray on his head and his beard was almost white. If he had been a large man, Rafe would have believed that was what Santa Claus looked like. As he was, the man was rail thin and tall. Rafe had to wonder how his body handled the recoil from such a powerful rifle.

"Rafe," he finally answered.

"You're that Duncan guy, right? Rafe Duncan?"

Rafe's fingers tightened on his gun as he tried to decide if he should raise it again. He hadn't made friends in town. The only people he spoke with were those he worked with. But this man acted as if he knew him. Issac reached behind him and Rafe didn't hesitate to raise his gun again, leveling it at the man's chest.

"Whoa there, son. I have something in my pocket you should see. It's not a weapon."

"Slowly," Rafe said.

Abiding by Rafe's demand, Issac slowly pulled something from his pocket and brought it to the front of him. He then reached toward Rafe with a folded piece of paper in his hand. Rafe stepped forward, only lowering his gun a few inches, to grab the paper. He stepped back immediately as he unfolded the paper with one hand. He read the sheet quickly and cursed under his breath.

"Charlie," Rafe said, just loud enough for her to hear.

He didn't have to turn to know she was coming up behind him. He could hear Aiden's sniffles getting close. When Charlie stopped next to him, he handed her the paper without looking at her.

"Do you know why those showed up around town?" Issac asked.

"Rafe..." Charlie's voice was barely a breath.

She stared at the paper that Issac had produced. In large color photos, Rafe and Charlie's faces were printed. Rafe immediately recognized his as the security photo he had to take at the facility for his security badge and assumed Charlie's was the same. Below the photos, the paper looked like a wanted poster out of an old western movie. They were listed as felons on the run from the government and if they were found they were to be captured and not killed. There were then instructions on a location that would be checked by members of the department looking for them. The location was the facility address.

"We don't know anything," Rafe finally said to Issac.

The one thing the paper seemed to be missing was the one thing people needed, the motivation to catch them. There was no reward. No promise of help. Just the accusation of them being on the run from the government. That part wasn't exactly wrong, Rafe had to admit to himself. However, there were no laws broken. They were being hunted like animals for the knowledge Charlie held. Rafe was seeing very clearly that the government was pulling out all stops to cover their involvement in what had caused the outbreak.

"What do we do?" Charlie asked, pulling Rafe's gaze to her.

"Nothing. We didn't do anything wrong. And we aren't doing anything about these," Rafe said. He took the paper from her and crumpled it before throwing it over a shelf.

"So, you did nothing, and the government just spent the time on those papers for no reason? At a time where the dead are walking and killing people? Seems extreme," Issac commented. The older man now had his thumbs hooked in his belt loops while he watched the two of them.

"We didn't do anything. It's what I know," Charlie blurted out.

"Charlie. We don't know this guy," Rafe said sternly.

"He saved us, didn't he?"

Charlie turned and handed Aiden to Rafe, who had to holster his gun quickly before the boy fell into his arms. Immediately the little boy's arms circled Rafe's neck and he laid his head on his shoulder. The day had taken a huge toll on the boy and Rafe realized he was young enough to still nap. Awkwardly Rafe patted his back and shifted from foot to foot. He watched Charlie as she stepped closer to Issac to put her hand out.

"I'm Charlie. I have a story to tell you," she said.

An hour later, Charlie was finishing the story of how she learned what was happening at the facility and how she was caught taking out data. She told him about Tammy and the mouse and then Aiko turning after she was bitten. Issac sat quietly, his face never showing surprise or disbelief. Charlie was animated when she spoke, anger and fear mixed into her words. She led him all the way to the moment he found them with the horde. When she was done, Issac just looked at her. He seemed to mull things over in his mind before he spoke.

"That is one story young lady."

"It's the truth," Rafe said.

He sat on the floor next to Charlie facing Issac. Aiden was cradled in his arms as he napped. They had moved into the back of the store for Charlie to tell the man everything they knew. She spoke the entire time, with little interjected from Rafe. The infected wandered by sometimes but sitting in the back of the store they weren't seen. Rafe would look up every time a vehicle passed them, his gut still not completely settled to believe this Issac was just a concerned citizen. Suspicion had Rafe wondering if Issac had a tracker on him and was leading the government right to them.

"I believe you," Issac finally said.

"You do?" Charlie said, clearly surprised.

"Yes. The terms you use, are clearly medical and professional. I saw how this man fought out there, so he's obviously in some sort of security or military. He's protecting you and this little boy. All that seems to check out. So why wouldn't the rest of the story?"

"Now you know why they are looking for us. Are you going to try and turn us in?" Rafe asked.

"Now, son, I wasn't planning on doing that even before I knew your story. I have no love for the government personally, especially after I saw how they were dealing with things now. If they were looking for you, I figured they were just wasting more time. Instead of saving people."

"What are they doing here?" Charlie asked.

"There were some emergency messages. Sending sick people to clinics and other locations. I stayed at my place. But when I went to the roof, I could see one of the places. They were killing those people. Before they even died or turned or whatever. They killed them straight away!" Issac exclaimed.

"They weren't trying to help them? Do tests? Take blood or other vitals? Nothing?" Charlie asked.

"No. They were separated from their families immediately. Taken through a tent. I could see where they brought them out and shot them through the head. The only way to end them. I don't know what happened to the family members. I didn't see them again."

Charlie sat back and Rafe could tell her wheels were spinning. He watched her as her lips moved soundlessly. As a doctor, he imagined this information was against all of the humane commitments she had made over the years.

"What are you thinking?" Rafe finally asked.

"This pathogen, it mutated from the mouse. Tammy would be the main point of information if they could find her. They have to know that. There must be teams of people looking for her or at least working on a cure. Without knowing how the pathogen mutated, I can't predict how curing it would work. I want to believe that someone can be cured before they die and reanimate. In addition to that, if the illness mutated from the mouse to Tammy, I can't be sure it won't change again. Or it could possibly affect some people differently."

"That's a lot to swallow. So instead of looking for a cure, they are just killing the infected. What does that tell you?" Issac asked.

"It tells me, they have no clue what they are facing. And

instead of fixing it, they are just trying to clean it up," Charlie said.

"They are thinking if they kill all of the infected before they turn, they will stop the spread. But it's not working," Rafe said.

It was then that Aiden woke up in Rafe's arms. He looked around at the group of adults that he barely knew before his face started to screw up in sadness again. Charlie instantly reached out for the boy and he easily went to her. He whispered to her and Charlie nodded. She pulled out a box of granola bars they had found in the store and Aiden happily sat munching on one.

"We are going to need to move if we don't want to sleep in this store," Rafe said.

"It's getting late. You are welcome to bunk at my place for the night, so you can walk during the day," Issac said and after seeing Rafe's look of distrust he added, "You'll be safe."

Charlie looked at Rafe for his decision. The options rolled around in his mind. He didn't want to hike at night with Aiden. The little boy would need to sleep. And they hadn't found his father yet. Though Rafe was pretty sure he was gone or infected. Hiking at night was dangerous enough in the woods, more so when you're hiding from the infected and the government. Staying in town one night would give them more time to scavenge what they could, pack additional bags to carry and sleep. He still wasn't sure they could trust the older man, but for now, it was a better option than sleeping in the open store.

They were careful leaving the store, checking for the horde. Issac told them it seemed to move as a flock, to whichever area drew their attention. Then they would change direction when something new seemed like food. Rafe and Charlie followed him through the alley behind the store to cross the street. Issac led them to the back of another store, which he opened with a key. When they all were inside, the locks were all turned again, and a board was placed under the door handle to prevent it from turning. Rafe had to approve of the precautions.

Turning into the store, the room was dark, the front windows covered with sheets. It was then Rafe realized they were in a dry cleaner shop. Rows of clean clothes hung all around them and the smell of chemicals reached his nose. Issac drew them deeper into the room, explaining that the business was basically one big room. So, he blacked out the front windows to keep anyone from looking in or from drawing the infected attention on accident.

"No one wants to break into a dry cleaner's anyway," he commented.

"You never know," Rafe replied.

"True. Which is why I bunk down behind the front counter. That way I'm near the front if anyone gets any crazy ideas. And I still have a direct shot to the back door if necessary. We'll set you guys up over against the wall. I happen to have sleeping bags and comforters you can use. When people don't have big enough washers, they bring that stuff to me. It's come in handy."

"Did you have the gun here already?" Rafe asked.

"No. I was home when this all happened. When I came to town to see the destruction for myself, I came here to hide and watch. I brought my gun and food with me at that time. Since then I've just scavenged all I needed from nearby."

"Wouldn't being at home be safer?" Charlie asked.

"I didn't think so. I live in a downstairs apartment. There seemed to be too many people around," Issac said.

Rafe had to agree with him. Staying away from any large population was probably the best decision. He remembered his father saying the same thing and saying that the reason there was so much land around the compound was that he had purchased a lot of it over the years. He did this to keep people away from his home, for when society failed. It made it unlikely for people to show up on their doorstep unless they already knew they were there.

Charlie created one big bed with sleeping bags, sheets, and comforters. Rafe watched as she worked, keeping her eye on

Aiden as well who played with some of the toys Charlie had brought for him. The little boy seemed to be over his little sadness from earlier, but his yawn indicated to Rafe that they would be facing the difficulty of bedtime.

"Where is he going to sleep?" Rafe asked her.

"Between us, I think. That way he can't get up and wander."

The trio sat together to prepare something for dinner. Aiden wasn't crazy about any of the options. However, Rafe was determined. Using a propane stove that Issac had in the back of the cleaners, he warmed water and added it to the small portable macaroni and cheese container. He let the orange powder dissolve, thinking about how he would prefer Aiden to eat vegetables and fruit. This was better than nothing. Bringing the macaroni to the boy, Aiden's eyes lit up and he ate the entire container without complaint. Charlie smiled at Rafe over her can of beans, happy that they could handle the boy together. Storm was quite happy to have a small child nearby who would accidentally drop food. The dog sat panting right next to Aiden during the whole meal with high hopes.

Darkness settled over the town and the group sat around a low lantern talking more about their stories. Aiden was happy to play in a corner with pens and receipts Issac gave him. Charlie told more of the story of how they found Aiden and Issac looked at the boy sadly.

"When I saw him running for the infected, I just couldn't figure out why he was doing it. Makes sense now," the older man said sadly.

"You don't have family nearby, Issac?" Charlie asked.

"No, my wife died about ten years ago of cancer."

"Kids?" Rafe asked.

"Nah, we never had kids. We were like kids ourselves. Always traveling and enjoying life. We didn't want to make children suffer because our attention was all over the place."

"You never regretted that decision?" Charlie asked, as she

glanced over at Aiden. Her eyes seemed to hold something else, but Rafe didn't have time to figure it out just then.

"No. I asked my wife the same thing when she got sick. She said no, because with kids we never would have had all the adventures we did. We had neighborhood kids who were always around, so we spoiled them when we wanted to have kids around."

"That sounds like a nice life," Rafe commented.

Issac smiled then and Rafe could only imagine his wife brought a look like that to his face. It seemed like he suddenly looked younger and was looking backward into the past. Rafe wondered what it was to have that in your life. Especially at a time when survival was so difficult. Protecting yourself was one thing, being responsible for others was another set of problems. He looked at Charlie and then to Aiden at that point. Charlie had needed him, and he didn't regret offering his help to her. Poor Aiden, if they didn't bring him with them, there was no telling what would have happened to him.

Shortly after their story time, everyone decided it was time for sleep. Rafe felt adrenaline draining from his body and exhaustion replacing it. His side was aching constantly, though he knew it was better now than a day or so before. Charlie checked the dressings again before they slept, changing the gauze and adding ointment to keep out an infection. They laid Aiden in the middle of their makeshift bed, but he immediately rolled toward Charlie, wanting to be cuddled. She easily abided, realizing the poor boy was looking for affection and comfort.

Storm whined as Rafe was thinking of falling asleep and realized the dog needed to go out. Taking his weapons with him, he quietly went to the back door with the dog. He peeked out first and didn't see movement. Allowing Storm to lead, the dog sniffed the air for a moment and then went about his business silently. That was all Rafe needed to know it was safe. He stopped out into the darkness with him, letting the cooler air brush across his skin. The stars were sparkling clearly above and Rafe found himself torn between feeling on edge and feeling calmed by the quiet night.

Back inside, Storm curled up on a pile of clothing that was at the foot of their bed. The dog was quite happy with something soft to lay on. Rafe slept well, until he felt small feet in his back, one kicking very close to his wound. He rolled back to find Aiden, laying perpendicular to Charlie and himself, head at Charlie's shoulder, feet at Rafe's back. Despite being kicked, Rafe had to smile at the antics of the little boy. The smile quickly faded as he realized that Aiden was dreaming and that was why his body was tossing and turning. He carefully turned the boy so he was laying centered again, and his little eyes opened and looked at Rafe.

"My mommy, I want mommy," he said quietly.

"I know, buddy. It's just not safe," Rafe replied, at a complete loss at how to explain the loss of his mother.

"She was going to hurt me?"

"She didn't know it was you. Your mommy loved you very much. Now she wants us to keep you safe," Rafe said.

"Safe..." Aiden mumbled as he fell back into sleep, with half of his body draped over Rafe.

Rafe patted his back softly, hoping the boy could fall into a dreamless sleep. He couldn't imagine what it was like seeing someone you loved turned into an infected. The thought caused Rafe anxiety, thinking of his sisters. Had they come to the compound yet? Found him gone? The idea that the mercenaries could be there, could attack them, made Rafe fear for their safety. He hoped the evidence of the attack was all the sisters needed to know something bad had happened before they arrived.

"You're good with him," Charlie whispered, awakened by Aiden and Rafe's conversation.

"I am? I'm not sure what I'm doing. I don't know what to say to him," Rafe whispered back.

"You did well. He's going to have to trust us, so we can make sure he's ok."

"He has no one. He'll have to stay with us," Rafe said finally, knowing the truth in his heart. They couldn't leave the boy with anyone else.

"I know."

They fell into sleep, both of them touching Aiden, to reassure themselves that the little boy was safe. Rafe dreamed of the little boy sleeping in the bathtub and his infected parents finding him like that. The parents were infected but, in his dream, Rafe saw them as conscious of their actions. They came after their boy realizing he was an easy meal. Rafe watched from an outside window and screamed out loud in his dream. The infected parents didn't even try to change their path, going straight at Aiden. The boy's cries of joy were quickly cut off and screams of terror replaced them.

He jolted awake a few hours later, sunlight trying to peek around the sheets on the windows. His heart was beating hard against his chest and his wound ached. Hair tickled his face and he realized Aiden was still laying across his chest. Charlie had moved closer to the two of them, her arm over Aiden and partially across Rafe. Shifting was impossible without waking them both, so Rafe took deep breaths working to calm his heart and to forget the gruesome nightmare in his mind.

The clearing of a throat pulled Rafe's attention to the side. He found Issac propped against the counter looking at them with a small grin on his face. Rafe realized how it must have looked and he had the need to say again they weren't a family. However, talking would have woken them and then Issac put his finger to his lips. He pointed outside and Rafe looked at the shadows crossing in front of the sheets. They weren't infected, he could see their movements were clear. He could also see they were all holding large weapons.

"The military is back," Issac whispered almost too low for Rafe to hear.

Panic must have crossed Rafe's face because Issac signaled for him to calm. No choice now, Rafe reached down and grabbed Charlie arm, shaking her slightly. She sat up lightning quick, her gaze flying around the dry cleaner's. When she looked at the clothes she calmed and Rafe knew she had just remembered where she was. He squeezed her arm and she slid it out of his hand, looking down at him. Rafe motioned to Aiden and she took the sleeping boy carefully from his chest, cradling him against her. She watched Rafe carefully and didn't say a word as Rafe held a finger to his lips as well.

Rafe quickly shifted to his feet. He checked his 9mm and his shotgun, knowing they were both loaded, yet he needed to be sure. He slid his arms through his knife belt, planning on a quiet fight as long as he could manage it. As Rafe prepared, Issac crawled over to him.

"You should stay hidden in here. They won't come in."

"Who is it?" Rafe whispered.

"The men looking for you I'm sure. They come by here, check the businesses, talk to us and then leave. I'm going to go outside and convince them to leave," Issac said.

"Or give us over and win their favor," Rafe replied.

"I guess I could do that *if* I wanted their favor. I have no need for them and their type of help. You're going to have to trust me. You can't go out there and take them all on yourself."

Rafe weighed their options. He realized Issac was right. They didn't know how many there were. He was only one man. After taking out the first group that came to the compound, Rafe had to assume they sent more men with more firepower. That left them with the option of trusting Issac. The part about Rafe that was like his father, the paranoia and distrustful part, had a very difficult time allowing anyone else to control his survival.

"I'm going to wait by the door. Hear what is being said," Rafe said, motioning toward the sheet covered door.

Issac didn't speak, just nodded once and stood to head for the door. Rafe followed and crouched nearby where he could hide without being seen. A key was produced from Issac's pocket and he unlocked the bolts on his door. He walked out with his hands up and quickly disappeared from view. The door was left a crack open and Rafe crawled over to peer out slightly. He jumped back when he realized Issac had been right, there was a group of mercenaries outside.

"Well, hello again, boys. What can I do for you?" Issac's voice drifted through the small opening of the door.

"Have you seen these people?" A voice answered.

"This is the same flyer you gave me a few days ago. And the answer is still the same. I don't know these two," Issac replied.

"We heard from some others that they were seen in town. But they had a kid and that's new."

Rafe cringed thinking about being watched as they were scavenging in town. People would cower to the military and government, believing they were the salvation they needed. Most people didn't question when the government said someone was a threat. They would accept it and turn Rafe and Charlie in without a thought. It was quiet outside, Rafe assumed Issac was pretending to look over the photos again.

"I'm not sure what you heard, but they didn't cross my path. I've never met these two."

"So, you'd be willing to let us check your place?" A second mercenary spoke harshly.

Rafe waited and held his breath. If Issac agreed to avoid a fight, they would need to escape. Rafe looked toward the back door they come through. Could they escape without the men finding them? He needed to get Charlie away to hide. And now he had to think of Aiden.

"Is this still America? To check my place don't you need a warrant?" Issac said, challenging the request of the mercenary.

"Is that a no, old man?"

That was all Rafe needed to hear. The men were going to come in and search, with or without permission. He crawled back to the makeshift bed where Charlie was sitting with Aiden. Storm was next to her, his teeth bared but the dog stayed silent. Rafe was astonished at how the dog seemed to know what was needed before anyone instructed him. The little boy was starting to wake up and Rafe knew that would also be a sound that would draw the mercenaries down on them. He started shoving things into his pack, glad they didn't take out much. Then he pulled Charlie to her feet and shoved all the bedding into a pile, so it didn't look like a bed.

"What is it?" Charlie whispered.

"We have to go out the back. Those men are coming in here. Issac can't stop them."

From the front, voices were raising and Rafe knew now he should have trusted Issac from the start. The old man was arguing with the soldiers, telling them they didn't have the right to come into his business and search. Rafe knew he was raising his voice to warn them. Charlie looked at Rafe panicked. He pointed toward the back door and the three of them rushed there. Aiden started to ask questions, but Charlie shushed him quickly. Luckily the little boy couldn't be heard over the dispute outside.

At the back door, Rafe pulled his weapons, hunting knife in one hand and 9mm in the other. At his feet Storm growled quietly and Rafe knew the back wasn't completely clear. The question was going to be if they could get away without the larger group hearing them. Rafe gave Storm a gesture to stay quiet and the dog lowered his body closer to the ground, preparing to strike. The door swung out slowly and Rafe could see one soldier walking the back alley.

A quick motion of his hand and Storm seemed to know he

needed to stay back with Charlie. Part of Rafe reviled the need to kill living people. His mind flashed back to Charlie and her fierce dedication to getting the truth out to people. Thinking of her, his resolve solidified, and he put his 9mm away. Light on his feet he slid along the wall following behind the soldier. Before the man could turn, Rafe had slid his hunting knife across the soldier's throat. The only noise was the man falling to the ground and the back door clicking closed. The group ran from the business area, not looking back.

CHAPTER NINETEEN

"Callahan, is it possible you are this incompetent?"

'The Suit' had expectations from those in his employ. The Major couldn't seem to meet those when it came to the two people he asked him to retrieve. In the three weeks since he gave Callahan the instructions to pick up Charlotte Brewer, there had been no progress. 'The Suit' had a team working on Patient Zero for a possible cure, but they hadn't had success either. He was at the end of his patience in many ways and Callahan was going to be the outlet for that frustration.

"They have stayed undetected. I have sent teams to the small town and though there was one sighting, we couldn't track them after that. The Duncan man has killed a number of my men," Callahan growled the last sentence.

"So, your men can't handle one man? One man and one woman are able to hide from you?"

"Sir, I do have some news," Callahan said.

"You should have led with that information. What news do you have?" 'The Suit' replied, impatience lacing his tone.

"We have captured his sister, Maxine. It was dumb luck that she stumbled into my base operations on her way to Montana. I am currently in the process of interrogating her. If anyone knows where Duncan is, it will be her."

"A sister? Communications have been down for weeks. If they weren't together already, what makes you think she will know where they are hiding?"

"Sir, from the research I've obtained about this family, they are very close. They would work together to survive this plague. I believe that's where Maxine was headed, to meet her brother and ride this out. I will get out of her whatever she knows."

"Callahan, pull out all of the stops, do you understand? Everything goes. Get that information," 'The Suit' said before he clicked end on the call.

'The Suit' turned to look through the glass wall he had in his office. The bunker was something very few people knew the location of. He knew it was wise to not allow Callahan to know exactly where he was. If the man ever did tire of taking orders, he could turn on him. Without a formal government in place, it was left to 'The Suit' to decide what direction society would go.

Below his office he could see into the lab where technicians worked around the clock. These people were those that could be saved from the facility in Kalispell and they were brought to the bunker with black hoods over their heads. If they ever questioned anything, they were shown the news and what they could be taken back to. Everyone fell in line with that warning. 'The Suit' recruited people without attachments for this exact reason. These technicians had no one to worry about, except themselves.

Patient Zero was in a cage at the corner of the lab. The floor around the bars was spotted with blood and black gore. They were already down one tech who decided to get too close to the infected without proper protection. Security had put down the tech as soon as the bite happened. The woman had sniveled for her life, but the protocol was clear. The infection would not break out in the compound. They would stay secure.

'The Suit' slammed his hand down on his desk, his frustration still at a peak. They needed a cure. If there would be anything left of the country, they needed to cure those that hadn't died yet. He tried to picture saving the world by going public with the cure. Then he would make people pay for it before getting inoculated. The plan was so clear in his mind. Yet, they didn't have the golden ticket. What they did have, was endless excuses. Excuses were not going to restart society with him at the helm.

He needed Charlotte Brewer. Prior to the incident, Charlotte had worked on the cure for every pathogen they had developed. According to his files, she had never found an illness she couldn't deconstruct and find the solution to. The lab techs working for him now continued to talk about how the pathogen wasn't what it was supposed to be and there were mutations involved. 'The Suit' didn't have the medical knowledge to understand how this was a problem. Yet, any problem he was faced with, he expected a solution. And that solution was Charlotte Brewer.

The Duncan man was proving to be a worthy enemy and 'The Suit' had to admire his determination. That determination was going to be his downfall because Duncan had something 'The Suit' didn't. People he loved.

CHAPTER TWENTY

One Month After Outbreak - Duncan Compound

Alex

"It's time, Alex, we need to go find him."

Alex Duncan stood in the barn, sorting through the milk they had in their freezer. A freezer that had been heartily stocked when they arrived. Her brother was meticulous with his chores, Alex remembered the trait from when they were children. When they arrived on the compound and he wasn't there, everything except the burned wall of the house was in order. Alex knew they had Rafe to thank for the plentiful crops in the garden as well as the greenhouse. The root cellar was full. The bunker was stocked. All because their brother was responsible.

So, then where was he?

"Let's go through this again. Two places to check," Alex said, turning to her sister.

Max was getting her fire back after being tortured by the man looking for Rafe. Alex was happy to see the light in her eyes and knew she had Griffin Wells to thank for that. At some point, she planned on cornering the man to find out his intentions with her sister, but she would wait until the family was complete and behind the walls of their compound.

"Those are the two we went to the most often when we would wander out on our own. You weren't really into camping with us for fun, only when Dad made you. But when Rafe and I went out on our own, we liked our particular places," Max replied.

"Ok. That makes sense. If we leave out the back of the compound, we can hike to both?"

"Yes. My guess is, if someone attacked while Rafe and his mystery woman were here, Rafe would have fled to the safety of the woods."

"They aren't that safe now," Alex pointed out.

Though they were safe inside the walls of their family compound, there didn't seem to be an end to the infected they found in the trees. It was unnerving to be out where you thought nature was safe, only to be hunted by the infected that had wandered far enough out to find a meal. Kalispell was nothing but the dead from what Alex had found. The infected weren't finding meals there any longer. While out hunting, she had come across a few small animals that looked torn to shreds. She guessed that if the infected were lucky, they caught animals to try and satisfy their urges.

"No. But we have to go, Alex. Tomorrow. We're ready. Everything is packed. Everyone knows their own roles for this to work," Max said.

Alex thought about the numerous meetings, which included a number of arguments as well. The sisters agreed they were both going for Rafe and everyone else could just do what they needed to do. That left the door open for all the adults trying to go, leaving Candace Reynolds, the thirteen-year-old, to run the compound. That was unacceptable and that was when the fights started.

Their survival group was now made up of two smaller groups. Alex arrived with her children Billie and Henry. As well as the teenagers Easton and Candace, the RV park owner Margaret and the know it all Marcus. Max stumbled into the compound with her daughter Jack, high school love Griffin, and grief-stricken Cliff. Everyone had their own stories and their own reasons for needing the compound. But only Max and Alex had the need to find Rafe.

Alex had already convinced Cliff to stay behind with the children. The man was emotionally broken. While Max hadn't known how to handle the situation with the man, Alex had quickly befriended him, giving him a shoulder to cry on. What Alex realized about him was, his need to protect Max's daughter was driven by the fact he couldn't protect his own son. When the discussions started, it wasn't a far leap to ask him to protect all of the kids on the compound. He took the job with pride and dedication. Alex felt good knowing the strong man was there in case a need arose.

Margaret was an older woman. She had tried to convince Alex she had already lived enough days, so if she were to die, she wanted it to be helping. Alex swallowed down the sadness that brought in her. Margaret was a force on her own, but Alex softly told her that she needed someone to maintain the animals and crops while they were gone. While Candace was capable of a lot, she would need guidance from a knowledgeable adult.

That left Alex dealing with the testosterone in the room. Griffin was refusing to allow Max away from him. Alex couldn't really blame him. After Max had been taken into custody and tortured within an inch of her life, Griffin had a real fear of her disappearing. Since the military wasn't only looking for Rafe, but most likely Max as well, Alex agreed that Griffin should go. Max didn't appreciate her disagreement on it, but Alex wouldn't budge.

Easton Reynolds, a quite capable sixteen-year-old, had served as Alex's backup on a number of occasions. However, all Alex could think of was keeping him safe. She had lost the teenagers once and it almost broke her to pieces. She couldn't do that again. She had pulled Easton to the side to hash out the argument with him privately. He had been furious with Alex for suggesting he stay behind. But she had been calm and clear with her needs and how she felt about it. She needed him on the compound, protecting Billie, Henry, and Jack. She knew she could trust him.

His largest issue was with Marcus being allowed to go, while he wasn't. Easton took offense to the attention Marcus showed Alex. While Alex didn't give the man much time, he still tried to converse with her privately or be overly friendly. Alex found the idea of love or flirting to be overly ridiculous at the end of the world, so she did what she figured was best. She ignored him. However, she couldn't ignore the fact that he was a fantastic shot and would be an extra set of hands in the group. Alex also knew that even if she left him behind, he wouldn't follow direction and would probably get himself killed wandering out on his own.

Dusk had given away to night and the sisters started their way to the house with a lantern. As they neared, the door burst open and Griffin came hurdling out.

"What is it?" Alex called out immediately.

"Soldiers, at the perimeter!" Griffin called back.

"Where are the kids?!"

"Coming down to go to the bunker! Candace and Margaret have them," Griffin said, as he ran by heading to the Bronco.

Alex looked at Max's pale face in the lantern light. Her eyes were cloudy with apprehension. Alex grabbed her sister and shook her a little to get her attention. She knew the old Max, the fearless, strong woman, was still inside the scared person in front of her.

"We have a plan for this, remember? They are not going to

take you, Max. Do you hear me?" Alex said, her voice calmer than she actually felt.

Max nodded and ran off to follow Griffin. Alex watched her for a moment before the kids came running out of the house following Candace, with Margaret on their heels. Alex handed off her lantern to Candace, so she had two in the bunker and quickly kissed her kids before sending them to hide. She then turned and faced the direction of the gate. Resolve pumped through her veins. These were the men that came for her brother. These were the men that tortured her sister. These men wouldn't last the night.

At the RV, her protector and savior from Las Vegas weeks before, Alex started to climb the ladder on the back. On the top of the machine, she pulled out the high-power rifle they had stored there. She checked, though she knew it was loaded for this exact reason. Making sure the ammo was within reach, she laid down on her stomach to adjust the night vision scope they had fitted to the rifle. Looking through the lens she saw everything was green but brighter than it would have been with a flashlight.

There she waited, for any sign of movement. On runs into town, Alex had seen evidence of the soldiers coming and going. A few of the living she found talked about the men who came but didn't help anyone. Without confirmation, Alex still knew those men were looking for her siblings. And at some point, they would come back to where they searched first, the compound.

Through the scope, she could see where Cliff and Marcus had run to the wall and waited with guns. There was no knowing for sure where the soldiers would come from. Safest would be from the gate side because of the road and lack of infected wandering in that area. But to be sure Griffin and Max would be watching the back wall for movement as well.

"Alex," a whispered voice came from the ladder.

"Come on up," she whispered back.

Easton crawled across the roof to her, bringing an additional hunting rifle that had belonged to her father. Easton didn't know how to shoot, though he asked Alex daily to teach him. Currently, he was more use to her on top of the RV, reloading for her as she needed it. She was the eyes for everyone on the compound. Easton also had a pair of night vision goggles that the kids had found in the long grass in the back of the compound. They had been just another piece of evidence of what had happened to Rafe before the family arrived.

With the night vision goggles to his eyes, Easton moved his position to check all the walls of the compound. Alex kept her gaze toward the front, waiting to see if the teen saw anything out of the ordinary.

"Movement at the gate," Alex said suddenly, as she saw soldiers pass next to the gated area where she could see through.

Easton, following the plan, flashed a light toward Marcus and Cliff twice. Once would have said not at their wall, two meant they were close. Easton then turned and gave Griffin and Max one flash. Then the boy settled next to Alex watching through his goggles.

"What are they waiting for?" He asked.

"To see if anyone is here or awake. They'll see the RV and know something is different from their last visit. It might be enough for them to investigate. We just wait and see."

Alex wished she was inside where she could watch the monitors. However, it was better to just be prepared for when the soldiers breached so they could take them out. If the soldiers were together as one, it would be harder to handle if they could at all. Alex's plan was as the soldiers tried to come over the fence, she took them out one by one. If they could avoid any hand to hand fight that was her goal.

Suddenly, a head showed above the rock wall. Alex waited, breathing slowly to keep herself calm. Was he just checking things out? Or was he coming over? She needed to know before she let off a shot. If they checked from the wall and then left, it would save them all from having to kill living people. Easton's breathing seemed to speed up as a second head and shoulders showed on the wall. They stayed still for a moment, before disappearing back down.

Not a second later an entire body hoisted on top of the wall. From Alex's vantage point she knew he couldn't see her on the RV roof, but if he looked down and to the side, he would find Cliff pointing a shotgun at him and Marcus with a 9mm. Alex centered her shot and with a squeeze of her finger, the soldier fell back off of the fence, dead before he hit the forest floor. The report of the rifle was quiet, a silencer helping, but the sound echoed slightly. Alex knew that the soldiers would know the shot was fired.

A flurry of movement at the gate told Alex they weren't going to turn around and give up. Suddenly two more bodies showed up on the wall, both with guns raised trying to find a target. Alex easily took out one and she saw Marcus step back to shoot up and knock the second back.

"That's three," Easton breathed.

"I'm sure there are quite a few more," Alex whispered back.

"Won't they give up a fight they can't win?"

"They don't know they can't win it at this point. Check the other walls, will you?"

Alex had a bad feeling about the whole raid. Why weren't there more trying to enter at once? Why would they just let their men die? Easton moved around the top of the RV carefully and quickly found out why the situation didn't seem normal.

"Alex, two coming through the field on our right!" Easton exclaimed in a whisper.

"Shit," Alex mumbled, as she adjusted her position.

She easily found the two soldiers in her sight and realized they were stalking toward Cliff and Marcus. The men were unsuspecting looking above them, relying on Alex and Easton to give them any signals they needed. Alex didn't have a hard time with moving targets and she easily shot them both in the bodies.

Marcus turned quickly realizing she was shooting somewhere else. Alex saw him tell Cliff something before running toward the fallen soldiers.

"Five," Easton said, keeping count.

Sickness rose in Alex's throat. Nothing in her was prepared for killing living people. Realizing her family was in danger pushed her to do the necessary things. She knew from Max's torture that this government faction would go to great lengths to get what they wanted. And they wanted her brother. She readjusted her position, fitting the gun against her a little tighter. They wouldn't find Rafe before she did. And she knew once they were together, they would be stronger.

Moments passed by. Easton continued to survey the walls with his night vision goggles. Alex moved from wall to wall, pointing the rifle in each direction to make sure they weren't missing anyone. She could see Cliff and Marcus moving along the wall carefully, checking for any breaches. After nothing moved for another ten minutes, Alex started to get stiff and the night air was starting to seep through her clothes.

"East, climb down and check the monitors. See if you can see anyone still out there or if any alarms are still tripped," Alex said.

Without question, the teen climbed carefully off the RV roof. He ran low, as Alex instructed him, and ducked into the house. Alex continued her sweep with the scope as she waited for his signal. She wasn't sure this group of soldiers would give up, even after five of theirs were down for the count. She watched as Marcus and Cliff went back to the two dead bodies inside the compound. They took all of the useable items off of the bodies, knowing anything could come in handy later.

"Alex!" Easton called from the ground.

"Yeah?"

"I'm not seeing anything on the monitors now. The sensors are all clear."

"Signal everyone and let them know. I'll stay up here just a few moments longer."

The walkie next to Alex crackled to life as Easton's voice came across with an all-clear message. Everyone knew if they broke radio silence they were fairly sure things were safe. Since Max had arrived with the information she had, they had made plans, backup plans, and plans to back up those in the event someone came searching for Rafe or Max again. Max had been fairly certain Major Callahan would not be letting go of what he wanted so easily. He would come for Max, even if it was just to kill her with his own hands.

With all of the adults gathered at the foot of the RV, Alex made one more pass with the scope, seeing nothing. She climbed down to join them. Max immediately hugged her, comforting her after having to use her skills in such a way. Alex appreciated her sister for trying to be warm and consoling, even when it didn't come naturally to her.

"They probably didn't have many more than the five you killed. When they sent out groups from the safe zone it was usually only seven to eight men assigned at a time. Two or three can't take this compound. They would know that," Griffin said.

"Which means they will come with more next time," Max chimed in.

"That only means you are right. We need to find Rafe soon. We need him and whatever this Callahan wants from him within the compound so we can fight this together," Alex said.

Max looked expectantly at Alex. The look of someone that had been taught to follow her older sister's guidance if anything should happen. Mitch Duncan was always unconventional. He often questioned Alex's dedication to his lessons. Yet, he still gave her the leadership of the family after him. He always said it mattered that she was the oldest and she was wise and compassionate. Her father had trusted her mind and heart to make the right choices. Alex struggled when those choices could put her family in danger.

"We leave tomorrow, first light," Alex finally said.

That night, Alex tossed and turned. Billie and Henry insisted on sleeping in her room, Henry in her double bed with her and Billie on an air mattress. Alex tried hard to keep quiet, not wanting to disturb the sleep of her children. She tried to make plans in her head of how they would go to find Rafe. First, she wanted to go into Kalispell. It was the nearest large town and she believed it would be the best place to find out information if they could find the living. She had avoided going there when possible because there were too many infected. However now, she would have enough back up that they could handle things.

When she finally did fall asleep it was fitful still. When Max poked into her room to rouse her with the sun, Alex was sure she hadn't slept a wink. But she was ready to go, adrenaline pumping through her veins in a frenzy. She softly kissed her kids goodbye, careful to not wake them. They knew they would wake with her gone, the plans explained to them the night before. Part of her felt guilty leaving them at all. Hard choices needed to be made to bring the family together, whole and safe.

In the cool morning air, Alex, Marcus, Max, and Griffin set out in their Bronco. The vehicle was packed with all of the supplies they would need for the trip that should take a few days according to Max. Alex was adding time by going to town first. The truck wouldn't get them all the way to the places Max wanted to check, so they had packs ready to go for when they traveled on foot. The group was quiet and reserved despite the obvious signs of nerves.

When they left the compound, Alex slowed to check the wall where the men she had shot had fallen. As she had suspected, the bodies and all of their equipment were gone. The living soldiers wouldn't have left their team members to rot in the wilderness. They also wouldn't waste valuable resources that could be salvaged from the bodies. Tire tracks could be seen where the truck they drove was pulled off into the trees, to avoid detection possibly. That told Alex they weren't aware of the security system installed. In her mind, she thanked Rafe for being so thorough with how he protected the compound.

Back in the vehicle the mood was still somber but seemed to crackle with energy. The drive to town was easy, luckily the roads weren't too congested with vehicles that had crashed or been abandoned. Each empty vehicle told a story of the plague. Some had dried blood splashed across windows, letting those that passed know the infected had been there. Some looked like they had just been parked and left, leaving Alex to wonder where those people went. Did they just walk into the woods hoping for salvation? They would be mistaken unless they were ready for what living in the wild was like.

At the edge of town, things became harder to get around. A semi had been tipped on its side, halfway into the road and half into the trees. The contents had been looted, though it wasn't anything useful in Alex's mind. Electronics seemed to always be the first thing on people's minds. Without a power grid running, those things were large paperweights. She carefully maneuvered the truck between the semi and the cars that had crashed on the other side of the road. It was tight, but she had done it before and knew it was possible.

It was like entering a ghost town when they pulled in. Alex hadn't seen anyone alive when she had come into town alone the last time. Though she assumed there was someone alive still. They drove slowly down the first few side roads. Alex watched the houses as they passed. The general disarray was disheartening. This far into the plague she had hoped to see more people fortifying and figuring out what they needed to make it. Instead, most homes were gutted. Doors stood open, windows were broken, garages ransacked.

"What are we even doing here, Alex?" Max asked.

Alex had been waiting for her to speak her mind. Her fingers were a constant drum against the passenger side door. Alex knew Max was frustrated with the pace her older sister was going. But Alex was about being safe and sane, so no one else was lost during their search.

"You never know what we could find in town. I haven't been here in a few weeks. Rafe might have come in for supplies."

"Why would he come here and not home?" Max asked, voicing the same question Alex had.

"I don't really know. I'm guessing he was trying to keep us safe and whoever he has with him."

The sisters had deduced that Rafe had someone staying at the compound with him. They guessed by some of the feminine items they found that it was a woman, but they were sleeping in separate bedrooms. They weren't sure what to make of that. Rafe had always been private with his personal life, not wanting to open himself up for the ribbing he would get from his sisters. Neither of them was aware of a female friend in his life. But if it was romantic, they had to assume they wouldn't be in separate rooms.

During Max's torture, Callahan had repeatedly claimed that Rafe had something that related to the plague. Max never believed him and would never give up the locations of her siblings. However, once Alex and Max put their minds together, they realized Rafe might have someone Callahan was after. If that someone had information about the plague, Rafe could be protecting that person. As well as his sisters, by not coming home.

"Coming into town is a waste of time. Rafe wouldn't stay here," Max said, expressing her dislike for their plan again.

"I don't think Rafe is here. I think he may have come here for supplies. Relax, Max, we will get to him eventually," Alex replied. She saw Marcus and Griffin look at each other knowingly, already used to the sisters and their bickering.

Alex progressed into town, driving through suburbs and near

strip malls. Something shiny caught Alex's attention and she slowed the truck to a stop in a parking lot. Max looked around, trying to figure out what Alex had stopped for. Alex herself wasn't totally sure. She looked from the pawn shop to the pot shop, to the dry cleaner. Nothing moved. But the shine she had noticed was on the roof. And whatever reflected the sun had moved.

"Something is up there," Alex pointed toward the roof of the strip mall.

"So?" Max asked, exasperated.

"If Rafe came into town and someone is being a lookout from the roof, they may have seen him," Alex explained. She tried to keep her voice even and patient.

"Ok. So, what do you want to do? Invite them over for tea? We need to figure out what there is to find and get going," Max said, as she popped open her door.

Alex followed her sister, noting that she was always brazen. They were both armed and they looked around warily. Walking to the windows of the shops, Alex pulled a piece of paper that had been taped up. She stared into the face of her brother under the word wanted in large letters. A woman was on the flyer next to him, smiling in her photo. Her name was Charlotte according to the flyer. Alex held it toward Max as she walked up.

"What in the hell?" Max asked.

"Our brother is apparently a wanted fugitive," Alex responded dryly.

A shuffling noise pulled both women from their conversation to the end of the strip mall. Both expected to find an infected coming their way, but instead, it was an old man pointing a rifle at them.

"So, Rafe Duncan is your brother?" The old man asked.

"What's it to you?" Max responded, her hand crumpling the wanted flyer before dropping it and pulling her tomahawk.

"Careful, Max," Alex warned, as she put her hands up.

"He said there might be people looking for him eventually. He had a message for two women. Two women that should look a lot like you two. What is the name of the plan you started the day this plague began?" The man asked.

"Sundown," Alex answered immediately.

The old man nodded and then a large smile spread across his leathery face. The smile changed everything about his presence, turning him into a loving grandfather, instead of a homeless man with a weapon. He pointed the rifle back at the ground and walked toward them. Max looked bewildered at his transformation, but Alex couldn't help but smile back slightly. He looked at each of them carefully and laughed a little.

"That brother of yours, he's a little crazy. But you're Alex," he said as he pointed to Alex. "And you're Max." He finished pointing to Max next. Both women did nothing but nod.

"It's very nice to meet you. I'm Issac. And your brother and I know each other well."

CHAPTER TWENTY-ONE

Max

She didn't do people. The old man that was currently ushering their group into his dry cleaner shop was friendly and talkative. He clearly enjoyed the company and welcomed them warmly into his makeshift home. For Max, he was overwhelming. The only reason she followed was that the man claimed to know Rafe. Her brother who was apparently a fugitive now. That made two of them she guessed. Yet, her face wasn't on a poster being plastered around town.

Inside the cleaners, it was clear Issac had lived there the entire month alone. The racks that usually held clothing were bare, except for what looked like drying laundry hanging around in places. A bed was set up to one side. Nearby that was a propane stove with stacked cans neatly in rows. Cases of water sat against the opposite wall. Max went to this wall and eyed what looked to be a second bed.

"Who else is here?" She asked, wary of an attack.

"Huh? No one," Issac said, turning to her.

When he saw where she was standing he motioned to the bed on the floor with a sweep of an old hand.

"Oh that. That's where your brother sleeps when he comes into town for provisions."

Max gritted her teeth at his answer. Looking at her sister, she saw that Alex's eyes were averted but there was still a smirk on her face. Max knew she'd hear about this later, Alex being right about Rafe coming to town. She still couldn't understand why he would come to town and not home. If it was to keep them safe, Max thought that was ridiculous. He knew his sisters well and should know they could defend themselves against whatever was to come.

"Issac, when did you last see Rafe?" Alex asked.

The old man moved them to a sitting area in the lobby of the dry cleaner's. A few chairs lined one wall and others had been added over the days. The group of five sat facing each other. Max fidgeted waiting for answers, so they could get on the road and find their brother. She wouldn't admit it to anyone, but she needed her family together in one place. Her hand hadn't healed, despite the ministrations by Margret working to keep it set and clean. Breathing could hurt at times, her ribs still bruised, possibly cracked. Max wouldn't tell Alex any of that though, because she knew her sister would delay the search. Or worse, leave Max behind.

"He was here maybe a week and a half ago. He's only come twice since the first time we met. But he knows he's safe here. I wouldn't turn him into those uniformed morons."

"That's kind of you," Alex replied.

It took everything Max had to not roll her eyes. Alex was always so good with people and Max still couldn't understand the need. She tried with those close to her, but strangers didn't rank for her.

"Where is he?" Max asked, jumping directly to the point.

"That I don't know. I asked him the first time he came back because he said he had hiked hard for almost two days to get to town. He slept hard and then got the supplies he needed before heading back. When I asked him, he said he wouldn't put me in danger by knowing where he and Charlie were hiding," Issac explained.

"Charlie?" Max asked.

"The woman. You saw her on the poster. She's with him. And the boy. Those two don't come into town with Rafe. He says it's safer for them to stay hidden."

"Wait, there's a child?" Alex cut in, her voice colored with surprise.

"I think I'll let Rafe explain what's been happening," Issac said with a shrug.

"He has a lot to account for apparently," Max muttered.

Issac insisted on feeding them while they were in his place. He produced packages of beef jerky, chips, apple slices and cans of sparkling water. They ate in silence, except for the short stories Issac felt necessary to share with them. He only left his dry cleaner's shop to get supplies. He stayed on the roof a lot to watch what was happening around. He explained that was how he met Rafe and Charlie when he helped them escape a horde.

Max sat back and just let the old man talk. If Rafe was his only company, the man was probably lonely most of the time. While Max wasn't a people person, she still couldn't imagine spending the apocalypse alone. The dry cleaner, though secure, was bare and lifeless. Issac had tried to make it homey with his candles, bedding, and blackout curtains in the front. Yet, in the end, it was still a dry cleaner's shop, not a home with people.

"Why do you stay here?" Max asked her need to have answers outweighing her desire to be quiet.

"It's in town. It's bigger than my apartment. And my apartment had too many people around. I knew they would all become the dead eventually and it would be less safe. This seemed better."

"And you never wanted to go with Rafe?"

"He suggested it once. But I said no. I didn't want to slow him down. Plus, if I'm in town, I can track the times the military men come in looking for them. It's valuable information."

"I would say it is," Max answered with a nod. As she was also trying to stay away from the military she could appreciate the need for extra eyes.

"We are going to find Rafe and bring him home. You said he had a message for us if we came to town. What is it?" Alex asked.

"He was pretty clear. He said to not come for him," Issac replied.

"What? That's absurd," Max sputtered. She quieted after one loaded glance from Alex.

"Issac, why wouldn't he want us to come for him? We're his family. We can protect him," Alex said.

"He believes that he and Charlie will lead the military back to the compound. He doesn't want anyone else to be at risk."

"Well, it doesn't matter if he's there. We've already had to kill some of them," Max said. Issac looked at her surprised at first, but then he grinned.

"Took some of them down, huh? That's fantastic. I'm sick of those boys coming in here acting like they run the town and we have to bow down and answer their questions."

"They aren't only coming for Rafe anymore. We are at risk if we are divided," Alex explained.

Issac just shrugged, looking at all of them for a moment.

"I understand where you girls are coming from. All I can do is give you the message your brother left. I can't stop you from doing anything."

Max knew that was the truth. Nothing Issac said was going to stop them from going for Rafe. The Duncan family needed to be together to weather the storm that was on the horizon. A shiver ran down Max's back, as Callahan's face flashed in her mind. Torture at the hands of the Major had been difficult. She hadn't walked away unbroken. But she did escape. Max knew Callahan was furious that his torture project had broke free and without giving him any of the information he wanted.

Griffin's hand ran up her spine and she looked over at him. She could see some of the pain in his eyes that she felt. His guilt was something he carried like a shroud, despite Max telling him numerous times that it wasn't his fault. There was no way he could know that all of the rules had been thrown out of the window by Callahan. Griffin held high regard for the military, after serving eight years himself. After he saw what Callahan was doing, he realized it wasn't his US Military anymore. The world was changing rapidly.

She took Griffin's hand in her unbroken one. He looked at her with a small smile and Max knew he was with her on this expedition, no matter what. Their relationship growing during the apocalypse seemed ludicrous. Something she felt the need to remind him daily. Her doubts and worries never phased him. He was busy convincing her they were solid and becoming the perfect father to Jack. Thinking of their daughter, Max had a worry that if they didn't make it, Jack would be alone in the world. For a moment she debated sending Griffin back to the compound, however, she knew he would never follow her request.

After they finished their meal and conversation, the sun was high in the sky. As Max, Griffin, and Marcus loaded back into the Bronco, Alex stood with Issac talking quietly. Max watched from her window trying to figure out what had Issac disagreeing with Alex. She had never been great with patience and reading lips wasn't in her bag of talents. Out of nowhere, Alex hugged Issac, the man looking as surprised as Max was.

Alex climbed into the truck and started it up. Max just looked at her, waiting for an explanation. When it was clear nothing was coming, Max sighed loudly.

"What was that about?"

"What?" Alex asked. Max knew she was playing dumb on purpose.

"Your conversation with Issac. He didn't agree with you about something. What was it?"

"Oh that. Well, I told him he should come to the compound with us and stay. He would be safer there. And we could use all the firepower we can get," Alex explained.

"Are you joking? Alex, you can't just invite every person you meet to our home!"

"No, I'm not joking. Max, Dad always wanted us to be open with those we could trust. And I know we can trust Issac. He hasn't turned in Rafe. He had multiple chances to tell the mercenaries that he was in town. But he never did. He deserves to be with us. To be safe."

Max flopped back into her seat, knowing she would never win the argument with Alex. Her heart was clearly better than Max's. It wasn't that Max didn't care about people. She did. Seeing the infected hurt her, as she watched them and tried to imagine what their stories were prior to the plague. But trust was a limited commodity now. She could appreciate that Issac hadn't turned in Rafe. However, they didn't know that yet. They hadn't found Rafe alive.

The drive was quiet. Max was lost in her thoughts of how to balance the scales between the siblings. At times she would shoot glances over at Alex, trying to think of something to say to her. A part of Max felt ashamed for not being more like Alex. She wanted to explain to her sister. Alex knew her better than most people. Did she even need to explain where she was coming from?

With instructions from Max, the truck pulled off of the main road. They bumped along a poorly maintained dirt road. A mile down the path, they were blocked by a fallen tree. The location of the tree had Max suspecting they were on the right path. She jumped from the truck quickly and went to where the tree had stood. As she had suspected the tree had been chopped, not splintered from falling naturally.

"This is the right way! Rafe did this to stop anyone from driving too close!" Max called to the car as the rest of the party got their feet on the ground.

Alex came to meet Max by the tree stump. She leaned down and touched the chopping marks.

"This had to take a bit for him to get done. He really wanted to make sure no one went any deeper into the forest with a vehicle," Alex said.

"Preventative measures. If this is here, that means they are at the cave location. We should go there first," Max replied.

With agreement on their plan of action, everyone began to strap on their packs. Each pack was equipped with everything they needed for survival. Being prepared was always the first priority. Though they had no plans on being separated from each other, that was always a possibility. Everyone carried waters, MREs, sleeping bags, tarps, ropes and cords, fire making kits, flashlights, and a number of additional items. Each person carried their own personal weapons, able and prepared to defend themselves and each other as needed.

Max set the pace from the truck. They marked the spot of their vehicle on a topographical map Alex had found. Though they were decent with a compass and natural markers, no chances were being taken. Max estimated they only had a day and a half of hiking if they moved quickly. Alex left the directions and plans to Max, as she knew the area better than anyone else.

A few hours later Griffin caught up with Max's lead, his steps falling in line with hers.

"Maybe we should take a small break, Max?"

"Why? We are making good time."

"How are your ribs?" Griffin asked.

Max didn't answer. She wasn't going to lie to Griffin, never again. Keeping the secret of Jack and Griffin being her father was the biggest regret of her life now. And that lie almost broke them beyond repair. She couldn't lie to him. But she also didn't want to tell him her ribs were screaming and that she couldn't take a deep breath without wanting to cry out.

"That's what I thought. We are going to take a break. We all need to catch our breath," Griffin said.

They sat near a small creek that ran through the trees. The babbling of the water was relaxing to Max. She sat on a large rock and leaned against a tree behind it. The pain in her side radiated through her entire body and she struggled to get comfortable in any position. She worked on concentrating on her breathing, slowing it so she didn't need so many deep breaths. Rustling brush over her shoulder caused her to jump and pull her tactical toma-hawk. Griffin was at her side a moment later, his rifle at his shoulder.

The smell was the first thing Max noticed. The infected seemed to decompose as they walked. No amount of living flesh that they consumed could stop the breakdown of their living cells. Max related the smell to roadkill that had laid in the sun for too many days. Putrid and nauseating. After all the fights she had with the infected, this was no longer a surprise for her. It was more of a warning system.

Alex and Marcus joined Max and Griffin, setting up at their backs so they were covered in a full circle. There was really no knowing what was in the trees. Max kept her eyes forward, waiting for the rotted body to show itself. When it did, Max had to cringe. There wasn't just one. Instead, there were five following as a group. The leader was a tall wiry man, once dressed in hiking gear. In her mind, Max created the story for him, assuming he was camping out somewhere not knowing the plague had come or to hide from it. It didn't take long to find him.

"Don't shoot. Noise could attract attention," Max said quietly.

Griffin nodded and slung his rifle onto his back. He pulled the knife he wore at his hip. Max knew Alex was wielding her knife and possibly the machete that she liked to carry. Marcus was another story. The man rarely listened to plans, so Max hoped he listened and didn't start shooting as soon as he saw the infected.

Waiting wasn't a game Max excelled at. She stepped forward with Griffin on her heels. She struck out with her tomahawk, shattering the knee of the wiry man, bringing his head into her reach. The body fell awkwardly, without the understanding of stopping or protecting itself. Max stepped back to let it fall and then swung her tomahawk again, embedding it into the skull of the infected. She used a booted foot against the head for leverage as she pulled the weapon free. The slurping sound was one Max heard in her nightmares sometimes.

Behind her, Alex and Marcus were engaging additional infected that appeared and Max began to worry they were in the middle of a horde. She watched Griffin assault the infected in front of them. Max forced her mind blank, forced the worry away so she could focus on defending them. Moving forward, she met with Griffin as they simultaneously worked to dispatch the infected in their sight. It was a fluid dance they had practice in, like riding a bike, they never forgot.

Almost before it started, the fight was over. The four living were left to breathe hard and look around, waiting for the next attack. Nothing came. Max walked back to her sister to check in and make sure she was whole. It was reassurance she needed, knowing she couldn't survive this world without Alex. They gave each other knowing looks, comfort without words. Sisters that were both unmarred.

Griffin suggested they move further down the creek to take their chance to rest, as none of them wanted to sit in the smell of the infected. Max walked at the back of the group now. Pain from her hand and side seemed to seep into every part of her body. She felt tired. And she knew they had the rest of the day before they set up camp. She tried to take a deep breath and almost let out a squeak when the pain intensified.

When they stopped, Max almost collapsed against a tree. She leaned her head back, focusing on her breathing again. Anything to take her mind from the pain and to calm her thundering heart. The infected were everywhere. She had assumed that of course, but it was still strange to see them in the forest away from town.

"Are you ok?" Griffin came to sit next to her.

"Yeah."

"You aren't great at hiding the pain," he said quietly.

"I'll be alright. Just need to get my breathing under control," Max replied.

"Is that it? Your ribs are hurting?"

Max cursed internally. Griffin knew how to get information out of her. She didn't want him to worry about her. They all needed to focus on moving forward.

"We can worry about finding Rafe. I can also worry about your healing. It wasn't that long ago that you were hurt," Griffin said, annoyingly reading Max's mind.

"I don't want any distractions. Especially not because of me. I can handle it. This will be over soon," Max said. She looked at him and smiled, hoping to give the illusion that she was fine. It was clear immediately that Griffin didn't buy it. Instead of smiling back, he handed her a bottle of water.

Night came faster than Max had wanted. She didn't feel like they had covered enough ground. Her impatience contended with Alex's unlimited optimism that they would get there when they got there. And that Rafe would be right where they thought he was. Max tried to think like her sister, tried to feel calm in her mind. But being apart from their brother gave her anxiety that wouldn't be cured until they found him.

Alex and Max worked together to gather materials for beds under their makeshift shelters. They had assisted the men in building two lean-to shelters against nearby trees. The foursome worked well in collecting the branches for the ribs of the shelters. Using the tarps, they had in their packs they covered the ribs and then started putting fallen branches over the tarps. They weren't expecting rain, but the shelters would provide some cover from anyone else that may be in the forest.

The sisters dumped the small fallen branches they had scavenged into the shelters. Once arranged there were four rough beds set up and covered with sleeping bags they had hauled. Everyone cut open their MRE dinners and left them to heat. They decided against a fire, worried that the light would attract attention. Instead, they used a flashlight covered in cloth in the shelters to see their meals.

The silence of the forest was the only company they had. As food was consumed the group was quiet, exhaustion taking over. Max ate her beef taco meal quickly. The taste wasn't perfect, but it was nutrition they needed. She was popping the small dessert discs in her mouth as Griffin finished his meal and started packing his things back into his backpack.

"I'm exhausted," Griffin said quietly.

A murmured agreement came from the other shelter, Marcus answering, Max assumed.

"I'm ready for bed myself," Max said after finishing her food.

"That's good, because I wasn't going to bed without you," he joked.

Laying together under the branches of their lean-to, Griffin held Max's hand. His thumb rhythmically rubbed over her skin, lulling her to sleep. When her eyes closed, she fell asleep deeply. Her dreams were always in turmoil, she expected it now. Tonight, was no different. Instead of the infected in the scenes, it was Callahan. A man she was sure she would never forget. His menacing smile with perfectly white, straight teeth was directed at her. It took all she had to not vomit. She tried to move away, and it was then she realized she was tied to the hook again, hanging by her wrists. Panic began to set in and she flailed her body violently. Callahan did nothing but look at her and laugh.

"Max...Max....wake up." Griffin's voice came through the haze and Max bolted up in her sleeping bag.

"What? What is it?" Max stammered, as she tried to wake and wipe the nightmare from her mind.

"You were kicking and lashing out. I was afraid you were going to break something on me," Griffin said.

Max recognized his light manner, but she could hear the concern behind his words. Suddenly Alex appeared with her dimmed flashlight. Her hair was rumpled, and her sweatshirt had been pulled on quickly. Max felt guilty to have woken everyone with her nightmare.

"Max, do you want to take a walk?" Alex asked quietly.

Max just nodded and pulled her boots on. She tried to pretend that she didn't notice the look her sister and her boyfriend shared. They both knew her mind wasn't right. She had been waterboarded, beaten, electrocuted, and starved. It was more than any normal person should handle. But Max was determined to not be broken in her soul. She may have broken bones still, but those would heal and so would her mind.

Walking away from camp, Alex waited until they were out of sight of the shelters. She turned to Max and pulled her into her arms. At first, Max was surprised. But that melted away and she found herself in her sister's warm embrace. She gripped Alex hard and she hugged her back. The feeling of her sister reminded her that she was ok, she had survived, and they were strong together.

"You can talk about it. That doesn't make you weak," Alex said.

"I know. It's just that Griffin already feels such guilt. I don't want him to know absolutely everything."

"It's easy to guess from what is on your body, Max. Maybe he's assuming worse than it was," Alex answered.

"I doubt that," Max said sarcastically.

"Then tell me."

Alex pulled her to a fallen log that they could see in the bright moonlight. Max sat heavily and looked at her sister for a moment. She studied Alex's caring expression and it made Max's heart hurt. Instead, she looked up at the stars, not able to see her sister's reaction to everything she was going to tell her. When Max got to the compound, she had told Alex a lot. Enough to explain why she looked like she did. She had been black and blue on most of her body. Even now the remnants of those bruises still lingered, green and yellow.

Everything started to spill out. From the first punch to the waterboarding, to her hallucinating while hanging from a hook soaking wet. She told Alex about the baton stun gun used on her wet skin. The threats Callahan made about Jack were some of the worst parts, which had set off Max enough to attack the man. That was how she ended up with a broken hand and cracked ribs.

To her credit, Alex didn't say a word the entire time Max spoke. Max knew it was taking all of her control to not lash out. Even Alex had her limits. Max finally looked back at her sister and wasn't sure if she should be worried about the eerie calm she saw on her face.

"Someday, we will find that Callahan and show him what happens when he touches a Duncan," Alex said, her voice dripping with menace. Max was almost taken aback.

"Wow, so all it took was for your sister to get tortured for the mean Alex to come out, huh?" Max said.

"It's not something to joke about, Max. I'm serious. We are going to get Rafe. And we will go on the offense if they keep coming after you both."

The talk had done wonders for Max. She didn't realize unloading to someone about her experience would help so much. But when they returned to the shelter, she laid next to Griffin easily. He reached over to touch her face as she started to fall asleep and her mouth curled into a smile. When she fell asleep then, it was into peace and darkness.

CHAPTER TWENTY-TWO

"Aiden! Don't go too deep into the water!" Rafe called, watching the boy like a mother hen.

Rafe didn't know how it had even happened, but somehow Charlie had convinced him to take Aiden fishing. And while they were at the creek she suggested Rafe get the boy cleaned up. Agreement seemed like his only option, so here they were. Rafe had a pole set up with bait in the water. The little boy had no patience for sitting calmly to fish, so he continually wandered into the water.

Catching the boy again, Rafe brought him back to sit and dry off. He ruffled his blond hair before settling him against the tree next to him. Rafe had tried to teach him about fishing, but the water called Aiden. Just like any four-year-old, he just wanted to play. The playing was a good sign after the boy had lost his parents. He was quiet a lot of the time, leaving Charlie and Rafe wondering if they needed to do something extra to help him through his grief. But then he would run around and play like nothing was wrong.

Suddenly the pole tugged in Rafe's hands. He let out a little cheer as he reeled in whatever was stuck on his hook. Aiden sat forward in fascination, waiting for something to appear from the water. Rafe concentrated on reeling evenly so he didn't lose what could possibly be their dinner. MRE's, canned foods, and macaroni and cheese only went so far. Rafe tried to fish every day that he was at the cave. He also had snares set around, hoping to catch a rabbit or something else small that he could skin and cook up.

The glistening scales of a small trout came out of the water as Rafe lifted his pole. He put the fish into a bucket with a little water. His mind began to wander over the last few weeks in the cave. He had gone on a few trips into town for supplies and information. He was thankful that Issac was always waiting for him with open arms. The hiking back and forth was a sort of therapy for Rafe. Solitude could be found in the trees when there was no sound but his own breathing.

On his trips, he did come across the infected. He dispatched those that were immediate threats. But he didn't go off his path to chase them down. After the first few days at the cave, he set up an early detection system around their area. That consisted of empty cans tied together and then tied to paracord that looped between trees. An infected wouldn't know how to avoid detection and the sound would give Rafe time to defend them if necessary.

Living in the cave with Charlie and Aiden was a new world for Rafe. He was used to being alone on his piece of land. Part of him really missed those days of habit and quiet. Before the plague, he always knew what he needed to do. Now, he was at a loss a lot of the time. He didn't know what Charlie needed to be somewhat content. And Aiden was a complete mystery to him. Even the time he had spent with his nieces and nephew couldn't prepare him for being one of the main parent figures for a child.

Somedays Rafe was sure Storm understood him. The dog would disappear into the woods for hours at a time. The first time he did it, Charlie was in hysterics afraid that the dog had been eaten. When Storm returned, he was panting and practically smiling. Rafe guessed he just ran the woods on his own and came home when he was ready. He could understand the dog's need.

The fishing trip that day proved fruitful, with three fish to take back to the cave for dinner. Providing for the group was one thing Rafe took pride in. It was the way he knew how to care for people. Shelter, food, water, repeat. Charlie appreciated it, as she told him often. But Rafe knew that almost a month in a cave wasn't the way Charlie wanted to survive the end of the world.

Arriving back at the cave, Charlie had the tarp and net pulled to the side, letting fresh air swirl inside their homestead. Over the month, items had been added to their shelter, making it more homey and useable. Rafe brought back a small solar battery so they were able to power up the laptop and charge it once it died. Charlie was bent over that now, working on her formulas and equations. Aiden ran ahead and plopped next to Charlie, leaning his head on her arm.

"Oh, you're clean. That's a nice change," Charlie joked, tickling the boy quickly before putting the laptop away.

"Fish for dinner," Rafe said as he set the bucket inside the cave.

"You aren't going to try and teach me how to clean them again, are you?" Charlie asked. Her nose wrinkled in disgust, making Rafe laugh.

"No. I feel like that was a waste last time. If you keep gagging, you'll never learn anything."

"That's why I have you," she said.

She turned to change Aiden out of the swimsuit he was running around in for his bath. During his runs into town, Rafe had collected a number of items, of all sizes, for Aiden. He wasn't always sure on sizes but when he told Issac, the man had laughed and explained what 4T and other sizing meant on kids' clothes. Rafe felt completely ridiculous, but he figured it out and made sure Aiden had all the proper clothing. Charlie wrestled the little boy into cargo shorts and a Spiderman T-shirt. The shirt made Aiden smile and he looked up at Rafe.

"My favorite," Aiden said, pointing at the shirt.

"Yup, that's what you said, buddy," Rafe replied. He had found the shirt in the Walmart after he risked the infected to go in and find items for the boy. He was so happy to bring back something that would make Aiden happy.

After he was dressed, Aiden sat with blocks in the section of the cave that had become his playroom. Rafe started on the fish, wanting them skinned and ready for frying for dinner. As he concentrated on his task he could feel Charlie watching him over his shoulder.

"You sure you don't want to learn?"

"No. I was wondering. You're headed into town again soon, aren't you?" Charlie asked.

"Why do you ask?"

"Well, it's been almost two weeks. And your habit is to go every two weeks it seems."

"Are you worried about something, Charlie?"

"You can obviously handle yourself. I just wonder. When can we go home or back to the compound, I mean?" She asked, uncertain.

"The compound is home for you too, Charlie, if you want to stay, Aiden as well. I'm sure Storm will love running around all the animals. But going back? I'm not sure. The military keeps going into town looking for us. They continue to put up those stupid posters. They must have gone to the compound by now," Rafe mused.

"What happens if they find your sisters there?"

"They didn't care about me. My guess is they'll find we aren't there and move on. If not, they will have their hands full with my sisters."

Charlie seemed to take that answer and didn't say anything else on the subject. Rafe looked around at the supplies they had.

He didn't really need to go into town. But getting the news from Issac was helpful for making decisions when it came to protecting Charlie. He also risked the military spotting him every time he wandered back into town. It was a risk he thought was negligible versus the insight he could gain.

He had turned back to the skinning of the fish when he heard cans clanging together. Dropping his fillet knife, Rafe jumped up to grab his hunting knife. Charlie was already at the mouth of the cave looking out. The cans were out of sight, far enough away that whatever came across them couldn't threaten them immediately after sounding the alarm. For a moment they both stood and waited, gazing out into the sunlit forest waiting for something to show.

"It's not the military. They wouldn't come during the day," Rafe said, as he laid his hand on Charlie's tense shoulder.

"You want me to come with you?" She asked.

"No. Stay with Aiden, keep him safe. I'll take Storm with me."

Walking out of the cave, Rafe gave a low whistle. From his left, he could hear the dog running toward him. The infected would have already caught his attention, but Storm was trained well enough to know not to attack without Rafe giving him the order. The white and silver blur popped out of the bushes, skidding to a stop at Rafe's feet. He looked up at Rafe with his mismatched eyes for a moment before barking once.

"Yup. Let's go, boy. You can handle my light work."

Rafe headed straight for where he heard the cans clang. The alarms were set no more than ten feet apart, so they were bound to find what was coming toward them. Storm's growls intensified as they got to the alarm. The paracord had been knocked down. The sound of growling nearby told Rafe where the infected had wandered off to. Without a known meal in front of them, they wandered aimlessly. Rafe looked down at Storm and whistled once to let the dog loose. That was all he needed to jet off, low and on the hunt.

The sounds of Storm ripping into flesh gave Rafe the direction he needed to go. He picked up his pace running to make sure the dog was safe. Rounding a tree, an infected stumbled directly into Rafe's path. Rafe pivoted quickly, almost falling directly into the infected's clawed hands as it reached out for the living meal it suddenly was upon. Finding his footing, Rafe spun quickly and plunged his hunting knife up under the infected's chin, puncturing the brain from below. Pulling his knife out he pushed the infected away from him.

Storm's fight was over, the dog now covered in black and red from tearing into the infected's head after he had attacked its knees. Rafe was impressed with the dog's intuition of how to handle the enemy. The dog sat, tongue lolling, at the feet of the infected, waiting for Rafe to check that it was truly dispatched. To be sure, Rafe thrust his blade into what was left of the temple of the infected. Standing, he waited for additional attacks or noises. The alarm was down now, so if there were additional infected they would have to find them the hard way.

"Storm, go. Find." Rafe said simply, letting the dog know he was to search the area. The dog barked once in agreement and took off again.

The paracord was down in two places, so Rafe traced the areas and reset his manual alarms. After setting the part he could see down, the paranoia rising to the surface made him trace the entire length of cord and cans. The walk calmed the adrenaline that had been pumping through him during the fight with the infected. The sun was warm on his skin, though the shade was still cooler. He stood in the sun for a moment, turning his face toward the light, closing his eyes. The sun was still normal. The heat still felt the same. The plague couldn't take everything away.

When Rafe arrived back at the cave, Storm was already back with Charlie. She tsk'd over the mess he had made with himself again. The husky's hair was thick and long, creating the perfect place for fluids to collect and dirty the beautiful white coat.

Charlie shot Rafe a look of mock anger as she cooed to the dog. Storm soaked up all of the attention, loving all the petting he received when Charlie was really dedicated to cleaning him up.

"I guess there were just the two we handled. Storm must have found it to be clear or he wouldn't have come home," Rafe said.

"Because he's a good dog," Charlie said, kissing Storm on the head. The dog licked her face in return.

"I fought them too," Rafe said.

"Yes well, we already know you are good at it."

"Second to the dog," Rafe muttered.

The smell of fish and hot dogs sizzling over the fire were an interesting smell together. Aiden refused to touch the fish, so Rafe dug out the last few hot dogs they had cold in the icebox he had created in the creek. Using a small plastic bucket, Rafe surrounded it with rocks and stacked rocks on top. The running water rushed by keeping the interior cold. It was helpful for keeping some meat items, like hot dogs, for short periods of time.

Charlie delighted in the opportunity to have a fire. Though it wasn't dark yet, Rafe wouldn't build a fire when it was dark, she sat close to it watching the flames. Aiden sat a few feet from her eating his hot dogs hungrily. The one thing they didn't have to worry about with the boy was his appetite. Once the hot dogs were done, Rafe went into the cave to grab a surprise he had scavenged the last time he was in town. He came out and handed a paper bag to Charlie. She looked inside, her eyes lighting up.

"S'mores?"

"I thought you and Aiden would enjoy doing them. Dessert?" Rafe said, shifting from foot to foot. He didn't understand how the little woman could make him feel so uncomfortable with just a look.

"Aiden, look! Do you want s'mores?" Charlie said, turning to the little boy. There was confusion on his face at first, but once Charlie explained what they were he was very excited about his dessert.

Rafe watched them roast the marshmallows and smash them between graham crackers and chocolate. Aiden was a sticky mess by the time Rafe said they needed to put out the fire. The sun had started to dip lower in the sky and he didn't want the light of the flames to attract any unwanted visitors. Inside the cave again, with the tarp and net swung into place, Charlie used a wet washcloth to scrub at Aiden's stickiness, much to the boy's disagreement.

"I am going to go into town tomorrow. I would feel safer knowing if things have changed or not," Rafe said, once Aiden was asleep in his bed.

"Are you sure you need to go?" Charlie asked.

"I wouldn't if I didn't think it was necessary."

"I know. I just feel so scared when you're gone. What if you don't come back at some point?" She asked, wringing her hands in her lap.

"You know that if I don't come back in four days, you head straight for home. Do you want to go over the map and compass again?" Rafe offered.

The first time he left Charlie and Aiden alone, she was scared. Rafe mapped out how she should get back home, to the compound, should the need ever arise. They agreed on four days. If he was gone longer than four days, she knew she had to go home. Rafe had kept his trips to town at three days so far and she was always extremely grateful to see him.

"No. I understand the map and what to do if you don't come back. I just don't want that to be the case. 'The Suit's' men are out there, hunting us all the time. You could stumble onto them on accident."

"They will have a fight on their hands if that's the case," Rafe said confidently.

She left the conversation for now and Rafe was glad. He didn't want to go to bed while they were at odds. Their harmony was important to him. They spent so much of their time together as a group, he didn't like when they argued or didn't talk. It made life uncomfortable in their makeshift shelter. Rafe preferred their easy companionship. Luckily, they rarely found reasons to disagree and have the hard silences. Rafe left Charlie to do what she was good at and she did the same with him.

Falling asleep was going to be difficult that night, knowing he was going out early the next day. Before going to bed, he worked to get his pack ready by the lowered light of a lantern. He crept around quietly to not wake Aiden, though they had found the boy could sleep through an avalanche. He made sure all his normal items were in his pack and added new MREs for the days he planned to be gone.

With the packing completed, he turned to climb into bed. He found Charlie laying in her own bed, watching him. Once he settled he looked over at her before he turned the lantern out.

"What's wrong, Charlie?"

"Just the usual. Wondering if you'll get eaten alive while you're gone. Wondering if you'll come back with my dog."

Storm lifted his head from Charlie's legs when he heard her refer to him. He looked around, trying to determine if anyone needed him. Charlie absently rubbed his head until he laid back down.

"He's definitely your dog," Rafe said with a low chuckle.

"Goodnight, Rafe," she said.

"Goodnight."

As planned, Rafe strapped on his bag early in the morning as sunlight was peeking over the mountains. Storm hopped and ran around, knowing they were going on a trip. He always went with Rafe, because he was such a good early warning system. Charlie surprised Rafe by hugging him after she kissed Storm on the head. He stood stock still for a moment longer than he should have, not knowing how to react to her. But he wrapped one arm around her and squeezed her for a second before she released him.

"Be careful," she said, as Rafe started to walk away.

"Four days. If I'm not back in four days, you know I wasn't careful."

Aiden came up from behind Charlie's legs then and looked up at Rafe expectantly. Kneeling down, Rafe brought himself face to face with the boy. His little arms wrapped around Rafe's neck.

"Bye, Rafe," Aiden said over his shoulder.

"Bye, buddy. I'll see you in a few days like before."

"Ok."

With that, Aiden pulled back with a big smile before running off toward the cave and his toys. Charlie watched him for a moment before turning back to Rafe. She looked at him for a moment longer before turning away as well. Rafe took that as his time to head into the trees. He whistled to Storm who pranced ahead a few feet before running back to circle Rafe's feet. The antics made Rafe smile, despite the heavy feeling he had. A feeling he hadn't felt when leaving the cave before. What had changed?

Into the trees, the sunlight was spotty between the leaves and branches of the mature giants around him. Rafe enjoyed the silence as they walked, the only sounds coming from the crunching of his feet on the dried brush. Storm ran around sniffing everything and marking trees whenever he had the chance. At one point he stood and looked off into the distance and Rafe stopped, waiting for the dog's cue. When he didn't make a sound and just continued on his way, Rafe guessed it was an animal that caught his attention.

Rafe always took a roundabout way back to town. In the off chance someone came across his trail, he didn't want it to lead directly to the cave. He often backtracked and would take different turns around trees that weren't necessary. If he hiked directly he was sure he could make it in just over a day. But that was a risk he wouldn't take for Charlie or Aiden. Storm also delighted in the new path every trip, giving him a million new smells and places to run.

Normally, Rafe would camp somewhere in the woods before getting to town, not wanting to walk during the night. Yet, this trip felt different. He wanted to push through. With Storm, he knew that they wouldn't stumble across any infected without warning. He kept his flashlight on the lowest setting, pointed at the ground. The moon gave a soft light, but it was blocked by the trees nearby. Storm finally slowed and walked with Rafe, realizing that walking at night was something they normally didn't do. His vision was far superior during the black night.

The first signs of the town began to show as they crossed an asphalt road, breaking into the fullness of the forest. Rafe decided to follow the road into town. Another thing he typically didn't do. But with the moon, he could follow the road without using a flashlight. He was on edge as he tried to be as quiet as possible. When he came to the first set of homes, he was careful to stay within the shadows. There was no knowing who had seen the wanted posters and who would turn him into the mercenaries given the chance.

Windows were lit in places, soft lights of lanterns or candles. Shadows of living people could be seen in some homes. It gave Rafe hope to know there were still living people in their homes. Though they didn't come out often, the safest way to be, they were still there. They weren't all part of the infected walkers, wandering aimlessly through the country.

Rafe headed directly for his normal hiding place. Issac had never failed to open his door to Rafe, letting him sleep in the dry cleaner. He would also bring the old man whatever provisions he could carry, knowing Issac couldn't get out as often as he should for food and water. Issac always said he didn't need it, but Rafe knew better. The old man would go without, making sure everyone else had what they needed before he did. He once remarked to Rafe that he had lived enough life, he was ready for what was to come. Rafe told him no one should want their life to end on the note of the plague. That had changed Issac's perspective, but not much.

As he rounded the alley that led toward the cleaners, Rafe was faced with bodies in the shadows. Storm's growl was low and menacing, but he didn't bound forward to attack. That told Rafe it was people, not infected. He immediately stepped back from where they had come from, hoping Storm followed without a whistle. Rafe didn't want to give away their position. He pressed his back to the building he was next to, hiding next to a large trash can that overflowed with disgusting waste.

He could now hear voices from the alley. He realized one was Issac. Storm came to Rafe's feet, still on alert and bearing his teeth.

"Shhh, Storm. Stay," Rafe said as quietly as possible. He needed to hear what was happening in the alley with Issac. Until now, the mercenaries hadn't come into town at night to look for Charlie and Rafe. They were clearly changing tactics.

"Boys, I've told you every time you've been in town, I haven't seen those two. Maybe they're dead," Issac could be heard saying.

"Old man, everyone we see says you know everything about what happens in this town. We know Duncan has been seen in town. How have you not seen him?" This voice was gruff and low, a new mercenary come to fight with Rafe.

"That's hogwash, kid. I rarely leave my place. How could I know for sure the comings and goings of anyone?"

"Listen, if we find out you're lying, you will pay for it. Our superior shows no kindness to those against the US Government."

"The US Government hunts down its own citizens now like this? What happens to local police? Trials? A jury of peers and all that fun?" Issac asked, his voice sarcastic.

Rafe cursed to himself. He knew Issac was a tough old man. But he didn't want him to push the wrong buttons with the soldiers he was faced with. Rafe knew firsthand what they would do to get what they wanted. They had no problem trying to use deadly force to get to Charlie, even if they weren't ordered to kill Rafe in the process. After killing most of the men that first night, Rafe was sure the orders had changed where he was concerned.

"If you see them, you need to let us know when we are here," the mercenary finished. Clearly, they didn't believe they would get information from Issac.

Realizing the conversation was coming to an end, Rafe wracked his brain on what he needed to do. He couldn't stay in his hiding spot; the soldiers could come his way and they would find him easily. Storm was itching to attack, his hackles high and his body prone for a charge. Rafe touched his head to get his attention and he realized he startled the dog when he turned and almost bit at his hand. Rafe looked at him in surprise for a moment before Storm realized what had happened. His ears twitched slightly, his head lowered, telling Rafe he was back.

Moving as quietly as possible, Rafe motioned to Storm with his hand as he slid along the wall away from the mouth of the alley. Suddenly Issac's voice could be heard again and Rafe froze to hear what was being said.

"I don't know why I need to do anything. I don't even know you are really the US Government," Issac said, defiance strong in his voice.

"Shit," Rafe muttered to himself.

He knew that Issac was trying to stand his ground but fighting with these men wasn't going to win anything. Things were quiet a moment. Rafe could hear murmuring between the soldiers. Suddenly the sound of flesh against flesh could be heard and a grunt as something fell. Without seeing, Rafe knew one of the men had hit Issac. Rage began to build in his gut, flowing through his veins like molten lava. They could come after him, an able-bodied man, all day. Rafe would give them the fight they wanted. But an old man, he should be off limits.

As a buzzing started in Rafe's ears he could hear the scuffle continue and he knew he had to act. He pulled two of his throwing knives and whistled to Storm, no longer worried about giving away their position. The dog lowered himself and began to stalk toward the alley. The go-ahead was all he needed to be prepared to handle the men that threatened them. Storm liked Issac as well, the man always having treats of some kind for the dog when they visited.

Rafe followed and just as they burst around the corner, Storm shot forward. He planted his front claws into the leg of the first soldier, causing the man to grunt in pain. And then sharp teeth were embedded in the calf muscle and the grunt turned into a scream. This caused the other soldiers to turn around to see what had happened, looking for the threat. Rafe took his chance of throwing his knives in the waning moonlight, unable to confirm he hit his targets. A curse and fall of one body told him one knife was true.

"No, Rafe!" Issac croaked from the ground.

Rafe could just make out the cut on his head and blood coming from his mouth. The livid rage that was in Rafe couldn't be contained. His hand went to his 9mm, pulling it quickly and pointing it at the nearest soldier. He shot him in the shoulder, knowing he wore body armor for protection. The shot spun the soldier to one side and the sound of the gun was all the mercenaries needed to pull their weapons. For a moment Rafe hesitated, wanting to get to Issac and protect him. Yet, there was no way to get through the attacking party without being killed.

"Run, boy! Run!" Issac yelled.

Making a split decision, Rafe called to Storm who was avoiding being hit by the soldier he had bit into. The dog turned at his name and raced after Rafe as they ran from the alley. Rafe zigzagged through buildings until they made their way into a neighborhood. His hope was to find an empty house to hide in until the soldiers gave up. The yelling and pounding of boots on the pavement behind him was a clear indication that they weren't stopping anytime soon.

Rafe ducked behind a hedge, hoping the men would rush by. He pulled Storm to hide with him and they waited, both panting from exertion. As they waited the group following them went by and discussions could be heard. Rafe listened, trying to determine their plan so he could go the opposite way. They were going to search the homes in the vicinity, sure they were hiding there. Rafe would have gone that way, but now he would backtrack once they started their search.

As the men got further away, Rafe stood in a crouch and began to go in the direction they had just come. Storm's bark was the first sign Rafe had that something was wrong. The second was the footsteps that seemed to come out of nowhere. Storm shot behind Rafe, causing him to whirl and find a gun pointed at his chest. The dog hit the man in the arm, going for the gun, but this soldier was prepared. He moved and kicked out, planting his booted foot cleanly on Storm's side. The blow caused Storm to slide to the side, whining in pain. It took everything Rafe had to not check on the dog, keeping his eyes on the gun.

"I knew you wouldn't just go into a house. So, I waited," the soldier said with a harsh laugh.

"Good luck doing anything about it," Rafe said as the knife he had concealed in his hand went flying toward the throat of the soldier. It embedded true and the soldier's eyes widened in surprise as he dropped his gun.

Rafe was just stepping forward to retrieve his knife when his world went black, a bag shoved over his head and arms roughly grabbing his. Storm began to bark wildly, his teeth slashing at whoever was holding Rafe. In his mind, he cursed at his stupidity. He should have kept running. He should have waited to move. He should never have come into town in the dark.

"Shut that dog up!" One voice called out.

"Damn it, you do it! He already bit my arm!" Another voice answered.

A thud could be heard again, and Storm's whine intensified. Rafe couldn't allow the dog to die with him. In his mind Charlie's face flashed, thinking of the worry she had over him coming into town. That picture caused Rafe to fight harder, getting one arm loose. Without his vision, he tried to use his hearing to strike out at who was holding him. His fist connected with something hard and he realized he had punched into the body armor of a soldier.

"Get his weapons before he does, idiot!" Voice number one yelled out.

Rafe's arms were grabbed again and roughly pulled behind him. He felt the zip tie and knew he was in trouble. Thinking again of Storm, his barking and whining were deafening, Rafe made his decision.

"Storm! Go home!" Rafe yelled.

The dog's noises went silent as Storm raced away. Rafe again was thankful for the training the dog had, knowing he would go straight back to Charlie and Aiden. He would be there to protect them when he couldn't. He could hear the panic about the dog disappearing. The soldiers' confusion around if they should try to follow the animal and wondering what home Rafe was sending him to. While other voices chimed in that they just wanted the beast gone, too many wounds from his sharp teeth already.

"Enough about the dog," a voice said. This voice seemed to be in charge because as soon as he spoke the other soldiers quieted.

"This man killed our brothers. We need to get him back to Callahan, he can decide what to do with him."

That was the last Rafe heard, before he was struck in the back of the head and his mind went black.

CHAPTER TWENTY-THREE

Alex

Clanging cans caused Alex to freeze in her steps. She looked around at Max, Griffin, and Marcus. With a sheepish look, Marcus looked up from the cans he had knocked to the ground. Alex just raised one eyebrow before following the cord of the obvious alarm system. None of them were looking for booby traps, but Alex realized then that Rafe would have found a way to alert himself to anyone approaching the cave.

Max stepped up next to Alex, whistling quietly under her breath. Alex looked at her, happy to see fewer shadows in her eyes. The talk they had the night before had created a vendetta inside Alex. When Max had arrived at the compound, broken not only physically but emotionally, Alex had known it was bad. Max had told them some of it when she told stories of Callahan looking for Rafe. But she had never given as much detail into the torture as she did the night before. Just thinking about it again made Alex feel sickening hatred in her heart, something she had never felt for anything in her life.

"Rafe definitely did this," Max said quietly. Then she gestured toward the trees ahead of them. "The cave is directly that way I believe. It's cut into that rock wall, but it's hidden by these trees from this vantage point."

"Then let's go and let our dear brother know that we aren't attacking him," Alex replied.

They carefully made their way through the trees. Alex was wondering why Rafe had the early warning system and yet he hadn't shown up yet to find out who had set it off. Maybe he wasn't at the cave just then and couldn't hear it. Alex's doubt was put to rest quickly. She wasn't sure if she heard the shot first, or if the tree five feet to her left started to shower bark, but she quickly realized they were being shot at.

"Get down!" Alex called. Everyone in her group ducked behind a near tree or rock formation.

"Rafe, you moron! Don't shoot us!" Max called out from her hiding place.

"I'm not Rafe," a woman's voice came back to them.

Max looked at Alex her eyes wide with surprise. Her sister then shrugged her shoulders and motioned for Alex to take over. Alex groaned inwardly, wondering when her sister would ever figure out how to handle people.

"So, then you must be Charlotte?" Alex said.

"Are you here to turn us in?"

"What? God no. We are here looking for our brother. Rafe Duncan. Where is he?" Alex said.

There was a long pause. Alex began to wonder if it was safe to show her face, or if she would look like Swiss cheese. She was just thinking about stepping out when Charlotte spoke out again.

"If you're who you say you are, what's the name of the plan? The plan your family has for the end of the world?"

"Sundown," Alex and Max yelled back in unison.

"Alex and Max?" Charlotte's voice held less malice now.

"Yes," Alex answered, knowing it was safe to show herself now.

When she looked to where Charlotte was standing, the woman looked small and scared. But she held the shotgun with confidence. It made Alex wonder if Rafe had been teaching the woman since he began to protect her. To be sure, Alex showed her hands were empty as she walked toward the woman. Alex took in the sight of the small beautiful Charlotte and started to wonder for the millionth time, who was the woman that Rafe was protecting?

"Could you put the gun down? I think we'd all feel much safer?" Alex asked.

Charlotte looked at the gun and put it down quickly, looking slightly embarrassed.

"I'm sorry I shot at you. But just so you know, Rafe taught me to use this and I would have hit you if I was trying to," Charlotte said, answering Alex's unspoken question.

"Thanks for the info. So, you're Charlotte Brewer? I'm Alex Duncan. It's very nice to meet you," Alex said.

She reached the woman and put her hand out to shake. Charlotte's hands were dainty, but her grip was strong and confident. Alex immediately liked her. Mitch Duncan used to say you could judge a person by the way they shook your hand. Alex had seen his hypothesis proven accurate many times in her life. And she would bet on the strength in this woman now.

"It's nice to meet you too. Please, call me Charlie. No one calls me Charlotte."

"Sure. Charlie, I'm going to have everyone else come out. Cool?"

"Yes, yes of course. I'm sorry. I need to get Aiden. Please come up to the cave," Charlie said as she turned away.

"Aiden?" Alex said to Charlie's back.

"You'll see," Charlie said with a slight laugh.

Max came from her hiding spot as Charlie walked away. Alex stood still, wondering where her brother was and who this woman was. There were too many questions in her mind. Max and the men came to stand with Alex.

"Well, that wasn't weird or anything," Max said.

"She was scared by the alarm, I'm sure," Alex replied.

She then motioned for them to follow and began the walk to the cave. It wasn't more than three minutes to get to the opening of the cave. Here they found the tarp and net pulled open for light to wash in. It was there that Alex and Max got their biggest surprise. Inside the cave, the small Charlie was standing with a small boy in her arms. Alex judged him to not be more than three or four years old. The boy had been crying, from the fear, Alex assumed.

"This is Aiden," Charlie said, turning so the group could see a small cherub face.

"Hold up one damn minute," Max said. She looked at Alex in astonishment. "Did you know about this?"

"Know what?" Alex asked.

"That Rafe got a woman knocked up and had a kid without telling us?"

"Wait, what?" Charlie interrupted.

"Our brother has never told us about his life here, friends, or girlfriends," Alex started to explain.

"Ok. I think we are having some misunderstandings here. First, I'm not Rafe's girlfriend. I've only known him just over a month," Charlie said before she started to laugh.

Max glared at her and Alex smothered the smile she wanted to show. Max wouldn't take kindly to being laughed at. It took Alex a moment to even catch on to what Max was saying and now that she realized it, Alex wanted to laugh as well.

"And the boy? Aiden you said?" Alex asked.

"Yes. Aiden. Can you say hi, Aiden?" Charlie asked the boy.

He laid his head on Charlie's shoulder for a moment before waving his hand at the group. Charlie turned and took Aiden to a corner of the cave. Now that Alex could focus on the entire structure, she realized Rafe and Charlie had set up quite the hideout. There was a laptop charging with a small solar battery. Stacks of canned foods and MRE's laid against one wall. Three beds were carefully placed near the back of the cave, where Rafe would have felt safest to sleep. And Aiden had a corner of small toys to play with.

After Charlie convinced Aiden that all was safe, and he could play for a little while, she gestured for the group of adults to follow her out of the cave. And out of earshot of the little boy.

"We found Aiden hiding in his home. In the bathroom. He was sleeping in the tub and eating whatever food he could reach. He says his parents went to chase the bad things away. We are guessing infected came to the home and they tried to draw them away. We saw the mother as an infected before we came here. The father is probably out there somewhere too. If not, he would have come for Aiden," Charlie explained.

"That's terrible. It's so good of you and Rafe to take him in," Alex commented.

"We couldn't leave him, not like the military did."

"The military? They found him?" Max asked.

"Yes. Aiden said he saw men in black with masks. They just found him and left him there, probably too concerned to find me."

"You? They are after you?" Alex asked.

"That's a very long story. Who are these two?" Charlie asked, motioning toward the still silent Griffin and Marcus.

"This is Griffin, Max's boyfriend. And this is Marcus, a friend I picked up along the way," Alex said, pointing to each man in turn. Both nodded to acknowledge Charlie.

"Speaking of long stories. Where is our brother?" Max asked.

"He didn't send you here? How did you figure out where we were?"

"This is one of the two places Rafe and I used to choose for our long camping trips. I knew he'd go somewhere he knew, that had fresh water and places to hunt," Max replied.

"The three of you are quite connected, aren't you?"

"I guess you could say that. So no, we haven't seen Rafe. Where is he?" Alex asked.

"He went into town. He left two days ago."

Charlie's face took on a slightly pale look as she said that. Worry crossed her features and Alex immediately saw that the woman cared more about her brother than she let on. She didn't have time to evaluate the situation, but she planned on speaking with Rafe to get to the bottom of things as soon as they found him.

"You're concerned. What is it?" Alex asked.

"Rafe and I have a deal. If he's not back in four days, I am to take Aiden and go straight back to the compound. I don't like when he goes into town. But he takes Storm. And I know the two of them are capable. I just worry about everything that can happen. Now you haven't seen him, but he would have been in the woods the same direction you came from I think. What if something happened?"

"I know our brother. He's smarter and tougher than anything he could face. He's fine. He'll be back just like always," Alex said.

"We easily could have missed him coming in. There are a bunch of different paths to take. If he even took a path we know of. Who's Storm?" Max added.

"My dog. Well, he's my dog now. That's another story. Are you hungry?" Charlie said after a moment.

The group sat around an early dinner of MREs, macaroni and cheese for Aiden, and canned fruits. Charlie chose to not delve into the story of how she and Rafe came together, saying she wanted to wait for Rafe, so they could all discuss what was happening. Alex studied her personality and how efficient she was with food preparation. She also was very good with Aiden, which was a surprise to Alex when she learned Charlie didn't have any small children in her family. Aiden clearly was attached to Charlie, turning to her for comfort or for food.

As they sat making small talk, a bark sounded far off from the cave. Charlie froze and listened. More barking followed, and Charlie was on her feet and out of the cave without explanation. Alex pointed to Aiden and told Marcus to stay with him, before she, Max, and Griffin ran after Charlie. She was fast for a small woman and Alex pushed to catch up with her.

"Storm! Here, boy!" Charlie was calling.

"Storm? The dog?" Alex asked, huffing while running to catch up.

Charlie nodded as she slid to a stop right at the place the alarm was set. She waited, listening again. Max and Griffin ran to a stop next to them and Max looked wildly around, her 9mm in her hand. Out of nowhere, a white dog bounded toward Charlie. Alex stepped back for a moment, mistaking the animal for a wolf. However, when he stopped in front of Charlie, panting hard, Alex realized it was a dog, a husky if she wasn't mistaken. She looked over at Max, who was staring at the dog in surprise.

Charlie knelt and rubbed the dog's head as he pushed against her. When her hands ran over the dog's side, it whimpered slightly and moved away. Charlie looked up, her eyes wild looking beyond the trees. She then moved closer to the dog again and tried to feel his side carefully. Storm whined, but he looked to Charlie with trust, a dog to his master.

"Where is he?" Charlie said quietly to Storm. The dog whimpered and put his head down.

"Why did the dog come back? Didn't you say he was with Rafe?" Alex asked. The panic rolling off of Charlie was infectious and it was settling in Alex's chest.

"He wouldn't have...Storm wouldn't have left Rafe. Unless Rafe made him. Or...."

"Or what?" Max demanded.

"Or he died. Storm wouldn't have left him otherwise," Charlie whispered.

As they spoke Storm seemed to become agitated. He pulled away from Charlie's arms and started dancing around yelping and barking angrily. Charlie stood up and watching him in confusion.

"He's acting strangely. He's never done this before. Rafe has always talked about his training. How Storm is an intelligent animal, sometimes even surprises him," Charlie said, talking to herself more than anything.

"Do you think he's trying to get us back into the woods? Like he's trying to take us somewhere?" Alex suggested.

Charlie looked at Alex hopefully, her eyes shining with unshed tears.

"That's possible. He's worked up about something. He wouldn't be like that if Rafe was dead."

"Then we need to go, now," Max said.

"I need to go with you. Storm won't automatically trust you. And I'm a doctor. If Rafe is hurt, I can help. We have a med pack. I'll carry that," Charlie said. She didn't wait for an answer, just turned on her heel and headed toward the cave.

Storm barked after her and she whistled him to her. Alex could actually see the dog huff in annoyance but still, he followed Charlie to the cave. When they entered again, Marcus was sprawled on the ground with Aiden playing with blocks. The little boy squealed when he saw Storm. The dog went to the boy, sniffed his head and licked his face before going back to Charlie. It was such a domestic action, Alex paused to watch.

"Aiden can't go. And he can't be left here obviously," Charlie said as she packed items into a black medical pack. "Can one of you take him home? Well to the compound? Would he be safe there?"

"Our kids are there. So yes, he'd be safe," Alex started.

"But if Rafe is in danger, we can't lose an adult right now," Max cut in.

"You're gaining one already. I might not be the fighter you are. But I've been learning, and I can help if anyone gets hurt," Charlie argued.

"Ok, ok. Let's discuss this," Alex said, holding up her hands to stop Max from continuing to argue the point.

Alex looked around at the four adults in her group. Max would never be convinced to leave without getting Rafe. Alex knew this because she felt the same way. That left Griffin and Marcus. She looked at the men for a moment and knew that Griffin needed to be with Max. After what her sister had endured, Max needed that support in a fight. Marcus was the last option. Alex looked at him still playing with Aiden on the ground and knew that was the best choice they had.

"Marcus, can I talk to you please?" Alex said. She led the way to the entrance of the cave.

"You want me to take Aiden," Marcus said before Alex could open her mouth.

"Yes."

"Ok," Marcus replied.

"Just like that? No arguing? Are you actually going to do it, or are you going to try and follow us anyway?" Alex asked. She was used to Marcus's antics.

"I wouldn't put that little boy at risk. If getting him home is a priority, that will be what I do."

"Ok. So, go straight back to the compound. We'll give you the directions. You might have to camp one night in the woods. Are you good with that?" Alex asked.

She realized a part of her was anxious about Aiden being with only one adult overnight in the woods. It wasn't that she believed that Marcus wouldn't do what was necessary to protect him should the need arise, but he was only one man. And he wasn't a

Duncan. Alex knew that she and her siblings were more equipped to handle tough situations than the normal person. Though Marcus had shown that he could shoot, build, and do a strange variety of things, he didn't grow up a Duncan.

"I know how to build a shelter and keep a boy safe," Marcus replied.

Alex gave him a nod of her head and they walked back into the cave. Charlie was busy packing up another bag and as she put toys in, Alex realized it was Aiden's bag she was packing. Aiden stood next to her, his face full of questions. Alex felt her heart twist for the boy. He had been through so much upheaval that month. Losing his parents, being taken in by Rafe and Charlie, living in the cave. And now here they were moving him again. Charlie looked at Alex, who pointed to Marcus. Without speaking Charlie knew the decision had been made.

"Aiden, are you ready for an adventure?" Charlie asked the little boy.

"What kinda adventure?"

"You're going to go on a hike with Marcus. Lots of fun things to find in the forest. Then you might get to camp under the trees. Wouldn't that be fun?" Charlie asked.

"Marcus? He's fun. Sure, that sounds like a good adventure," Aiden answered. He looked around at the adults. Despite his words, his face looked unsure. He looked back to Charlie.

"What about you, Charlie? You coming too?"

"Not this time, buddy. I have to go get Rafe. And then we'll meet you at home. Marcus is going to take you to our new home. There are more kids there. Wouldn't you like to play with some kids?" Charlie answered.

She knelt so she was level with Aiden. Alex watched the emotions pass across Charlie's face. The woman was attached to the boy and Alex could see how much she struggled to leave him. Alex could understand the feeling of being a mother to a child that wasn't yours. She had the same emotions when it came to

Easton and Candace. A new level of respect was starting to form in Alex's mind for Charlie.

Charlie put her hands on Aiden's shoulders as she gave him instructions to behave and listen to Marcus the way he listened to Rafe. She reminded him how it was so important to do what he was told immediately because there was so much danger out there. Aiden then threw his arms around Charlie's neck. Charlie squeezed him tightly to her and kissed his cheek before releasing him.

Marcus took the instructions he was given. Alex was appreciative when Charlie provided the topographical map and compass Rafe had left for her. Using that, Alex and Max were able to give Marcus a clear path straight back to the compound. They gave him the code to the door located on the back wall, which is what they were leading him to. If the military were watching the front gate, Marcus should be able to slide in with Aiden undetected.

Alex and Charlie watched as Marcus led Aiden away from the cave. The man wore his pack and carried the second with Aiden's things. They stood watching until they could no longer hear the chattering of Aiden as he talked about every plant and tree they passed. Alex noticed Charlie's hands gripped into her shirt by her sides as if she was holding herself still. She didn't know the woman, but she could imagine the feelings she was having. Alex laid her hand on Charlie's shoulder and squeezed. Charlie looked over at her.

"He has no one," Charlie said quietly.

"Not anymore. Now he has us," Alex replied.

"You Duncans. You are all a force, aren't you?" Charlie asked.

Alex had to laugh out loud at her observation.

"You could say that. We just want to be together. And we'll do whatever is necessary to make that happen."

"Then let's go get Rafe."

Alex wasn't sure what she had expected being out with Charlie. But the woman didn't slow them down at all. She was full of energy and seemed fueled by her concern over Rafe. They took turns carrying the medical bag, as Charlie was also carrying her own bug out bag on her back. Rafe had taught her a lot about necessities and survival during their time staying in the cave.

After a few hours of walking in silence, Alex called for a break and everyone found places to sit and take time to drink water. She watched her sister for any stress or pain. Max was good at masking things, so Alex had to watch her closely for any changes. When Max met Alex's eyes, she just nodded at her, letting her know she was ok. Then her eyes shifted to Charlie and took on a different look. Alex had a feeling Max was planning on mischief with the woman.

"So, Charlie, what are your intentions with our brother?" Max said loudly.

Alex almost choked on her water at the question just as Griffin spit his across the forest floor. Max had a slight smile on her face, clearly saying she knew what she was up to. Alex looked over at Charlie and saw her face had turned pink and she was looking down.

"You don't have to answer that," Alex said, attempting to save the woman.

"Why not? Seems we should know what's happening with our own brother," Max pressed.

"Rafe's personal life is none of your business, Max," Alex replied.

"Sure it is. Especially now. Come on, Charlie, give us the details."

"There's nothing to tell. Rafe is the man that has been protecting me. He's been kind and prepared. I'm not sure what would have happened to me without him," Charlie replied.

"So basically, he took you in when the dead started to walk?" Max asked.

"Not exactly. We came together before the plague started."

"Before? Why?"

"Max, that's enough. She already said it's a long story," Alex cut in.

"It is. And I think it would be best if Rafe was with me when I tell it. He has his own side of the story to fill in," Charlie replied.

"So, you have no intentions with him? Why not?" Max asked.

Griffin laughed out loud this time and Max punched him in the shoulder. He tried to stop his laughter, but he ended up snorting instead and that caused everyone to laugh as well. Suddenly, a bark from Storm stopped them all from laughing. Charlie shot to her feet and looked at the dog. Alex didn't know what was happening, but she followed Charlie's lead just in case.

"Storm is, how do I put this, well trained," Charlie said, whispering now as if she believed they were being listened to.

"Trained for what?" Alex whispered back.

"Rafe calls him his early detection system. He's good about notifying about the infected or any strangers."

Alex picked up her machete and pulled her 9mm from her hip. She waited and watched the dog for his signals. Storm growled and lowered his body to the ground, his gaze locked on the woods. The sound of rustling needles was the first sign of something approaching. The smell reached them next. Alex looked back to Charlie waiting to see what she would have the dog do.

"It's the infected, I think," Alex said.

"Storm, attack!" Charlie said to the dog.

The white dog took off like a shot, weaving through the trees to his victim. Charlie didn't hesitate to follow, and Alex was on her heels. She didn't need to look to know Max was following. Not far from where they had been sitting and laughing, the group ran up to find Storm attacking an infected. It was only one of a group of five that had stumbled through the forest. They had heard the living laughing not far away and it brought them closer to the living flesh they needed to feast on.

The infected that Storm faced was a small woman. Woman was a general idea, as Alex couldn't be sure. The small stature of the infected gave Alex the idea that it was at one-time a female. One month after dying the infected's body was decomposing in places, skin hanging from wounds that would never heal. The skin was gray and mottled with gore and filth from wandering looking for its meals.

Charlie didn't hesitate. She carried a knife that Rafe had given her. The blade quickly embedded into the back of the skull of the infected that Storm was attacking. The infected had been trying to grab the dog, but Storm just danced around its legs nipping at her, biting off fingers in the process. Alex had to swallow back the bile that wanted to rise in her throat as she saw the dog's muzzle covered in black and red smears.

Alex immediately slid into fight mode with her machete swinging down with a mighty strike against the nearest infected to her. The infected was larger and less decomposed than the woman. Alex pivoted from in front of the infected, to gain the angle to chop at the head. Wearing overalls and rubber boots the infected seemed to follow Alex easily. The quicker movements threw Alex off and she slid back the other direction, testing the infected. Its head followed Alex with no problem, though there was no intelligence or understanding in its black eyes.

Max joined her, with her tomahawk chopping at the temple of another infected. She looked at the infected that Alex was dancing with and looked at Alex as if she had lost the last shred of brains she had. Alex motioned to the infected to show Max what she was seeing. Max stopped after pulling her tomahawk free and was shocked when she saw the infected's hands shoot out and almost grab her sister.

Alex still was faster, but the faster infected reminded Alex of what she had seen almost a month ago before arriving at the compound. Infected that seemed faster. Since then she hadn't seen the same thing, making her think that it was just an off incident. Maybe an infected that was newly turned. Maybe they just seemed faster because she was panicked in the woods looking for her daughter Billie after she had run off.

Thinking of that time made Alex's steps falter. Billie had run off when she found out that Alex had not told her about her father being dead. Blake, her husband, had been the first infected she had killed. She had kept the secret from her children, protecting them, she had told herself. But when the explosive information was revealed, Billie had run headlong into a forest. A forest she hadn't known was crawling with the infected.

It was there that Alex had thought she had witnessed a change in the infected. Some seemed to run after their targets. They were faster as one almost took Alex out, knocking her to the ground where she was wounded. Though they were faster, the healthy humans still got away safely. However, since that time, in all of the infected that Alex had faced, none seemed to move like the faster ones she saw. With all of the other worries on her mind, she had pushed it aside and worked on what was right in front of her.

Alex, done with her testing, finally ended the large infected with a blow to its head. When she turned she found Max watching with her mouth hanging open. Griffin and Charlie stood over the infected they had dispatched. Alex cleaned her machete, using the coveralls the infected was wearing.

"What was that, Alex?" Max asked.

"Did you see it? How it moved faster than they normally do?" Alex asked.

"Yeah. It moved easier, though not smoothly like someone that's alive."

"What are you talking about?" Charlie asked.

The immediate issue handled, Charlie had turned to Storm to look him over. From where she was crouched with the dog, she looked up at the sisters.

"Before I got to the compound, we ran into a horde of infected. It was a mess of a situation. I thought I had seen infected that were almost running, but not quite. It was dark, and

I was panicked, so when I hadn't seen something like that again, I started to figure I just imagined it," Alex explained.

"But that was exactly like this? I mean it hadn't been running. But it turned and followed you quicker than anything I've seen," Max added.

"So, you've seen different behaviors? From the infected?" Charlie asked, standing up now.

"Maybe? I'm not really sure." Alex answered.

"This can't be happening," Charlie said, as she began to pace around the small clearing they were standing in.

"What can't be happening?" Max asked, standing in front of Charlie to try and make her stop.

"I can't be positive. I would need to see more of the infected. Compare them. But for changes like that, large changes, that could mean something in the disease is changing. And that's never a good thing."

"How could it just change?" Alex asked.

"Nothing about this pathogen is normal. I have worked daily trying to discover if there is a way to create a cure..." Charlie trailed off, stopping herself from saying more.

"And?" Max demanded.

"I haven't found anything that would work. The only thing I know is to prevent infection you must avoid a bite. If things are mutating somehow again, I have no way of predicting how that could manifest, " Charlie replied quietly.

"This is it. This is what Callahan was after," Max exclaimed, as she turned to Griffin.

He walked to Max to be a physical support if she needed it. Alex could see the wild look in her sister's eyes and knew she was seeing things she had been through. Griffin pushed her hair from her face and looked into her face. Max's hand gripped his wrist, grounding herself in the moment.

"Callahan?" Charlie asked.

"That's the man that threw me in a cell and tortured me. He

punished me for not telling him where my brother and sister were. He said Rafe knew things about the plague and he wanted what he had. I didn't believe it. Couldn't understand how Rafe was mixed up in something that was ending the world as we knew it," Max said, her voice soft and even.

"There's so much for me to tell you."

CHAPTER TWENTY-FOUR

Max

Her palms were hot and sweaty. She knew it, but Griffin held on tight anyway. They sat around a small fire listening to Charlie retell her story of the facility, meeting Rafe, her car being ran off the road, her house being broken into. Max believed every word the woman said, even without knowing her well. Not only had Rafe trusted her and taken her in, but Max had been tortured by the same man that was sending the soldiers after Charlie.

Alex had insisted on the fire, though Max had tried to argue. The fire at night wasn't safe. But after seeing Storm react to the infected, Alex trusted the dog to let them know of any intruders long before they showed. Max knew her sister was thinking of her, keeping her warm and comfortable as they heard how things tied together. A part of Max was thankful to know she wasn't tortured for nothing. It was true. Rafe did have information about the plague. He had Charlie. And Charlie's head was full of everything Callahan wanted.

"Rafe knew you would come to the compound. He also knew you were a force to be reckoned with. He believed the soldiers wouldn't bother you, because they hadn't come for him originally. They only wanted me. That's how we ended up hiding in the cave. We thought we were keeping you safe by hiding," Charlie said, finishing her story.

She looked at Max, her eyes full of sympathy. Max looked away, not wanting the sentiment. She did better with anger and the thoughts of revenge. Callahan's face was always in her mind, smug, with his perfectly straight white smile, pressed uniform, and impossible hair. Max fantasized about knocking the perfect teeth from his head. She lost herself in the idea of beating the sadistic bastard with her bare fists.

"Max?" Alex's voice broke into her daydream.

"Huh? Oh, what?" Max replied, realizing she had missed something.

Griffin squeezed her hand and looked at her. At least he didn't always show her sympathy. When she looked into his eyes now, she saw love. That she could accept, especially from him.

"I was saying, Rafe would never have stayed in the cave if he knew what had happened to you, Max. I'm sorry. He was so worried about keeping me and the information safe," Charlie repeated.

"There's no one to blame for anything but Callahan. Rafe did what he thought was right. As far as I'm concerned, he made the right choice. I trust my brother. He knows that the information you have is more valuable than my life," Max replied.

"No, it's not," Griffin cut in.

"He's right," Charlie said. "I don't think Callahan wants this information for the cure. I'm not even sure I can cure it. I haven't found anything that indicates it's curable. I think the man we call 'The Suit' is trying to cover their tracks. I have the proof that this all started in that facility. I have the proof that the government was working on chemical weapons and one went wrong."

Charlie's words hovered in the air, silence closing in on them. Max watched the flicker of the small flames. She then snorted and laughed ironically. All heads turned to look at her, even Storm.

"Dad was right. I can't even believe it," Max explained. When she saw a blank look on Charlie's face, she continued. "Our dad always said it would be the government that would kill us all. It wouldn't be some enemy from a different country. It wouldn't be terrorism. It would be our own government."

"I imagine he's laughing at us right now," Alex added.

"Well, I guess it's good that your father believed that. Because look at you now. You're ready for anything," Charlie said.

Max and Alex agreed, but everyone was lost in their own thoughts. Max wasn't sure where this left them. Even without knowing Charlie, Max knew Rafe wouldn't allow Callahan to have her. If she were to be captured, death was the only way for them to silence her completely. It was clear to Max now that the US Government had fallen to the plague. This faction controlled by 'The Suit' seemed to be calling a lot of the shots with the military. That gave them a fair amount of power over the country.

The fire burned out and they all climbed into their sleeping bags. They opted for no shelter building that night, so they could move faster if the need arose. They didn't want to leave too many signs of their presence through the forest. Rafe missing had everyone on edge. It was hard for Max to believe that Rafe was taken down by the infected. He was a skilled fighter and smart. He wouldn't be taken unaware by an infected. That left the military. And that option turned Max's stomach into knots.

They were moving before the sun had broken the horizon. Everyone had a silent understanding that they needed to move as fast as possible to track down Rafe. Storm had his nose to the ground everywhere. Max was partially expecting him to suddenly start running off and show them where Rafe was. Nothing was that easy, though.

It was when they arrived into town, driving the Bronco they

had retrieved, that Storm took lead. He barked once at Charlie and she watched him. He looked toward the alley that led the way to Issac's building. Charlie gave the dog a one whistle signal and he started trotting away. The group followed him carefully, watching for anyone that might be in hiding looking for them. Finally, at the back of the dry cleaner, Storm pawed at the door. It was quickly opened by a battered and bruised Issac.

"Oh my god, Issac!" Charlie exclaimed.

The old man ushered them inside before locking the door solidly behind them. He limped his way into the larger room and Charlie immediately opened the medical pack. She made Issac sit on the counter while she looked at the cuts on his face.

"What happened?" Alex asked.

"Those damn soldiers were back," Issac said, wincing slightly at the crack in his lip.

"They did this to you? Why?" Charlie said.

"I guess I said more than they liked. They were looking for you and Rafe again. I wouldn't tell them anything and then I might have opened my mouth. They have little patience I guess."

"Was Rafe here?" Charlie asked.

"Yes. Oh god, that boy should have gotten away. But he cut one of them and when they realized who he was, they all went after him. Leaving me here. I heard this morning from another survivor living nearby that they saw them dragging a hooded person with their arms secured behind his back. It had to be Rafe," Issac said sadly.

"Oh god. Was he alive?" Charlie asked, her voice taking on a panicked sound.

"I don't know for sure. But why would they have a dead man hooded? They didn't want him to know where they were going."

"Do you know where they were going?" Max asked.

"Not exactly. Some of us survivors keep in touch. We try to track their movements around town. They come from the east usually. That's my best guess."

Max began to pace, plans trying to form in her mind. They only had a general idea, but Max knew they would be going back to the safe zone that Callahan controlled. That would be east, then they would have to turn south at some point. If they could catch them before they got too far away, it would be easy to handle the soldiers and get Rafe back. Alex stopped Max from walking and pulled her to the side.

"What are you thinking?" Alex asked.

"We need to go now. Try to run them down before they get to Callahan. If they get back there, Callahan might not hesitate to kill Rafe."

"Ok. Let's go. They only have one way to get out of town and head the direction they need to go. They wouldn't know we are after them.

The sisters moved back to where Charlie was bandaging Issac and applying ointment to his wounds. The old man looked as if he was only putting up with the ministrations because he didn't want to upset Charlie. Max waited only a moment before breaking the silence, her patience on the very thin side.

"Is he good? We need to catch up with them. They are almost a day ahead of us."

"He'll be alright if he stays inside and rests. Can you do that, Issac?" Charlie said.

"Young lady, I'll follow whatever your orders are. You're the doctor. You know best," Issac replied, with a little wink of his eye that wasn't swollen half shut.

Charlie set Issac up with ice packs and medication to help with pain and swelling. As they were leaving Alex had turned back to the old man and told him they would be back to get him. He couldn't stay alone in town anymore. He looked like he was going to argue, but Alex settled it by closing the backdoor.

"Going to move everyone into the compound, Alex?" Max asked.

"Anyone that we can trust and needs help. Issac can't keep

fighting this fight out here by himself. He's better off with us," Alex replied.

"Maybe he likes to be alone."

"I don't think that's true. He enjoys the company when people are here. You can see it on his face. He would be better behind the walls with us."

Max had just scoffed at Alex and her streak of saving the world syndrome. It wasn't that Max didn't care about people. She did. She cared about her people. But it had never crossed her mind to offer a place for Issac to stay. Her sister, of course, knew what was right and did it without question.

Back inside the Bronco, Alex drove while Max sat in the front seat with a road atlas. The pages were bent and creased from use. Highlighter was streaked across some pages. Max knew from the stories she heard that this map got Easton and Candace to the compound after they were separated. The map now had a forever home in the truck for when anyone left the compound.

Max traced a path with her finger. It was the most direct route to get back to Callahan's base of operations. It was the way they had come to the compound. She felt if they followed that route, they had a good chance to find the soldiers and Rafe. She directed Alex as she drove, both sisters feeling panic at the prospect of losing their brother.

"The drive back to the safe zone is two days if they stop to rest," Griffin said from the backseat.

"Do you think they'll stop?" Charlie asked.

"If they don't believe they're being followed, they'll probably not rush," Griffin replied.

"Callahan would want them back with Rafe immediately," Max said quietly

"Rafe wouldn't tell him anything," Charlie said.

"No, he wouldn't. That doesn't mean Callahan wouldn't try to get it out of him anyway," Max said.

That image settled into everyone's minds. Max knew firsthand how it could be. Stopping them before they got back to Callahan was going to be the best plan. Max was lost in thought as she stared out of the truck window. The trees flew by and she barely registered anything. Suddenly she caught sight of something that made her sit up in her seat.

"Alex, stop!" Max cried out.

Alex slammed on the brakes causing everyone to sit forward against their seatbelts. Storm barked from the back indicating his dislike for the quick stop. In front of the truck were skid marks that started in the middle of the road and ended near the tree line. At the end, the body of a soldier was on the ground. Max looked at Alex who was studying the scene.

"That has to be from the men that took Rafe," Max said as she jumped out of the truck, her tomahawk in her hand.

Behind her the driver's door slammed, Alex joining Max to investigate. The sisters followed the marks on the street. Max bent and brushed her fingers across the black skids and decided they seemed pretty fresh. There hadn't been rain to wash away any of the residues and they were still dark against the lighter asphalt. She stood and joined Alex at the soldier.

Max used her booted foot to turn the soldier. Once he was sprawled on his back, they could see there must have been a fight. The man was bloody on his face and there was a cut across his throat.

"That could have been Rafe," Max said pointing.

"If he got ahold of a knife, yes. He could have been fighting to get out," Alex replied.

"How long ago do you think?"

"It couldn't have been more than four hours. Look at the blood on the ground. It hasn't congealed or anything."

Max began to pat down the pockets of the man, not hopeful that anything was left. If the soldiers were smart, they would have taken everything off of him before dumping him. Patting one pocket, she heard the crinkle of paper. She reached in and pulled out what was a piece of the wanted poster for Rafe and Charlie. Turning it over Max gasped.

"Alex, oh my god!"

Max held the paper to show her sister. On the back in what looked to be blood, the word "ALIVE" was written. Alex dropped to her knees next to Max.

"That has to be from Rafe," Alex said softly.

"He got loose in the truck and killed the soldier to slow them down and leave us a note. That has to be it," Max replied.

"Smart. But we need to hurry to catch up. He won't be able to keep killing people to leave them on the side of the road," Alex said.

With that, the sisters ran back to the truck. Max was barely in her seat before Alex jumped on the gas, the tires screaming on the road before they shot forward. Griffin demanded to know what was going on. Max showed them the note and Charlie took it from her gingerly. She stared at the paper, her eyes clouding with tears. It was then Max knew without a doubt that Charlie had feelings for her brother.

"Bodies as breadcrumbs?" Griffin asked.

"So it seems," Alex replied ironically.

CHAPTER TWENTY-FIVE

His head throbbed, and he fought the urge to throw up. Somewhere in his mind, he wondered if these were signs of a concussion. Not that it would be his first. As he forced his eyes open he realized he was still wearing the black hood the soldiers had put on him. With the sun up, the material was less dark, he could barely make out the shadows of four men in the back of the truck with him. Turning his head carefully he could see at least one in the driver's seat.

"He's awake," one of the men in the back said.

"Keep an eye on him. We can't lose him now. Callahan needs him," a voice came from the front passenger seat. Rafe added another in his count.

Six soldiers in the vehicle with him. His mind was foggy from being knocked out and he worried he was going to pass out again. His hands had long since lost feeling from the zip tie around his wrists. He tried to flex his fingers and couldn't seem to get any blood flowing through. He tried to evaluate the rest of his body. His head was the worst of the pain he felt.

Rafe thought about Charlie, hoping Storm had gotten back to the cave. She would have known he wasn't coming back. He had instructed her to take Aiden and go to the compound, find his sisters and be safe. Once his sisters knew the truth about what Charlie knew, they would keep her safe just as he did. He could admit to himself now, in the dark of the hood he wore, that Charlie meant more to him than the secrets she held. He wondered if he would have the chance to tell her that.

Thinking about his sisters, he realized they wouldn't give up on him. They would come after him. His mind circled around the implications of them looking for him with the military. Would they even know he was alive? Rafe wondered if anyone had seen him carted away by the soldiers in the middle of the night. Issac would have expected him to come back if he were ok.

He wondered about this Callahan they spoke about. Was 'The Suit' behind the name, or was this someone else entirely? His resolution was already set, there was no way he'd give up Charlie or any of the information she gave him. Though part of him guessed they weren't going to keep him alive no matter what he said. He was a liability who knew too much.

Ideas began to form and Rafe decided he needed to leave his sisters and Charlie a message if he could. He knew Alex and Max were smart. They wouldn't stop looking for him until they found him alive. If they found him dead, the world would come crashing down on whoever caused it. For now, he needed them to know he was alive. All pieces of his plan had to fall into place correctly for his message to get out.

Rafe began to cough, violently and loudly. The soldiers didn't care in the beginning. The sound of the coughing hid the noise of Rafe pulling the flyer he had in his pocket. When he had come into town on one of his trips, he had pulled down a wanted poster and kept it. He had meant to burn it, just to make a point and make him and Charlie feel better. But he never got around to it. Now it would be the medium for his message.

He could feel the warmth of blood where the zip tie had cut into his wrist in one place. He guessed they carried him by his arms, pulling his wrists taunt against the plastic. Carefully he used the blood to write his message. He hoped it was clear because it wasn't like he would have time to inspect his work. After it was written and had dried a few minutes, Rafe crumpled it in his hand for when he needed it again.

Using the little bit of sight he did have, he placed the four soldiers that sat with him in his mind. He created a map of the interior, so his movements could be accurate without him seeing perfectly. He took a few deep breaths, preparing himself. Then he started to breath harder, panting loudly. This sound drew attention from the soldier next to him.

"What the hell, man?" The soldier said.

"I'm going to puke!" Rafe called out.

"No, you're not, sit still and swallow it."

That voice came from the front seat. Rafe decided that was the leading officer. And he was clearly cold. Exactly what Rafe needed for his plan to work right.

"No, no, I can't. I'm going to puke," Rafe said, making his voice quiver with panic.

He then stood up, as if he was looking for a way out to empty his gut. The soldiers around him scattered to the sides of the large cargo area, trying to avoid any spray. That was exactly what Rafe had hoped for. With gagging noises, Rafe bent at the waist. Once, twice, and on the third thrust down of his body, he was able to snap the zip tie at his back. With no hesitation, he tore off his hood.

Immediately he was faced with four soldiers that looked shell-shocked at what he had just done. Their indecision was all Rafe needed to move. He snapped out with a punch, landing it solidly on the nearest soldier's face. The sound of his nose crunching was exactly what Rafe was shooting for. If he could escape, he would. But in his mind the calculations made that seem unlikely. The man with the injured nose went to his knees and Rafe turned to the next.

The second solider to face Rafe had exactly what he was looking for. On the man's utility belt, a bowie knife was sheathed. Rafe grabbed for the man's vest, yanking him in and down as Rafe raised his knee to meet his face. The blow glanced off slightly and hit the soldier's cheek. Slightly dazed the man stepped back, trying to defend himself. Instead, Rafe jumped to one side, grabbing the man by the throat and stepping behind him. In the confusion, he thrust the message into the man's front pocket before unsheathing the knife.

The truck slammed to a stop and if Rafe hadn't been holding onto the solider, he may have gone down with the jolt. The soldier from the front seat turned with a handgun pointed at Rafe.

"We need you alive, but that doesn't mean I can't maim you in some way. Do you want to be in pain the rest of the trip?"

"You think I'm worried about pain? Just kill me," Rafe replied.

The leader audibly sighed at his response.

"Do you think I'm stupid enough to be tricked into shooting you? Because you run your sarcastic mouth?"

"How about if I kill your guy?" Rafe said.

Before the gun-wielding man could answer, Rafe plunged the blade into the neck of the soldier, cutting across his throat. Rafe had to separate himself in his mind, putting the humanity away where he couldn't see it. Humanity would stop him from doing what he needed to do, would stop him from protecting himself the best he could. Any compassion he had for soldiers following orders had no place in the front of his mind right now. It wasn't something Rafe did naturally. He had to grit his teeth against any outward reaction to what he had done. He couldn't show the rest of the soldiers any weakness.

The wounded soldier grasped at his throat on the ground. Panic broke out in the back of the cargo truck. One soldier bent to try and save the man, while another knocked Rafe to the ground with a blow to the head. He didn't go out this time.

Instead, he was face to face with the man he had murdered. Rafe's eyes made contact with the soldier's. The disbelief and fear in the man's eyes, caused Rafe to wish that they would just knock him out. Or just shoot him.

"He's not breathing," one soldier said.

"We'll need to leave him here. Callahan doesn't bury the dead. Take his ammo and throw him out," the lead soldier said as he turned around in his seat.

"And tie that asshole up. Better this time."

Rafe watched as they checked the dead soldier for ammo. He watched the front pocket, willing the men to stay away from it in his head. When they just casually patted him down and left the note where it was, Rafe had to fight against releasing a huge gush of breath. Instead, he worked on regulating his breathing and really not throwing up this time. The second blow to the head was making his vision blurry. He wanted to close his eyes and go to sleep; however, he knew that could be a death sentence for someone with a concussion.

Moments later, the body of the soldier was left on the side of the road and the cargo truck was moving again. There was a general silence in the truck now. The soldiers no longer felt jovial with their catch. They were all quiet, thinking of their fallen brother and how easily Rafe had overtaken them. Rafe wondered if they would learn anything from this. He hadn't given away all of his knowledge, so he hoped he had the chance to escape again later.

An hour later the truck pulled over again. This time for the soldiers to eat their meals and take a bathroom break. Rafe was left with one soldier at a time, who pointed a gun at his head the entire time. Rafe disregarded the gun as if it was nothing more than a water pistol on a hot day. He ignored them as they changed shifts for each to have a moment to eat and relieve themselves. He tested his wrists, which were now zip tied and circled with duct tape.

Rafe couldn't be positive about where they were. The soldiers either didn't feel the need to talk or they wanted to make sure he had as little information as possible. He could tell it was midday and from the direction of the sun, he believed they were moving East. But that was only a guess from what little he could see through the windows and the doors when they were quickly opened and closed.

When the soldier's changed the third time, the man sitting across from Rafe was one he had been keeping an eye on. He was clearly a younger man and Rafe made him nervous. That made Rafe grin evilly at the man now, who paled as his eyes grew larger.

"So, this Callahan, he's your superior?" Rafe asked.

The man said nothing, just narrowed his eyes slightly at Rafe.

"Not supposed to talk to me, huh? I doubt I'm long for this world, so what's the problem with telling me anything?"

The soldier wasn't good at hiding his emotions. Rafe could easily read the doubt cross his eyes. This practical boy didn't know the final plans for the man he had helped capture.

"Don't think so? You seem surprised to hear that I'll probably be killed. Do you know why?"

"No," the man finally answered.

"What's your name?" Rafe asked.

"Smith," the man answered quietly.

"You seem really uncomfortable with me, Smith, why is that?"

"I'm not uncomfortable. You don't scare me," Smith said, his chin raising in defiance.

"Ok. Whatever you say. So, who's Callahan?"

"Major Callahan. He controls the military now," Smith replied. He clamped his lips shut quickly as if he felt that he had said too much.

"The military? Like all of it? Where are the generals and people that were in power before?"

"Where do you think? Dead."

"For sure? Communication has been down for weeks now. How does Callahan know he's in charge?"

"I don't question the Major," Smith said.

"That seems dangerous," Rafe replied.

"It's what I enlisted to do. Listen to my superiors."

"So, what does Callahan want with me? You have to know something about that."

"The information you have about the plague. You are keeping the cure to yourself," Smith said.

Rafe looked at the man in disbelief. It seemed the soldier really did just fall in line with his orders. He just blindly believed whatever Callahan fed him. Including that there was a cure for the disease that was wiping out humanity.

"That's ludicrous. I would never put the entire human species in danger to keep a cure for myself," Rafe scoffed.

"That's what your sister said too," Smith blurted out. Then he sat back in shock, realizing he had made a mistake.

Rafe's eyes snapped back to the soldier. He leaned as far forward as he could, staring down the young man.

"My sister? How do you know my sister?" Rafe growled out.

"Be quiet. Sit back," Smith said, waving the gun in front of Rafe.

Rafe was not phased. Fear and anger were raging inside his mind.

"What does my sister have anything to do with this?"

"I said be quiet," Smith practically yelled.

"You know something!" Rafe yelled back.

His fury was too much to handle. All he could see were his sisters' faces in his mind. He had no idea which one Smith was referring to. But the fear that one of them just didn't make it home, made Rafe homicidal. The humanity in him died as he thought of his sisters. Thought of them hurt or worse, dead.

No longer caring about the gun that was pointed at him, Rafe stood, large over the smaller man. Smith's hand with the gun shook and Rafe looked down at him menacingly.

"You saw what I did to the other soldier. I will do something even worse to you if you don't answer my questions."

"I'm the one with the gun," Smith replied, his voice shaky and uncertain.

Rafe stepped to the side suddenly, out of the aim of the gun. He pulled his leg up and side kicked the arm holding the gun. Smith grunted, the gun sliding to the far end of the truck. Rafe then stepped back in front of the man. When he tried to get up and get to the gun, Rafe kicked him in the chest, causing him to fall back into his seat. Then Rafe strategically placed a booted foot between Smith's legs, letting him know where the next blow would be if he moved again.

"Which sister?" Rafe bit out, his voice an icicle directed toward Smith.

"Ma...Ma....Maxine," Smith stammered.

"Max? Where is she? Did you hurt her?" Rafe said, pushing his boot against the man's groin. Smith involuntarily shrunk back and grimaced.

"I don't know where she is. She escaped!" Smith cried out.

"You didn't answer the last question. Did you hurt her?"

"I....I...."

"Smith, what in the hell is happening here?" The leading soldier bellowed. He had opened the door and found Rafe stepping on Smith's genitals.

"Sir, he...he attacked me!"

"We were just having a friendly conversation," Rafe said, nothing friendly about his voice. He also didn't remove his foot from Smith's groin region.

"Sit back down, Duncan!" The soldier yelled.

"Nope. I want to know where in the hell my sister is and what this prick did to her."

The sigh from the soldier was full of annoyance. The truck

shifted as he climbed in. With no one else in the truck, it was easy for him to strike Rafe for the third time in the head. This time Rafe didn't have a choice, his world went black again. The last thing he saw was Max's face. But it wasn't the face he knew and loved. It was the face of an infected.

Rafe couldn't tell how long he had been out this time. He awoke to chaos. The barrage of bullets woke him with a start. He was lying face first on the floor of the cargo truck. The door was wide open, and he was alone. That was the first thing that struck him as strange. They left him alone. And he wasn't tied up in any other way. His arms starting at his shoulders down to his fingertips were numb, telling him he'd been laying that way for quite some time.

More shots sounded outside and Rafe realized again that it was bullets that had woken him. He tried to turn himself, but he had to squeeze his eyes shut against the pain lancing through his skull. He looked around at the benches in the truck and quickly found a sharp edge on one. Working slowly to not make himself vomit, he moved into a sitting position, with the duct tape on his wrists aimed at the sharp edge.

He tried to work as quickly as he could. From the shouts he was hearing outside of the truck, they were dealing with a horde of infected. He doubted the soldiers were concerned with keeping him alive now. With no weapons and his arms behind his back, he was an easy take-out meal. He could feel the sharp metal cutting into the duct tape. He continued to saw until he felt the tape give.

Then needing to deal with the zip tie, Rafe stood and performed the same maneuver he had done earlier, breaking the tie after a few tries. His arms now free, Rafe bent at the waist and began to vomit onto the truck floor. He couldn't hold back the pain and vertigo he was experiencing from the head wounds. Once his stomach was empty and he was gasping for air, he realized he heard a different pandemonium outside now.

Yelling voices reached Rafe's ears. Voices he knew. He was

beginning to think his mind was playing tricks on him, his concussion-causing some sort of hallucinations. Putting aside what he thought he was hearing, he began to search the truck. In the front seat where the leader had been sitting, he found his weapons. Feeling lucky at the moment, Rafe took the time to strap everything on. He wasn't going to get eaten by the infected and he sure as hell wasn't getting taken by the soldiers again. He would kill every single one of them.

The sound of gunfire began to slow until it was only voices outside now. Rafe couldn't mistake them now. He pulled his 9mm and stepped to the open door of the truck. The soldiers fighting a horde was an understatement in Rafe's mind. When he looked out he couldn't count the number of infected heads outside of the truck. Luckily none of them knew he was inside.

Some were on the ground, tearing into the flesh of the soldiers they had taken down. Closest to the truck was the leader of the team. It almost seemed like he was running for the truck when the infected began to consume his meat, his arm was outstretched toward Rafe. The infected tore his flesh from his bones, shoving muscle, skin, and gore into their mouths. Some bent with their faces pressed against exposed places where the man's uniform had been torn. Rafe just stared, without much idea of the next steps to take.

Many of the infected seemed to wander away from the truck and Rafe could hear fighting still happening. But it was silent, the sounds of chopping and cracking of bone could be heard. Every once in a while, a lone shot would sound out, but the majority of the fight was quiet. Over the sea of infected, Rafe could finally see in the sunlight. And what he saw brought his entire life into focus.

Both of his sisters fought, side by side, killing every infected that came near them. Rafe could see Max's tomahawk fly as she wielded it with deadly precision. And his older sister, Alex, had a machete. Rafe had to smile at her choice of weapon. Only Alex would find something exotic and use it during the zombie apocalypse. There was a man fighting with them as well. Rafe couldn't be sure who it was, but he was clearly on their side.

A small blonde head pulled his attention from his family. Charlie was outside the truck they were driving, fighting the infected with all she had. His sisters were watching her, he could see them glancing her way often. Rafe could see she was wielding the crowbar she had from the beginning.

Seeing her fighting the infected gave Rafe a start and he could no longer stand in the shadows and watch. He pulled his own 9mm and shot the first few infected that were near the truck. The sound pulled the attention of some of the nearby infected, who turned in Rafe's direction. He was fine with that. He was primed for a fight after what he had been through that day. He jumped from the truck and immediately stooped to grab the rifle one of the soldiers had dropped. With a quick pull of the trigger, he knew there was still some ammo.

For safety, he shot away from his family, not wanting a stray bullet to strike someone. The noise he was making brought more infected his way. He easily took them down with the rifle. When it clicked empty, he pulled his hunting knife and started the dance with the undead. Minutes passed as the bodies continued to fall. Rafe took a few moments to pull his throwing knives and using them with deadly accuracy. He whirled and moved as blood and black gore flew from the infected near him.

Rafe was left, heaving for breath, in the middle of infected bodies everywhere on the asphalt. He looked over to his family and saw his sisters ending the last few infected that were in the horde. Now seeing them laying around, Rafe didn't believe there were any less than fifty infected. The soldiers weren't prepared to handle them, as he could also see the bodies of them laying around. He tried to count, but he thought one was missing. That was a concern.

However, first, he needed his sisters. The three locked eyes over the sea of infected bodies. Even at the distance they were at, he saw Alex's eyes fill with tears and Max smile like a lunatic. Immediately the three of them moved, stepping on the bodies in their way until they met in the middle. His sisters threw their arms around him, Alex at his neck and Max at his middle. He awkwardly tried to hug them back without them all tumbling into the disgusting gore that was across the ground.

"I can't believe we found you," Alex said, her voice full of tears.

"I can. He left breadcrumbs," Max replied sarcastically.

"You found my message," Rafe said.

"It was hard to miss," Alex replied.

Suddenly remembering soldier Smith, Rafe pulled back from his sisters. He looked at Max and gasped when he saw the green-ish, yellow bruises on her face. She cradled one hand and he almost saw red when he realized it was broken.

"That son of a bitch, where is he?" Rafe said, spinning around.

He moved around the infected dead looking at the dead soldiers. His sisters followed him, confusion on their faces. Grabbing the first soldier that he found, he flipped him over. Alex couldn't hide her gasp behind him because the infected had ripped most of the face off of the soldier. Looking down at the bloody mess, Rafe knew it wasn't Smith. He moved on to the next.

"Rafe, wait. What is it? What are you looking for?" Alex called as she tried to catch up to him.

"Smith, I need to find that weasel," Rafe called over his shoulder.

When his sister didn't answer, he turned to look at them. Max was frozen still and the man that Rafe hadn't recognized was reaching for her. Seeing the fear on her face made Rafe even more angry that he turned and continued to the next soldier. After searching he realized there were only five bodies. And the one missing was Smith.

"You saw Smith?" Max asked quietly.

"Little weasel soldier that was too small to look like an adult? Yeah, he was in the group that took me. But his body isn't here. He got away," Rafe replied.

He looked at the man standing with Max, his arm protectively around her. And it dawned on Rafe who the man was.

"Griffin?" Rafe said, surprise on his face.

"Yeah. Hi, Rafe. Long time," Griffin said as he held out his hand for Rafe to shake.

"Rafe?" Charlie's voice came from behind him.

He spun and looked at the small woman that he hadn't been able to stop thinking about. His vision swam a little and the pain was starting to return as the adrenaline drained from his body. Charlie must have seen the change because she automatically reached for him. Rafe took it as a sign that she wanted to hug him again and he wrapped his arms around her, resting his cheek on her head.

"You found my sisters," he said.

"Well, no. They found me."

"Oh. That's good."

It was then that something bumped into Rafe's legs and he jumped away from Charlie to reach for his weapons. The small bark brought his attention down to man's best friend that was waiting for his acknowledgment. Rafe immediately dropped to his knees. He hadn't been able to see Storm during the fight. The dog had clearly done his job because he was filthy.

"There's my good boy! You went home like I told you to. Good boy," Rafe said as he rubbed Storm's head where it wasn't wet with bodily fluid. The dog reached forward and licked his face.

"He did. Him coming home without you was what set us off to find you. He was a little sore, but ready to fight" Charlie said.

"Yeah, he took a couple of kicks before I sent him back to you."

Rafe tried to stand up, but he wavered. Sitting back on his knees, he took some deep breaths. Charlie made her way behind him and she cursed. Rafe tried to turn and look at her because he rarely heard her use foul language. She pushed his head back, so she could look at his wounds.

"You are a mess. How many damn times did they hit you?" Charlie asked.

"Uh, three I think? Twice where I passed out."

"You are bleeding all over yourself. I might need to stitch you up."

"Oh good, I'll owe you again," Rafe replied sarcastically.

"How do you feel?" Alex said as she stepped over to see what Charlie was looking at.

"A little woozy. And my head is starting to hurt again."

Rafe could hear Charlie murmuring to Alex. Alex walked away and the next thing Rafe knew, Griffin was hauling him to his feet.

"It's all good, man, lean on me," Griffin said.

Rafe didn't have much of a choice. As soon as he was on his feet again, his head swam, and he could barely see where the ground was to put his feet on it. Griffin had to practically drag him to their truck. Once there, Charlie climbed into the back and helped Rafe sit and lay on his stomach. She wanted the wound available to her, so she could work.

"Rafe, I'm going to drive the military truck. We could use it back home," Alex said, looking into the Bronco from the back.

Rafe didn't answer, just murmured in agreement. Any additional heavy-duty vehicles would be useful. He was glad he was with his sisters. They could think while he couldn't. They could make sure their family was taken care of while he couldn't think straight. While he let those thoughts flow through his mind, Alex reached in and ran her hand over his face.

"I was worried about you, brother," she said softly.

Rafe reached up and took her hand and pressed it against his cheek.

"I'm sorry. I wanted to protect you."

"They came anyway. We handled it."

"Did you kill them?" Rafe asked.

"Some."

Rafe felt sadness flow over him. He knew Alex would feel that pain the heaviest.

"I'm sorry."

"Stop saying that. You're my brother. I love you. I would do anything to protect you," Alex said. She leaned down and kissed his cheek.

"I know. It's just, this is so much worse than you realize."

"Charlie told us what she has. With what she has and what Max knows, we've put a lot of it together. You did the right thing protecting her."

Suddenly Rafe lifted his head before Charlie pushed him back down.

"Aiden! Where's Aiden?" He exclaimed.

"Shhhh, it's ok," Charlie smoothed her hand over the area where his head wasn't injured.

"He's probably at the compound by now. We sent him with Marcus," Alex replied.

"Marcus?"

"Another story, brother."

"We have so much to talk about," Rafe said.

"We have time. Rest now. Let Charlie fix you up," Alex said, closing the tailgate of the Bronco.

Rafe fought hard to keep his eyes open. Dizziness continued to wash over him in waves and he was worried that he would throw up again. That idea made him chuckle.

"There really isn't anything funny right now, Rafe," Charlie said.

"Wait till Alex figures out I puked in that truck," Rafe replied.

Charlie let out a light laugh at that and the sound warmed Rafe. Laying on his stomach, he couldn't look at her, but he could see her hands fussing with medical supplies. He reached up and took one of her hands and pulled it to him. He kissed her knuckles lightly. Her breath hitched and Rafe wished he could see her face.

"I'm sorry," he said.

"You're sorry? For what?" Charlie asked.

"I should have listened to you. Not left and gone into town."

"Well it's not like I had a good reason, just a feeling," Charlie replied.

"If I had listened to that feeling, we wouldn't be all the way out here. And you wouldn't be patching me up again."

"Patching you up is better than finding your body," Charlie said. Her fingers threaded with his, cradling their hands in her lap.

Rafe squeezed Charlie's hand again before she let go to work on his wound. She poured disinfectant across the gash and Rafe hissed at the burn. Whispered words of sorry and comfort came from Charlie and Rafe just wanted to wrap his arms around her. Her soft voice lulled him. While he knew that he shouldn't fall asleep, he couldn't stop the blackness as it swallowed him.

CHAPTER TWENTY-SIX

Max

Seeing Rafe resting peacefully gave Max some solace after what she had been through. She raised her eyebrow at Charlie when she saw them holding hands, but she fought the urge to say anything. When all she wanted to do was yell "I knew it!" She was happy to see her brother finding someone to care about. Charlie had already proven her feelings for Rafe by putting herself in harm's way to save him. Just as Max would do the same for Griffin if the roles were different.

Griffin stood off to the side waiting for Max. She went to him and laid her head on his shoulder.

"Smith," Griffin said.

"Smith," Max repeated.

"He's out there. I found a trail leading away from the road," Griffin said. He motioned toward the woods with his chin.

"He'll go back to Callahan. Tell him everything," Max replied.

"What do you want to do?"

Max thought about his question. What did she want to do? She couldn't even be sure that she would make the right choice with everything she had been through. Fear lanced through her when she thought about Callahan having any more information about her or her family. He would know now that they were together. He would send more soldiers to their home.

"We have to track him down," Max finally said.

Griffin nodded and went to reload his weapons. Max went back to the Bronco where Charlie was dressing Rafe's wound. She lowered the tailgate again carefully.

"We need to track down the solider that's missing. Can Storm help with that?" Max asked.

The dog was sitting outside the truck, waiting for his companions to make a move. At the sound of his name, his ears twitched. He jumped to put his paws on the back bumper of the truck. Max could clearly see his gaze on Rafe and if she wasn't imagining things the dog looked concerned.

"We've never had him track anyone. But he's proven to be trained in a number of things," Charlie replied.

"Will he go with us?"

Charlie seemed to think about that for a moment before looking at the dog.

"I think if I give him the command to follow you, he will. He's good at giving warnings when the living or the dead are nearby."

Max nodded and waited for Charlie to talk to the dog. She rubbed his ears and head, letting him know they were all proud of him. Then she pointed to Max and told him to follow. As Max moved away from the truck, the dog heeled easily and seemed to be waiting for his orders. The pair met with Griffin again at the edge of the woods. He was kneeling down near footprints he had found in the softer soil.

"See here, these are pointed out of the forest, unlike the others from the infected when they were coming out. The infected wouldn't have gone backward," Griffin explained, pointing to what he was looking at.

Max agreed with his findings and they started to walk into the forest. A call from Alex stopped Max in her tracks.

"Max, are you sure you should be doing this?"

Max spun to meet her sister's eyes. Her first instinct was to be mad at the implication that she was weak and couldn't handle tracking down one weasel. But when she looked at Alex, she could see her sister was only concerned for her.

"I need to. We can't have Callahan getting an update from him. Griffin will be with me. We'll handle it," Max replied. And then more softly she added, "Don't worry, Alex."

Alex stared at her for a moment before nodding her head. Max knew she didn't need her sister's approval to do anything. They were all trained in the same lessons, the same talents, the same knowledge. All three Duncan siblings were capable of protecting themselves as well as the family. Max knew that Alex was thinking about the different ways those tasks got completed by each of them. If she was honest with herself, Max didn't know how she was going to deal with Smith when they found him.

Under the shadows of the trees, the silence ground on Max's nerves. Storm stalked at her feet, his nose to the ground. Without being given direction it seemed the dog knew they were looking for something or someone. He immediately went into search mode. Griffin walked slightly in front of Max, looking for additional footprints or signs of anyone moving away from the road in the trees. The shadows of the trees provided too many places for someone to hide if they wished.

Suddenly, Storm barked and took off like a streak. Max froze for a moment, waiting to see what the dog was after. However, as he started to wind through trees, she took off at a run to follow. Griffin was close behind, both of them holding their weapons, preparing for anything. The barking of Storm pulled them closer to his location. Before they reached the dog, a human cry let out as snapping teeth could be heard.

Max came to a sliding halt in a small clearing where Storm had Smith pinned to the ground. The dog had his teeth on the soldier's shoulder, but Max could tell he didn't bite down enough to wound mortally. Again, Max found herself wondering where her brother had found this dog that seemed to just know what his companions wanted from him.

"Storm, off," Max said, snapping her fingers and bringing the dog back to her. He easily obeyed, accepting that Max was now part of his pack and he was to listen to her.

When Max looked at Griffin, she knew her face was pale. She tried to control the shaking of her extremities, but it took everything she had to not just shoot Smith where he laid. Griffin stepped up to her and placed a warm hand on her shoulder. His fingers slid to her neck, where he massaged for a moment. His touch had a calming effect on Max, reminding her she wasn't alone here. Not alone in dealing with Smith.

"Don't let the dog hurt me," Smith gasped out.

"Did he already?" Max bit out.

"I don't think so."

"Well stop your whining, you would deserve that and more if I had my say," Max said.

Smith lifted his head and looked at Max. She could see it was then that he realized who had come after him and a new fear crossed his features. His eyes moved to Griffin as he crawled on his hands and knees to a tree to help him to his feet. Griffin stepped toward him, fury flashing in his eyes. Max knew he was seeing how he found her, hanging in that torture room. She had been delirious, injured, and broken inside. At that time Griffin had given Smith some of his own medicine, the bruises from that encounter still showing on Smith's face.

"Are you going to kill me?" Smith stammered.

"We should," Griffin replied simply.

"Why do you do what you do?" Max asked. It wasn't the question she meant to ask. But once it was out of her mind, she realized she wanted to know.

"What?" Smith asked.

"Why do you do what you do? Why are you causing pain and havoc? You don't seem to enjoy it," Max said.

"I'm just following orders."

"So you blindly follow orders, even those that are wrong? Like beating a woman for information she doesn't have?" Griffin said. He continued to move closer to Smith, his rage uncontrollable.

"He...Callahan...he would have killed me, or anyone that didn't do what we were told."

"So it was ok to kill her?" Griffin roared.

Max flinched at the noise and looked around to ensure there are no infected. She looked down at Storm who was focused on Smith. If the dog wasn't reacting to anything else, Max felt confident there were no other threats nearby. When she looked back to Smith, Griffin had him by the back of his uniform. He pushed the man into the clearing again, so he could no longer hide behind trees. Griffin pushed him to his knees and held a gun to his head.

It felt like an out of body experience for Max. She watched Griffin take the actions he was taking, she knew what he intended to do. Part of her was happy. She wanted Smith gone. She wanted one less threat to her family to be walking. She wanted to satisfy the hunger for vengeance in her heart. Yet, as she looked at Smith, a man that couldn't have been in the military but a year or two before the plague, Max felt something twist. The soldier shook like a leaf and squeezed his eyes shut, waiting for the inevitable end to his life.

"Griffin, stop."

Griffin looked at her in surprise. His face was hard lines and it made Max sad that something was broken inside him too. She was the one beaten, but everyone suffered from the wounds she carried.

"We can't kill him. We aren't cold-blooded killers, Griffin."

"We can kill him. It's not cold blood. It's self-defense," Griffin shot back.

"He's on his knees. How is that self-defense? This is about revenge," she said softly.

She walked to Griffin's side. He watched her, trying to read her eyes. Storm followed, his beautiful eyes never leaving Smith's face. When Smith looked at the dog, Storm would bare a threatening smile of sharp teeth, begging to dig into the enemy. Max gave the dog the command to watch and she almost laughed ironically at how Storm did exactly that. He was almost nose to nose with Smith by the time he settled into his watching mode. Smith couldn't have gotten away if he was the world's fastest track star.

Max turned back to Griffin. He still held his gun point blank at Smith's head. Her unbroken hand circled his wrist and pulled the gun away from Smith's head. She looked up into his face, the face she had loved all those years they were apart. His hazel eyes, the exact shade of their daughter's, were full of anguish and anger.

"I know. I feel it too. I hate what they have done. But what does it say about us if they can strip us of our humanity? We aren't natural killers, Griffin. We do what we have to, to protect our family, our people. This isn't that."

Griffin seemed to want to speak, but he made a choking sound instead. He pulled Max to him and crushed her against his body. Max let him do what he needed, as he buried his face in her neck and breathed deeply. She patted his back, trying to soothe his pain. He carried guilt that she had tried to take from him, but he refused to let it go.

"Nothing that happened to me is your fault, Griffin. It was Callahan. What we do going forward, those are our choices," she whispered against his cheek.

Griffin finally nodded his head and pulled back. His eyes were red from unshed tears. It made Max even more angry at the situation, but she couldn't bring herself to kill the man at their feet.

She moved to be in front of Smith's eyesight again. The man looked at her and back to Storm in a comical fashion. He couldn't decide which was a bigger threat and his fear was too physical at the moment.

"Storm, heel," Max said, to ease the man's panic a bit. Griffin stayed behind him, so he wasn't going anywhere.

"Here's how this is going to go, Smith. Listen carefully. You are going to be our prisoner. We aren't killers. But we also can't have you running back and telling Callahan what you know."

"I wouldn't..." Smith started.

"Don't interrupt her," Griffin growled from behind him, causing Smith to flinch forward.

"Yes, you would. So, lying about it isn't going to change anything. You've already proven you will do what you need to, to survive, to save your own ass," Max continued.

"Where are you going to take me?"

"That I haven't figured out yet. But I'm sure we can find something secure between the truck you were driving and the supplies we have at our home. Understand you aren't a welcome guest and your life is only being spared at my kindness. Even after what you did to me, I'm sparing your life," Max said. She leaned close to him, making sure her point was being taken clearly.

"I...I understand," Smith said quietly, his eyes down in surrender.

Griffin continued to keep his gun pointed at Smith as they wound their way back to the road. Storm stayed at Max's side, prepared to fight or defend however he needed to. Max took a mental note to talk to her brother about the dog. There was something comforting having the beautiful creature watching your back. And it felt odd to give an animal such trust.

Despite her decision to keep Smith alive, Max kept her distance from the man. His face was a painful reminder of what tortures had happened to her at the orders of Callahan. The scared part of her believed this man was going to turn and hurt her again. She had to grit her teeth against changing her mind and letting Griffin bury the man in the forest.

When they arrived back at the vehicles, Charlie and Alex waited. Their reactions to Smith were vastly different. Charlie's face colored red, while Alex nodded her head in understanding. Max knew without saying anything that Alex would agree with the decision made. But Charlie seemed of a different mind.

"Why is he here?" Charlie asked.

"He's our prisoner," Max replied.

"Prisoner? Why aren't we just leaving him for the infected or killing him ourselves?"

"Because if he somehow makes it back to the save zone, he can tell Callahan everything. And we aren't killers, Charlie," Max explained.

"Rafe isn't going to like this," Charlie replied, crossing her arms in front of her. Max realized she had a stubborn streak. She wanted to laugh about it, but she decided to save it for another time.

"Maybe he won't. But this was my decision to make. And it's the one I'm going with," Max said.

"I'm proud of you, Max," Alex said, breaking the tension. Charlie looked at her wildly but didn't speak. She smartly realized she wasn't going to win the argument, especially when the sisters agreed on something.

"We aren't killers," Max repeated.

On advice from Charlie, they decided they couldn't drive all the way home that day. Rafe needed to be stable with his head injury and she doubted the drive would be smooth enough. Max and Alex agreed, and they pulled the vehicles off the road a mile down from the infected carnage. Rafe slept through the movement of the vehicles and the noise they made as they prepared a small camp.

Dinner time came, and Max worked on MREs for everyone.

The routine tasks helped clear her mind of the cloudy chaos. Griffin had insisted that Smith didn't leave the military truck. He was secured with each arm separately attached to the truck bench with zip ties. Though it was extremely unlikely he would get out of the ties, Griffin stood guard at the truck with his rifle at the ready.

Max didn't doubt that given a reason Griffin would kill Smith. And she wanted to save Griffin from that. Smith's life meant nothing to Max. Her hate for him was real and radiated throughout her body. Yet, she believed their humanity, how they were going to live from now on was important. If they gunned down every person that crossed them, bodies would stack up. And so would the guilt of actions being taken.

Meals prepared, Max took one to Griffin. He began to eat standing up. Without saying anything, she started to open the truck door.

"Max, what are you doing?" Griffin asked.

"We aren't going to starve him to death either," Max replied.

"Do you think this is safe?"

"You'll be standing outside, right? I'll scream if there's even the smallest hint of danger," Max said. She flashed him a small smile and stepped into the truck.

It was dark inside. The front of the truck was pointed toward the trees and the shade blocked any sun from seeping through the windows. Smith looked at her warily when she sat across from him. She sat and studied him for a minute.

"When did you eat last?" Max asked.

"Yesterday, I think."

Max mixed the beef stew she had in front of her and watched as Smith's eyes went to the bag. She pulled the spoon out with a bit of stew on it. Holding it across the gap between them she waited for Smith to lean forward to take the bite.

"You're feeding me?" Smith said after swallowing his food.

"If we weren't going to shoot you, why would we starve you.

Plus, I thought we could have a tit for tat here," Max said. Smith's regarded her warily.

"How old are you?" She asked.

"Nineteen."

"That's younger than I had guessed. So, did you even finish boot camp?"

Smith shook his head no, as Max held out another bite to him. He quickly took it and swallowed. Max guessed he wanted to take the food while it was being offered since he couldn't be sure they would always feed him.

"So you were immediately brought to the safe zone, to report to Callahan?"

He looked at her for a moment and Max just sat stirring the stew. Seeing his hesitation, Max pulled out some of the other foods that came in the MRE. She put a bottle of water down next to her. Then she pulled out a brownie, pretzels, and bread. Smith stared at the items and then back to Max again.

"I'm sure you're thirsty," Max said. When Smith didn't answer she continued, "This is how tit for tat works, Smith. I ask questions. You give me answers. You get food and water."

"I...I can't betray my government," Smith stammered. Max could see the war between his need for loyalty and his need for food.

"Callahan isn't the government. The things he's doing, they aren't for the betterment of the country. They are to take over what's left."

"That's not true. Callahan is getting his orders from somewhere. I've heard him on a satellite phone."

Max raised an eyebrow at the offered information. Smith seemed to realize suddenly that he had said too much before he clamped his lips together.

"So back to my question. Were you just swooped in and brought to Callahan?"

"Callahan sent men to get us. He took us. Brought us to his safe zone," Smith replied.

Max nodded, forming a picture in her head. She unscrewed the cap of the water and held the bottle to Smith's lips. Giving him just a sip, she sat back again. Callahan was taking orders from someone. Max could guess that was 'The Suit' Charlie had told them about. And he wasn't following any sort of procedures. Just grabbing soldiers wherever he could. Callahan had to know that taking barely adults from boot camp would give him an army of malleable people to follow his every order.

"What did Callahan tell you about my family? About why you were torturing me?" Max asked.

Smith seemed to think about answering. So as an incentive, Max opened the snack bread, taking a piece from the package. She held it in Smith's direction, letting him know an answer meant a piece of bread.

"He told us you were keeping the cure from the government," Smith said.

"Well that's ridiculous," Max replied. She leaned over and put the bread in Smith's mouth. The man chewed and swallowed quickly, waiting.

"How would we know that it was ridiculous?" Smith asked.

"By using your brain? Why would anyone keep a cure to themselves and just let everyone die horrible deaths like this? My family, we aren't political. We aren't military. We aren't associated with the government in any way. What would we gain from keeping the cure?"

Smith seemed to mull this over. Max wondered if a part of him felt ashamed of what he did. She fed him a few more bites of the stew and another piece of bread before asking another question.

"So what will Callahan do if none of you return?"

"I guess the same thing he always does. Send more men.

Larger groups each time," Smith answered easily this time. He was rewarded with a large gulp of water.

"Since I escaped, what have you heard about my family?"

"He was so angry when you escaped. The men that were on the watch that night...well..." Smith stammered.

"Well, what?"

"They disappeared. Just gone."

"What do you think happened to them?" Max asked.

"There were rumors of course. We don't have people go AWOL often, you know absence without leave," Smith explained.

"I'm aware of what AWOL means," Max said sarcastically.

"Right. So there were rumors. I never saw anything myself. But the rumor was Callahan took them off post himself and shot them," Smith finished.

Max wasn't surprised at that information. Callahan was cold blooded. He would do anything he wanted in the running of his post. And as it seemed he wasn't reporting to any official government entity, he could get away with it. Max fed Smith the last few spoonfuls of the stew.

"So what else did he say or do after I escaped?"

"I'm not sure..."

"Don't clam up on me now, Smith. You won't be going back there, so Callahan will assume you're dead. The information you're giving me will never be routed back to you," Max said. She wasn't positive any of that was true. Protecting Smith from Callahan was the least of her concerns. Smith sighed and pointed to the water. Max gave him another sip before placing the cap back on.

"He told us that you escaping and working against us was a sign that you knew where your brother was and what information he had. You were added to the wanted list, along with Rafe and Charlotte Brewer. He put a bounty on you and the men you were with."

"Didn't you ever wonder why he was so quick to kill those that apparently had information about the cure? Wouldn't he need what we knew?" Max asked.

Smith seemed to think about that, looking down at his feet. Max knew she had given him enough to think about. As they were taking him with them, she would continue to press for more information. The boy was easily manipulated by Callahan, and the Major kept him close. Max knew there was more information in his head. She let him finish the water and even fed him the brownie before leaving the truck.

The sun had almost set when she exited. Griffin was waiting for her, as she knew he would be. Alex stood off to the side, also waiting to see her sister. Max guessed Alex was concerned about her resolve to not kill Smith. Griffin stopped Max first and made her look him in the eyes.

"I'm fine. Everything is fine," Max said to reassure him.

"Are you sure?"

"Yes. Are you going to stay out here all night? I was getting used to you sleeping next to me," Max joked. Her banter had the desired effect, making Griffin smile.

"I think we can rig the doors from the outside to keep him in. We'll lock the interior gate between the bed of the truck and cab. Then we'll rig the doors outside. That way we can let him loose, so he can sleep," Griffin explained.

"That's a good idea. I'm going to talk to Alex. I'll see you when you're done."

With that, Max kissed him softly and met with her sister. Alex immediately hugged her. Max, though never one for a lot of affection, could always use a hug from her sister. She hugged Alex back just as hard. When they separated, Alex searched Max's face much like Griffin had. It made Max snort.

"You and Griffin. You're both worried I'm going to fall off of some ledge and going on a killing spree. Don't worry, dear sister, you aren't on my list," Max said.

"I'm not worried about a killing spree, Max. I'm just worried about your emotional health."

"Does anyone have emotional health right now, Alex?"

"I guess not. Help me set up some areas to sleep?"

It was easy to slide into setting up camp. It felt natural to work side by side with her sister. They needed three beds as Charlie insisted on sleeping in the Bronco with Rafe. She said it was in case he woke up and was in pain. She also wanted to keep waking him often to make sure his concussion didn't make him never wake up again. Max and Alex shared a smile over Charlie's bumbled explanation of why she wanted to sleep with their brother. The little blonde's fair skin turned a nice shade of pink before she just turned away and went back to the truck.

They had parked the vehicles in a v, leaving one open side. The open side was toward the road, making sure nothing could easily sneak up on them from the forest. As the sun went completely down and the area went pitch black, they used a lantern on a very low setting and hidden under a truck to see to the last of their set up. Everyone had their weapons next to them and flashlights in case. Their early detection system, namely Storm, slept near their feet.

Max rolled in her sleeping bag, so she was as close to Griffin as she could be. He held out his hand for hers and they entwined their fingers.

"Thanks for following my lead today," Max whispered.

"We are a team, baby. I might not always agree, but we work together."

She didn't expect to sleep well that night. It took time. She heard Griffin's breathing deepen as he fell off. Even Storm could be heard lightly snoring. Max couldn't stop thinking of Callahan and the threat he was to their family. When they reached the compound, they would all have a lot to discuss, as they decided the way to move on in their survival.

CHAPTER TWENTY-SEVEN

Sunlight shone into the back of the Bronco, waking Rafe. The pain in his head was still there, but it wasn't as glaring as before. He had shifted, only to encounter someone sleeping next to him. Blonde hair spilled across a makeshift pillow. There was no mistaking Charlie, her small form curled on her side facing away from Rafe. He laid and watched her a moment before he noticed Alex looking through the window at him.

He had carefully climbed out of the truck to meet his sister. Alex hugged him again, longer this time.

"Hey. I'm fine," Rafe said.

"I know. I just needed this. I've been so worried. Seeing the house damaged, I was afraid..." Alex trailed off as she pulled away.

"What's wrong with the house?"

"You weren't there when it happened? When I got there the front wall was burned. Luckily, it's not a load bearing wall, so we have been rebuilding it."

"Burned? No. That didn't happen when I was there. They probably went back looking for us again after the first attack."

"Charlie told us about that. She was quite impressed by your fighting skills," Alex said with a silly grin.

"Stop it, Alex," Rafe warned.

"Stop what? I didn't do anything."

"What didn't she do? I probably did it," Max said as she walked up. She also hugged Rafe again. But her's was tight and quick. His little sister, never one for overly affectionate moments.

"Our brother doesn't want me talking about Charlie," Alex explained.

"Leave it be, you two. There's nothing to tell," Rafe said. He led them further away from the truck, afraid they would wake Charlie with their conversation.

"She cares about you, Rafe. There's nothing wrong with that," Alex chided.

"She cares because I've been taking care of her. That's all it is. She feels like she owes me," Rafe replied.

Their conversation was cut short when Griffin walked by with Smith at gunpoint. Rafe saw red as soon as the man entered his vision. Smith saw Rafe at the same time and shrank away. Griffin noticed Smith's movements and he looked around. Rafe began to walk toward Smith, his fists balled at his sides. He wished he had his knives strapped to him. In his mind, all he could think of was hurting Smith the way he was sure they hurt his baby sister.

Griffin stepped up to Rafe to stop him. He handed his gun to Alex who led Smith the rest of the way to the truck. They stepped up where Rafe could no longer see what was happening. Griffin kept a hand on Rafe's chest.

"You need to talk to Max," Griffin said simply.

"What is he doing here?" Rafe yelled.

"Rafe, calm down. Jesus, you have a head wound. Relax," Max replied, rolling her eyes.

"Max. I'm going to kill him. Get out of my way," Rafe said to Griffin as he pushed his arm away.

"No, Rafe. Stop it. We aren't going to kill him. We're going to use him for information. We'll lock him up back at home. He's really just a child. Nineteen-years-old. He has done bad things. I know that. But I do not want blood on anyone's hands," Max said. She stepped in front of Rafe now. She looked up with her blue eyes, so similar to his.

"He hurt you," Rafe replied.

"Yes. Under orders. I don't think he would hurt anyone if he wasn't ordered to. He's too scared. He's already told me some things. I know I can get him to tell us everything he knows about Callahan and 'The Suit'."

Rafe tried to rein in his fury. His thoughts were running rampant with hurting the man. The sensible part of him said he knew where Max was coming from and she was right. And in the end, it was the choice for her to make. He looked at Griffin and without saying anything he could tell he was also barely restraining himself. Rafe started to calm a bit, deciding that if Smith was imprisoned with them then maybe he would get a little payback.

"Hey, wait a minute. I didn't get to ask. What are you doing here?" Rafe asked Griffin.

Looking between Griffin and Max, he could tell some things had been happening that he wasn't privy to.

"Well, I went and got him," Max said.

"And?" Rafe prompted.

"He knows everything. He knows that he's Jack's father. I also found all of the letters from him that Dad hid from me eight years ago," Max explained. Rafe looked at her in surprise. Then his instincts to protect came back.

"And, what do you think about being a father?" Rafe asked Griffin.

"I'm quite content with it actually. Jack is wonderful," Griffin replied, a lopsided grin on his face. He slid an arm around Max then and Rafe raised an eyebrow at them.

"Yes. Before you say anything, this is also happening," Max said pointing between herself and Griffin.

"Oh, well I see. We'll have to have a conversation later, Griffin. About your intentions and all that fun," Rafe said. He kept his face very serious while Max's face colored.

"Rafe Duncan, why are you up and walking around?"

Rafe's wince made Max laugh out loud. She and Griffin walked away, leaving Rafe with a Charlie that wanted to give him a piece of her mind. He turned to find Charlie standing with her arms crossed over her chest. Storm sat next to her feet, his look saying he knew Rafe was in trouble.

"I didn't want to wake you," Rafe said.

"I don't know how I didn't wake when you left the truck. I guess I was tired. You still shouldn't have gotten up until I was awake. How are you feeling?"

"Great. Back to normal," Rafe lied.

He immediately knew Charlie didn't believe him. She gave him a squinted look before stepping forward to reach behind him and touch the sizable knot that was on his head. Her movement brought her close to his face and he looked down at her. She wasn't being nice, pushing on the wound, to make her point. Rafe hissed and tried to move away. He didn't want to admit to Charlie that he still felt lightheaded and had trouble focusing.

"I know when you're lying. Get back in the truck and lay down please," Charlie ordered.

"We need to get moving. I can't be on my back the whole time," Rafe replied.

"Yes, you can. There are three other adults that can drive the vehicles if need be. You will be laying down with me until I'm sure you are ok to be up and around."

"You get real bossy when you go into doctor mode, ya know?" Rafe said.

Despite wanting to argue with her a little more, he followed her orders and climbed back into the Bronco. Charlie climbed in after him situating him comfortably on a pillow. She fussed over him with her doctor tasks. She cleaned his wound again, checking for any sign of infection. Once he was patched up again she climbed out of the truck to talk to Alex about leaving.

Rafe heard Charlie give Storm an order. The next thing he saw was the dog jumping on the tailgate and coming into the truck. He carefully laid down next to Rafe, his muzzle pushed against his shoulder.

"She tell you to watch me?" Rafe asked the dog.

Storm lifted his head to look at him. He then licked Rafe's face before laying back down. Rafe put his arm around the dog, running his fingers through his soft fur. Storm rolled slightly so his body was pushed against Rafe and he could receive belly rubs. Rafe had to laugh a little at the dog's actions. They laid like that until the truck started.

"Storm, I told you to watch him. Not go soft because he gave you attention," Charlie chided as she climbed into the back of the truck too. Storm just let his tongue hang out of his mouth and Charlie laughed.

"We're headed home," Max called from the driver's seat.

"Who's driving Smith?" Rafe asked.

"Alex. Griffin is with her to keep an eye on him. But he's tied up well. They didn't think it was good for me to be in there. I'm stronger than you all think," Max said, the last bit under her breath. Rafe still heard her and knew his strong sister couldn't handle so many people trying to baby her.

"Everyone knows you're strong, Max. Whether you like it or not, we love you. And when someone you love gets hurt, you want to protect them," Rafe called back to her.

Max didn't answer as they pulled away from their makeshift camp. Her silence gave Rafe time to think about what they would do with Smith when they got back to the compound. His plans were derailed by Charlie sitting close to his side. She gazed out of the window, lost in her own thoughts. Rafe studied her profile and he knew he needed to handle the feelings he had for her.

As if she could hear his thoughts, Charlie turned abruptly and met his gaze. He fought the need to look away and she stared into his eyes. A soft smile showed on her face and she crawled to be sitting closer to him.

"What's on your mind?" She asked.

"Are you going to stay with us, Charlie?" Rafe blurted out.

"What? Of course, I am. Where would I be going?"

"I didn't want you to feel obligated to stay or something."

In his head, Rafe knew he sounded awkward. But he wasn't used to dealing with women in relationship type situations. He had shied away from anything serious. Now here he was in the apocalypse, with the first woman he ever really fell for.

"Why would I feel obligated to stay? You're the one that has been protecting and providing for me. Do you want me to go?" She asked quietly.

"No. God no. I want you to stay. With me. Charlie, I want you," Rafe said.

He felt like he was waiting on pins and needles as her eyes widened for a moment. She looked over the seat at Max and then back to Rafe. Without warning, Charlie leaned down and pressed her lips to Rafe's. The kiss was soft and tentative at first. But Rafe didn't hesitate to take advantage of her advance. He threaded his hand through her hair at her neck and pulled her closer, deepening the kiss. When she pulled away, she had a blush spilled across her cheeks.

"What took you so long?" Charlie asked in a husky whisper.

Later that afternoon they pulled into town. Alex and Max had agreed when Rafe suggested they go back into town to check on Issac. The old man didn't need to stay in town alone anymore. Now that they were going home, Rafe wanted to bring the man with them. He had been helpful to Rafe and protected them from the soldiers that came into town.

Arriving at the dry cleaner's, Issac was already coming out the front door. He was holding his gun at the ready, clearly not sure who was sitting in the military vehicle. Rafe started to climb from the back of the Bronco with Charlie's help. The two of them went to Issac, who was sporting darkening bruises on his face. But his wounds were still cleanly dressed.

"Boy, it is good to see you alive," Issac said to Rafe. When Rafe put his hand out to shake, Issac grabbed it and pulled him in for a half hug.

"Issac, I'm sorry this happened to you. If you hadn't been lying for us..." Rafe started to say, but Issac cut him off.

"You can stop that right now. What those men are doing, by hunting you down, is wrong. It's not the country we live in."

"We are going home. With my sisters home, we are safer together," Rafe said, motioning to Alex and Max behind him.

"Hello, again ladies. It's good to see you all healthy and walking. Where is the boy?" Issac asked.

"He's already home. You should come with us, Issac. There's nothing left in town for you. We have plenty of room," Rafe said.

"Please, Issac?" Charlie asked.

Issac seemed to think about it for a moment. He looked at Rafe with his arm around Charlie and he smiled at the couple.

"Ok. I think I'd like that. Should we load all of the supplies you've been bringing here?"

Rafe was surprised that Issac agreed so easily. But he was thankful. He knew he would worry about Issac in town on his own. If anything happened to the man, when he could have been safer at the compound, Rafe wouldn't forgive himself. Griffin and Smith under the watchful eye of Issac started loading cases of water and boxes of food. Rafe watched as Smith pulled his weight. The man never tried to disobey an order that was given to him and he worked hard moving supplies to the vehicles.

Issac also packed up all of the bedding items he had in the business. Alex agreed with him that they could never have too much. As they worked, Rafe could hear Alex telling Issac about the compound and about how they had plenty of room for everyone. Rafe thought about the bunkhouse their father had built for this exact moment. They could use the bedding from Issac and make sure everyone had a comfortable place to sleep.

The ride back home to the compound was uneventful. There were a few close calls of infected wandering in the road, but Alex didn't hesitate to use the military truck to her benefit by running them down. The bodies would bounce from the front, leaving a clear path for the Bronco to pass as well. When they pulled up to the gate of the compound, Charlie gave Rafe permission to sit up. He was so anxious to be home.

The trucks pulled into the compound and Griffin closed the gate behind them. When they pulled up the gravel drive, Rafe first noticed the large RV that was parked next to the house. He next noticed the new wall that was being created for the burned section. He had to admit it looked good. There were people milling around that he didn't know, but he wasn't surprised that his sisters found other survivors to join their fight.

As everyone spilled from the vehicles, Rafe heard screaming from the kids as they ran to their parents. When Rafe rounded the Bronco, his nieces and nephew all flew in his direction. They all asked questions and hugged him. Rafe had to go to his knees to hug each of them. He was so happy to see them all behind the walls of the compound, safe.

Looking around, he found Aiden coming from the house holding an older woman's hand. When he saw Charlie and Rafe, he cried out and tried to run down the stairs. Charlie ran toward him first and swept the little boy up in her arms. He squeezed her neck and told her he had missed her. Then he looked over her shoulder to Rafe who was slowly making his way to them. Aiden's arms reached out behind Charlie so Rafe circled them both in a hug.

They stood like this for a long moment. Rafe leaned down to breathe in Aiden's little boy scent, a mixture of dirt, food, and shampoo. His calm was broken by Max who yelled out loudly behind them.

"Alex! I told you!" Max yelled.

"Max, stop it. Leave them alone," Alex called back.

"I don't want to. I want to know what her intentions are with our brother," Max said.

"Stop being a brat. Get over here and help me," Alex replied.

Rafe refused to acknowledge them. He smiled against Charlie's hair. He could feel her giggling at the exchange. Rafe knew it was just starting. And he couldn't say he didn't enjoy the teasing. It reminded him that his sisters were with him. It reminded him they were family and that they knew him better than anyone else.

Finally releasing Charlie and Aiden, Rafe realized there were a few faces he didn't know. He walked up to the older woman that was standing on the porch watching him still. She smiled warmly at Rafe when she came down to meet him.

"Hi, I'm Rafe Duncan," he said, holding out his hand.

"I'm Margaret. It's really nice to meet you. Your sisters have been so worried," she replied as she gripped his hand.

"Hi, Margaret. How were the kids while we were gone?" Alex asked when she walked up.

"Oh, angels of course. We had a great time learning how to take care of the animals and the gardens. You've done a really good job up here," Margaret said, looking at Rafe.

"It's home," Rafe said, shrugging.

"Come, I have more people to introduce you to," Alex said, taking Rafe's arm.

That evening, Rafe stood at the pasture, watching the cows feasting on their grass happily. He had taken the time to greet each of them, letting them know he was home. He had missed their routine and being home. The stars were starting to wink from the sky and Rafe stared up wondering if Mitch Duncan was watching his kids survive like he taught them.

"It's so different being here with a full house," Charlie said as she walked up to stand with Rafe.

He looked down at her and grinned like a fool. He slid his arm around her and pulled her to stand closer to him. He leaned her head against his chest.

"So, I'm thinking we should take my room. I want to give Alex Dad's room because she has Billie and Henry sleeping with her. Then Easton can have Alex's room downstairs. Issac said he's fine sleeping in the bunkhouse with Cliff and Marcus. Margaret and Candace said they are happy in the RV for now," Rafe explained.

"Hmm, sharing a room?" Charlie murmured with a small laugh.

"If that's not ok with you we can do something different," Rafe said quickly, feeling ashamed for not asking her about his plan first.

"I'm teasing, Rafe. It makes sense for us to share your room. Aiden can sleep on a small cot there with us. Storm already has his bed in there too," Charlie said.

"I just don't want to be away from you. The month in the cave, we were never apart for long."

"I know. I got used to you sleeping near me. I don't want to lose that either."

Decided, they walked hand in hand back to the house. When they walked in the kids were watching a cartoon movie and the adults were gathered around the dining room table. Easton sat next to Alex as well, considered a part of the adult group after everything he had been through. Rafe was impressed with the boy after hearing about his story from Alex.

Rafe and Charlie took places at the table. There wasn't room for everyone, but they made it work like a war room. Alex sat at the head of the table, the natural leader of the Duncan family, thus the natural leader of this group of survivors. Rafe waited for her to start the meeting she had called. They all had information they needed to share, and it was better they shared it sooner rather than later.

"I can't tell you how happy I am to have everyone here now," Alex started.

The adults all automatically quieted when Alex started to talk. Rafe knew she wasn't trying to run anything. It wasn't like Alex to take charge. But people respected her and looked up to her, himself included. She was most qualified to keep them in line and on task.

"We've been comparing notes between Max, Charlie, and Rafe. We don't have a perfectly clear picture, but we know more than we did. And understanding the motivations behind who we're dealing with is going to be important to survival. I wish I could say we are only dealing with the infected."

"I'm sorry for that," Charlie added. Alex smiled warmly at her. Rafe appreciated the kindness Alex showed the woman he had decided was for him.

"That is not your fault, Charlie. You can't blame yourself for this. The actions of the man you call 'The Suit' and Major Callahan are what have spurred this war between us and the military."

"The fact is, Callahan and 'The Suit' want to kill Charlie and anyone else involved with her. We won't hide the truth from anyone here. If you are a member of this house, you are family. And as a family, we won't keep secrets. You need to know how serious this is," Rafe added. Alex nodded for him to go on.

"Charlie knows this plague was caused by experiments the government was commissioning. The people, including Charlie, that worked on these projects didn't know what was happening with their research," Rafe continued.

"I thought I was helping. I was creating cures for every type of plague that could be manufactured in a lab. Now I know they were only looking for the one we couldn't cure. I don't believe they even knew this could happen. I didn't. And neither did the other doctors I worked with. Something happened with this pathogen that wasn't planned," Charlie said.

Rafe squeezed her leg under the table, giving her reassurance. He knew she carried a lot of guilt about the outbreak.

"Charlie can't cure the plague. She's been trying to figure it out since we went on the run," Rafe said.

"It's possible also that it has mutated. Alex mentioned seeing faster infected before," Charlie added.

"We all did," Easton spoke up. "It was a much faster walk than what seemed normal, as if they could have run at us if they tried. Not that any of this is normal."

"Right. I can't even begin to understand what's happened without my lab and specimens to test," Charlie said.

"I don't think that's what Callahan is after. He claims he wants the cure. But he isn't worried about any of us living. I think they just want to silence the information," Max said quietly from her seat.

Rafe looked at his sister. She looked at the table when she spoke about Callahan and Rafe had to tap down the anger that wanted to burst out. He knew Max didn't need his anger. He thought about Smith, who was still locked up in the military truck. Until they created something more solid in the barn, they agreed they could keep him locked in the truck. Smith didn't argue, clearly realizing he was lucky to still have his life.

"I think Max is right. I think this is about getting rid of the evidence of what they have done. And about taking control of what is left of the country. So this is the deal. Living here we are relatively safe. We have the security systems in place. Rafe has suggested barbed wire at the tops of the fence. This will take time and manpower. But it would stop the soldiers from trying to jump our walls again," Alex continued.

She had everyone's attention. Looking from face to face she made sure they heard her and understood what she was telling them.

"This is the time we tell you, no one is required to be here. If you decide it's too unsafe, you are welcome to leave with as many supplies as you can carry. We understand this isn't exactly what you signed up for. But we are a family and we won't put out anyone," Alex finished.

Everyone looked at each other, no one spoke up. Alex, Rafe, and Max knew what they were doing. They would stay together no matter what. They stood for each other and their family. But their new additions didn't have to stay if they didn't want to.

"I think I speak for everyone here when I say, screw 'em," Issac said finally.

Laughter broke out around the table, lightening the mood. Alex made eye contact with Rafe over the table. They smiled at each other, knowing they were building something important there. The conversation turned to chores and responsibilities. Because Rafe had been on the compound alone for so long, Alex turned to him to head the assignments for everyone.

Rafe wasn't prepared for the extra hands, so he used the time to discuss what was needed and people volunteered their knowledge. Margaret had worked with gardening before, so she was assigned to the planting and harvesting, with Candace as her assistant. Candace was also going to help with the cooking and children. Rafe would continue to work with the animals and Easton asked if he could learn as well. Marcus was going to finish the wall on the house and create a secure cell in the barn for Smith.

The rest of the adults were given other tasks. Alex and Max agreed they would go to find the barbed wire as soon as possible. Issac had some suggestions of businesses that had it before the plague. They discussed being able to clip off the wire and carefully winding it to bring it home to be used. It was then agreed as a rule no one went out alone and that three people or more was the best option. No one wanted to be trapped outside of the walls with no backup.

As the meeting ended, everyone went their separate ways. Rafe promised to join Charlie soon in their new room. He said goodnight to Aiden who hugged him tightly.

"It's good to be home, right, Rafe?" Aiden asked.

"Sure is, buddy. Do you like your new home?"

"Yes. I like the kids here. I miss my mommy and daddy. But Charlie said they always watch over me. So I know I need to be a good boy."

"That's a good plan. Off to bed with you," Rafe said, patting his head affectionately as he grabbed Charlie's hand and asked for a bedtime story. Before she could walk away, Rafe kissed her quickly and she smiled sweetly at him.

Outside, Rafe joined his sisters on the hill that overlooked the front gate of the compound. He stood behind them, his arms around their shoulders. They looked out over the place that was theirs. They had completed Sundown, finding their way behind the walls that were built by their father. Being prepared had gotten them through the days since the plague. Rafe found pride in what they had accomplished so far. Being with his sisters, in their home, made survival feel possible.

"This isn't over," Max said, breaking their comfortable silence.

"No, I guess it's not. But for now, maybe we can enjoy a night of safety," Alex replied.

"Together we can handle anything," Rafe said.

"Dad would be proud of us," Alex said.

Thinking about their father, they all fell silent. Rafe knew he would be proud of his children. In upholding his beliefs after he was gone. For completing Sundown, bringing their family back together. Rafe thought about the struggles they all had to go through to get to where they were now. Mitch Duncan would never have said it in so many words, but he would have been proud. His children were strong survivors.

"What's going to happen to us?" Max asked.

Rafe wasn't sure how to answer her question. Alex also stayed silent, in her own thoughts.

"I mean, where do we go from here?" Max continued when neither of her siblings answered.

"This is it, I think. Take it day by day. Keep the compound safe. Continue to be as self-sustaining as possible. Protect ourselves," Rafe finally answered.

"Stay alive," Alex said.

The siblings turned to find their own beds. As they walked back inside, Max poked Rafe in the side.

"So about Charlie," she said.

"Don't start, Max," Rafe replied.

"Do we need to find a priest that's alive?" Max asked.

"Max, leave him alone. If you tease him, he'll never tell us anything," Alex cut in.

"I'm never telling you anything anyway," Rafe replied as they made their way up the back stairs.

"Oh come on, Rafe," Max whined as Rafe opened the door.

With the door open, Storm shot out of the house. Rafe watched him sniff around the yard. The dog ran to the hill the Duncans had stood on. He looked out over the wall, standing still watching. Rafe came up to him and knelt. He rubbed his hand over the dog's soft head, massaging his ears and followed his gaze. Though Storm wasn't giving his normal signals of intruders, Rafe knew threats were out there.

"It's quiet for now, Storm. We're alive. Let's sleep tonight. Tomorrow you can hunt down the boogiemen," Rafe said, standing and heading back to the house.

Storm stood, gazing out beyond the fence. He didn't turn to follow Rafe. White silver fur shone in the moonlight, like a beacon of hope and protection. There he would wait because the dog knew. In the feral part of him, Storm could see that the world outside their walls would come calling. The dead and alive.

CHAPTER TWENTY-EIGHT

His fist smashed into the cool metal desk he sat at. 'The Suit' couldn't listen to the excuses from Callahan and his men any longer. Every shred of hope they gave him over the last month was quickly quashed by the next update. Listening to Callahan's voice now made 'The Suit' want to travel out of his bunker to handle the Duncans himself.

"Sir, we will have this handled soon," Callahan said.

"You have said that each time you've called. And yet you have nothing but mistakes and excuses. I'm beginning to think I picked the wrong man for the job."

"If you have someone else to assign this to, you are welcome to....sir," Callahan said, adding the last word in a sarcastic tone.

'The Suit' didn't like being stuck between a rock and a hard place. Callahan was aware that 'The Suit' didn't have any other subordinates to reach out to. The plague had wiped out many of the reserves from their faction and he was grasping at the last few threads they had. He could feel the power slipping through his fingers. He grasped his hand in a fist, working to catch the metaphorical omnipotence.

"What do you suggest, Callahan? How will you handle this one family?"

"We are still making plans, sir. But we know their weakness."

"Well, don't leave me in suspense, enlighten me," 'The Suit' replied.

"Their family, the people they have at that house. They are emotionally connected. Start cutting them down, one by one. Eventually, they will give us what we want."

'The Suit' stood and walked to the windows that overlooked the lab space. Patient Zero was alone in its cell, the lab technicians working in another room. Without focus, the dead woman bounced off of the bars. 'The Suit' watched as she continually hit her head into the metal and realized that was exactly how he felt. The Duncans were a barrier he was slamming his head into and yet, they didn't budge.

Turning back to the pile of papers he had on his desk, he spread out three color photos. Alexandria, Rafe, and Maxine stared back at him. He knew they had nicknames, but he refused to use them. They weren't people to him, they were obstructions. Standing between him and what he wanted, keeping him from achieving his ultimate goal. To cure the plague.

Truthfully, 'The Suit' wasn't concerned with the cure. With fewer people to control it would be easier for him to restart the government in his image. However, he knew if he had a cure to offer people, that would only pave the way to becoming the hero he wanted to be. Hero wasn't a word he typically used for himself. He knew it was a fake idea. People liked a hero. And that was who they would follow.

Once he had the remaining American people falling into line, he would become the ruler he saw himself as. *It would be well deserved*, 'The Suit' thought to himself. He had worked behind the scenes, in the dark, for too many years. It was time his successes and power were recognized by the public.

"Sir?" Callahan's voice came from the phone. 'The Suit' realized he had been in his own musings for too long.

"Their loved ones," 'The Suit' repeated, bringing them back to the plan Callahan was hatching.

"Yes, sir."

"I like that plan, Callahan. These people are a thorn in my side. If we allow them to continue as they have, believing they can have victory over us, this will only fester and grow. I need them to go away, however that must happen."

The pair hung up and 'The Suit' sat down heavily at his desk. The eyes of the Duncans seemed to follow him. Lashing out, he threw the photos and papers across the room. He straightened his suit jacket and pushed his glasses up his nose. After a few deep breaths, he felt back in control of his emotions.

He watched the images he had pulled up of Kalispell. It was here that he watched as the plague had raced from its origins in the facility to the streets of the nearby town. Now the streets were home to the dead and the living were the minority. As he watched, a white truck stopped, and people began to jump out with their guns at the ready. He immediately recognized the Duncan siblings.

Sitting forward to get a closer look, 'The Suit' watched as they methodically checked corners and shadows for threats.

"Soon the shadows won't be so easy to deal with. Take your last breaths, Duncans. We are coming for you."

ACKNOWLEDGMENTS

Thank you so much for joining the search for Rafe Duncan! I hope you enjoyed the exciting story of how this infection started and how the Duncan family came together. To keep up with more of their stories, be sure to follow along on my website court-neykonstantin.com. I also post updates on my Facebook page at https://www.facebook.com/AuthorCKonstantin.

As always my brainstorming bestie was by my side during the writing of ALIVE. Thank you for reading every message I sent, no matter how long and all over the board it may have been. You always know when to rein me in when necessary, and push me further when I need it.

Thank goodness for a fantastic editor that keeps my comma mess to a minimum!. Pam Ebeler from Undivided Editing keeps me on track with those evil little things, making sure I am able to concentrate on the bigger picture. Thanks for all your hard work Pam, I appreciate you!

Thank you to Podium Publishing for the fantastic cover for ALIVE. Seeing Rafe portrayed so well really brings the story to life!

Made in United States
Troutdale, OR
12/10/2023